# JILLIAN'S ISLAND

*a novel*
Kimberly Webb

For my friends.
If you think that includes you,
it does.

# 1



*JILLIAN*

Grandpa hit the jackpot.

That's not even a figure of speech; he won $4.7 billion playing Powerball, and his days managing a scuba diving shop in New Jersey were done.

Such newfound wealth would have prompted some seventy-somethings to finally retire – live in a mansion on a hill and spend the rest of life in the lap of luxury (or blow it all on more lottery tickets and frivolous lawsuits), but not my grandpa. Scott "Skippy" Hamilton used the money to realize his lifelong dream of becoming a sea captain. His vessel was a multi-million-dollar yacht that he used to transport the rich and famous from the Florida coast to exotic, tropical destinations in the Bahamas and back. Essentially, he ran an exclusive cruise line for people too good for regular cruise lines. He christened it The Flying Honeymoon.

It was fantastic.

I wasn't normally one to think inanimate objects were sexy, but dang, this was one foxy boat! Sleek, curving lines, long banks of black-tinted windows along the sides, and three sun decks. Inside, it was all leather couches and marble tabletops, plush carpets, and stained-glass murals. It was a floating palace – just, you know, smaller and more watertight.

We left port at noon on the day of The Flying Honeymoon's last voyage with ten passengers and five crew members, myself included. The day had been packed with passenger arrivals, check-ins, and ship tours. Escorting clients to their staterooms, then running to the kitchen for a glass or two of bubbly that just couldn't wait.

Grandpa's business, The Flying Honeymoon Tours, was a rising star in the travel world. Only in business for six years, he already had high-profile clients booking with him regularly. Thanks to an endorsement from a certain late-night talk show host (Nice show last night, Jimmy!), tour reservations were booked out a year in advance, with most clients ringing in from the 1-Percenters Club.

Three years ago, Grandpa reluctantly hired me as a stewardess on the yacht, and I had been working to earn his approval ever since. Skippy's admiration was hard to come by ... for me. I'd never been a favorite grandchild. But I was always determined to prove myself to him. I sailed with him on every voyage, never took a sick day, and always strove for excellence. Grandpa would never accept anything less. Through the years, he showed his approval and appreciation by begrudgingly promoting me to Head Stewardess. Metaphorically, this meant I was not only in charge of the circus, but I also got to shovel the elephant poo at the end of the show.

This week's guest roster was uniquely star-studded. Along with a sweepstakes winner, a richer-than-Midas banking tycoon, and two university professors, I had the distinct pleasure of welcoming aboard none other than Bridget Foster: singer, actress, and America's Sweetheart.

Was I a 27-year-old woman working with the rich and famous? Yes. But did I still scream a little and nearly wet my pants when I heard that the country's beloved idol, Bridget Foster, was going to be joining our next voyage? Of course!

I would like to say that meeting Bridget would go down on my list of "Best Life Moments." But I can't.

Bridget Foster arrived with an entourage of assistants, all bustling about to unload her luggage and buff her nails and hairspray her already-perfect hair. I exaggerate a tad, but they were busy. Despite the army of assistants on the dock, in the end, only Bridget and her bodyguard, Patrick O'Neil, boarded the ship.

She was just as stunningly polished in person as she appeared on her Instagram. Dressed from head to toe in designer fashions, she would have stood out in any crowd, no matter their average bank account sum. She wore a red and white striped dress, sleeveless to show off toned and tanned arms, and cut a few inches above the knee to display equally sculpted and caramel-colored legs. She wore wedge heels so flawlessly white I wondered if they had ever been exposed to air before this very moment. A string of pearls circled her throat, with a matching bracelet mimicking it on her wrist. She carried a sleek white leather handbag in one expertly manicured hand. (I had seen the day before on her Insta that she'd chosen a nail color called Caribbe-Yesss for the trip.) Money could buy nice clothes and shoes, but one look at this woman's face proved that there were some things that people were just born with.

Bridget Foster had toffee-colored eyes that made her olive skin look even more exotic. Thick eyelashes and full red lips, elegant brows, a perfect nose that was neither too small nor too long. Cheekbones that poets could (and did) write sonnets about. And shiny, perfectly styled mocha-brown hair that, even when pulled back in a high ponytail, fell halfway down her back.

She was a vision. It was no wonder she was the most recognized face in most U.S. households and a semi-deity among young adults and teenagers. I had memorized every song she released and watched her in every cameo movie appearance she made.

Huge fan.

Not that I would have, but I didn't get a chance to geek out over meeting my celebrity girl-crush. When she reached me, Bridget greeted me with a distracted, "Hello," before passing me off to Patrick to complete their check-in. That cursory greeting was the only acknowledgment I got before she pulled out a cell phone and began tapping at the screen like she was sending an S.O.S.

I stared after her for half a moment before, feeling firmly put-in-my-place, I turned to the bodyguard to speak lackey-to-lackey.

Patrick-the-bodyguard was professionally distant, not even sparing a glance as we conducted business. With the forms signed and room keys allocated, Patrick took a welcome packet from my hands and muttered, "Let's get this over with," before following the preoccupied Bridget Foster up the gangway.

I reminded myself that getting the cold shoulder from a celebrity was a sort of calling card of the service industry. Still, I had hoped that Bridget would be nicer.

After the last passengers had checked in and each group was shown to their staterooms and given a ship tour, we were ready to set off for adventure.

It was a magnificent day to be at sea. There was a breeze, as always, and the air was richly humid. The sunshine was warm but not overbearing, and the ocean seemed less malicious than usual. It was shaping up to be an uneventful trip.

"Jillian!" Skippy calling out my name across the ship was a trademark of the yacht. Ever since Jimmy had done a bit about it on his show, Grandpa had really hammed it up and now our guests came to expect it. It was part gag, part legitimate beckoning, and I never failed to show up when he called. You never knew when he'd need, I don't know, an emergency Vitamin C tablet or an iced tea.

From my position in the aft lounge, I laughed along with the nearby passengers when Grandpa Skippy's call rang out from the bridge. I had been serving crudités and wine to the guests who were already bored of their staterooms, and I excused myself with a playful *what are you gonna do?* shrug that earned an extra laugh from the sweepstakes winner, Kenya.

Grandpa was at the helm on the bridge, his first mate, Eric, at his side double-checking coordinates and speaking on the radio. Grandpa looked up when I entered the room.

"Jillian, good. Go get my sunglasses from my room. The prescription ones in the black case."

"I know the ones."

"Hurry, Jillian," he added with more impatience than was called for. I chalked it up to him being old and crotchety.

"Aye-aye, Skippy," I said with a mock salute.

He glared at me, but the smirk on his lips betrayed the gravity of the look. "Don't get lost."

I wound my way around guests and furniture, through the narrow halls down to Captain Skippy's stateroom where I found his sunglasses just where he always kept them. Snatching them up, I reversed course and headed back to the bridge. As I emerged from the staff area, I rounded the corner without slowing down and ended up knocking shoulders with Kenya Adamson, one of the first passengers I had greeted that day.

The first thing I had noticed about Kenya was her arresting presence: she was easily 6 feet tall, slender but with strong shoulders, curly black hair that glistened in the sunlight, eyes so dark they were almost black, and skin the color of iced coffee. She might have been utterly intimidating if she hadn't been grinning broadly, thanking me personally for the sweepstakes she had won. "This is the trip of a lifetime!" I half expected her to pull me into a hug, and she was so gregarious that I wouldn't have protested if she had!

As I crashed into her in the hallway, the half-full glass of orange juice and rum she carried met a disastrous fate: it splashed out onto my clothes and hers, and the glass fell from her hand, shattering on the deck.

Tumbling over my words, I apologized for the disaster and crouched down immediately to sweep up the shards of glass. Kenya, to my surprise, dropped down as well, picking up the larger glass segments between careful fingers.

"Please, let me do that," I said, trying to take the glass from her.

"It'll go faster if we do it together," Kenya replied, sparing me a brief look that dared me to disagree. I didn't, and in just a minute the mess was cleaned up and we were both back on our feet.

After discarding the broken glass in a nearby trash can, Kenya brushed her hands over her navy linen pants, examining the orange stain that bisected her cream-colored blouse. I winced, knowing that the clothing was ruined and the cost of replacing it would likely come from my own paycheck.

I opened my mouth to offer a fifth apology, but Kenya spoke again before I could. "Mom will be pissed," she said. Was that glee in her voice? Who would feel gleeful about being doused with a tropical drink ten minutes into a luxury cruise?

Kenya looked down at me with mischief in her dark eyes. "She gave this to me as a wedding present, and she told me that I should have given it back to her since I didn't get married." She shrugged one shoulder. "Guess that serves her right for buying me clothes as a gift instead of a vacuum."

A response to this sentiment was slow in coming. Kenya didn't let the silence last more than a second or two before continuing to speak as though I'd given some witty reply. "I was just off to the top sun deck to scout for prospects." She waggled her eyebrows at me with a cheeky grin. "Care to join?"

In six years of working aboard The Flying Honeymoon, I had never been invited to go on a manhunt. First time for everything! "I'll pass this time," I said, at last getting my proverbial feet back under me in this conversation.

Kenya shrugged again. "Just as well. I'll bet all the men on this boat are taken anyway. But," she fluffed out her hair and grinned widely, "it never hurts to look!" She started to walk away but paused long enough to say over her shoulder, "If you change your mind, you know where to find me!"

"Noted," I said with a chuckle. "I will come find you – with a fresh drink."

She gave me a final grin before disappearing around the corner.

"Jillian!" The clarion call sounded again, and I suddenly remembered Grandpa Skippy and his sunglasses. I made it back to the bridge without further incident. After handing over the sunglasses, he gave me a "Get back to work," and then I was off and running again.

***

My coworker, Alexis, and I spent the rest of the morning flitting around the ship helping guests retrieve luggage and unpack luggage and stow luggage and fetching drinks and appetizers. Meanwhile, Mikey, our ship's chef (and Alexis' husband), was in the kitchen preparing a gourmet spread for our Sail Away luncheon, and Captain Skippy and his first mate were making final preparations to embark on our journey.

It was 12:30 p.m. when Skippy weighed anchor, and the yacht began its graceful glide away from the port and out to sea. Our guests took time away from the start of their vacation to stand at the railing and wave goodbye to the dock workers and anybody else watching our departure. While they waved, I made another mental headcount:

Bridget Foster and bodyguard, Patrick.

Kenya Adamson, travelling solo.

Two professors from the University of Miami – Dr. April Yung and Dr. Carter Buckley.

Howard Lovell and fiancée, Elodia, and their three assistants: Portia, Tyron, and Gordon.

Ten passengers, five crew members. We were all accounted for and ready for our five-day cruise.

When we were far enough from the shore that we couldn't make out faces anymore, most of the guests turned away from the railing and wandered off to find food or drinks. Howard Lovell found me right away. I had spent the majority of my morning in their stateroom helping Elodia unpack and stow her empty luggage in the hold. I was used to their type: wealthy, entitled, world-on-a-string thinking. They say, "Jump," and you said, "How high?" I had become adept at making people like this happy. The key is to accept their thinking that they are the all-knowing rulers of the universe, and you are the lowly peon who is just lucky enough to be graced by their presence.

It's hogwash. But making them think they're right about that is key to earning generous tips.

Elodia Francom was elegant in every conceivable way: clothes so on the cutting edge that they still had price tags attached and notes tucked in the pockets from the designers, hoping she would "see them next season!" I lost count of the number of hair products she had requested to be unpacked and organized neatly by the vanity. Lotions, creams, anti-aging serums, moisturizing buffers, and every imaginable shade of cosmetic products. As I set up the room, Elodia and Howard stood by the porthole window, discussing something in low voices that didn't carry to me.

Elodia was dressed in a flowing, multicolor dress with a plunging neckline that showed off a physique that was questionably God-given. Her platinum blonde hair was pulled up in a neat bun that paired well with the sun hat she wore whenever she was on deck. She had dark blue eyes and porcelain skin that she likely lathered with sunscreen every day to keep from freckling or burning. She was Scandinavian fairness paired with the best plastic surgery money could buy. I couldn't help but wonder what this woman had looked like before she decided to take matters into her own hands.

Howard Lovell hadn't had much to say in our interactions to that point. His manner was gruff but quiet, his thick, salt-and-pepper eyebrows pinched together in a perpetual scowl of disapproval. He grumbled out a direction or two before taking up his station in a comfortable chair and pulling out his jumbo-screen phone to check his stocks or something.

Howard was older than Elodia and clearly did not share her concern about aging. Her seventeen stay-young elixirs were set up next to his single bottle of aftershave, a black comb, and a bottle of lotion. He was shorter than Elodia by three or four inches, but the fact that her high heels added an additional four inches to their height difference made me suspect that he didn't mind her being taller than him. He was handsome in his own right, but he had still gone way up when paired with Elodia.

Neither of them were unkind to me or any of the members of their entourage, but they weren't warm and cuddly, either. This was a couple who had enough money and influence in their pockets that you didn't want to step on their shoes in the grocery line unless your first cousin was a lawyer.

As they stepped away from the railing, the firsts to finish waving goodbye to U.S. soil, Howard flagged me down to request a whiskey sour be sent to his room, along with a cold compress and a plate of food from the luncheon.

Elodia didn't stop beside her fiancé, continuing her march to the dining room where lunch was served with flair. Neither of them seemed upset that the beginning of their romantic getaway was being spent in separate corners of the ship.

After informing the rest of the guests that lunch was served, I went to the bar to pour Howard's drink, assemble the rest of his requested items, and take it all to his stateroom. There was a "Do Not Disturb" sign on the door handle, so I set his room service tray on the floor and slipped a receipt beneath the door.

With that job done, I returned to the deck, expecting to find it cleared of passengers, but I was surprised to find one lone man holding his original position by the railing.

Dr. Carter Buckley stood at the bow, his folded arms resting on the rail, eyes closed, leaning his face into the wind. The pair of professors intrigued me.

Dr. Buckley caught my attention the moment he stepped onto the dock. His light brown hair had natural highlights from hours in the sunshine, and his skin had a healthy sun-kissed glow, but it was a little pink like he often got burned if he wasn't careful. He was tall with a confident posture but a relaxed expression on his face that conveyed no egotism. And his eyes! Ocean blue with intriguing gold rings in the center and laugh lines crinkling the skin at the corners. Even though he wasn't smiling when I had met him, he had the appearance of a happy man.

I had met a lot of movie stars in this job, and I'm not saying Carter Buckley rivaled them in good looks, but he was attractive anyway. More approachable and real than any celebrity I'd ever known. I liked him at once, even though we hadn't had a chance to talk about anything other than paperwork and "Welcome aboard" and whatnot.

His companion starkly contrasted his easygoing appearance: Dr. April Yung wore a red and white crop top and a white tennis skirt with white sneakers, and Dr. Carter Buckley was dressed in basketball shorts, tennis shoes, and a plain grey T-shirt. I knew from Dr. Yung's profile that she was in her mid-fifties, but she didn't look a day over thirty. Dr. Buckley was 32, not much older than me, which was remarkable because he was a highly respected marine biologist and a college professor. His career made me feel like I had been working a lemonade stand since high school. Well, that wasn't far from the truth, actually ...

Captain Skippy had offered the university a discounted rate to have the two professors join on this sailing. He wanted to break into the intellectual crowd that might be more interested in nature tours on remote islands than staying up all night drinking and throwing up on his deck boards. The partnership with the University of Miami was a trial run, and I was under strict instructions to make sure the professors had no complaints about the trip.

Seeing him then, enjoying the sunshine and the breeze, I didn't want to interrupt, so I stopped at the top of the stairs and turned to go, leaving him in solitude. But he must have heard my steps, and he waved me over.

"It's Jillian, right?"

I returned his happy smile, pleased that he remembered my name from our brief meeting when he boarded. "That's right. Are you enjoying the sailing so far, Dr. Buckley?"

"It's unbelievable," he said with feeling. "I've never been on a ship like this. It's ... immaculate."

"Thank you," I accepted the compliment on behalf of Grandpa Skippy and the crew. "Glad to have you and your colleague aboard."

He kept his forearms rested on the railing but nodded toward me with a friendly grin. "Do you have a minute for a break? You've been running around like crazy every time I see you."

I forced out a laugh and joined him by the rail. "I can spare a few minutes. What are you looking forward to most about your vacation?"

"I'm excited to get to the islands," he said. "April and I plan to scuba dive and check out the Andros Barrier Reef that we heard has an unusually high population of an invasive species of algae that's likely causing a pocket of coral bleaching. Of course, the obvious answer might be climate change, but April and I are interested in conducting some further studies to see if there's more to it than that. In fact, I learned about another test we could try to learn more about the algae, and I'm eager to collect some samples for the lab..." He stopped himself, and I watched as a blush crept up his neck to shine from his cheeks. After clearing his throat, he pushed his fingers into his shaggy blonde hair and rolled his eyes at himself. "Sorry to bore you."

"I wasn't bored," I claimed. Then, at his disbelieving look, I grinned and added, "I just didn't understand every third word."

He laughed at that. "My friends tell me I get carried away." He shrugged, though, and finished, "But it's not my fault they don't like really cool stuff."

This surprised a real laugh from me, and it made Dr. Buckley grin. "What about you?" he asked then.

I quirked an eyebrow. "I like cool stuff," I said semi-defensively, "but I don't know much about coral."

Another laugh. I liked how easily he laughed, and the sound brought a smile to my face. I thought briefly that if I wasn't working and he wasn't my client, this might be a man I'd be in danger of developing a mean crush on.

He turned to fully face me, still chuckling as he asked, "I meant what are you looking forward to about the Bahamas?"

The question caught me off-guard. "Nothing really," I said after a moment's hesitation. "I'm just working. I probably won't even get off the ship."

Dr. Buckley scowled a little then. "You don't get any time off?"

I shrugged. "A few hours, probably. But I usually don't bother disembarking. I'd rather just take a nap in peace."

He shook his head. "I can't believe it. You get to be at the doorstep to paradise, and you don't even get to enjoy it."

"It's not exactly my first time," I defended. "We make this trip every other week. I've seen Nassau plenty of times."

He looked thoughtful, then looked out over the frothy waves, the beckoning horizon, the cloudless blue sky. "I hope you get to enjoy it this time," he said earnestly.

This was the first time a guest had ever asked what I did during our days at port, and I was weirdly touched by his concern for my enjoyment. "Thank you, Dr. Buckley."

He looked at me again, and I noticed the way his grey eyes were rimmed in the center with a shine of gold. "Please, call me Carter," he invited with a friendly grin.

And I felt like we were friends already. "Thanks. I won't keep you away from the view," I said, excusing myself. "But let me know if you need anything."

"Thanks, Jillian. I will."

As I turned to go, Dr. Yung stepped onto the deck from the dining room, clearly looking for her missing partner. She gave me a curt nod before walking past me to speak to Dr. Buckley.

***

I returned to the galley kitchen and found Alexis there preparing a tray of hors d'oeuvres. I washed my hands, then joined her in refreshment preparation.

"Folding more socks?" she guessed, noting the delay of my return to the kitchen. I began to help her spear tiny blocks of cheese onto sword-shaped toothpicks.

"Hopefully I'm done with that for this trip," I replied with an eye roll that helped relieve some of my annoyance at the jobs we were given. "I was actually talking with Dr. Buckley." Carter, I mentally corrected with a private smile.

Alexis' eyebrows rose slightly and her eyes lit up. "Ooo. He's kind of yummy, huh?"

"Is he? I hadn't noticed." I hoped she didn't see the blush that I could feel in my cheeks.

Alexis clucked her tongue. "Girl, you must be some kind of messed up not to notice that tall drink of water."

I rolled my eyes again. "What makes a man 'yummy' anyway?"

She scoffed at my apparent stupidity. "Well, in this case: 6'1", wavy hair, tan skin, and beautiful eyes. He's got that soulful look, you know? Like he could recite some sappy love poem then fistfight a bear to protect you."

I quirked an eyebrow. "Bears get into fistfights?"

Alexis ignored this. "Did you see his forearms? A man doesn't get muscle-y forearms and not have muscles everywhere else."

"Maybe he uses one of those grip strength tools while binge-watching Netflix."

"He's too smart for that," she waved my comment away. "He's a professor," she added, as if I wouldn't have already known that.

"Marine biology," I supplied, not sure why I wanted to prove that I knew anything about yummy Dr. Carter Buckley.

Alexis nodded firmly. "Even better. He's hot and he cares about the planet. Marine biologists always talk about saving our oceans and protecting whales and stuff."

"On TV," I interjected.

She ignored this and moved along to the point her mind had clearly been conniving, "You should ask him out."

How my friend was able to read my secret thoughts like a book was always baffling to me. I had barely realized myself that I had a micro-crush on Dr. Buckley. How did she know? I decided to play dumb. "Out where?" I asked with a suppressed snort. "We are on the ocean."

Her expression plainly said, don't be stupid. "So take him a drink, then sit and talk for a while. There's always a way to make sparks – even floating on the ocean." She then pondered a moment and added, "Maybe especially on the ocean."

"Great. In between turndown service and dish duty, I'll take him out of his vacation to have an awkward, forced date ... that wouldn't make this trip uncomfortable for everyone."

"We'll have to be stealthy, then."

I laughed. "You just let me know what your evil little mind comes up with, and I'll make sure to wash my hair that day."

She winked at me, flipping her dark ponytail behind her shoulder. "Don't think I won't."

# 2

## *CARTER*

**D**r. Yung took relaxation in stride. She lasted about twenty minutes after lunch before she traded her white tennis outfit for a bathing suit and a sheer cover-up, huge sunhat, and sunglasses. She tried to convince me to come sunbathing with her. I think she was flirting with me, but sometimes it's hard to tell. She batted her eyes at me and told me I was really missing out. I wasn't interested in inviting skin cancer into my life, though, so I declined, opting instead to sit in the air-conditioned lounge. So she went outside without me, and for two hours, I don't think she moved from her position on a reclined deck chair with an ever-present tropical drink within easy reach.

Several of the other guests followed April's lead and basked in the sun, steadily drinking themselves to dehydration. Rather than join them, I settled into a cool leather armchair in the quiet peace of the lounge and pulled out my iPad to catch up on a new marine biology article, sipping a very cold Dr. Pepper with a cherry bobbing inside.

Call me a nerd, everyone else in my life did. They were right: I was a nerd. After graduating college, I decided to stay for two subsequent degrees and then teach there. I was obsessed with learning. It wasn't even that I wanted to be an expert, I just felt like a sponge. If someone talked about the ocean, I wanted to be able to hold my own in that conversation.

I was midway through reading a fascinating paper about the effects of climate change on kelp when one of the ship's stewardesses entered the lounge from the kitchen, carrying a large black tray topped with full glasses. She caught my eye over the top of my iPad and offered a nod and smile.

Jillian. Her brown eyes had lit up earlier when I had called her by name. It can't be that unusual for someone to remember her name, can it?

She had been attentive and helpful to me and every other passenger since our excursion began, but other than the niceties of order taking and delivery, and our brief conversation on the upper deck, we hadn't spoken. She was one of four staff members aboard besides the captain, and with so many guests to attend to (and with the demanding personalities of several of my fellow passengers), she hadn't had a spare moment. I wondered if she expected to run around nonstop like this for the next five days. I found myself hoping that she was paid very well for this job.

As I watched her walk back out to the sun deck, I found myself smiling at the way her hips swayed with each careful step she took. She wore a pair of well-fitting tan pants, white deck shoes, and a blue button-down shirt. Her wavy brown hair was pulled up into a smart ponytail, the ends playing in the wind as she stepped in and out of the lounge. I swallowed hard, fighting back the temptation to stare at this beautiful woman for the rest of the trip. She took my breath away.

It was the confident set of her shoulders and the angle she held her chin. The sun flashed across her face as she stepped through the glass door and illuminated her rich root beer brown eyes. The sun caught sight of her hair and brought out a red tinge that mesmerized me. As she took the final step out of the lounge, those eyes swung over toward me, and her progress stuttered slightly. A smile hitched up the right corner of her red lips, and then she was gone.

Busted.

Feeling my face burn, I lifted the publication and attempted to resume my reading. Five minutes later, I had read one paragraph – six times – and by then she had returned, empty tray tucked beneath her left arm. She didn't look my way as she returned to the kitchen, a fact I observed despite my instructions to my own eyes to keep to themselves.

Blessed distraction arrived then. A man and a woman emerged from the hall that led to the staterooms. The man was shorter than the woman, and he had a full head of white hair. It was difficult to guess how old he was because his forehead and cheeks had an almost eerie smoothness. I could only guess that he had had many Botox injections. The woman's age was a clear discrepancy between them: first instinct would put her in her early forties. I had to assume that she was his daughter. He held a phone, his eyes locked on the screen. She followed two steps behind him, delivering a monologue that he clearly was not listening to.

"–if we go that way it will mean losing two guest rooms. I think it'll be worth it, though, because we hardly ever have overnight guests. Most of my friends would be happy to be put up in a hotel rather than actually stay at the house..." The sound of her voice followed them out of the lounge and onto the sun deck.

I changed my opinion: the way she spoke and the way he ignored her, I had to assume this was a married couple. Bummer for them.

I shook myself out of distraction and returned to the article. Nobody came through the room again for a long while, and eventually I was able to settle back into my research. It was decidedly stuffy of me to hide inside, reading articles, while on a state-of-the-art private cruise. This was a prime example of how my career had overtaken my life.

I hadn't told anybody else, not even April, but this trip fell over the unhappy anniversary of my divorce. Six years had been a long time to sequester myself in the world of academia, hiding from most relationships that didn't include scholarly advancement.

Staring at the doorway Jillian had exited through, a smile ghosted across my face. She had been friendly, and she was lovely and smart. Not much like Melanie. Was there any reason I shouldn't look for a woman like that?

Maybe it was time to let a little life back into my life.

***

# *JILLIAN*

"Excuse me."

I looked up from the bar where I was midway through mixing a cocktail. Kenya Adamson stood before me with a shy grin on her face and a large sunhat perched on her head.

"How can I help you, Miss Adamson?"

She rested her elbows on the bar top. "Just call me Kenya. I'm not so fancy like everybody else." She lowered her voice and added, "Meaning, I don't have a huge stick up my..." She broke off and cleared her throat loudly to emphasize her self-censorship. I tried not to laugh. "I mean, can you believe how much Mr. Big-Shot Fancy Pants tipped Alexis for his drink? I think he might have doubled my yearly salary. I'm for real. I've never seen that much money in one place before. It's more proof that I'm way out of my zone on this ship. I wouldn't be surprised if there were $100 bills rolled up in the ravioli tonight."

"Oh, don't be silly," someone else chimed in, breezing into the conversation with ease. "They would never serve anything so pedestrian as ravioli on a barge like this. It's caviar or nothing."

Kenya looked at the newcomer, and her jaw instantly plopped open. "Oh, my word," she whisper-yelled with stars in her eyes, "Bridget Foster! I can't believe you're Bridget Foster. I am in the same room as Bridget Freaking Foster. Would it be totally inappropriate to ask for your autograph? Oh, what am I thinking, of course it would. You're Bridget Foster."

Bridget deserved an Academy Award in Not Running Away from Crazed Fans. She was whipped-cream-smooth, and she smiled like Kenya's outburst had no power to embarrass either one of them. "It's no trouble." She threw a subtle look over her left shoulder, and Patrick, the bodyguard who lived in her shadow, walked away. "Patrick will get you a picture from my things, and I'll write whatever you want."

Kenya looked like she had been promised the key to the city. "You are too amazing."

Bridget, in contrast, perched serenely on a barstool. "Could I get a bottled water? And maybe some nuts, or something?"

Kenya, still starstruck, followed Bridget's example and slid onto a stool of her own — with, I might add, much less grace than her idol had. "Same for me."

I stepped back to fetch their requests and unabashedly eavesdropped on their conversation while my back was turned.

"I'm a big fan," Kenya told Bridget, her voice trembling slightly with excitement. "And I'm a day-one 'Foster Kid.' Your Sym-Pathetic tour was my very first concert. I went with my best friends in middle school."

"I'm always happy to meet a fan," Bridget gave a somewhat canned answer.

"Can I ask you what—"

The deep voice of Bridget's bodyguard cut off Kenya's question. "Bridget would prefer not to talk about her music," he said gruffly. "This is her vacation."

I'm sure Kenya blushed. Hell, I blushed, and I wasn't even part of the conversation!

"Oh, I'm so—so sorry!" Kenya blustered. "Of course you don't want to talk about work. And I'm sure you're just sick of fans gawking at you."

"It's fine," Bridget answered, her voice quiet but cool. "I'm always happy to meet fans."

The way she repeated that same phrase made my brow pucker. She certainly didn't sound like she meant those words. And she sounded exhausted.

As I returned to the bar with water bottles and two bowls of mixed nuts, I observed Bridget's posture: straight back and firmly squared shoulders, but her chin dipped down, her eyes cast toward fingers that strangled a cocktail napkin, her lips pressed in a tense line.

Patrick stood at her shoulder but faced away, watching the door. Kenya looked like she might cry.

I handed over the water bottles and a bowl of nuts, and both women thanked me in subdued tones. Feeling the uncomfortable tension, I offered the only solution I could think of, "Can I turn on the TV for you ladies? We're still in satellite range."

Kenya declined and lifted her water and nuts, stepping away from the bar and crossing the lounge to sit by herself near a window.

Bridget watched her go, then released an unhappy sigh. "I hate when I do that," she muttered under her breath. Then, noticing me watching her, she said, "The TV would be great. Thanks."

I turned on the flat screen behind the bar and gave Bridget the remote, then excused myself to deliver the drink I'd been mixing before the two ladies arrived.

As I crossed through the lounge to take a drink to Portia on the deck, I found Carter still tucked into an armchair with his iPad. Alexis's charge to ask him out flittered through my mind. He was pretty cute, and he had been really nice... Maybe getting to know him better wasn't completely out of the question.

Refusing to let my insecurities talk me out of action, I took a quick breath and took a step in his direction, not sure exactly what I was going to say to him but determined to flirt. Then, before I got there, I saw Kenya cross the lounge and situate herself in the armchair beside him.

She sat with her knees angled toward him, leaning forward as she spoke and showing off bright white teeth and a red-lipstick smile. He lowered his iPad cordially as she started talking. I couldn't help but notice that he kept the screen unlocked, obviously ready to start reading again as soon as she left.

"I heard you were a marine biologist," her voice traveled to me from across the lounge. "Would you mind looking at something I found on the beach?" Then she reached into her bag and extracted a large, pale pink seashell.

Carter's expression morphed instantaneously. He took the shell from Kenya's outstretched hand, turning it over in his fingers almost reverently. He held it close to his face, nearly touching his nose as he examined the bottom. Then, without taking his eyes off the shell, he reached into his shirtfront pocket and withdrew a pair of glasses. He slipped them on and continued his study of the shell, speaking to Kenya about it all the while.

I found myself grinning at the scene. I could see why Kenya had sought out Dr. Buckley's opinion on the shell rather than the stonier Dr. Yung. Plus, Dr. Buckley was really cute.

Alexis came into the lounge then and leaned on the bar across from me, easily following my eyeline and correctly deducing that I'd been staring at our university professor for longer than I should have.

"Could you want him more?"

My cheeks burned with a humiliated blush, and I purposely averted my gaze. "I don't know what you're talking about."

Alexis wasn't buying my obvious lie. "Cut the crap. He's hot, you're hot. You should go for it."

"We don't even know if he's single," I protested. "He's probably married with seven kids. All the good, handsome guys are, you know?"

She leaned across the bar conspiratorially. "Well then, aren't you in for a surprise? I happen to know that he is single. He owns a condo in Sarasota, and he also owns a beach house in Destin, Florida, that he rents out as an Airbnb most of the year."

I stared at her. "How on earth do you know all that?"

She shrugged one shoulder elegantly. "I Google everyone before they come on board. You know that."

She had told me that before, but I never knew the depths she researched. "You're scary."

"I know. So. What are you going to do about Dr. Yummy and the interloper?"

I guffawed at that. "You might have stalking skills, but your nickname game needs some improvement."

"Granted."

"I'm not going to do anything," I told her, dropping my voice. "I am working."

"You are a chicken," she accused.

"I never even said I liked him," I pointed out.

She gave me a sidelong look. "Didn't you, though?"

"No, you invented this forbidden romance just because you're bored of being married."

She gasped. "Too far, Jill." But she jumped back on track immediately. "Don't think I haven't seen the way you've been watching him. You can't pretend you didn't know where he was every minute of the day."

That was undeniably true, but I tried to deny it anyway. "I know where everyone is. It's not that big of a ship."

"Admit it, you would like nothing better than to go over there, throw your arms around him, and drown in those beautiful brown eyes."

I clucked my tongue. "His eyes are blue."

"Aha!" I had fallen into her trap. "So you think he's hot, and we know he's smart, but still you are too afraid to ask him out because... of the husband thing?"

"Oh my gosh, will you drop the husband thing already?"

"I will. On one condition."

"Oh boy. I can't wait to hear it."

She grinned mischievously. "If you go out there and flirt with Dr. Buckley — blatantly, so there's no way he could miss it — then I promise I will never again ask you about your husband."

I studied her for a moment. For some people this would not have been the slightest temptation, but the truth was that Alexis was relentless in asking about what happened with my ex. She had asked me for information about the breakup every day — multiple times a day — since we met. I was about ready to tear my hair out... or hers.

So, I caved.

"Fine. I will go flirt with him, have him laugh in my face, and then you have to leave my love life alone. For good. Agreed?"

Now she beamed and put down the carafe of water she had been holding to extend her hand to shake mine. "Deal. But this had better be some Grade-A flirting. No simple hair toss and a wink. I want words."

Sighing heavily, I lifted a tray of salads that Mikey had prepared and followed Alexis back to the lounge. "Fine. After my break."

She glanced at her wristwatch. "Better take it now. Dinner prep starts in 45."

***

Even though we were surrounded by water, the sun was oppressive. I inhaled deeply through my nose and then let air out in a burst, trying not to break into a sweat. It was cool enough inside the cabins, but out here on the deck, it was all sunshine and heat. It was a testament to my fatigue that I was unwilling to walk the thirty or so steps back into the staff cabin area. Instead, I just kept my right arm crooked over my face, blocking the white sunshine and maybe .2% of the heat. I had collapsed into this unused deck chair on a vacant part of the deck, choosing to start my break right here, right now. My feet ached, and my cheeks did, too. Smiling all day can feel phony, even when you do like your job. My mind drifted toward the memory of cool blue eyes and sandy blonde hair, catching the sunlight as it tousled in the sea breeze. Dr. Carter Buckley was a handsome man, but as good as he looked, it wasn't his face, hair, and biceps that had me thinking about him.

It was the glasses.

I never had a nerdy glasses fetish before, but I grinned as I remembered how he had whipped them out of his shirt pocket and casually put them on to get a closer look at the seashell Kenya had shown him. Like taking a close look at something like that was so ordinary for him that he didn't need to think twice about it. It was so immediate. Seashell? I've gotta get a better look at that!

The man was a marine biologist. At no point in his career had one seashell not become just like any other? Evidently not.

There was a childlike innocence to curiosity like that. The irresistible need to know more about something. To think that an ordinary shell—any shell—was cool enough that it needed its own special time. I just loved that.

And then, in my imagination, the scene continued differently. In my mind, Dr. Buckley then pushed back his hair and met my gaze, eyes sparkling, the corners wrinkled in a grin; he wanted to talk about it. With me! As if I knew anything, as if my thoughts mattered at all to him. And somehow, I knew that they did matter to him. Not scientifically, maybe, but person-to-person, he cared what other people had to say and was open to opinions.

That kind of trait is too rare.

And then, my mind began a leisurely stroll down "What If Road," contemplating just how many butterflies would take flight in my stomach if he had placed that shell aside, strode across the lounge and taken me in his arms ...

Then, as if summoned by my imagination, I heard someone sit down on the lounge chair beside me. I moved my arm from my eyes and startled to find Carter Buckley settling into a reclined position, copying my previous position by slinging his arm over his face.

I allowed a few seconds for my face to cool from my fantasy before addressing the man beside me. "Comfy?"

"Mmm," he hummed happily. "You made this look so good, I had to try it out for myself."

A little thrill tickled its way from my toes up to my cheeks. The pose looked great on him, too. He had changed into board shorts and a white T-shirt, a pair of leather flip-flops, and a pair of mirrored sunglasses (which he had taken off just before covering his eyes with his elbow). His sandy hair was hidden beneath a navy-blue cap. And I noticed just a speck of white on his jaw where he hadn't rubbed in his sunscreen completely. He looked even better than my memory could justify.

"Is it always so hot at sea?" he asked, sitting up slightly and uncovering his face so he could look at me.

"Of course not," I quipped, "sometimes it storms."

"Hmm. Between those choices, I'll keep the heat. I don't have any interest in making the news this week."

"A storm would make the news?"

"It would if it sank our boat, and we all died." He shuddered theatrically.

I suddenly recalled the way he had clutched the white life jacket in his fists during our muster drill, how he had eyed the lifeboat apprehensively, and the tension that had locked up his shoulders when he climbed the gangway. "I get the sense that you're not as comfortable on a boat as I expected, for a marine biologist."

He flinched but didn't deny it. "I'm not afraid of the ocean ... I just have a healthy aversion to drowning."

"And this was never an issue when you chose to study the ocean. For a living."

"I study ocean life," he clarified. "And a great deal of that can be found much closer to shore. And a lot of times, in a lab, under a microscope."

I hummed thoughtfully. "I respect that, but if you're so afraid of ..."

"Drowning at sea," he supplied.

"Right. Then why are you here?"

He smirked. "I was assured that in the event of death at sea, I would be given a full refund."

"75%," I chuckled. "Tips not included."

He laughed at that, then settled himself down onto the lounge chair again, closing his eyes and replacing his sunglasses. "I like you, Jillian. You're the only person on this boat who doesn't take themself seriously."

Pressing my lips together to keep a giddy little giggle at bay, I reminded myself that Dr. Buckley was probably just a very friendly guy. I was sure he liked lots of people. Don't read into it. "Thanks. I like you, too, Carter."

It was his turn to smirk. "You're only saying that so I'll leave a big tip after dinner."

"He's onto me."

Listening to his rich laughter could easily become habit-forming. To distract myself from his handsome face, I reached down for my water bottle. Was the heat out here ramping up, or what? My face felt like it was scorched.

After I replaced my bottle on the deck and reclined on my chair again, Carter and I sat together in companionable silence for a minute or two, listening to the waves slap the hull of the ship, feeling the salty coolness of the spray from the sea. At least, I assumed that's what he was enjoying. Personally, I was trying to figure out what I could say next to rekindle our conversation. Another part of my mind scolded my stupid hormones for considering involvement with a client. Although there wasn't technically a company policy against client/steward romance, I didn't have to be told that it was not a stellar idea.

So, yeah, right. Don't let myself crush on the hunky marine biolo—

"Can I ask a personal question?"

Never mind. I'll get back to that thought later.

"You're welcome to ask. But I reserve the right not to answer."

"Fair enough. So, I was kind of eavesdropping earlier," he admitted with very little chagrin, "and I heard the other stewardess mention your husband."

"Oh."

He paused for a moment, a pink blush creeping up his cheeks. I let him sit with the awkwardness until he got to the actual question he'd alluded to. "Yeah, and I also noticed you don't wear a ring." He gestured somewhat pathetically toward my left hand. "So do you, like, not want people to know you're married? Does that help with ... tips?" By the time he'd finished the question, his face was lobster-red and his voice had nearly petered out. As if he'd realized while he was talking that this was not only a personal question, but an insulting one as well.

I wasn't about to let him off the hook. "So you think I pretend to be unattached so guys will flirt with me and give me more money?"

His Adam's apple bobbed with a gulp, and he pushed up to sit straight, his eyes wide behind his sunglasses. "That is not what I— meant to—I just, I mean I don't... People do that sometimes. Not that it's good... or bad... or... anything. I don't want to imply that you're unfairly taking advantage of your looks."

I raised one eyebrow, perfectly aware that letting him stew in his own stupidity was a special brand of torture.

"Be-because... uh... you're good at your job. And you deserve all kinds of tips, regardless of your looks. Or your... marriage... status. But, uh, all I'm saying is that, uh... I'd be jealous. If I was, um, your husband. He's a lucky guy, you know? And I guess I hope he knows that."

I took a moment before answering. It would be easy to be deeply offended by his careless question. Assuming I would not wear a wedding ring to increase my tips was a slight against my character. But... what did Carter know about my character? Certainly not enough to make any kind of judgment like that. So, maybe I could give him the benefit of the doubt. Just this once.

With a sigh, I relaxed my head on my cushion again. "I guess I can take that as a compliment, then. But you're wrong about my husband."

Carter looked partly relieved to be seemingly forgiven for shoving his foot in his mouth, but the relief was overshadowed by confusion. "Oh?"

"I don't have one." I shrugged one shoulder. "We never made it down the aisle. And just so you know, I wore his ring everywhere until the day I dropped it in a manila envelope and mailed it back to him."

My explanation deflated some of the embarrassment between us, and the tension in Carter's shoulders eased.

"I'm sorry," he said at length. "I really didn't mean to imply—"

"I know. It's okay."

My watch beeped then. "My break's up," I told him, sitting up and stretching briefly. "Guess I'd better get back to it. But feel free to let me know if you have any other potentially embarrassing questions." I grinned at the flummoxed look he gave me. "I'd love to talk to you some more." And with that, I walked away.

***

The afternoon wound down with the usual requests: help store luggage below, bring a drink, take a tray, find the first aid kit, reprint the itinerary. On and on. I was exhausted by dinnertime. When our formal Bon Voyage dinner party began, all the staff assembled in the lounge to welcome our guests. Alexis and I took up posts by the doors to greet everyone, and Mikey sat at the piano and provided beautiful background music. The Bon Voyage party was a Flying Honeymoon tradition, and everyone always enjoyed dressing to the nines for our first dinner together. Our guests always tried to impress each other by dressing in their finest attire. It looked like the living cover of a magazine with all the sparkle and shine and expensive clothing. I felt dowdy in my work uniform.

Kenya Adamson was the first to arrive. She looked stunning in a royal blue dress that shimmered with sequins. She caught my gaze across the room and gave me a little wave, then she went to the bar to get a glass of champagne.

Bridget Foster and her bodyguard, Patrick, came next. She made her way directly to the piano and asked Mikey if he could play a special song. Patrick stood a few feet back, his dark eyes scanning the lounge as if waiting for a gunman to appear at any moment.

Elodia and Portia entered next, followed a minute later by the rest of their party. Howard watched Elodia as she chatted with her friends, his expression unfriendly. The two men that followed him in looked bored. Tyron eyed the bar, and Gordon eyed Alexis.

Better warn Mikey about him.

I welcomed the large group and invited them to help themselves to the buffet. Howard asked me when the captain would finally make an appearance, and I promised him that Captain Skippy would be there shortly.

"What kind of name is 'Skippy'?" he asked dubiously.

"It's a nickname," I explained, infusing my tone with more patience than I felt. "His name is Scott, but he's gone by Skippy most of his life." I smiled at Gordon and Tyron, who did not return the expression. "He's always loved the ocean, and being a ship's captain was his lifetime ambition."

Howard muttered something I didn't care to understand, and I moved along to the next guests to arrive: April Yung and Carter Buckley.

April looked fantastic in a clingy red dress that left little to the imagination. I wondered whose eye she was trying to catch. Was she interested in Carter? He wore a black dress shirt with a blue tie paired with jeans and some nice shoes. Compared to the gentlemen in tuxedos around him, he looked dressed down, but anything fancier would have looked silly with his collar-length hair and surfer-dude vibes. I thought he looked great.

April placed her hand on Carter's arm and leaned close to speak to him. I didn't miss the way he pulled back slightly. Maybe her admiration was unrequited.

My heart perked up a little, and I walked toward them with my perfect smile in place. "Welcome. So glad you could make it. Please, enjoy some food and drinks. Our captain should be with us shortly."

April gave me a brief nod, then walked toward the bar, pulling Carter along by the sleeve. He shrugged a little helplessly and followed his colleague, but he sent me a wave.

As promised, Captain Skippy arrived and greeted the guests with genuine enthusiasm. He made a speech about his hopes for the voyage and his wish that everyone would enjoy their time on the peaceful ocean and make lifelong friends along the way. When he was through, he mingled with the guests, sipping his sparkling water after toasting their champagne.

The rest of us tried to follow his lead and get to know the passengers even while we served them food and drinks and helped clean up the occasional spill. It was a tightrope walk.

An hour after the party began, I finally got a chance to catch my breath. Stealing into the corner to take a sip of water, I scanned the room for impending chaos. Nothing looked ready to explode, to my relief, but I did notice that Carter had slipped out at some point.

I snagged Alexis when she walked by. "Did you see where Carter—Dr. Buckley—went?"

Alexis's eyebrow rose. "Lost track of your quarry?"

"Shut up. I just wondered if you saw him."

She laughed, then gestured toward the door. "He's out on the deck."

She left, and I stood alone for a moment, fighting back the impulse to run out there and talk to him. Then again, I reasoned, everyone deserves a break. And there was no reason why I shouldn't go out there.

For once, I acted on my impulse, picked up a tray of appetizers, and wove my way out of the party and out into the cool evening breeze. I found Carter at the bow in the same position he'd been in that afternoon, face to the wind, eyes closed. Only this time, the light of the sunset painted the scene in romantic brushstrokes.

I approached on measured steps, not wanting to seem over-eager. Even though I was. I'd been thinking about Carter Buckley all day, and I was anxious to talk to him again. He turned when he heard me coming, and I was relieved when he gave me another one of his cheery smiles.

"Hi, Jillian."

"Sorry to bother you," I said, reverting to my 'service mode' out of self-preservation. It turned out to be harder to flirt with my crush than I remembered.

Carter kept smiling and gestured to the tray in my hands. "If you were bringing me food, I'll just tell you that you're welcome to 'bother' me with that anytime."

"I noticed you didn't stick around for dessert, so I thought I'd tempt you. With the cake, of course."

His eyes twinkled, clearly not missing my accidental double entendre. "I could definitely be tempted."

I swallowed convulsively and dropped my gaze, and then, in the klutzy move of the century, dropped the whole tray. Cake and icing splatted to the floorboards, and I dropped to my knees instantly to clean it up. I couldn't believe that I'd made a gigantic mess in front of a guest twice in one day!

Carter knelt beside me in a flash. "Woah! You okay? Let me get that." He lifted a plate from my hands and replaced it on the tray. There were three or four more plates scattered around, and he helped me gather them together and scooped up the splatters of cake and icing. Then, both of us with sticky hands, we stood and examined the mess.

"Well," I stated, feeling the weight of my utter ridiculousness.

Then he snorted, and we both burst into laughter.

"I'm so embarrassed!" I finally said between peals of laughter.

He responded simply by laughing harder. I knew he wasn't laughing at me. But even if he wasn't, well, it's hard not to laugh at a perfect clown.

"I'll go get another piece of cake for you," I said, lifting the tray full of ruined desserts and propping it on my hip.

"Why don't you make that two?" Carter said, laughter still dancing in his eyes.

I noticed his height for the first time. He was taller than me, but he didn't tower over me. It was nice to be able to look into his eyes without craning my neck. I liked his eyes. They were a greenish blue—like a still mountain lake in the sunshine. There were small crinkles around them, like he smiled a lot. Which I knew he did. I noticed, too, that he had a faint suntan line on the bridge of his nose and on the sides of his face. From sunglasses, I surmised. I wondered vaguely if his sunglasses were prescription, like his reading glasses, so that he could use them when he was working. Or if he just wore them when he was driving. Or if...

I suddenly realized that he looked at me expectantly, and I remembered that I hadn't understood what he had just said. "Two?" I repeated, my brain struggling to derail from my fantasies about Carter Buckley's face and retrench itself in my present conversation with the man.

His smile was bemused, but he graciously skipped over my obvious lack of attention. "Yeah, it seems like you could use a break." Then again, maybe he hadn't let it go after all.

Why is it that when an attractive man pays the right kind of attention to a girl, her brain shuts off? There's got to be some evolutionary lesson there. But there I stood, falling victim to chemistry—or biology—and I was really struggling to keep up with Carter. He went on, "Maybe we can sit and talk."

"Over cake?"

"Ideally."

Idiot that I was, I realized I was smiling. "Okay. I can do that."

He grinned. "Then it's a date."

A date! Was I allowed to date a guest? At that moment I cared less about that than I did about my un-date-like attire. "Give me ten minutes to change?"

"Take all the time you want. I'll get us some cake."

Have I mentioned how much I was beginning to like this guy?

***

In my stateroom, I opened my wardrobe hoping that my fairy godmother had made a surprise visit and changed my work clothes

30

into a stunning ball gown. No such luck. Not knowing what else to do, I grabbed my radio and asked Alexis to come to my room and help me.

She arrived two minutes later with Grandpa Skippy hot on her heels. "What's going on?" he demanded, bursting into the stateroom as if ready to fight off an intruder with his bare hands.

"Nothing's wrong, Grandpa. I just need Alexis to help me get dressed for a date."

Alexis squealed delightedly, but Grandpa looked like he'd been slapped. "You have a date?"

I steered Alexis to stand before my woeful wardrobe and asked her to pull an outfit together for me. Then, to Grandpa I sniped, "You heard what I said."

He folded his arms across his uniform with a scowl. "I don't understand. How could you have a date?"

I suppressed the impulse to roll my eyes. "I met a man, cast a spell on him, and tricked him into wanting to get to know me better."

He laughed through his nose. "That, I believe."

"Grandpa!" I cried as Alexis scolded, "Captain Skippy!"

His eyes narrowed. "Which one of these guys is it? Not the beefy guy?"

I mentally flipped through our passenger list and came up with the only man who fit the description 'beefy.' "Patrick?"

Alexis asked, "Is he the bodyguard?"

I shook my head. "Yes, Patrick is Bridget's bodyguard, but no, that's not him." I took a quick little breath then said, "It's Carter. Uh, Dr. Buckley."

"Buckley?" Grandpa Skippy repeated with a furrowed brow. "I thought he was with the other lady. Dr. Yung."

"They came together," I explained, "but they're colleagues, not partners."

The captain harrumphed disbelievingly. "I bet she wouldn't say that, if you asked her."

"What does that mean?"

"I may be old, but I'm not blind. She watches him, follows him. The woman wants him. Bad."

I pursed my lips. Grandpa Skippy had, before becoming a yacht captain, made his living selling diving equipment. He was a born salesman. He could read people better than anyone I'd ever known. "It doesn't matter. He asked me on a date, and I said yes."

Skippy hmphed and turned to leave. "Hope he's ready for a disappointment."

I didn't let on how much that comment stung. I should have been used to Skippy's barbed words by now: it had always been this way between us. He had his reasons for keeping me at arm's length, but it didn't lessen my desire to be close to him.

Grandpa grumbled something about the room getting too crowded and he left.

Alexis didn't acknowledge the awkwardness between me and Grandpa. Still thinking about my date, she was as giddy as a kid at Christmas. "I'll give you $100 if you kiss him," she said with barely contained glee.

Mikey's head popped into the room through the open door. "I'll double it."

Shaking my head slightly to focus less on my strained relationship with my grandfather and more on my upcoming date with Carter. "You don't even know what we're talking about," I retorted to Mikey. Then, back to Alexis, I said, "Just find me something to wear!"

Mikey just shrugged. "I know whose side to be on."

Alexis stood in front of the wardrobe with her hands on her hips, then she looked at me with a pained expression. "This is a hopeless wreck. You're going to borrow my LBD."

I knew the little black dress she was referring to, and I didn't bother trying to hide my pleasure at this offer. I grinned and followed her to her stateroom. "You're the boss!"

# 3

## *JILLIAN*

Carter stood by the rail when I arrived at our spot. It was dusk now, and the sun had painted the sky with brilliant pinks and purples. *Dang, he looked good in this lighting, too.*

When he saw my new outfit, his eyes did an up-and-down perusal, then his smile widened into a broad grin. "Wow. You look ..." He looked at the dress again and couldn't come up with anything more than, "Wow!"

I felt heat rush to my cheeks, and I was glad it was dark out so he wouldn't see how much his compliment made me blush. "Thanks."

Alexis's dress was gorgeous, of course. It didn't fit me perfectly, but I made do. It was a simple black cocktail dress, but what made it sensational was the perfect sweetheart neckline and the high slit over the left leg. It wasn't incredibly revealing, but it was a knockout all the same.

"Hi," he said, approaching the table with a silly grin. Then he gestured toward the plates of cake I'd just put down. "I could have gotten those for us. I was planning to sneak into the kitchen, but there's a really scary-looking lady in there."

"That would be Alexis," I provided, sitting across from him at the little table and sliding a slice of cake to him. "And I'd like to say that her bark is worse than her bite, but I'm pretty sure I heard her husband once claim that she used to be a UFC fighter, so I wouldn't cross her."

"Noted. Still, I feel weird that you brought our dessert. I just want you to know that... I mean, you don't have to be a server on the date. You're on a break, and I don't want you to feel like ... um, I don't know what I'm saying ..."

His embarrassment was just the cutest. "I think I do."

He sighed with relief. "So, uh, can I get you a drink?" His earnest expression shifted slightly to one of puzzlement, and he dropped his voice, "By the way, where can I get a drink?"

I laughed. "Don't worry about it. Alexis is going to come by in a minute. I bribed her with Lindors to play waitress so I really can take a break."

"Are Lindors the most accepted currency in international waters?"

"Sailor's preference," I claimed with a half shrug.

As though summoned by the use of her name, or perhaps by the talk of Lindor Truffles, Alexis came up the stairs then with a tray on her hip.

"Hello," she said as she stopped at our table and placed a Dr. Pepper in front of Carter and a Sprite before me. Then she scowled at the plates of cake. "I see someone brought contraband."

"Life's short," I said with a broad smile. "Thanks for the drinks."

Alexis picked up her tray then turned to go. But before she disappeared back down the stairs, she gave me a knowing look and waggled her eyebrows. I could have killed her.

I picked up my Sprite and took a little sip, then I noticed an extra, folded napkin stuck to the bottom of the glass. I pulled it off and found writing inside the fold.

$100 if you kiss him! – A.

Yeah, I definitely wanted to kill her.

I crumpled the note and tucked it under my thigh, turning my attention back to Carter. He had taken a long drink from his soda glass and was now fidgeting with his dessert fork.

"I've got to tell you something," he said suddenly.

I set down my glass. "Okay."

"This is my first date with a woman in a couple of years."

I responded only by raising my eyebrows.

He cleared his throat, and the fidgeting redoubled. "I mean, I don't exactly date very much. Or ... at all."

"How come?"

"I had a tough breakup a few years back, and, I don't know, I just threw myself into work and studies and stuff and didn't leave any room for anybody else." His expression shifted slightly. "Come to think of it, maybe I was always like this and that's what caused my breakup."

I didn't have a ready answer for that, but Carter didn't seem to mind waiting for my response. Finally, I said, "What changed your mind about this date? Did I rope you into something you don't want to do?"

"No," he answered right away. "That's not what I'm saying at all. I definitely want to be on a date. With you. I just wanted you to know that if I seem uncomfortable, it's not because of you."

"So, you don't date ..." I started.

"Anymore," he added helpfully.

I grinned. "You don't date anymore. I tried that a few months ago, but my mom wouldn't get off my back."

He laughed. "Your mom sounds just like my dad. He can't understand why I don't want a whole houseful of kids and a golden retriever in the backyard. Although, technically, I already have the golden retriever."

The breed of his dog was so fitting for his personality that I nearly burst out laughing. "What's your dog's name?"

"Malibu. My niece wanted her name to be Malibu Barbie, but I thought that was taking things too far."

"I love that. So, you're a successful university professor who loves the ocean, has a dog, and doesn't need a family."

He took a sip of his drink. "Is it a bad thing to be happy where I am?"

"No."

"People are always complaining that they want more of this or more of that, and I just ..." he shrugged one shoulder, "I guess I just want things to stay the same."

Here I was, a yacht stewardess who looked for adventure at every port, on a date with a man who wanted his life to stay exactly as it was. A match made in Heaven.

Suddenly, I felt lighter and more relaxed. He and I were so different that there was zero possibility of this thing becoming an actual relationship. So there was no pressure. I could just enjoy a date with a handsome man and not worry about what happened next.

For an untethered, travel-the-world woman like me, it was good to know this house-and-family man wouldn't be a good fit. ... Right? If that was true, why did I feel oddly disappointed?

"That's good to know." I took another sip of my Sprite, and Carter practically chugged his Dr. Pepper.

It was time for a new subject.

"So," I said, smiling, "can you tell me why your university would pay to send two professors on a cruise of the Bahamas? I assume it has something to do with research, since Dr. Yung brought so much equipment."

Carter relaxed a little. "It's actually not an assignment. There was a raffle last Christmas, and this trip was the grand prize. Dr. Yung won and since it was a trip for two, and we're the only two single professors in our department, she invited me to come. She brought her research equipment to prove a point."

"What point is that?"

"That this isn't a romantic getaway and that she's not coming on to me."

This information eased my mind, but it didn't answer all my questions. "Why did she need to clarify that? Did you think it was a romantic thing?"

"Not at all," he said. "I think it was my fault, though. I had heard a rumor that she was interested in me, so a few weeks ago, I asked her if she had romantic interest in me and wanted her to know that I only saw her as a friend. I told her that if that changed anything about the trip, I'd be glad to bow out. But she told me everything I'd heard was untrue, and she, in fact, had a lot of work to do."

"So you think she brought all the lab equipment to prove to you that she's not interested," I surmised.

"Exactly."

I hummed thoughtfully. "I don't think she's being totally honest about that."

He ran his fingertip along the rim of his glass. "Does it make me sound conceited if I agree with you?"

"Not at all. It takes a wise man to admit that someone else is right," I teased.

He toasted me with his Dr. Pepper. "Touché."

Our conversation turned then from work to home life. I found out that Carter lived in Sarasota with Malibu Barbie, and he liked to take her jogging on the beach before work. His parents divorced when he was a teenager, and his mom died a few years later in a car accident. His dad lived in Washington state, and his only sibling, a sister named Claire, lived close to their dad. Carter had grown up in northern California and learned to love sea life when he'd gone on a field trip to the aquarium in the fourth grade. He liked to read spy novels, and his favorite movie was The Rock.

From there we moved on to a game of rapid-fire questions and answers.

"What's your favorite dessert?" I asked.

"Chocolate cake." He lifted a forkful of the stuff into his mouth then asked his question, "How many boyfriends have you had?"

"Six. Where do you see yourself in three years?"

"Same as now. Boring, I know. Maybe I'll go crazy and get myself a girlfriend. What about you?"

"I don't think I want a girlfriend," I teased.

He laughed. "Where do you see yourself in three years?"

I didn't hesitate with my answer. "Working for Grandpa. I think I'll keep this job until he retires."

"So, is this your career or his?" Carter asked.

"I'm helping him," I defended. "I want him to succeed."

"What would you do if Captain Skippy retired tomorrow?"

That stumped me. I thought about it for a few moments before finally shrugging. "I guess I'd have to go back to the drawing board."

He accepted this answer with a slow nod. Then he looked at his watch. "It's getting kind of late," he observed. "But I have one more question."

I looked at the time, too. It was nearly ten o'clock. "Okay. One more question each. You first."

He leaned toward me slightly, his head cocked to one side. "If we had met somewhere other than this ship, and I had asked you out, would you have said yes?"

I countered his question with my own, "If we hadn't met on this ship, would you have asked?"

"Is that your final question?"

"It is."

"Yes," he said.

I grinned. "It's a yes for me, too."

Now he grinned at me. "Good."

We stood from our little table, and I resisted the urge to bus the dishes. I remembered I was wearing a borrowed cocktail dress, and I was off the clock. Instead of busying my hands with cleaning, I found myself reaching for Carter's hand and walking toward the deck railing. He didn't hesitate to follow my lead, and my heart warmed at the way he looked at me and squeezed my fingers.

I stepped up to the railing and took a few moments to breathe in the sea air as I looked out at the eternal star-scape around us. It was a stunning night. "I need to do this more often," I breathed.

I felt him turn to look at me. "Date your passengers?"

I bumped his side with my shoulder. "I mean stop and smell the roses—so to speak."

"It's a good idea. But you know, I wouldn't mind if you went on another date with a passenger. At least, this passenger."

I turned to face him. "Are you asking me out again?"

"Not yet." He cleared his throat. "Jillian, would you go out with me again?"

"Yeah."

"Good."

And then another person must have possessed my body because my next move was out of character. I took a small step toward him, lifted onto my toes and pressed my lips to his.

It was a brief kiss, and I pulled away almost as soon as I'd realized what I'd done. I didn't retreat, though. My face was near his, and his eyes opened. Then his hand cupped my jaw and pulled me back in for another warm kiss.

When I pulled away again, it was with a huge grin on my face and a delighted tingle pinging through my entire body.

"I'll see you in the morning," I murmured, delighted with the way he continued to hold my hand and gaze at me like he would like to keep me here longer.

"Good night, Jillian." Then he leaned down and pressed a kiss to my cheek. "Thanks for a great date."

I floated back to the kitchen where I found Alexis and Mikey cleaning up the last of the dishes. "You owe me $100."

***

I had intended to take the rest of the night off and let Alexis handle any service calls, but the truth was I was too wound up to sleep right away, and Alexis looked dead on her feet. I told her to head to bed and promised I'd sit up in the kitchen until the room service "last call" at 11:30. All our passengers had seen themselves to bed not long after I'd returned from my date with Carter, so I expected a quiet shift.

There was a high-powered radio on board that sometimes let us pick up radio chatter, so I used the lull in work to tune in and try to get some juicy gossip. I happened upon a channel where two fishing rig captains were discussing a recently reported sighting of an escaped convict. I recognized the name and story from the newsreel I'd caught earlier that day.

The convict's name was Giovanni Accardi, and he'd escaped from police custody in Italy, but just that afternoon he'd been reportedly spotted in Nassau, Bahamas. The fishermen were discussing the bounty on the man's head, hoping that one of them would be able to collect it. If they found him swimming across the ocean, they said, it'd be like noodling catfish to bring him to justice.

I rolled my eyes and switched off the radio. Like a hardened criminal would be stupid enough to just start swimming. I sat back in an armchair and had just pulled out the mystery novel I'd been halfway through for two months when I heard the door to the lounge open and close. The lounge and kitchen were separated by a metal door that usually stayed closed, but I'd left it open a crack after Alexis had gone to bed.

I set my book down and started to rise to greet whomever had entered the lounge, but my motion was halted by a sharply raised voice. It was Bridget.

"Let go of me!" she cried. "What has gotten into you tonight?"

"I'm sorry," a male voice replied. It was her bodyguard, Patrick. "Did I hurt you?"

She didn't answer the question and asked one of her own. "What's so urgent it can't wait until tomorrow?"

I reached the door and stepped up silently, angling myself so I could see into the lounge without being spotted right away. I saw Patrick standing beside the outer door with his hands stuffed in his pants pockets, his gaze downcast and his shoulders slightly hunched. Bridget strode away from him with straight shoulders and a scowl, rubbing a spot on her forearm. When she was ten paces away, she sat primly on a sofa and faced him with her mouth set in a hard line, folding her arms tightly across her stomach.

"I feel like I've been more than compassionate until now," she went on when he remained silent. "I had the rest of the team stay back, like you asked, so we could have a chance to talk privately. So ...? Start talking."

"You already know what I'm going to say," Patrick said in a murmur so low I barely caught it. He looked up at her then, his dark eyes sad and pleading.

She must have already known, because her posture and expression did not change. Still, she didn't let him off easy. "Why don't you do us both the courtesy of saying it out loud. Then we can talk about it like adults."

He crossed the room and dropped to his knees before her, his hands resting on either side of her hips on the sofa, his face inches from hers. The empty room carried his whisper like a shout. "I love you, Bridget. You're the most beautiful and amazing woman in the universe to me. I have to be with you. I'll die if you don't let me ..." He reached up and touched her face.

She flinched away from his caress, and he let his hand drop to the cushion, his head falling forward with defeat. All at once, he collapsed into her lap, wrapping both arms around her and pressing his face into her thighs.

"Change your mind," he begged. "Please give me another chance. I messed up last time. I know that, but please. You don't know what you're doing."

"Pat," she tried, placing a hand softly on his hair. "It's not that you're not—"

"No!" he reared back, pulling away from her hand but not releasing her waist. His motion pulled her forward off the couch and down onto the floor in front of him. "I'm not giving up, B," he said, his voice turning hard as his grip strengthened around her. "We belong together," he claimed wildly. "You belong to me!"

He bound her tight against his chest and began to kiss any part of her face he could reach. She shouted at him to stop. I was already halfway across the room.

My 5'9" frame was no match for his 6' wall of muscles, but I had the element of surprise on my side. I grabbed him by both shoulders and pulled him backward, breaking him from Bridget, who scrambled away and got to her feet.

I pushed Patrick away from me, and he stumbled and dropped to a knee on the carpet. He knelt like that for a long moment, not trying to stand. He just put his face in his hands and hunched into himself on the floor.

I spoke to Bridget when I was fairly sure Patrick wouldn't jump at her again. "Miss Foster, you can head back to your stateroom if you'd like. I'll have the captain radio the Coast Guard and have them take him away."

Bridget had been backing away from Patrick, but she stopped then, obviously torn by indecision. "I don't think he should be arrested," she said.

I looked at her, waiting for her to say exactly what she did want to happen to her assailant.

"I—I'll deal with it," she told me. She straightened her shirt and her shoulders. "Thank you for your help. Patrick," she waited for him to look up at her. When he did, she went on, "You've always been my friend, and a good bodyguard. I don't want to jeopardize that over something so ..." she searched for the right word. I had several come to mind, but I kept them to myself. She finally settled on, "overblown."

Patrick jolted slightly at the word, his expression changing from misery to offense. "Overblown?" he repeated.

"Yes. I think you're just ..."

Patrick got slowly to his feet, his demeanor darkening along with his scowl. "This isn't some stupid crush, Bridget. And I'm not overreacting. I'm in love with you. I could make you happy. I could satisfy every desire ... even the ones you didn't know you had. You need me." He stepped toward her. "I can't live without you ... I won't live without you. And you ..."

I had heard enough. "Patrick," I interrupted. "You need to stop. This isn't going to happen."

It seemed that Bridget was done listening, too. "I'm going to bed. I want you to leave me alone until you get your head back on straight." She took a quick breath then went on, "And I can't work with you anymore. Not until you get away from the crowd you're in." Her shoulders straightened again and she gave him a serious glare. "I'm not your woman, and I don't want to be. But I am your friend. If you want me to stay that way, you've got to straighten out your life." With her piece said, she nodded at me then turned and left the lounge.

Patrick started to charge after her, but I stepped in front of him. "You'll leave her alone," I growled, feeling like a butterfly trying to intimidate a wolverine. "Go back to your room, and in the morning, we will bring this before the captain."

Patrick scoffed and shouldered past me. He left the lounge, but he didn't follow Bridget's path to the staterooms, heading instead out onto the deck, digging in his pocket for a cigarette as he went.

The residual adrenaline in my system made my arms and hands tingle. I took a different route to the staterooms and made sure Bridget was safely locked in her room before I returned to the kitchen and paced for a while, trying to convince my heart to return to its normal rhythm.

It was about forty-five minutes before I felt normal again. And, predictably, boredom returned not long after that.

***

It was after midnight when I received my final room service call of the night. It was from the Lovells' stateroom, requesting a bottle of wine, crab dip, and crackers.

With a tray cocked against my hip, I balanced the wine bottle and upturned glasses while I briskly knocked on the stateroom door. There followed a few moments of muffled shuffling and the exchange of voices before the door cracked open very slightly and Howard Lovell stuck his nose and one eye through the opening.

"Who is it?" he demanded waspishly. "Don't you see the Do Not Disturb sign?"

Glancing at the conspicuously vacant doorknob, I took a short breath to fix my professional mask into place before offering an undeserved apology. "Terribly sorry to disrupt, Mr. Lovell. I'm just bringing by the room service order. Your Do Not Disturb sign must have been knocked off. Don't worry, I'll get you a new one, and we can be sure this won't happen again."

He harrumphed in such a way that let me know that, in a former life, he was either a walrus or a mustachioed villain. "Well. We'll just see about that, won't we?"

Ah, Mr. Lovell was going to be a tough fish to fry, I could see. Did it make me a little crazy that I got satisfaction from winning over grumpy rich people in three days or less? The jury is still out on that one.

"Please, allow me to comp this bottle, for the trouble," I said, using my placating cheerful-but-not-in-your-face voice.

He snapped the tray out of my hands with a perfunctory growl. "It had better be. And don't expect any tip, either, young lady. You won't be getting any handouts from us!"

And with that sour declaration, he retreated into the stateroom and the door thudded closed. I closed my eyes as I turned to go, letting my winning smile slip away, ironed into a flat line as I pressed my lips together, hard. In my first year as a stewardess on Grandpa's yacht, exchanges like this were more likely than not to make me cry a few stubborn tears alone in the staff room. These days, used as I was to being treated like the gum on the bottom of a $500 loafer, I practiced my quick meditation and recited my mantra internally:

You're worth more than they could ever afford, billionaire or not. He probably ruined his own day long before you got here; don't let him ruin yours.

This mantra had to be coupled with at least one minute of deep breathing to keep the tears at bay. That's what happens when you are "overly sensitive," as my mother used to say.

I was about fifteen seconds into my breathing ritual when, without warning, the stateroom door opened again. I jumped back, startled, expecting Mr. Lovell to rail into me again. Breathing could only do so much to waylay tears if someone was actually yelling in my face.

It wasn't Mr. Lovell, though. It was Elodia Francom. She was wearing a satin nightgown and the kind of fluffy feather slippers that you only see in Old Hollywood movies. Her blonde hair was neatly braided back into a long plait that slung over her shoulder like a sleeping boa, but wispy curls framed her cheeks and ears, softening her look. The corners of her still perfectly-lipsticked lips were downturned in a disapproving frown. She closed the door behind her, and then, feeling the draft in the hallway from the sea air, wrapped her arms firmly around herself.

"I'm so sorry about the mis—"

But she put up a hand to stop me before my apology could really get rolling. "No, please. It's us that should apologize. Or,

Howard, really. But I haven't ever heard him apologize to someone in the six years I've known him, and I'm not holding my breath." She laughed lightly, and I wasn't quite sure what to do with myself. She went on before I could get my footing in the conversation. "Anyway, please don't bother comping the wine. I'm happy to pay for it, and," she unfolded her arms and extended some money, folded between her ringed fingers, "here's a tip. I included extra for having to deal with ..." she inclined her head back toward the stateroom door. "He can be ..." Her cheeks flushed then as she seemingly realized she was about to start gossiping with a mute servant. She cleared her throat. "Again, I apologize for the rudeness. I will answer the door myself, in the future."

She smiled at me with quiet kindness, previously masked behind money and arrogance. "Thank you, Jill. Good night." Then she let herself back into the stateroom and closed the door once again.

Feeling mollified and more than ready to crawl into my bunk, I left the stateroom hallway and returned to the deck. I had just ascended the top step when a voice from the darkness startled me to a halt. It was a male voice speaking impatiently. "Antonio, wait." I paused, listening for a response, but none came. The voice fell silent momentarily then he spoke again.

"I told you I'm working on it," he growled loudly enough for me to understand. "Just give it an hour." Another pause, and I realized he was on the phone. "Yes, I'm sure I can handle it. I'll take care of the starch-shirt and meet you there." Another long pause then he said in a low growl, "Fine. Do what you want, let's just get going." Then there was a faint beep—he had ended the call. Footsteps started in my direction. Without really knowing why, I retreated down two steps so he wouldn't see me as he passed the stairwell. The shadowy figure of a man scuttled past my hiding place without turning an eye toward me. When he was gone, I released the breath I'd been holding.

I wondered how he had gotten service to make a phone call. Then I reasoned that it must have been a satellite phone, and I put the matter from my mind. The passengers' affairs were really none of my business. As long as it didn't interfere with the ship, whoever-he-was could make as many phone calls as he pleased.

I tucked my empty tray under my arm and returned to the kitchen, ready to clean up and finally call it a night. I was exhausted, and I knew the next morning would start far too early.

# 4

## *JILLIAN*

When my alarm sounded the following morning at five a.m., I shut it off without opening my eyes, allowing myself a few moments to breathe the cool, salty air before facing another busy day aboard the ship. In those peaceful moments between sleep and being fully awake, I drank in the rocking of the ship, usually so peaceful at this time of morning. But my brow furrowed slightly, and I propped myself up on my elbow when I recognized that this morning's rocking was not gentle at all. In fact, now that I was listening for it, I could hear heavy waves slapping the sides of the hull, and the vessel swayed ominously with each clap. If I hadn't spent an hour the previous night going over the weather forecast with Grandpa, I would have guessed we were in the middle of a storm.

"This can't be right," I said to myself, swinging my legs out of my berth. The boat rocked, knocking me off balance, and I caught myself on the wall. With growing concern, I changed from my pajamas into my work clothes and slipped on my deck shoes before making my way out of my stateroom. My room didn't have a porthole window, so it wasn't until I was out of the crew member quarters that I finally caught a glimpse of the sky.

It was still early, and the sun should have been peeking its face above the horizon just now. Instead, I saw the sky enshrouded in near blackness, with dark, angry clouds churning all around us. A flash of lightning split the sky, illuminating rain that came down in sheets, falling at a steep angle in the gale-force winds.

How did we wind up in such a terrible storm when the forecast called for clear skies?

Before venturing to the bridge to check on Grandpa, I grabbed my raincoat and, out of habit, a life jacket. With both items secured around my shoulders, I opened the door and stepped out into the storm.

The force of the wind took my breath away. Being in the Caribbean, it wasn't a cold wind, but it brought with it enough rain that every exposed article of clothing was drenched instantly. Grabbing the railing on the wall, I turned my face into the wind and made my way, one forced step at a time, toward the bridge. Unsurprisingly, there was no one else out in the early morning storm. I scooted along the railing as quickly as I could, eager to get out of the rain and into the warmth of the bridge. When I reached the door, I opened it with cold but grateful fingers, ready for the warmth and light to wash over me as it always did from the control room. When the door opened, I was met by no shaft of light, though. I opened the door fully and slipped inside, closing it firmly behind me before turning to address Grandpa.

"Where did this storm come from, huh?" I asked the back of his Captain's chair. The room was warm, as I had expected, but dimly lit—the only lights emanating from the control panel and monitors. I shook some water droplets from the end of my ponytail and approached the bench.

"Boy, it's dark in here. You're not sleeping on the job are you, Skippy?" I asked with laughter in my voice.

When he didn't immediately respond with a snarky quip, my eyebrows raised, and I closed the distance between myself and his chair.

"Something going on?"

No answer. That's when I saw his coffee mug overturned, cold dark liquid soaking the control panel.

"Grandpa?" I reached out and turned his chair to face me, and I gasped, my blood running cold in my veins when I saw his face. He was slouched in the chair, mouth open and eyes half shut. A dark red streak of blood cut down the right side of his head, pooling in the white fabric of his collar. His skin was pale, and I could hear raspy, shallow breaths rattling his chest.

"Grandpa!" I dropped to my knees beside his chair, reaching for his head and pressing two fingers to the side of his neck. His pulse was weak. I patted the cheek on the side of his face that wasn't crusted with dried blood and said his name again, trying to rouse him back to consciousness. My efforts were wasted: he didn't move any more than to continue with shallow breathing.

My heart pounded in my ears, panic threatening to overtake me. I needed help. I could administer first aid, but—I suddenly realized—no one was controlling the ship. And it was unclear just how long we'd been moving fast with no one at the helm. I hesitated briefly between continuing to try to rouse Grandpa and taking the controls.

Remembering the ten passengers aboard, my responsibility to them won out. I left Grandpa's side and took control of the ship.

The motors were running at a moderate cruising speed, making the whole yacht fight with every crashing wave. My first move was to kill the motor. The vicious rocking of the ship lessened right away, but I knew there was more to rescuing a ship from a storm than killing the motor and praying for the best. Unfortunately, my knowledge of the ship was limited to basic controls and emergency navigation. I certainly needed the latter now, but getting ourselves to land was secondary to making it through this storm.

To emphasize the urgency, lightning flashed across the dark sky once again, illuminating the dim room with shocking white clarity. My heart thundered in my throat just as real thunder roared from the heavens. The sound was so loud and so close that a scream was startled from my throat.

Hands shaking, I reached for the short-range radio. My fingers slipped off the talk button twice before I was able to make the connection and call for our first mate. "Eric, do you copy?" For a moment there was no response. I tried again, "Eric, this is Jillian on the bridge. Are you there?"

"Copy, Jillian," Eric's voice finally sounded back through the radio. "Who drove us into Hell?"

Knowing that this radio wave was shared by all the crew members, and not wanting to cause more alarm than the storm was already creating, I kept my message to the point, "I need you on the bridge ASAP."

There was a few seconds' pause before Eric's voice finally crackled back, his tone lower and tinged with some of the urgency I felt, "Copy. I'm on my way."

With help on the way, I turned from the control panel and knelt beside Grandpa again. He hadn't moved in the few moments since I'd left him. I thought his awkward position on the chair might be causing the shortness of breath, so I slid him slowly from the seat to lie flat on his back on the floor. Right away, his breathing evened out. Feeling slightly calmer, it occurred to me to turn the lights up to better assess his condition. On my way back from the light switch, I grabbed the first aid kit that was clipped to the wall. With the lights on and tools in hand, I sat beside him again and examined the wound on the side of his face.

All the blood seemed to be from a single shallow gash just above his right temple.

"What happened?" I whispered, gently cleaning blood away from the wound with a moist towelette from the first aid kit. I could only imagine that, for whatever reason, he had fallen forward in his chair and hit his head against the control station, causing the wound and knocking him unconscious. But how long ago? Grandpa Skippy was spry, but he was not a young man. A head injury and blood loss at his age was a very serious matter.

A nurse, I was not. I didn't know what else to do but wipe the blood away, cleanse the area, and bandage the bloody gash. By the time Eric burst through the door, I was just wrapping a bandage around Grandpa Skippy's head.

Eric's eyes were wide and his face ashen. "What's going on? What happened to the captain?"

"I don't know, but I need you to take charge of the controls," I said. "He's alive, but he won't wake up. He needs help fast. Can you tell how far we are off course?"

Eric had taken the helm and was studying the monitors before I'd finished speaking. He had been in the Navy when he was in his early twenties, so he was a natural at taking charge of perilous situations at sea. He looked at the monitor for a few moments, then I saw his Adam's apple bob as he swallowed hard.

"Skippy insisted on taking the night shift," he began in a low, slow voice, "and he was going to set our course for the Nassau. Right now, we're about a hundred miles southwest of there. We're halfway between The Bahamas and Cuba."

"So ... we've been adrift for hours?"

"Not so much adrift as much as charging forward in the wrong direction. The storm certainly isn't helping."

I gulped, taking in this information with a growing feeling of panic in my chest. "What ... what do we do now? Is the ship okay?"

"I'd need to do a walkabout to be sure, but it seems like everything is functional now. But unless one of our upper-crust passengers happens to also be an EMT, we ought to get the Coast Guard out here to treat Skippy. I don't like how pale he is."

I gulped in another quick breath. "Agreed. Okay, yeah. Call for help. I'll go see if any of the passengers are awake and try to keep everyone calm."

Another great wave battered the boat, and I stumbled into the door. Eric clutched the captain's chair for support, and several frightened screams reached us from the main part of the ship. Eric and I exchanged alarmed looks. "Better get going."

Then we each said at the same time, "Good luck." I opened the outside door again, cast one final glance back at where Grandpa Skippy still lay on the floor, then stepped back out into the wind and rain.

I didn't know how long I had been on the bridge, but it wasn't long enough for the sun to make any change to the darkness of the stormy sky. It still felt like the dead of night, and the storm had intensified. With my feet slipping on the rain-slicked deck, I once more held the railing as I made my way to the first door leading into the main part of the ship, which led into the dining galley.

After securing the door behind me, I pushed wet strands of hair out of my face with shaking hands. I couldn't get the image out of my head: Grandpa slumped helplessly in that chair, bleeding. He must have been there for hours. I cursed myself for not checking on him after the party last night. I shouldn't have let myself get distracted—I should have been there to help him ages ago.

Worried and distracted by thoughts of Skippy as I was, I had taken several steps into the dining room before I realized that I was not here alone.

"Jillian." Carter stood along the starboard bank of windows, his hands wrapped in a white-knuckle grip around a dining chair. His eyes were wide and his brow was creased with obvious alarm. "I hoped I'd see you."

After our warm conversations and obvious connection last night, those words under other circumstances probably would have made me blush. Now, though, the anxiety in the room swirled like the wind outside. Tension abounded, but I was the professional here.

I tried to put on a convincing face of reassuring confidence. I'm certain that I failed.

"Sorry to keep you waiting," I said. "Is the storm upsetting your stomach? We have some patches or seasickness bracelets, if you need one."

He rubbed a hand on the side of his face. "I'll admit that is what woke me up." And now that he said that, I could see that he looked a little green. "But once I saw the storm ..." he trailed off and released a ragged-sounding breath. "I'm not a huge fan of open water," he admitted in a strained tone. "I'm afraid the storm isn't helping to ease my fears."

My already dry throat got a little drier. I was still searching for words to begin breaking the news that we were hundreds of miles off course and in the heart of a major tropical storm when Carter caught sight of my expression, and his face paled.

"What's going on?"

I cleared my throat twice. "First, you need to believe me when I tell you that we're safe, and that we've got everything under control."

"You're scaring me, Jill."

After briefly closing my eyes and breathing in one more dose of courage, I blew out a quick burst of air and tried to begin with, "Grandpa Skippy …" But emotion suddenly clogged my throat as the memory of that beloved old man lying broken on the floor.

Carter's grip tightened on the chair momentarily before he rounded the table, closing the distance between us and placing one hand on my shoulder. The fear that had been apparent on his face before was gone, completely replaced by concern. "The captain?"

I fought through the tightness of my throat to draw a breath. "He hit his head somehow. I found him just now, and when I left he was still unconscious. I … I don't know if he's going to be okay. And … even worse, the engines were going full speed when he … when whatever happened to him so …" I had to break off as my throat closed up painfully again.

Realization dawned in Carter's eyes as he fit together the unspoken pieces. "So … for hours we've been just … speeding through the ocean? With no one steering?"

Licking my lips, I nodded once. "Eric is trying to pinpoint exactly where we are right now. And he's sending out a signal for help."

His eyes drifted toward the storm-darkened windows again. "That would explain the sudden change of forecast, I guess," he said dryly.

I snorted a humorless laugh at his quip. "Guess so." I rubbed my hands over my face. "I need to tell everyone what's going on." My gaze crept to the galley doors, and I thought I heard voices on the other side. I found myself chewing on my bottom lip. What on earth was I going to say? If this conversation was any indication, I was not going to be able to do this smoothly.

Seeing the anxiety on my face, Carter seemed to wipe out all of his own fear and misgivings and the confident scientist from the day before returned with stars. "What can I do?"

Gratefully, I gave him a little smile. He really was so sweet. "Just come with me and, I don't know, stab me with a fork if I start acting ... unprofessional again."

"Unprofessional," he repeated with one eyebrow raised. "You mean, if you act human at all."

This time my little laugh had the slightest tinge of real humor. "Yeah. That."

We crossed the dining room together, and he held the door open for me to precede him into the lounge, where it seemed the entire occupancy of the yacht was milling around, waiting for me with about a thousand questions.

I took a breath, sent a prayer to heaven, pasted on my professional air, and dove in.

***

With the exception of Howard and Elodia, all of the passengers had been abruptly awakened by the last huge wave that had rocked the ship. Dr. Yung complained about falling from her berth and spraining her wrist trying to break her fall. She was huddled on one of the sofas, wrapped in a blanket with one hand firmly clasped around the opposite wrist. No one else claimed any injury, but nearly all of them were livid at the storm. Portia griped about the poor quality of the stateroom cabinet because she had lost her cell phone in the rough waters. Bridget and Dr. Jung made similar complaints, but Howard snapped at them to pipe down because they didn't have service out here anyway. His demand was to know how the weather had been forecasted so terribly. Naturally, they tore into me right away, demanding to know how our forecast had missed a hurricane's approach. It took several minutes for the din of shouts and complaints to die away enough for me to finally speak.

Speaking calmly and miraculously emotion-free, I explained that our captain had suffered a medical incident, and that help was on the way.

I was unimpressed when the next question I received at this pronouncement was from Portia, "So how long until we get back on course?" she asked in a voice that clearly indicated that her vacation itinerary was much more pressing than saving a man's life.

"I have not yet gotten an update from our first mate," I explained, fighting back the urge to grit my teeth and yell at this airheaded woman about priorities. "As soon as I am able, I will go back and get an idea about when help will arrive."

"Well, I hope you know that if we don't get to Nassau today, we will be demanding a full refund," Tyrone snapped in a tone that hid none of the glee he felt at wielding such a threat.

What wonderful people I have surrounded myself with, I thought glumly.

As if he'd read my thoughts, Carter stepped up at that moment, proving yet again that he was a cut above the rest. "The staff have enough to worry about right now without you making stupid threats about refunds." He turned then to the rest of the group. "Does anybody else have anything productive to add to this conversation? If not, I'm sure Jill is eager to get back to her grandfather."

His brief speech had the desired effect: no one else made any argument or demanded a refund. The conversation that followed was more subdued. I explained that, while the ship was seaworthy enough to survive these waves, it would be in everybody's best interest to keep a life jacket nearby until the waves died down. This information served to further dampen the spirits in the room, but it couldn't be helped.

Although this meeting certainly wasn't the highlight of my career, I felt confident that at least everyone would be safe for the time being. Chef Mikey offered to prepare breakfast as usual, and I gratefully agreed that that would help the mood. He invited all of the guests to wait for a meal in the dining room, and with only a few grumbles, all of the guests filed through the door Carter and I had recently come through. I was pleased to note that each of them was carrying a life jacket under an arm, if not wearing one, fully buckled, like Kenya and Bridget.

Once they were gone, I looked up at Carter. "Thank you. That was ..."

He cut me off with a shrug. "It could have been worse."

"If you say so. I'd better get back to Grandpa. You should go enjoy some breakfast. I'm sure we'll get some answers from the Coast Guard really soon."

"I'd rather be with you," he said with a transparency that, I think, surprised him as much as it did me. "If you don't mind."

For the second time, amidst the insanity that had been the last half hour, I genuinely smiled, and I found myself reaching for his hand. "I don't mind."

"Good."

The thrilling feeling of walking hand-in-hand with a guy I was crushing on was squashed as soon as we stepped out of the warm galley and back into the swirling storm.

Being that our sailing courses usually took us through calm, sunny waters, it hadn't occurred to me before how inconvenient it was to have access to the bridge from outside doors only. The rain hadn't eased up, and the journey back to the bridge was as treacherous as before. Water sloshed into my shoes and dripped from my hair, and a great gust of wind caught my breath and whisked it away to the sea.

I tightened my grip on Carter's hand, and he squeezed my fingers in return. Reassuring.

I led him to the bridge as quickly as I could, and soon we ducked back through the door to find Grandpa Skippy and Eric, just as I had left them. Eric was surprised to see Carter with me, but not wanting to get into the whole thing, I just introduced the two of them and moved into the heart of the matter.

"How's Skippy?"

Eric shook his head. I could see strain clearly etched into his face. "No change."

Swallowing back a surge of fear, I kept focus on the important highlights I needed. "How far out is the Coast Guard?"

The lines on Eric's face seemed to sharpen and I saw his hand clench on the radio he held in his left hand. "I haven't been able to reach them. I haven't been able to reach anybody."

"What?" I gasped. "Why not?"

His expression was grim, but he shot a glance at Carter, obviously hesitant to share too much with a passenger present.

"Just tell us," I urged. "He deserves to know what's going on as much as anybody else."

Eric took in a short breath, blew it out again, then ran his hands through his hair. "Something's wrong with our transmitter. I can't get any messages out or in. And, from what I can tell, our navigation system isn't working right either. I have no idea where we are. We are stranded in the middle of a hurricane, somewhere in the ocean, with no way to call for help."

And here I had thought the morning couldn't get any worse.

Carter's face was white as paper and his mouth had dropped open.

Eric, noticing Carter's blanched complexion, with a mirthless grunt added under his breath, "Told you we shouldn't tell him."

I was not any better composed after this devastating revelation. The rational part of my brain seemed to have staggered to a halt. Stranded? Who gets stranded these days? What happened to our technology? This could not be happening.

I stammered a few times. Closed my mouth, gulped twice, then started stammering again. "I-I—we ... What are we going to do?"

Eric looked like he had been slapped across the face a few times and was struggling to recover. Granted, he was further along on this acceptance pathway than Carter and I were, but it was still a lot to take in. "I can keep sending out our S.O.S. beacon, and hopefully somebody nearby will pick it up."

"That one is still working?" Carter asked in a hoarse voice.

Eric nodded. "As far as I can tell. But the chances of another vessel being within range in this kind of storm are very low. Our best bet would be to get up on the roof and see what's going on with our antennae. My guess is the wind has broken it."

"Do we have a replacement?" Carter asked.

This, I knew the answer to. "Yes. I can get it from storage and climb up there."

"You're not climbing up there in this storm," Eric protested firmly. "I'll go."

"You need to keep us from capsizing," I countered, gesturing to the control panel. I could feel my rationality slowly returning. I had been trained for this eventuality. Granted, I never dreamed I would ever have to employ the training I got years ago, but still. It was in my brain somewhere.

"I'll do it," Carter offered. "At least if I get struck by lightning, we still have a full crew to take care of everybody else."

"Don't be stupid. You're not risking your neck—"

Eric cut me off. "I agree with Jill. No passenger of mine is risking his neck on my watch."

"But—"

"You can help, though," Eric continued. "You go together, just make sure she doesn't fall."

Carter accepted this plan with a nod, and we were just preparing to head out into the storm once again when the floor seemed to be yanked from beneath our feet.

With a great groan, the yacht tipped perilously toward the starboard side. This was the worst lurch yet, and I fell to my knees, sliding several feet across the floor before the world was righted again. There was hardly a second before it happened again, this time in the other direction. I heard Carter call out, but his yell was covered by my own scream as I fell bodily to the floor and was thrown, hard, against the door.

Eric had been tossed against the control panel and was fighting to get back to his feet to retake control of the helm. My head was spinning, and I felt throbbing pain behind my ear, all before I even realized I'd smacked my head in my fall. I clutched my head, groaning, and I opened my eyes enough to see that Carter was doing the same. And, distantly, I heard screaming.

I pushed myself up to my knees, holding onto the door handle for support. Was someone hurt? I had to go help!

"Jill," I heard Carter say as I jerked myself to my feet, "don't go out there!"

"I have to help," I said, yanking on the door as my head swam. Was that from the hit or was the ship falling again?

The door opened under my insistence, and the rain and seawater met me with full force. So much water poured down on me, I felt like I had fallen into the ocean. I felt someone grab my arm from behind, then I heard the door slam shut again behind us.

Lightning split the sky, followed instantly by the loudest clap of thunder I had heard in my life—so loud I instinctively threw my arms over my head and crouched to the deck. Carter had done the same, and we stumbled together toward the outer railing as the sea tossed the ship yet again.

But then ...

The horizon disappeared, and over the side of the ship I saw nothing but dark, angry skies. All sounds seemed to evaporate except my own gasp as my stomach dropped, and I lost touch with the deck.

I fell.

It felt like I might fall forever, but it was really only a second or two before my fall was broken by the wall, just outside the bridge. My shoulder hit first, and pain sliced through the joint from the impact as the rest of my weight plowed into the wall. With a sickening *whump*, Carter hit the wall beside me. We locked eyes, our expressions conveying equal amounts of terror.

Though shocked from the fall, I hadn't lost my sensibility entirely. I knew that, pain or not, we were still on the ocean being tossed by titan waves, and the age-old adage was ever true: what goes up must come down.

If we were tossed this direction, it was nearly certain that we would be thrown, with as much force or more, the other way. And if we fell the other way ...

I blinked myself out of whatever stupor I had been under. "We've got to move!" I screamed over the wind. We needed to get inside or lashed to the deck. One more wave like that, and we were certain to be thrown overboard.

My logic couldn't make my body move, however. The ship had righted again, enough that Carter and I found ourselves yet again on the deck, but there was no time to run, nothing to grab hold of, nothing to keep us tethered to the ship as, inevitably, a wave pulled the ship upward yet again—drastically, dramatically, dizzyingly. Sideways. More than sideways.

My body pitched, and I fell again.

Headlong, flailing, screaming.

Momentum carried me off the ship completely, tossing me into a black wave, my terrorized shriek flicked away in the wind.

I hit the water with a slap, more pain spearing my skin as I landed. And then the cold sea entrapped me in her icy fingers, tugging me down, smothering me, drowning me.

# 5

## *CARTER*

Completely drenched and my forehead stinging, I pushed myself up from the deck floorboards. I must have been knocked unconscious from my last fall, and I had no recollection of the last few moments. My leg was twisted painfully around the post of the railing, and as I tried to move, searing pain wrenched through my knee, thigh, and hip on that side. My stomach turned, my seasickness rearing up again, paired with the pain, making it impossible to keep from vomiting. As I finished being sick on the deck, the boat teetered nauseatingly to the left again, and I clutched the post with both arms, squeezing my eyes tightly shut. The storm, the sea, and the unhappy creaking of the boat filled my senses, and I was inches away from panic.

*Why, oh why, had I ever agreed to get on this boat? People were not meant to travel by water. That's why we invented airplanes!*

On the brink of hyperventilation, I heard it. A call in the wind, barely discernible above the wind and the waves. And suddenly, my eyes flew open, remembering with a shock that Jillian had been beside me right before I hit my head.

"Jillian?" I croaked, looking around desperately. I saw only water, darkness, and an empty deck. "Jill!" I pushed myself up to my feet, my right leg nearly buckling beneath my weight, and I braced myself up on the post again as I continued to scan the area for Jill. There was nobody around.

How long had I been out?

My only hope was that she had gotten back inside the bridge to safety, which was exactly what I needed to do at that moment. The ship lurched again, and I stumbled away from my safety post toward the door I had come through not long before. As I reached for the handle, it turned, and the door swung inward. Captain Skippy stood there, looking wild-eyed and ghostly pale. He grasped my arm and yanked me through the door just as the floor beneath us tilted dizzyingly once again.

"Captain," I gasped. "You're awake! Is Jill in here with you?"

The first mate was still at the helm, and he turned wide eyes to me as Captain Skippy snapped the door closed behind us. "She's not with you?"

A quick glance around the small room made my stomach drop several inches. "She's not here?"

"How long has it been since we left?"

"Five, ten minutes maybe," Eric answered. "I haven't kept track of the time – I've been trying to keep us from capsizing."

My brain was spinning. The last thing I remembered before waking up on the deck was walking along the open railing with Jillian when the ship swayed dramatically, causing us to fall and land on the wall. I'd slid down the wall and my leg got wrapped around that post before the ship had lurched again. I remembered falling again, but my leg was stuck, so I hit my head instead. But Jillian ...

I felt whatever blood was left in my face drain in a flash. My lips felt numb and useless as I breathed, "I think she fell overboard."

Eric goggled at me, but Captain Skippy didn't hesitate for longer than a second before grabbing the microphone and announcing over the P.A., "Man overboard. Man overboard. All available personnel, secure yourself to the outer railing and scan for life overboard."

"She was wearing a life jacket," Eric piped in urgently, "so she's probably bobbing."

The captain took this in with a nod and added into the microphone, "Be advised, victim is wearing emergency flotation."

He then repeated this information once more before hanging up the microphone again and taking a step toward the door.

"Whoa!" Eric cried, grabbing Captain Skippy by the arm to stop him from charging outside. "You're in no condition to be a rescue swimmer. And I need you in here in case—"

"If you think I'm leaving my granddaughter out there to drown—!"

But he never got to finish the threat. Just then, a deafening crash shuddered through the whole boat, and all three of us stumbled. The captain and I fell to the floor. The first crash was followed almost immediately by another.

Eric had landed on the control board and had a good view out the front windows. He gasped after the second crash, then swore loudly. "Rocks!" he yelled, scrabbling to get back to his feet. "Captain, we're about to—"

His warning was cut off by a third crash, this one so loud and violent that I threw my arms over my head, convinced that the ship was being crushed all around me.

The noise from the engines was suddenly roaring, wailing. The ship tipped forward a final time before halting with smashing finality and the screech of metal against rocks. The deafening roar of the engines suddenly died, and in its absence was just the sound of the sheeting rain pounding on the roof and deck, and the waves continuing to beat against the hull.

Screaming was once again heard over the rain. And I looked at Eric and the captain, stunned and dry-mouthed.

"Did we just ... crash?"

Eric's jaw hung slack as he blinked out the window. I looked out and immediately realized my question was stupid. Sharp, black rocks the size of cottages speared upward out of the still-churning water. And one thin, lethal-looking dagger of a rock had impaled the front of the ship, piercing straight through from bottom to top. We were pinned on the rocks like a bug on a corkboard.

And to make matters worse, a hole the size of a steamer trunk had been punched in the side of our hull, and we were taking on water. Fast.

Captain Skippy came to his senses first.

"Lifeboats!" he gasped. "Life jackets!" He ran to the door and was outside in a heartbeat. Eric and I followed right behind him. There was clearly nothing left to do on the bridge.

The three of us ran to the lounge, where every passenger and crew member was present—some standing by windows or holding on to furniture to keep upright, and others sprawled out on the floor. Several were bleeding.

"Everybody put a life jacket on," Eric commanded. "We've hit ground and are taking on water. Captain," he turned then to address Captain Skippy, "I'll ready the lifeboats. You help the passengers and crew." Back to the larger group, he said, "Leave everything and head to the lifeboats immediately." Then he turned and ran from the lounge back outside to prepare the life rafts.

Since I already had a life jacket on, thanks to Jillian, I followed after him. I knew nothing about sailing, and I knew I was basically useless, but I didn't have to feel useless. "What can I do?" I asked when I caught up with Eric at the stairs. He was heading down to the lowest deck.

"Stay here and make sure no one gets lost. We need all heads accounted for."

"Wait!" I cried as he started to sprint away from me again. "How long do we have?"

He stopped long enough to turn back and make eye contact with me. His face was ashen and his eyes wide. "Minutes."

A chill flooded my veins that had nothing to do with the rain still pouring down the back of my collar.

Lightning flashed across the dark sky, and two seconds later, thunder roared. But the storm was easing up slightly, and the ship, pinned as it was on the rocks, no longer rocked and reared on the waves. My queasy stomach settled slightly now that we were stationary, but the physical relief did nothing to ease the sick feeling in my heart. I stayed near the stairs, waiting for the others to come, all the while scanning the ship and the sea for any sign of Jillian. I saw nothing. Where was she?

A rush of anxious babble met my ears just before the throng of other passengers turned the corner and, with a good deal of shoving and jostling, took the stairs two abreast. I counted heads as they passed me:

Lovell ran down the stairs first, dragging his fiancée along by the hand. In her other hand, she clutched a suitcase and a handbag. She was wearing stilettos.

Next, the superstar, Bridget, followed by her muscular shadow, Patrick. He carried two suitcases in each hand and had a murderous look on his face.

Dr. Yung jogged behind Bridget, clutching the case for her experimental equipment, and on her shoulders was the backpack that I knew held the transcripts from her latest experiments. She barely spared me a glance, even as I encouraged her. "What are you waiting for?" she barked as she hustled by. "We're not going to wait for you."

Imagine, people think we ought to be a couple...

Bringing up the group was Lovell's entourage and Kenya, who seemed to be the only passenger—besides myself—that had heeded Eric's instructions to leave everything behind.

Captain Skippy came very last, holding on to the ship's railing for balance. His face was pallid and his footsteps halting. "Jillian?" he asked weakly. "Jilly..."

I didn't want him to panic about Jillian and keep himself off the lifeboat, so I stepped to his side and wrapped his arm over my shoulders. "Nearly there," I said automatically, having no idea just how far the lifeboats were from this spot.

We took the stairs in tandem, arriving with the others on the lowest level and finding Eric easily on the swim deck. He had inflated two large life rafts, and he and Patrick were muscling them into the water, still tethered to the ship for security.

With the boats in the water, Eric directed everyone into one of the two boats, barking irritably at those who insisted on bringing their luggage, but he didn't stop them, either. Captain Skippy and I took the last two seats on the second raft, and Eric untied our tether.

Before he shoved us off into the sea, he called over the storm, "Jillian?"

I shook my head. He nodded gravely, shoved us off, then took his place in the other raft. When both life rafts were untethered, Eric and the captain started each of the engines on the back, and we motored through the choppy water away from the wrecked yacht. I couldn't keep myself from looking back in awed horror at the massive ship. It had seemed so petite at the port, next to the other cruise ships—it had been dwarfed. But now, locked still with its white hull speared through by jagged rocks, I was struck by how large it was, how much of the ship had always been hidden under the waterline. It was a beautiful boat.

I glanced at the captain, wondering how he must feel at driving away from his dream and his livelihood. He kept his face forward, however, his eyes on the oncoming waves, constantly scanning the wavesr for a sign of his granddaughter.

My stomach was churning again, but it had little to do with the rocking of the lifeboat anymore.

I turned back and watched with horror as a gigantic wave crested over the rocks, crushing against the yacht with ear-splitting force. When the water receded, the sides of the ship showed further damage, gaping black holes yawning into the rain-soaked sky.

Shaking the rain out of my eyes, I turned to the captain again, my heart thundering in my throat. "We're not safe out here," I yelled over the wind. "What do we do?"

"The rafts each have S.O.S. alerts that send a distress call to the Coast Guard immediately," he answered in a voice loud enough for all of the passengers on our lifeboat to hear. "If anything goes wrong with the boat, keep hold of your life jacket and stay together. Help will come for us soon."

His voice held such assured confidence that I easily believed his optimism ... for about four seconds. A wave crested high over us, and our lifeboat rose on the water, angling, arcing with the wave until, with screams and the roar of our motor, the boat capsized, dumping all of us into the angry sea.

# 6

## *JILLIAN*

**I** **heard the roaring first,** even before I was fully awake.

*Whoosh. Pause. Swish. Pause. Ruuush. Pause. Swoooosh.*

I was drenched, and my salty hair stuck to my cheeks and lips. My lips were dry, even with my face pressed against the wet sand.

Then came the ache. It was a whole-body thing: pain wringing through me from my toes all the way up to my chin. And then those aching muscles remembered the great fatigue they'd earned by swimming and treading water and clinging and desperation.

I remembered fighting for my life in the waves. I did not remember losing consciousness. And I had no idea what sand I was lying on.

With a great deal of effort, I opened my eyes and, with agonizing movements, lifted my head off the beach.

The day was overcast and gloomy, with dark, murderous clouds menacing on the horizon. The wind was stiff, making the seawater mist over me. I shivered and pushed myself up to my knees.

It wasn't raining anymore, but the sand was pockmarked by the raindrops of a torrential gale. Seaweed, leaves, branches, and shells littered the shoreline. My gaze moved landward, where the dishevelled sand met a line of tropical trees and foliage, less than twenty yards away. I saw no buildings, no pathways, no roads, and no people.

Bile rose in my throat, and my attempt to swallow it back was met with protests from my esophagus: my mouth was full of seawater. The saltwater already in my stomach somersaulted viciously, and I had no option but to bend over double and let it all pour from me in a noxious, cough-inducing stream. I spent the next few miserable minutes coughing up more water than was ever in the ocean to begin with, before finally sitting back on my heels and staring up at the dreary sky.

I was bone-tired, my throat rasped with every breath, and worst of all, I had no idea where I was.

Fell overboard. Washed away somewhere in the Caribbean Sea. Emerged nearly drowned on an unknown beach. This situation had the makings of a made-for-TV movie.

It was a long time before I found enough energy to drag myself up, and even then I had to put my hands down on the sand more than once to regain equilibrium. Finally, with annoyed desperation, I pushed myself to my feet, staggered only once, then turned and faced my reality.

Facts:

1.   I needed fresh water and, eventually, something to eat. My throat burned from puking as well as dehydration.

2.   I wasn't on Mars, so I had to be somewhere. Just because I didn't see any buildings immediately didn't mean this was a deserted island. This wasn't the 1800s—there were people everywhere on this planet. I just had to find one.

3. Carter and the crew must have realized that I had fallen overboard, and I couldn't imagine them not looking for me.

4.   I needed to stay calm.

Still, it was with my heart hammering in my throat that I set off walking down the beach. Surely there were clues to be found—something that would help me figure out what to do.

I walked slowly, scanning the horizon as well as the tree line as I went. As far as I could tell, I walked north, toward a large rockface that jutted out into the ocean. I thought maybe I could climb to the top of the rocks and look for help. There hadn't appeared to be anything of interest to the south of my position, and that was the best plan I could come up with. The distance was deceptive, however, and after trudging along for what felt like hours—but was likely about twenty minutes—it seemed I was no closer to the rocks than I had been before.

Feeling defeated, I stopped to catch my breath, my hands on my knees as I panted like an ill-trained marathon runner.

With a growl at my own fatigue, I straightened again and took three more halting steps through the sand before I, once again, stopped cold. This time, though, it was the sight of what lay on the shore that stopped me. It was a large, white-painted piece of thick metal that was jagged around the edges and crumpled so badly that every surface looked dangerous to touch. It was the size of a dining table but crushed into itself. My breath stole from my throat as my feet moved me forward toward the torn metal—I recognized that paint color and the former texture of that hull. This was a piece of The Flying Honeymoon.

My blood chilled in my veins, and my tongue went numb. This was no inconsequential scrap on the shore. This was evidence of a shipwreck. My shipwreck.

Suddenly, I turned toward the sea, scanning for more signs of the ship. I didn't see anything right away, but after a few minutes, I spotted something yellow bobbing in the water about a hundred yards from shore. A lifeboat!

Without a second thought, I charged into the water toward the raft. My still-wet clothes were immediately saturated again, but I plunged forward anyway, hell-bent on reaching whomever of my friends was in that boat. I struggled forward for several minutes until a huge wave crested toward the shore, bringing the lifeboat in with it. The water slapped into my chest and drove my head under the wave, but after a moment, I found my feet again and half swam, half walked toward the boat that was finally within my reach.

"Hey!" I cried out, finally grasping a rope on the side of the lifeboat. Using my elbows and a huge kick of my legs, I hoisted myself up on the rim of the boat. But a major problem presented itself right away: instead of finding friends huddled safely in the lifeboat, I saw the bottom canvas of the raft. Somewhere along its journey, the boat had capsized.

The adrenaline that had propelled me to the raft drained from my muscles like snow slipping from a tin roof, leaving an icy slush in its wake.

A few shallow breaths pumped my lungs before my brain came back online. How long ago had the boat overturned? It was possible that my fellow passengers had been dumped only recently—they could be nearby. With some effort, I leveraged myself higher onto the raft, slipping my knee up beneath me so I could kneel on the overturned raft's bottom. Cupping my hands around my mouth, I began to shout toward the sea, "Hey! Is anybody out there? Can anybody hear me?" I paused to listen for any response besides the roar of the ocean waves. A few seconds passed with no answer, so I raised my hands again to holler some more, but just before I yelled again, I heard something.

It was a cough followed by some muted splashing, and it was coming from the other end of the raft. Acting before I had a second thought, I leapt toward the other edge of the raft, flopping onto my stomach and army-crawling across the still-moving raft to look over the side.

"Hey!" I exclaimed.

Her sodden hair stuck to her face, and her arms were so tightly wound around a side rope that she didn't have a hand to move the sticky hair from her eyes as she looked up at me. It was Bridget. Shocked amazement lit her expression when she recognized me.

"Jill? I can't believe it. We thought you were a goner!"

Just then, a huge wave crested over us, nearly upending the raft. When I was able to breathe again, I leaned over the edge once more and extended my arm to Bridget. "We're nearly to shore," I said with a glance landward. "But let's get you up here anyway."

She took my hand, and after a few failed attempts, we managed to hoist her out of the water and onto the relative dryness of the raft's bottom.

Panting, she lay on her stomach beside me, her tired eyes trained directly on the shore. "I can't believe we found land." Then she pushed herself up onto an elbow and speared me with an amazed look. "How long have you been here? How did you get here? Last we heard, you'd fallen overboard."

"The details are still fuzzy," I said truthfully, "but we can sort all of that out later. What happened to everyone else?"

"Howard and Elodia were holding onto the raft with me until just a few minutes ago. They were holding onto the other side. I could see them, but it was so loud in the waves that I couldn't understand them. They shouted something to each other and tried to tell me something before they both let go. A big wave came over then, and I didn't see what happened to them. Maybe they saw the land and decided to swim for it. I couldn't see the beach from where I was, but I guess they could."

"I must have just missed them when I swam out," I guessed. "Who else was in the raft with you?"

Hypothermia or panic—or both—were starting to overtake Bridget, and she had tucked her head under her folded arms, shuddering fiercely. "I—I don't know. Everyone. Me, Howard and Elodia, the captain... Um, one of the professors and that girl... Kenya, I think? But... I don't know what happened to them." Her head came up again, and she began to look around frantically.

I put my hand on her arm in a feeble attempt to help her focus. "Bridget, how long ago did the raft flip?"

She shook her head. "I don't know... it's all blurring together. Maybe like twenty minutes? There was a huge wave, and we tried to balance out, but it was just too big."

A part of my brain wanted to help Bridget re-center and calm down, but the survival impulse was stronger. "Let's get to shore," I said, then added hopefully, "maybe the others will be there waiting for us."

She took some coaxing, but eventually I was able to convince her to get into the water and swim the few hundred feet to where our toes were able to touch the sand. A few minutes of tough swimming later, we emerged from the ocean completely drenched, coughing, and shivering but, at last, safe. Bridget crawled on hands and knees from the water and collapsed, wheezing, onto the sand. I'm sure I didn't look much more elegant, but I managed to keep myself upright as I scanned my surroundings yet again, searching for castaways. With each beat, my heart sank further. I couldn't see anybody around, nor were there any footprints on the sand apart from my own. I cast a glance back toward the rolling sea, dreading the possibility of having to go back in to rescue my companions, but then I heard a shout.

Swivelling on my knees, I scanned the beach until, at long last, I spotted them. Elodia and Howard were stumbling along the sand toward us. I waved an arm over my head, and as she recognized me, Elodia broke into an uneven run. "Jillian—you're alive!"

She reached me before I was able to get to my feet, so when she threw her arms around my neck, we both tumbled to the sand. She pushed herself off me with a hurried apology. "Are you okay? We thought you drowned."

"I'm okay," I assured her as Howard joined us at a more sedate pace. "I'm so glad to see all of you. Have you seen any of the others?"

"Not yet," Elodia said with a shake of her head. "But we just got to shore a little while ago. We saw you two swimming in from down the beach, so maybe we'll see the others from here, too?"

Howard sat heavily in the sand beside Elodia, his face pale and drawn. He was breathing heavily, and I noticed his hands were trembling. He hadn't yet spoken.

Elodia pulled her knees to her chest and rested her forehead on her crossed arms. "What are we going to do?"

My mind hadn't gotten that far yet, as my eyes were still scanning the grey water for any signs of swimmers. And then I spotted a dark shape as it emerged from a wave. I was on my feet before I could make out who it was, but it looked like a person struggling in the water.

"Hey!" I cried, running on numb legs toward the water. "Someone's out there!"

As I splashed into the surf, the figure in the water slowly came into focus. It was a person—a woman—Kenya—holding onto something with one arm. A suitcase. She was hanging tightly with one arm onto the floating suitcase, and with her other arm she struggled to keep something above the water's surface. A head? It was a man. With a captain's hat.

"Grandpa!"

I struggled toward them through the waves, swimming the last several yards before grasping onto the opposite side of the suitcase from where Kenya held on. Without speaking, I used all my available energy to kick my legs against the water, jerking the suitcase as hard as possible toward the beach. Kenya seemed to revive some energy upon seeing me, and she and I kicked with all our might until, an eternity later, our feet touched the rocky, sandy bottom, and we were able to walk the rest of the way out of the ocean, dragging Grandpa Skippy and the suitcase between us.

We emerged from the sand on hands and knees, barely managing to hoist Grandpa from the water before we each collapsed, gasping, onto the wet sand. Elodia and Howard arrived by our sides moments later. Elodia began to thump on Grandpa's back, and before long he spit out a lungful of seawater and coughed hard until his airway was clear.

When he could breathe again, he looked up and found me watching him anxiously, and relief swept over him. "Jilly," he cried, "you're okay!"

I threw my arms around him and held him tighter than I'd ever done before. His head had started bleeding a little bit again, but the fact that he was awake and talking was more encouragement than I'd ever expected to find on a lonely beach in the middle of nowhere.

I pulled back enough to look him in the face. He was pale, with deep worried lines etched into his skin. I'd never seen him look his age before that day. Suddenly, I believed he was seventy-three.

"What happened?" I whispered, my thoughts jumbled and adrift. So much had happened, and I felt like I didn't understand any of it.

"I don't know," Grandpa growled. "I can't remember anything that happened since last night. I woke up on the bridge with Eric, and then Carter came back and said you were gone, and—"

He hugged me again. I could count on one hand the number of times this man had embraced me, and I reveled in the warmth.

"I'm okay, Grandpa," I assured him.

But I knew that I had more to worry about than my own safety. I looked about and counted the people around me. Howard, Elodia,

Skippy, Bridget, and Kenya, plus myself made six. There had been ten passengers and five crew members aboard, and I knew there had been two lifeboats. They must have split in half when they abandoned the ship.

"Is this everyone that was in your boat?"

Kenya pushed up onto her hands and counted under her breath before groaning and sitting up. "Carter's not here?"

I turned to look out at the swirling surf, hoping to see a person swimming in with the waves. No one was there.

"How long has it been since you last saw him?" I asked the group.

No one seemed to remember seeing Carter after the raft overturned the second time. The story unfolded that the raft had flipped once when they had first launched from the ship, but they had worked together and righted the boat, getting everyone on board again. By the time they had gotten everyone out of the water, they had lost sight of the other lifeboat that had Alexis, Mikey, Portia, Tyrone, Gordon, April, Patrick, and Eric on board. Carter had been on the raft before the second capsizing, but he hadn't been spotted in the water since. Thankfully for all of them, they had been within sight of the island when they tipped.

Knowing that Carter was the last passenger from the boat we needed to pull ashore spurred me back to my feet. Kenya and Bridget got up to help me search for him, and Elodia and Howard stayed with Grandpa on the sand. I was grateful that they volunteered to stay with him, because he still looked green and unwell.

Because we didn't know where Carter might turn up in the water, the three of us split up. Kenya and Bridget went north along the beach, and I walked south, scanning every wave and rock in search of my friend.

After I had walked for a long time, the exertion of the day caught up with me again, and my knees buckled. I sat on the sand, drained and exhausted, ready to burst into tears. I sat with my back pressed to a cold, wet rock, my knees drawn to my chest, staring without seeing toward the stormy horizon. This, I thought vaguely, must be what shock feels like. I didn't know what to do with that information, so I shoved it toward the edges of my mind.

Groaning, I dropped my face into my hands, my fingers curling into my tangled, wet hair. Pain throbbed behind my eyes as a tension headache made itself known. I sat that way for a long time, coaching myself in a practice of deep breathing to keep panic at bay. The scene around me didn't change as I curled in on myself, except for the addition of some cawing seagulls.

Eight or ten birds swooped down, crying out to one another as they dug in the sand with their beaks. I rested my head on my knees and watched them. The ocean breeze touched my face, cooling the hot tears that wetted my cheeks. How long had I been crying?

The birds leapfrogged one another as they scavenged for food in the wet sand, gradually getting nearer to my position by the rocks. Finally, one spotted me there, startled, and flapped backward with a cry. His mates followed suit, and within moments, they had all flapped away. I could hear them calling to each other—or maybe shouting insults at me—for several long moments after they'd flown off.

A sigh shuddered out of me. Alone again. The birds called again, mocking me.

"Jillian!"

I lifted my gaze upward when the sound of the birds' cries changed. I hadn't heard a seagull sound like that before.

"Jill!"

There it was again. I sat up and swiveled around to my knees. That was no bird call. I looked up and down the beach until I saw... I shot to my feet, not caring about the sand that coated my hands and legs.

"Carter?"

It was him! Down the beach a few hundred yards, emerging from the foliage I hadn't yet explored, Carter Buckley jogged toward me, waving his arms. My lack of energy was now a forgotten memory, and I ran, kicking up sand as I pelted toward him.

We met somewhere between the water and the trees, and, without thinking twice, I launched myself into his arms.

"You're alive!"

His arms encircled me instantly. "You're okay!"

"Oh my gosh, I can't believe it's you. You're really here."

"I was so worried about you."

Then, just as quickly as I'd thrown myself into his arms, I pushed back with a gasp, registering the red streaks across his face.

"What happened to you?"

Carter shook his head, and I looked at him fully for the first time. His face was pale and ashy, making the long cut on his cheek stand out with sickening contrast. There was a trail of blood streaked down his neck, leading to a watery brown stain on the collar of his T-shirt. There were at least two rips in the shirt: one on the left shoulder and one across his left side. Each of these tears was accompanied by another bloodstain.

He grabbed me again around the shoulders and hugged me to his chest. "I've never been so scared."

My mind conjured a scene of him fighting off a shark and an octopus with a saber.

"I thought I'd lost you," he whispered, then murmured again, "I was so scared."

Be. Still. My. Heart.

My fingers curled into the back of his shirt, and I pressed my nose into his shoulder, breathing in the scent of seawater and sand.

"I'm here," I said softly. "It's going to be okay."

# 7

## *JILLIAN*

Carter told me that after the raft overturned the second time, he was caught in a riptide and dragged away from the rest of the group. After struggling in the water for a long time, he finally got free of the current and was able to see the island in the distance. It was a long swim, and he was surprised that his stamina had held on so long. When he got close to the land, he was so tired that he couldn't fight against a huge wave that tossed him into an outcropping of jagged rocks — the miniature version of the ones that wrecked the yacht.

The cuts and scrapes all along his left side were from his run-in with the rocks. Thankfully, the cuts were shallow, and he hadn't lost any mobility. By the time he finished telling me what happened to him, the bleeding had stopped. Now the biggest risk was infection. Hopefully, the raft's first aid kit hadn't gotten lost in the surf.

We walked together along the beach, back to the rest of the group.

I had never taken a walk along the beach with a boyfriend—not that Carter was my boyfriend—but I had imagined it to be much more romantic than the over-exhausted, breathless stumble that this walk was.

When we reached the others, Kenya greeted Carter like a soldier returning home from enemy lines, rushing to him and wrapping him in a huge, teary hug. Grandpa gave him a handshake and a clap on the shoulder, and he got a solemn nod from Howard.

My trembling legs finally gave out, and I collapsed onto the sand. Fear-soaked adrenaline had been powering my actions since I landed on the beach, but now that everyone was accounted for, my body was done. Carter sat heavily in the sand at my side, resting his arm on a bent knee and putting his forehead against his arm, portraying the perfect image of desperate exhaustion.

Kenya sat with her arms wrapped around herself, tears silently trailing down her cheeks. Bridget sat beside her, slumped forward with her fingers curled into her hair, face downturned, unmoving.

No one spoke for a long time, each of us staring in different directions: at the sand, at the water, at the sky, at the jungle to our backs.

I had been on plenty of islands in my time working for Skippy, but this abandoned stretch of beach felt especially foreboding. I didn't know that I had ever been so removed from society that I couldn't hear sounds of humanity from just beyond the trees. My skin prickled as I watched a handful of birds explode upward out of the canopy of palm trees, screeching and crying to one another as they fled whatever danger had spooked them.

After a long time, Kenya finally broke the silence. "What do we do now?"

No one moved, no one answered. But that was the question of the day. What are you supposed to do when your yacht crashes and you find yourself washed up on an island with no signs of human habitation?

"The lifeboat has an emergency beacon," I said after a while, my mind feeling so slow it might have been working in reverse. "Someone should get our S.O.S." Then, trying to convince myself, I repeated, "Someone will come."

Just then, Howard startled everyone by launching to his feet. "How could this happen?" he thundered at Skippy. "You incompetent old man. You've killed us all!"

"Howard," Elodia said, looking thunderstruck, "this isn't his fault."

He whirled around and snapped at her, "He's the captain. Who else should I blame for a shipwreck?"

"He's right," Skippy said in a gravelly voice. "This is my responsibility. Your safety is my responsibility."

"So what do we do now?" Howard demanded. "Just sit tight and wait for a magic rescue? What if one doesn't come? What if we die out here?"

Kenya laughed mirthlessly then and said under her breath, "Then there wouldn't be anybody for you to sue."

Howard heard her words and glared fiercely at her. Kenya didn't shrink from his ire, though. He began a verbal attack, but Bridget interrupted, looking up from her curled-over position for the first time.

"Oh, shut up," she snarled at Howard. "You're not any more important than anybody else on this beach. This isn't Kenya's fault any more than it is yours or mine or even Captain Skippy's. It was an accident." She shot a fiery look at Skippy and added, "Right?"

Grandpa bristled. "If you're asking if I wrecked my yacht and destroyed my business on purpose..."

"No one is saying that," Kenya defended Bridget. "We're all in the same boat here... figuratively speaking. And we're not going to get through this by shouting at each other."

This did nothing to calm Howard's temper. "Someone will be held accountable for this."

"Yes, they will," I said, "but not until everyone is home safe. It's stupid to place blame now when there's nothing to do about it."

Elodia spoke up then, raking her blonde hair out of her face. "So what are we supposed to do? Just wait?"

"Do you have a better suggestion?" Kenya challenged.

Silence followed that, and nobody could make eye contact for several minutes. Bridget had wrapped her arms around herself and was rubbing her biceps, goosebumps standing out on her skin as she shivered.

The wind had picked up again, blowing cool, humid air in from the ocean. The light was beginning to fade from behind the clouds. Even though it was summertime, there was a real chance we could get hypothermia if we sat out on this beach overnight.

"We need to build a fire," Carter said, as if reading my thoughts.

Howard rolled his eyes. "And how do you expect to do that, Boy Scout?" he asked sarcastically. "Did you pack a blowtorch with your scuba gear?"

Carter's face reddened with some combination of irritation and embarrassment.

Kenya was the one to come up with a solution, however. From the pocket of her hoodie, she pulled out a white Bic lighter. She gave it a test click, and a spark easily ignited the fuel within.

I stared at her with my mouth agape. "Why do you have a lighter?"

Kenya shrugged lightly. "Scouts are always prepared." She gave Carter a playful wink, then she added more seriously, "My ex was a smoker, so I got in the habit of carrying these around. I forgot it was in here."

"That's lucky," Bridget said, looking at Kenya with sincere appreciation. "Do you think we'll be able to find any wood dry enough to burn after this storm?"

Carter answered that, standing up as he said, "Can't hurt to look."

Exhausted as I was, I got up as well, and Bridget and Kenya volunteered to gather firewood as well.

Grandpa Skippy suggested that he and Howard go out into the surf and retrieve the lifeboat from where it was still churning with the waves. Elodia heroically volunteered to stay at our makeshift base camp, "So no one will get lost."

At least four of us rolled our eyes at that, but no one argued, and we split up to gather our assigned items.

This was the first time I'd really looked at the island or moved around without adrenaline giving me tunnel vision. If we hadn't been stranded, the pristine beauty of the island would have blown me away. I was somewhat jaded from my many trips to the Bahamas, and I had thought that if you'd seen one island, you had seen them all. And that was still mostly true, but walking from the white sand beach into the cover of towering palm trees gave me newfound appreciation for nature's handiwork.

The beach was strewn with seaweed and other plant life that had been shaken free from the trees during the storm, and there were sections that got very rocky and difficult to walk around. The beach was perhaps 100 feet wide from waves to the start of the tree line. It was like the dividing line between two worlds. Vast, open horizons and endless oceans were swallowed up the second you stepped into the palm tree forest. Thick shrubs, grasses, and ferns covered the forest floor, and vines snaked their way up the thick trunks of palm trees. It was thick and muggy in the trees, water plopping down from the canopy above so steadily I half-wondered if it was raining again. The sunshine, already filtered through thick grey clouds, barely made itself known in the jungle.

When we entered the trees, we thought we would split up to gather wood from different directions, but the feeling inside the jungle was so eerie and otherworldly that we instinctively stayed together.

Most of the fallen branches and limbs we found were soaked through from the rain and constant humidity, but as we forged deeper into the trees and got braver about lifting fallen leaves and looking under brambles, each of us was able to gather an armload of semi-dry wood that we carried back out to the beach.

When we left the trees, I was surprised to realize that we had gotten off-course. I might have sworn that we left the same way we went in, but unless Elodia had wandered half a football field down the beach, we had gotten turned around along the way through the trees. I made a mental note that, if we ever had to go in there again, we should try to make a path so we didn't get lost.

Skippy and Howard had wrestled the lifeboat from the water and dragged it up to where Elodia sat. We hiked the stretch of beach between us and the lifeboat and deposited the wood in a pile next to it.

"I'll get started building the fire," Kenya volunteered.

Bridget looked at her with a furrowed brow. "You know how to build a fire?"

Kenya might have taken offense at the assumptions interlaced with that question; instead, she held up her hand in a three-fingered salute. "Gold Award Girl Scout Ambassador at your service."

Howard scoffed. "Great. So you're going to sell us overpriced cookies?"

"Ha ha." Kenya rolled her eyes, then bent down and started organizing the wood. "Like I haven't heard that a million times." After a few minutes, she had constructed a campfire base and, with the help of some dry tinder she had stuffed into her pocket and the lighter, she had started a nice, warm fire.

She sat back on her heels, warming her hands near the flames, and very proudly did not rub her success in Howard Lovell's face.

It was clear that our meager firewood pile wouldn't last us very long, so a few of us made more trips to the jungle to find more wood. By the time we'd gathered a good pile, the fire was roasty-toasty warm, and I knelt beside it gratefully.

With the immediate threat of hypothermia squelched, the seven of us gathered around the fire and felt 2% more comfortable.

The group conversation turned then to the other nine people who were in the other lifeboat. "Gordon, Tyron, Portia, Patrick, Dr. Yung, Alexis, Mikey, and Eric," Grandpa Skippy said, counting off the souls on his fingers. "If they didn't capsize like we did, hopefully their motor survived and they were able to make it into the path of a passing ship."

"Wait, your motor died?" I asked. That information hadn't been passed along to me yet.

Skippy nodded. "When we capsized the first time, I heard the boat smack against the wrecked yacht. After we all got back in, the motor wouldn't start, and it looked like when it hit the ship, a piece of the motor broke off. That's why we drifted for so long before we got to the island."

"The other boat didn't flip, though," Bridget pointed out. "I saw Patrick take control of the motor before we went under. By the time I came up again, though, they were gone."

I scowled, but Kenya spoke, voicing my thoughts before I could. "Patrick left you? Isn't it literally his job to protect you?"

"If you saw him at the motor before we capsized, you would think that they would have seen us go over."

"Why didn't they come help us?" Elodia asked.

Skippy shook his head. "People do unexpected things in life-and-death situations."

That information was received unhappily, but no one could debate its truth.

Then Elodia said, "At least we can hope they're safe. If they didn't tip like us. Portia can't swim."

"Tyron can swim," Howard said, "and Gordon was so big, he'd probably float."

I asked Bridget if Patrick was a good swimmer, but she just shook her head with a shrug. With the effort of remembering something that happened a lifetime ago, I recalled the altercation I'd witnessed and broken up that night before. It wasn't surprising that she didn't want to talk about Patrick.

Alexis, Mikey, and Eric worried me, too, but at least I knew that they had been trained to handle a situation like this. Alexis was certified with CPR, Eric was former Navy, and Mikey was too stubborn to let anything happen to any of them.

"If they're rescued, they'll send someone to find us," Carter said with surety.

The conversation petered out, and silent, worried boredom crept in.

With nothing more to do, the seven of us settled in on the beach. Grandpa leaned heavily against the side of the life raft, Kenya and Bridget sat together by the campfire, watching Carter stoke the flames, and Elodia and Howard sat a ways apart, keeping to themselves.

I sat close beside Skippy, drawing my knees up to my chest and burying my cold toes into the soggy sand. "I still don't understand what happened to you, Grandpa," I said, making the most of our few moments of relative privacy. "What happened to your head?"

Grandpa shook his head, though, looking befuddled and, rightly, upset. "I don't remember. Last thing I remember was getting back to the bridge after the party and re-checking the course I'd set earlier. I told Eric to go to his bunk for some rest, then I took control. But I don't remember much of that at all. Next thing I remember is waking up on the floor of the bridge. I just don't understand it," he continued with a growl. "We shouldn't have been anywhere near rocks that high. Unless we ran off course at full speed all night." His ashen face paled even further. "But from the way things look, that might be exactly what happened."

I rubbed his arm, trying to infuse comfort and warmth into his skin, even though my own mind reeled with questions and worry. "Did you take all of your medications?" I wondered. "Or take anything new?"

He shook his head, rubbing at a spot on the back of it. "No, I did everything right. I'm sure of it."

Following a feeling in my gut that made me ill, I leaned in closer and whispered, "At the party, did you have anything to drink?"

"Of course not," he shouted. Kenya and Bridget, sitting nearby, jerked around to stare at us at this outburst. I gave them a grimace of a smile until they turned away again. Grandpa lowered his voice, but his tone was still defensive. "You know I would never drink while I'm on duty. Especially with clients on board."

Feeling chided, I sat back and leaned my palms into the sand. "I know. I'm just trying to cover all of the possibilities."

He let out a frustrated puff of air and then, wilting, he dropped his face into his palm. "None of that matters much now anyway," he said with no small amount of despair. "The ship is gone. My career is over."

I did not point out that worrying about his ship seemed selfish, considering our stranded-on-an-unknown-beach circumstances.

"We'll figure all that out," I said placatingly. "Let's just get home first."

I looked around at everyone sitting close to the fire. Howard had his head on Elodia's lap, his rounded shoulders shuddering even as she stroked his hair and spoke gently to comfort him. Despite the comforting presence she apparently was for Howard, her eyes were wide with obvious distress, and her gaze was trained, almost unblinkingly, on the swell of the sea. Her fingers shook as they combed through Howard's salt-and-pepper hair.

I let my gaze fall from them and drift across the sand to where Bridget and Kenya sat together, talking in low voices. Unlike Elodia, they were not staring at the water; Kenya's eyes were directed down the beach, staring without taking in much, locked on the large rock formation on the north edge of our beach. Bridget's eyes were on the trees. Their voices were too low to carry to my position, but their unguarded expressions and weary postures indicated that their conversation was not serious.

How did this happen to us? I thought for the umpteenth time. And what do we do now?

Carter approached us from where he'd been gathering more firewood in the jungle. "Captain, you said there's a homing device on the raft," he said, looking meaningfully at our lifeboat on the sand. "What activates that?"

Grandpa's vacant expression sharpened, and he sat up a little straighter—he was always at his best when talking shop. "It should have begun to emit the moment we inflated the rafts. And there's an alert with the signal that notifies the Coast Guard, or any nearby vessels, with our S.O.S."

"Did you happen to check the time when you inflated the rafts?" I asked.

Grandpa shook his head, but Carter nodded. "I did. It was 8:24 a.m." He shook back his sleeve to check his shiny silver wristwatch. "And it's 3:56 p.m. now."

I did the quick math. "Almost seven and a half hours." Carter nodded. I looked at Grandpa. "How long will it take someone to respond?"

"I'm surprised no one has come looking for us yet," Grandpa admitted with a heavy expression. "From what I've been told, most SOS signals have a response of some kind within an hour, even if it does take longer for a rescue group to come together."

"A response?" Carter repeated. "What do you mean by that?"

"A radio response," I explained. "The device on the raft is equipped with rudimentary radio. It's not great for talking at long distance, but at the very least we would get a ping and Morse code."

Carter looked unimpressed. "I guess I hoped for something more sophisticated."

Grandpa bristled a little at this. "It's not the most expensive life raft money can buy, but it's not cheap, either. Not everyone has University money. And really, who ever expects to have to use their rafts?"

Carter cleared his throat and turned away, but I could have sworn I heard him mumble, "Ever heard of the Titanic?"

I jumped in before a fight started. "A radio is a radio, right? Would we be able to hear a response from here?"

The question wasn't brilliant, since we couldn't have gotten much closer to the radio unless we were sitting right by the raft. Of course, Grandpa confirmed that we would hear the radio anywhere along the beach, since he had turned up the volume.

"I'm surprised," Carter commented, frowning at the radio.

"That such a cheap raft would have a volume knob?" Grandpa intoned sarcastically.

Carter managed not to roll his eyes. "No, that we don't hear anything at all, even with the volume up."

Agreeing with him, now that he had pointed out the oddity, I leaned over the side of the raft to peer at the radio dials. Sure enough, the volume knob was turned to MAX, and the red light beside the SOS transmitter was flashing, as it should. Still, it was weird that it would be completely silent without any static or popping noises. Silent radios were often not very silent at all, especially when seeking a signal. I fiddled with the knob, but there was no change.

In the back of my mind, the voice of my tech-guy brother sounded with an oft-repeated line: "Have you tried turning it off and turning it back on again?" Knowing that was often the first, and best, step to fixing electronic issues, I did what the voices in my head instructed, and flipped the switch off, counted to five, then clicked it back on again. The system beeped loudly at me once, and the SOS light resumed its flashing, but there was still no other sound.

Carter, who was crouched beside me and had watched all of my monkeying with the device, leaned in a little closer to the radio, trying to see the backside of it. "Does it need a longer antenna, do you think?"

I studied the black rectangle once again, trying to remember everything I had learned about radios. A longer antenna certainly would help us achieve a longer range and clearer sound; all we needed was a long piece of aluminum to connect to the existing antenna. "It's worth a try."

"Can you find the antenna and maybe figure out a way to secure something onto it?"

I nodded and, after Carter had gone a few steps away, turned to Grandpa again. "Do you remember where the radio antenna is?"

Grandpa had closed his eyes, the pinched state of his eyebrows expressing the agony of his headache. He shook his head and said, "It should be right on top of it."

Another look at the radio box proved that notion false. In fact, I looked around the whole thing again, even climbing into the raft so I could look underneath and all around it. There was, apparently, no antenna. But I did find a round hole in the back of the radio box labelled ANT, and, broken off inside that hole was a bit of jagged aluminium.

I sat back on my heels, barely stifling a gasp. The antenna had been snapped off—intentionally or accidentally, I didn't know. But without any kind of antenna, it was clear that our distress signal had never made it a single yard into the air, much less the hundreds of potential miles we needed to span to call for help.

Panic rose in the back of my throat, and I felt my fingers and toes begin to tingle. "Grandpa," I said, keeping my voice deliberately low and calm. "Will you come look at this, please?"

My calm voice got Grandpa's attention right away. With deliberately calm movements of his own (albeit slow and painful), he got up and stepped into the raft beside me, crouching down to see what, I was certain, was a damaged radio.

Grandpa's jaw set, and his face paled even further as a sailor's curse word slipped through his lips.

Goosebumps raised on my arms as my blood ran cold. "Do you think...?"

He jerked his head side to side, his mouth set in a grim line as he muttered, "It hasn't been transmitting. At least since it's been broken. And who knows how long that has been."

"I haven't seen anybody messing with it," Carter's voice sounded from behind me, making me jump. I hadn't heard him come back. He crouched down beside me to examine the radio along with Grandpa. "And, honestly, it looks the same as when I first saw it."

"So you think it's been broken this whole time?" I asked, feeling my fingertips prickle with a cocktail of adrenaline and dread.

Carter shrugged one shoulder as he sat back on his heels. "At least since we capsized." He looked at Grandpa. "It's possible it could have broken when we capsized."

But Grandpa was scowling. "The raft would have been designed with that possibility in mind. I can't imagine one dunk would ruin what's supposed to be an indestructible radio."

"Two dunks," Carter corrected mildly.

"Maybe we're wrong," I proposed, knowing even as I spoke that I was grasping at proverbial straws. "It could be an internal antenna. Or a satellite. Someone could still be on their way to our beach right now."

Grandpa's eyes were lined with worry, but I saw him try to lighten his expression for my sake. "You're right. We might be overreacting."

"Sure," I agreed instantly. "The ANT port could be for... anything. Right?"

Ever the scientific mind, Carter was shaking his head. "I'm no expert in radios, but this isn't behaving like any functioning radio I've ever encountered. And, while it is possible that our distress call made it out there, it's probably a better idea to move forward with the reality that no rescue is coming."

We sat in silence for a few moments, letting this harsh reality wash over us.

"So..." Carter finally ventured, "What do we do now?"

"Signal fire?" I suggested.

"Not a bad idea," Grandpa agreed. "We can operate under the assumption that the other raft's radio is intact, and if so, they'll be found within hours and be able to tell the rescuers that we're out here somewhere. Someone will be looking for us."

I was worried about him, still. His color hadn't returned as much as I would have liked, but I knew that the best thing I could do for him now was to try to get us off this beach, into dry clothes, and get some medical attention.

"I guess we'd better tell the others what's going on," I said at length. "They're in this just as much as we are."

Carter got up first and offered his hand down to me to assist me in standing. Then we both helped Grandpa up onto his unsteady feet.

"Let's get this over with."

# 8

## *JILLIAN*

The bandages I had wrapped around Grandpa's head on the ship were crusted with sand and salt from the ocean spray. The lifeboat had a small first aid kit with a few bandages and gauze, disinfectant, and antibiotic ointment. In one of the few strokes of good luck for the day, the bandages were individually wrapped in waterproof plastic so they weren't ruined by seawater. I did my best to doctor up Grandpa's head then turned my attention to the others. A couple of Carter's scrapes were deep enough that they could have used stitches, but with my limited supplies, we had to make do with a heavy bandage and generous disinfectant. No one else seemed hurt — at least not physically.

Grandpa's wound was the greatest worry. His head wound had stopped bleeding, thankfully, but beautiful red and purple bruises bloomed on his forehead. It looked tender, but I was more worried about how addled and confused he felt. He couldn't remember what had happened after taking over the helm last night.

The rain finally stopped, but there was still a stiff breeze that eventually dried our clothes. I was grateful to be dry and that we were able to keep our fire lit, even if the wind did blow. After we explained the situation with the radio, there was a long circular discussion that led nowhere helpful. The discussion eventually fizzled out, leaving everyone more tired and grumpy than before.

As the afternoon progressed, Carter, Kenya, Bridget, and I had taken turns gathering more kindling for the flames, so we would have enough to keep the fire aflame through the night. As the sun began to set, Carter and I volunteered to go together into the trees. I offered simply to give myself something to do other than stare at the beach and the popping fire.

When I first got up, my legs immediately began to shake, my knees weak and trembling from a long night of sitting on the ground. My head spun a little, too, from dehydration and hunger, and somewhere around midnight, a headache had begun to claw at the back of my eyes. So, with my head pounding with each beat of my heart and my balance swaying in the breeze, I hiked with Carter toward the trees where we had found the best firewood yesterday.

Carter, noticing me wobble through the sand, hung back and extended his left hand toward me. Gratefully, I took it in my right, and we walked together, my footfalls plodding unevenly through the sliding sand. He was remarkably steady at my side. With my head drooping and my shoulders hunched in a distinctly unattractive manner, it was no surprise that Carter knew I felt lousy.

"We'll get through this," he murmured as we drew near the tree line. "Someone will rescue us."

I began to nod, but my headache redoubled at the motion, so instead I said, "I hope so. I want to be optimistic, but in a few hours it will be a whole day since the ship ran aground, and we haven't seen a single vessel on the horizon. I can't help but feel like there's nobody out there." With a bit of effort, I lifted my chin enough to look up at Carter. He was watching the ground as we walked, the corners of his mouth turned down in a serious, worried expression that aged him.

We crossed over the line of rock separating the beach from the forest, then picked our way through the foliage, searching for dry wood that would burn hot.

As we worked, my mind continued its nonstop replay of the day's events. The wreck, falling overboard, washing up on the beach, finding the others one by one, huddling together and trying to figure out what to do, having our hopes dashed when we realized our beacon wasn't emitting our distress signal. In my wildest imagination, I never dreamed that I would ever end up in this situation: cast away on a deserted island.

"I just don't get," I started after we had worked for several minutes, "how, out of all of the mapped and chartered and claimed islands in the Caribbean, we managed to find one that is abandoned. I mean, why couldn't we wash up at a Sandals resort? There seem to be a billion of those to choose from."

Suddenly, Carter stopped walking, and a few of the sticks he'd gathered tumbled from the crook of his arm. Alarmed, I turned to look at him. The aged, haunted look had cleared from his expression, and a quizzical furrow puckered his brow.

"That's a good point," he murmured after a moment. "I wonder..." The rest of the wood fell from his arms then, as he turned abruptly and marched back through the trees the way we had come.

Startled by this rapid change in demeanor, I dropped my own load of wood and followed him. "Carter?" I called, jogging as best I could through the thick vegetation, trying to catch up. "What's going on?"

I caught up to him back on the beach, where he had stopped again, his arms crossed over his chest with his right hand lifted, massaging his jaw, his body turning slowly from one side to the other as he, apparently, studied the trees.

"What?" I repeated. Following his gaze toward the tops of the trees, I asked, "What are you looking for?"

"Something. Anything." This enigmatic response was followed by silence for a few more beats until he shook his head a couple of times and looked at me with bright eyes. "You're right, Jill, the likelihood that we've washed up on a deserted island in this day and age is extremely remote."

"Okay..." Blame it on shock and exhaustion, but I was not following.

"What if we are on an inhabited island—we're just on the wrong side?"

It took only two seconds for my brain to catch on to his train of thought. My mouth was dry from my light jog, and I licked my lips. "Do you think we should..."

"I think we should finally explore our island," he finished for me. "Best-case scenario, we find that Sandals resort that you want, just half a mile around the bend. Worst case, we find nothing and are no worse off than we are right now."

I wholeheartedly agreed, but a glance at the sun dipping down beyond the horizon put a damper on the plans. "If we're not rescued by morning, we spend the day exploring," I proposed.

He nodded. "Deal."

***

We returned to the fire and our companions with markedly increased enthusiasm. Bridget and Kenya noticed the excitement on our faces, and Kenya got to her feet right away. "Did you find something?"

"Not yet," Carter said, confidently taking charge, "but we hope to."

He explained our joint theory to the group and proposed that, in the morning, we split into groups and go exploring.

Carter had scarcely finished his proposal before Howard cut in grumpily, "I'm not going anywhere. If a boat comes looking for us and no one is here... well, we might as well sign our own death certificates. Besides, that SOS signal could be working all this time, and a rescue boat could be here right now."

"He's not saying we should go right now," Kenya said impatiently. "And honestly, if no one finds us tonight, I'm willing to do whatever it takes to get off this island."

Bridget was nodding. "I agree. And I don't want to just sit here and fry in the sun. We need to do something."

Howard was not to be swayed, however. "Didn't your mother teach you that if you get lost you need to stay still so someone can find you? It doesn't do any good for everyone to be chasing each other around, using up all our energy. I think we should stay right here."

93

Elodia sat beside Howard on the sand, holding his hand with a white-knuckled grip, her expression etched with worry and indecision. When Carter had proposed looking for help, she had looked relieved, intrigued, and almost ready to volunteer, but Howard's words now held her back.

I opened my mouth to encourage her to speak her mind, to stand up to her condescending fiancé, but before I could say anything, another voice beat me to it.

"You're absolutely right," Grandpa Skippy said. "We'll need a couple of us to stay here in case a rescue does come."

Carter nodded, knowing that with the captain's say-so, it was as good as decided that we would be exploring the island tomorrow.

***

During the afternoon, we dragged ashore several suitcases that had fallen out of the lifeboat and ransacked the contents. There were four suitcases in total, one of which was completely filled with Elodia's beauty creams. We deemed that useless, except for her three bottles of expensive sunscreen. Two of the cases had various women's clothing items, including a gold sequined dress with matching high heels, six bathing suits, a satin top and leather pants, some not-very-comfortable-looking underwear, and, blessedly, six sets of women's joggers, socks, and t-shirts. Plus four waterlogged novels. We were all relieved that Bridget had packed for both stunning evening events and relaxing in her room with a book. Who would have guessed?

The smallest suitcase was Howard's, and it contained basketball shorts and t-shirts, khaki shorts, and button-down shirts with loud tropical patterns. He had packed two hoodies and one quarter-zip sweatshirt.

Without really asking permission from the owner of the clothing, Kenya and I divided the clothes among the group. Bridget and Elodia's clothes were too small for me or Kenya, so we dipped into Howard's clothes for warmth and comfort. I ended up with the quarter-zip sweater and a pair of crew socks. The marginal warmth they provided felt wonderful against the wind. I bypassed the sleeves and kept my arms wrapped around myself beneath the sweater, pretending the material was as thick and lovely as the duvet that was now sleeping with the fishes at the bottom of the ocean.

Carter covered his shredded t-shirt with a button-down covered with pink flamingos wearing sunglasses, then topped that with a gray hoodie. Skippy kept his long thick pants and captain's uniform shirt, but I draped a couple of t-shirts over his shoulders for a blanket. The rest of the group picked through the clothes and found enough to keep them moderately comfortable and change out of some still-wet socks and underclothes.

So, aching, sore, and cold, but at least dry, we hunkered down by the fire, and the seven of us tried to get some sleep as the night stretched out before us.

Grandpa rested with his head against the lifeboat, and after an hour or so, he dropped into a restless sleep. I sat on his right side, watching him in the dancing light of the fire until my eyelids grew too heavy and I rested my cheek against the raft, just for a minute.

The next thing I knew, dawn was creeping across the sky, and I heard the shuffling movements of someone tending to the signal fire. It was Carter, looking like he hadn't slept a minute, dark circles hanging beneath his eyes and his complexion ashen. His chin was shadowed with stubble, and, paired with the bandages and cuts on his face, he looked rugged and dangerous. But then he looked over at me and grinned, and I couldn't help thinking he was more Labrador than Rottweiler.

I got up carefully, stretching my aching back and stiff joints slowly as I hobbled over to where Carter crouched beside the fire. "Didn't you get any sleep?"

He shrugged. "Maybe a little bit. Kenya and I took turns keeping the fire lit."

A twinge of guilt crackled through me. "You should have woken me up to help."

His eyes narrowed slightly with confusion. "You don't have to do everything, Jillian. You need to rest, too."

I didn't know what to say to that. Was it too whiny to think that it was unusual for someone to not want me to do everything for them?

Kenya returned to the circle then with an armload of wood. She had an incredible knack for finding great firewood. As she set her load on top of the small pile, I complimented her unexpected survival skills.

"I never would have guessed you would be so good at being a castaway," I said lightly.

Her color darkened a little, but she looked pleased all the same. "All the credit goes to my daddy," she said proudly.

Carter sat back on his heels, warming his hands by the flames. "Was he outdoorsy?"

"A lumberjack?" I guessed.

Kenya laughed. "Nothing like that. He was an accountant. After he and my mom split up, he needed something to keep him going when he didn't have us kids during the week, so one of his friends got him into the scouting program. He became a Scout leader and would take me to every campout on our weekends together." She looked wistfully at the fire. "I lived for those weekends in the mountains. There were always a whole bunch of boys around, but I was just there to be with Daddy." She looked up at me then with sadness in her eyes. "He died when I was twelve. That's when I begged my mom to let me join the Girl Scouts. I wanted something to keep Daddy with me. I only got good at all this stuff because it made me feel close to him." She laughed lightly and tossed a stick into the center of the fire. "I guess it finally came in handy."

"I'm sorry about your dad," Carter said gently. "I'm sure you miss him."

She nodded. "Thanks. I do. Is it weird to say that I feel like I've felt him with me since we got here? Something about being out in nature... I don't know, it sounds crazy. I guess maybe I'm never still enough when I'm in my real life."

"What do you do for work?" I asked, realizing I had never thought to ask her.

Her face lit up a little and she grinned. "I'm a kindergarten teacher. Six years now."

I groaned. "That sounds exhausting."

Kenya shrugged but nodded. "You get used to it."

"Hey," Howard snarled from the other side of the fire, "can't you three shut up? Some of us are trying to sleep."

I flushed, embarrassed, and was about to apologize when Kenya said with an eye roll, "Shut up, Howard. We're all doing the best we can to stay sane."

She wasn't wrong, but even still, I sat back away from Carter and Kenya and let our conversation die. I watched Kenya with a new understanding as she carefully tended the fire, thinking of her father and how his passion had very well saved our lives.

***

The sun made slow progress up over the trees, waking the tropical birds who began to sing heartily as the light warmed their feathers. The bugs that had pestered us all night long retreated from the sunshine, and we had a small window of reprieve from the buzzing and biting of flies and mosquitoes.

It was a picturesque morning. The ocean on one side, a lush green jungle on the other. A blue sky littered with thin clouds.

The only thing that would have made it better was food. A working toilet. A toothbrush, maybe. A shower. Room service...

My stomach burned with hunger and my mouth and throat ached with thirst. We hadn't found any fresh water sources in the trees so far, so we had tried to collect some rainwater in one of the hard-sided suitcases. None of us trusted the cleanliness of the water, and I wished we had a pot to boil it in. But a few sips of questionable water were better than absolutely nothing, which was the alternative.

There wasn't anything to eat, and certainly no espresso machine on the island. So after everyone got up (no one really slept very well) and took a drink of water, there seemed like nothing better to do than start our exploration of the island.

Carter didn't waste any time jumping into the planning. He stood with his fists on his hips and studied the jungle as he asked, "So, who would like to go and who would like to stay?"

Howard, Elodia, and Grandpa Skippy opted to stay at our little camp (Grandpa sheepishly suggested that he may not be well enough to go on a hiking expedition, and I was grateful that I didn't have to be the one to talk him into staying behind). That meant that Carter, Bridget, Kenya, and I would split up and explore. Kenya suggested that we walk the perimeter of the island, following the beach, rather than trying to trek through (and ultimately getting lost in) the jungle. We decided to split up to cover the most ground. Bridget asked to go with Carter, so Kenya and I paired up. We agreed to walk in one direction until midday, then turn around and come back to the camp. That way, no one would be out after nightfall. Kenya and I headed north, and Bridget followed Carter southward.

Our trek north brought us first to the large rocky outcropping that jutted into the sea for several hundred feet. It was steep enough, too, that climbing over it seemed foolhardy, so Kenya and I decided to head inland to get around it. The rocks, large and sharp-edged, jutted right out of the sand, and fragments of them had drifted outward onto the beach. Even with our shoes on, we still had to step carefully as we approached the rocks so as to avoid slicing open our soles or even an ankle. After picking our way up the beach and entering the shadows of the trees, we found that the rocks continued inland much farther than we had expected, with trees and grass growing thickly through the cracks and crags of the rocks.

Not seeing an easy path, we stopped and studied the ominous obstacle before us. Even through the trees, we could tell that the rocky outcropping that drifted into the sea was the short end of the feature, and as it went inland, the higher it climbed. Even a short walk away from the tree line proved that the rocks were larger here—more like cliff faces than boulders.

"How are we supposed to get around?"

My head swiveled back and forth, my eyes scanning the line of rocks before us, my mind whirling with indecision. To follow the cliff and hope for a break, go back to the beach and try to climb over the boulders there, or go back to camp and hope that Carter and Bridget had better luck?

I voiced these options aloud to Kenya, and she joined me in mulling them over for a few minutes. At length, she broke the silence. "I think we try the beach first. At least there we know what we're up against. Who knows how far this cliff goes inland before it becomes passable—if at all—and the last thing we need is to get lost."

"So, it's the devil you know versus the devil you don't, huh?"

She grimaced but said, "Yeah. You any good at rock climbing?"

"Does the two-story wall at the mall count?"

She chuckled mirthlessly. "I get the feeling that wall will be a walk in the park after today."

We retraced our steps and stepped back onto the beach a few minutes later. Knowing how the cliff escalated once it was hidden beneath the trees did nothing to diminish the task that the beachside rocks presented. But, as Kenya reminded me, there was nothing for it but to get started. So, tentatively at first, we both stepped onto the rocks and began a slow, cautious climb.

The rocks along the top of the outcropping were not as sharp as those that had been scattered to the beach, and after a few minutes, I settled into a slow but steady rhythm—testing boulders for steadiness before grasping them and pulling myself forward, stopping then to find a secure foothold before moving on. The path we picked wasn't completely vertical—more like climbing a steep staircase on all fours. Of course, this staircase was made out of sharp and crumbly igneous rocks that had a proclivity for slicing and crumbling beneath our weight. More than once, even after testing a foothold, the rocks crushed beneath my foot as I exchanged my weight from the other foot, making my leg slide out from beneath me, brutally scraping my knees, shins, and forearms. From the grunting and cursing behind me, I had to assume that Kenya wasn't faring much better. Not exactly a comfort.

Without watches, it was impossible to know just how long we had been climbing before we both needed to stop to catch our breath.

"Ugh," Kenya groaned after finding a secure resting place. She lifted the front of her t-shirt to wipe the sweat from her face. "I'd kill for a Dasani right about now." She paused to gulp in a breath then added, "Better yet, a piña colada. And a whole tray of curly fries."

My hands and arms trembled as I stretched them out, trying to shake off the fatigue and pain. I had more cuts than I cared to count, and the adrenaline that had fueled the beginning of this venture had smoked out about a quarter of the way up this rock pile. "I just hope we find something good on the other side," I said, throwing a glance up toward the pinnacle of the rocks, still about thirty feet above us.

"Like an Arby's," Kenya posed, eyes closed and head resting against a rock. "Or a Hyatt."

I chuckled lightly, then inhaled a long breath, following her lead and resting my head against the softest rock I could see. Spoiler alert: it wasn't soft at all.

"So," Kenya said after a few moments of exhausted silence, "what got you into being a yacht stewardess?"

"Nepotism," I said with a smirk. "Grandpa started the business and asked if any of his grandkids wanted to help out for a few months until he could build up his employee base."

"And you were the only one to take him up on it?" she guessed.

I let out a little sigh. "Actually, almost all of us volunteered. We got some training and certifications together, and for the first year it was a purely family-run effort. Then, one by one, all my cousins left to pursue other interests until the only ones left were me and Grandpa Skippy."

Kenya took a beat of silence before asking, "You liked it the most, huh?"

Normally, I would fib the answer to that kind of question, but something about being stranded and exhausted made it easy to be perfectly honest. "It's not exactly my dream come true. I mean, I never wrote a report about this in elementary school or anything. But Grandpa... I guess I do it for him."

"Because he needs you," Kenya assumed.

I wanted to agree, to say that my life's work was all in the desire to help my grandpa reach his dreams. That's certainly what I told my parents, my friends, even myself sometimes. But in reality... "Skippy doesn't need me," I admitted. "He doesn't need anybody.

He could find someone to hire to fill my job in about two seconds, and he's certainly made it no secret that there are better-qualified people than me."

Kenya's brow furrowed. "You make it sound like he keeps you out of pity."

I was too exhausted in every way to lie. "Sometimes I think that he does."

Her confusion didn't ease. "But you're so good at your job. I can't imagine that he doesn't feel lucky to have you. Plus, he's your grandpa, right?"

The depth of that statement felt like a dagger through the ribs, reopening a wound Kenya had no idea existed. "Grandpa and I... our relationship is complicated."

Kenya didn't answer, just rested her chin on her knee and watched me, waiting for me to continue.

"I was..." I broke off, cleared my throat, started again. "When my older siblings were in high school, my father had an affair and got the other woman pregnant. When my mom found out, she kicked my dad out and wanted a divorce. But then, the woman called my mom from the hospital and told her that she didn't want to keep the baby. She wanted my mom to take me, to raise me like her own baby, with my dad. I don't know how my mom ever agreed to that, but she did. She let my dad move back in, adopted me, and raised me with all the love a parent can give. She and my dad patched things up and tried to be a normal, happy family. To let the whole thing go."

Kenya's mouth was open, in an amazed expression I knew was the perfect companion to this story. I had only told it to a handful of people in my life. In fact, I had only learned the truth of it when I was in high school. It was a shocking revelation.

I continued the story. "Even though my mom eventually forgave my dad and tried to put the past behind them, Skippy never forgave him. He hasn't spoken to my dad since then. When I was a kid, I recognized that Skippy didn't come around like my other grandparents did. I thought it was just because he was busy or that he lived far away. I guess it all started to make more sense when I learned that I was adopted. Skippy wasn't really my grandpa, so why would he make any effort to get to know me?"

"Jillian," Kenya breathed, "Oh my gosh."

"Yeah... heavy stuff." I rubbed my hands down my face and blew out a long breath, then I pushed myself back up to my feet and dusted the sand from my backside and palms. "Enough moping. We've got to keep moving if we're going to find you that Hyatt." I extended my hand to her, and she took it and let me help her up. Then I turned to resume climbing the rocky hill.

"Hey, Jillian."

I paused and looked back at her. She grabbed my shoulder and squeezed gently. "I'm sorry you've had to go through all of that. I can't imagine."

Tears pricked at the corners of my eyes, but I blinked them away, too dehydrated to cry. "Thank you."

"Whether your grandpa ever tells you this or not, I want you to know that I think you're amazing at your job. You're an incredible woman, Jillian. And I'm glad I know you."

Now I really wanted to cry. "Thanks, Kenya. Ditto."

***

It took us less time to climb the last half of the rock face than it had the first, and when we finally crested the last stones, we were able to get our first view of the other side of the cliff. What we found made a curse slide from Kenya's tongue. The cliff we had just summited was matched by an immediate downward slope on the other side. We stood on the top of a long, narrow tongue of rock that jutted away from the body of the island, and on the other side was another stretch of sandy beach, edged by dense green jungle. The land curved to the right, disappearing into itself less than a mile past the edge of the rock, presumably curving around to make up the north side of the island. To the east, we saw more trees and hills that would be torturous to climb, and beyond that, the ocean. To the south, we could see the wisps of the beach campfire drifting upward from the beach, but the land turned sharply again, and we couldn't see much more than trees beyond it.

The island, what we could see of it, was small and looked as hopelessly deserted as we had feared. We really were all alone on this rock. My heart sank to my toes, and tears stung my eyes and clogged my throat. I wouldn't have gone so far as to say I'd been certain we would find help, but seeing for myself that we were on our own cut deeply.

"We're really stranded, then," Kenya said in a hollow voice.

I copied the curse she'd muttered moments before and turned a helpless circle, hoping to see something that wasn't there—anything that would disprove my heartsick knowledge that we would die out here. Panic welled up in my chest, flattening itself against my diaphragm, constricting my chest. I suddenly felt breathless, and my hand clutched at my throat, grappling to allow more air into my lungs.

"We're going to die," I rasped, my knees buckling and landing me on the rugged rocks. "I can't believe it. We're really going to die out here."

"Jill..."

Blood began to pound in my ears, drowning out Kenya's voice, and the urgent throbbing of my heart deafened my other senses.

"This can't be happening."

"Jill," Kenya tried again, but I paid no heed, my panic threatening to blacken my vision and throw me headlong down the rock face we had just tediously climbed.

"What's the point of swimming across the ocean if we're just going to die here?"

"Jillian!" Kenya shouted, shaking my shoulder and finally wrenching me from my terror.

I looked up, startled, half expecting to find her staring at me with wide, frightened eyes, placating me with empty words of comfort. But she wasn't even looking at me. Her attention was riveted northward, down the unexplored beach and toward the trees there.

"Look. Do you see that?"

Her focus broke me from the daze of panic I'd been suffocating in, and I pushed myself back to my feet. "What?"

"Halfway between here and the end of the island, and then in a little bit," she started, pointing to the spot she described, "do you see a kind of break in the trees?"

I squinted, following her directions and, after a few seconds of searching, I saw the same break she described. Perhaps a quarter mile inland from the beach, a group of trees was missing. It was difficult to tell just how big that clearing was, and it could have been a little meadow, but then I saw, leading away from the clearing, a thinner, straight line of cleared trees climbing eastward up a slope.

"Is that..."

Kenya stood on her tiptoes, trying in vain to see where the line went. "I think it's a road." She turned to me, eyes sparkling excitedly. "Maybe it leads to a village on the other side of the island—just like you thought!"

I couldn't help feeling that she was right. "Do you think we can get there?" I asked, peering toward the initial clearing that she pointed out. "Maybe it's a cabin or something. If someone is there, they might be able to help. And if not, we could follow the road to... wherever it leads."

"It may take a couple of hours to get there," Kenya said, glancing back toward our camp. "But I think we can get there and back to camp before sunset."

Invigorated by a real slice of hope, I bobbed a nod. "Agreed. Let's hurry though. I don't want them to worry."

And with that, we started northward, down the rock face, along the beach, and toward where we guessed the clearing was. The trouble was, we didn't know exactly where the clearing was in relation to the beach, and down off the rocks, we couldn't see it anymore. I estimated a mile, but Kenya thought it might have been farther. As we walked along, we kept our eyes peeled and our focus on the trees, watching for anything that might indicate where we needed to turn inland.

Then, seemingly out of nowhere, we found the entrance to a path. It wasn't wide enough to be a true road—maybe eight feet across—it could have fit a vehicle. But it wasn't paved, and it was so overgrown that it clearly hadn't been accessed in years.

Kenya stepped onto the path tentatively, her head on a swivel, taking in the surrounding wall of jungle on each side. I stayed on the beach, scanning the exterior landscape for clues. Why would this path be here? It wasn't narrow like a game trail, and a closer look at the ground revealed ruts on each side—where it had once been worn down by wheels. In my modern mind, I assumed they were tire-sized tracks, but they were so overgrown that it was impossible. Still, it was clear that this trail had once been regularly trafficked.

I turned my gaze back to the ocean. Had there once been a dock or a port here? The waterfront directly before me was nearly identical to every other stretch of beach we had encountered so far, but when I scanned the area back in the direction we had come from, I noticed a gradual dip outward, where the sand seemed to reach longingly toward the sea, and I could almost imagine that this would be a good place to build a dock, if one was ever needed. Maybe there had been one there once.

As if summoned by my imagination, I spotted a large wave crash spectacularly against a boulder, previously hidden beneath the water. As the water retreated back into the ocean, I saw, sticking awkwardly upward, a tangle of planks that were stuck together at one end but splayed out at the other, as if they had been properly aligned once, but were now reclaimed by the ocean.

I pointed this out to Kenya, and she agreed with my guess that perhaps this had once been a landing site of some kind, and whoever had landed here was likely responsible for this little road.

"Well," Kenya said on a sigh, "you know what they say, 'All roads lead to Rome.'"

I peered down the grassy jungle path and rubbed my forehead. "I don't know about Rome, but it's worth checking out. Maybe your Hyatt is down there."

She grinned at me. "Now you're talking."

***

Never in my life had I wished for a machete. But as we bushwhacked our way along the road that time forgot, the encroaching tree limbs, vines, and razor grasses made known their displeasure at our disturbing their isolation. Palm trees flourished near the beach, but after a little distance, we found yellow pines and ironwood trees surrounded by thick ferns. In any breaks in the trees, we saw wildflowers and greenery beyond my imagination: yellow elder flowers, wild sage, jacaranda, sea grape, Bahamian buttercup, yellow pine, southern bracken fern. It was as breathtaking as it was wild, and it attacked us at every opportunity. Bugs circled our heads, and more than once a spider found its way onto our clothing or skin. We heard wasps buzzing beyond the trail; mosquitoes nipped at our arms and faces. Birds flitted in the trees above us, squawking insults at us. Sweat poured from my brow, and exertion mixed with humidity made me feel soaking wet and burning up.

After twenty minutes of dodging fauna, nursing scratches, mopping humid sweat from our faces, and grumbling against the apparent futility of this trek, I noticed that the path had been gradually widening, and the plant life hadn't been as territorial over this area. The walking got easier and easier until, after what was probably a one-mile walk, we finally stepped off the road and into the clearing we had seen from above. My breath caught in my throat.

"No. Freaking. Way."

It was a village, the likes of which I had only ever seen in movies. The clearing was a circular acre of land, and around the inner perimeter of the trees stood nine small huts with bamboo walls and thatched roofs. The doors of every hut faced inward, a well-worn path leading toward each. In the center of the circle was a circular stone wall topped with a lattice of tightly woven bamboo and strapped down with vines.

Kenya and I stood at the village entrance in awe. Had we actually found civilization? There didn't appear to be anybody here, but a village like this didn't happen on its own.

"Hello?" I called into the clearing.

My call was answered only by the sounds of wind through the trees, humming insects, creaking branches, and rustling leaves.

Was it my imagination, or had the oppressive heat of the afternoon suddenly turned colder?

I shuddered, and goosebumps prickled on my arms. I looked at Kenya, who had her arms wrapped tight around her torso. Her eyes were wide, and she swallowed hard.

There was a low moan from the jungle behind us, followed by an enormous gust of wind that flattened our clothes against our backs and pressed us a step closer into the village.

"Is it just me," Kenya said over the wind, "or does this place feel super haunted?"

I was not superstitious, but as the temperature continued to drop and the wind howled ferociously around us, I couldn't help but wonder what spirits we had disturbed.

"L-let's get out of here," I stammered, turning away from the village, ready to run into the jungle and escape the haunting within this circle. Something felt really wrong about this village.

Kenya agreed wordlessly, grabbed my hand, and the two of us ran back onto the road, against the wind, and into the noisy jungle. Adrenaline spiked through us, and we ran the entire mile, stopping only to cross over fallen trees and skirt around the sharpest of plants. Panting, shaking, and sweating, we emerged from the jungle, back onto the beach.

The haunting storm had, seemingly, not just affected the jungle surrounding the village. The sky, which had been stunningly blue and brightly sunny, was now boiling with dark gray and black clouds. A fierce storm had blown in from the ocean. The wind slapped our faces with salty water, whipping and tearing at our clothes and hair.

Kenya's eyes were wide and fearful. "Did we anger the gods and call down a hurricane?"

My mind immediately wanted to dismiss such a ridiculous, superstitious notion. But... the timing was beyond coincidental.

The clouds above took their cue and unleashed a fierce torrent of icy rain. We were instantly drenched. The wind was so great, I felt like I might be blown off my feet. Lightning cracked the sky, blinding me just as thunder followed with a roar.

"Come on," Kenya cried, grabbing my arm, "we need to take cover."

We dashed back into the jungle, but we stayed on the road we had followed away from the beach. After a quarter mile, both of us were gasping for breath, and we had to stop and regroup. Kenya leaned heavily against a palm tree, and I braced my elbows against my knees, sucking in oxygen like I had never exercised a day in my life. Thank you, malnutrition and exhaustion.

After a few moments, my heart rate had returned to a semi-normal rhythm, and I stood and looked at the jungle around me. Rain trickled through the canopy overhead, but the stand of trees dispelled most of the ferocious wind.

Kenya straightened from her hunched and gasping position by the tree and joined me in the middle of the overgrown road. Her eyes were still wide with alarm, but she wasn't panicky anymore.

"What do you think we should do?" I asked. "It'll take a couple of hours to get back over those rocks again. But we'll kill ourselves if we try to do it in this storm."

"I don't want to sit here on the road to that village all night," she countered with a dramatic shudder.

"So... we just wait for the storm to pass. And hope we have enough time to get back before dark." This sounded like a terrible plan, but I didn't see many options.

Kenya nodded vaguely, but her attention had been snared by something in the distance. I followed her eye line but only saw thick trees.

"What?" I asked.

"What if we could get back without going through the storm?"

I raised one eyebrow. "Do you have a magic portal you haven't told me about?"

But she shook her head. "No. But I've been thinking that maybe we took the long way around. What if we cut through the trees here," she pointed into the trees, "and bypassed the length of shore we followed to get here? I'll bet we could avoid all those rocks and save a bunch of time. And the trees would keep us out of the storm."

Her suggestion to hike through unmarked and unknown terrain went against my instincts, which usually stayed in the realm of 'Stay where you are until somebody finds you.' Then again, I'd learned that as a six-year-old who had lost her mom in a grocery store, so the situations didn't exactly align.

"I don't want to get lost," I said, not ready to plunge into more unknown territory.

"What's the worst that could happen?" she countered. "We'll keep straight that direction and, worst case, we end up at a different stretch of beach than we expected. If we walk long enough, we'll find the ocean, no matter which way we go."

I wasn't convinced. "Maybe..."

"And I am not going back to that haunted village again. I'm not too keen to stay here and wait for the ghosts to come looking for me, either."

I didn't disagree. "But..."

"Look, we'll mark our path." She stripped off the oversized hoodie she had worn since our marooning, then pulled off the thin t-shirt she wore underneath. She found a small tear in the hem, and she worked at it for a minute until she was able to rip a strip of fabric free from the bottom. She tied this to a tree branch at eye level then looked back to me, waiting for me to be impressed.

I couldn't decide if I was impressed or too tired to argue, so I gave in with a "lead the way" shrug. And we plunged into the unknown jungle, marking our trail every dozen feet or so so we could find our way back to the road if we needed to.

The direction Kenya had chosen to take was, blessedly, easy terrain, and before too long, the trees opened up and we were able to see the ocean. The sudden storm that had attacked us half an hour ago had died off, and while it was still cloudy, there was no rain and no wind to speak of. We were still about a quarter mile away from the shore, but from our vantage point, we could see that we had indeed bypassed the rocky outcropping and were within easy reach of our beach camp. I could see three figures standing around a scraggly fire.

I let out a low whistle as I stopped to stretch a cramp out of my calf. "You were right, Kenya. Good thinking."

She accepted this praise with a huge grin. "Smarter than I look, huh?"

I laughed lightly. "I'm just glad your gamble paid off."

She shrugged, still grinning. "I've always been lucky."

"How does this shipwreck play into all that luck?" I asked, dryly.

Rolling her eyes, she started walking again toward the beach. "No comment."

Taking Kenya's shortcut, we crossed the distance that had taken us most of the morning in just an hour. It was midafternoon, but the low and dark clouds made it feel later than it was.

When we reached our beach at last, we found Grandpa Skippy sitting alone in the sand, slowly poking at the low flames with a long bamboo pole. The sight of his expression nearly broke my heart. His cheeks seemed to sag with fatigue and sorrow. His eyes drooped, and the wrinkles on his face seemed to stand out sharply in the afternoon sun. His shoulders were hunched, and his slow movement spoke of bone-deep weariness and mountains of regret.

I approached him first and he looked up in one fast motion, like I had startled him out of a reverie. A ghost of a smile flitted across his lips as his eyes locked onto my face.

"Hey, Jilly. Glad you made it back."

With his face turned toward me, he looked pale and weak. I wondered why he had been left alone when it was obvious that he was unwell.

"You here alone, Skippy?" Kenya asked as I started to fuss with his bandage.

He shook his head and pulled away from my probing fingers. "Quit fussing over me. The Lovells just went out to get some more wood and cool down for a bit."

"Cool down?" My mind immediately conjured the image of Howard Lovell threatening a fistfight with my ailing grandfather. "What happened?"

He waved off my concerns. "Just too much sun. Elodia was starting to get a headache, so I suggested they take a walk in the trees for some shade and look for a spring for some water."

My shoulders relaxed. I hadn't even realized how much I had tensed.

"Have Carter and Bridget come back yet?" Kenya asked, settling herself down on Grandpa's other side and promptly flopping backward into the sand. It had been an exhausting day.

Grandpa Skippy shook his head. "Not yet. Should be soon, though." He looked at his watch. It was nearly 4 p.m. "They said they would be back before sundown."

I nodded and watched the sky with him for a few moments.

"Did you find anything?" he finally asked.

Kenya propped herself up on an elbow and looked at me, some of the fear from earlier returning to her eyes.

"Maybe," I said. "Things got kind of weird, though."

Grandpa opened his mouth to reply, but he was cut off by a shout from the trees.

"We're back!" It was Elodia. I turned in the sand to watch as she and Howard emerged from the trees, a broad grin on her face and her arms full of coconuts. Howard was not smiling, but he carried a load of mangoes. Her grin was infectious. "And we brought food!"

# 9

## *CARTER*

**U**ntil that morning, I hadn't spoken much to Bridget. When we were on the ship, she was always shadowed by her bodyguard or sequestered in a corner alone. It was clear that this superstar was untouchable, and no low-life marine biologist was going to break down the gates to have anything as trivial as a small-talk conversation with her.

That was true during the 24 hours we'd spent on this island, too. When we first left the group that morning, we walked southward in silence for a while. There wasn't much of interest besides the abandoned stretch of sand, rolling waves, and looming jungle to our left.

Bridget was quiet as we walked, staring off at the sky or the trees. I didn't know what to say to her, and the walk was strenuous enough to make conversation difficult anyway. After an hour of walking in silence, we agreed to take a break. Bridget found a driftwood log to sit on, and she left enough space for me to sit beside her. We stared at the ocean for a few minutes, catching our breath.

Then, she sighed deeply, drawing my attention.

"Something on your mind?"

She shook her head. "I just realized this is probably the longest I've been around a stranger without them asking about a tour or needing an autograph or telling me that I'm a sellout." She shot a little smile at me, trying to mask the unexpected pain that statement held.

"You don't like to talk about your work?"

She shrugged one shoulder. "I love what I do. I love to sing, and I've really liked doing movies and stuff lately. But... I don't know, I guess when I started, I never expected that my job would become my whole life. You know?"

I was no international pop star, but I could relate to having my life overtaken by work. "It feels like you don't have a life if you're not working?"

She shifted on the log, turning to face me more directly. "Exactly. Like, no one will let me be anything but Perfect Bridget Foster. When... sometimes I just want to eat a hamburger and get ketchup all over my chin and not have anybody print it in a tabloid."

"Now, that I can't relate to."

She shook her head. "Do you know the last time I went on a date—like a real date? Not one tailored to further anybody's career or get a perfect picture or raise money for a foundation?"

I couldn't even hazard a guess. I never would have thought her fame would spill over into who she dated. Dating was hard enough without politics. "Sounds... awful."

She gave a hollow laugh. "I haven't had a normal life since I was sixteen. Don't get me wrong, I'm not complaining. I love what I do, and I'm so grateful for everything I have and for the people who listen to my music. But sometimes... I just wish I could turn it off."

I pursed my lips and looked around at the island we sat on. "Well, you can't get much farther from the paparazzi here," I said. "Maybe this could be the escape you're looking for."

She laughed at that. "I never would have thought that my only way out of the spotlight was to get stranded in the Bahamas."

I shrugged, smiling. "Stranger things have happened."

Laughing again, she said, "Thanks."

We lapsed into silence again for a few moments. Then, Bridget said, "So, you're into Jillian, huh?"

I felt heat creep up my neck, but I couldn't resist a small smile. "Is it that obvious?"

"I didn't think you were trying to keep it a secret." She considered me with her head tilted to one side. "I like you two together. You're both down to earth. I think you'd be good for each other."

"Thanks."

After a few more minutes sitting on the log, we stood and continued our trek down the beach. Bridget continued to chat with me as we walked, telling me about some of her hobbies—her real hobbies, not just the ones her publicity team fed to the tabloids. She told me she liked to play badminton and soccer, but in her downtime, she was an avid reader with an affinity for dime-store romance novels.

"The worse the plot, the better," she said, laughing. "I don't want to believe a word of the story. That's true escapism for me."

I confessed that I wasn't much into fiction, and she recommended a couple titles that might get me hooked. "They're not romances," she clarified. "But they're still really good."

I remembered that the suitcase we'd opened on the beach had equal parts fancy clothes and comfortable ones, along with several novels. I wondered if that wasn't a perfect representation of Bridget's personality: half work, "Perfect Bridget Foster" with the expensive outfits and glossy hair; half comfort and novels, wanting nothing more than to curl up with a good book and let some time slip away.

I looked at her differently after that. I had never been a fan of her music before, but now I could look past her veil of fame and the sheen of money to see the real person beneath. The young woman who wanted real connections, to live the life she wanted, to find meaning and fulfillment. I hoped she would find those things.

As she told me more about her life and the expectations embedded in that life, it became clear that she was lonely. Even surrounded by people, she didn't feel like she got to connect with most of them.

"And," she admitted, "I'm a complete introvert. I was super shy as a kid, and it took a ton of coaching to get me to ever get on stage."

"It's impressive that you were able to overcome that," I remarked.

"I still have to work on it. Some nights, all I want to do is stay home with a cup of tea instead of facing all those people."

She described some of the mental exercises she has used for years to help her get out of her comfort zone. She spoke about her life, her struggle to accept being the center of attention, the strain that fame had taken on her family and her friendships. After high school, she confessed that she had to quietly sever ties with most of her friends because they only ever wanted favors or money from her. Nobody wanted to be friends with the popular singer and not have anything to show for it.

I hadn't expected to feel sympathy for a rich megastar, but I did. I knew that she probably wasn't looking to make a random 35-year-old man her new best friend, but I was willing to listen and be a sounding board—one that it seemed like she had needed for a long time.

We spent the day talking as we walked the empty beach. We never saw anything more interesting than some pop bottles that had washed up on the shore and some torn, discarded fishing nets. The most valuable thing I came away with was a tentative friendship with Bridget.

It was mid-afternoon when we returned to the others at the beach, tired and dehydrated. I wished we had found even a tin can we could hold over our campfire to boil water in, but no luck in that department.

Jillian and Kenya had returned before us, and we waved tiredly as we approached. Since we didn't have much to tell about our search, it only took a couple of minutes before we were ready to hear from Jillian and Kenya's journey.

Elodia sighed, disappointed, and said, "Too bad you didn't find anything." She turned to Jillian then and asked, "What about you guys?"

Jillian exchanged an apprehensive look with Kenya. My hair immediately stood on end, and my spine straightened in anticipation. They'd found something.

Hesitatingly at first and then with increasing agitation and nervous energy, the tale came forward. An overgrown path, an abandoned village, and the real possibility that the place was either haunted or guarded by evil spirits—or both. The menacing storm that had chased them out.

When the story was finished, a prickly silence followed. Then, like a volcanic episode, questions erupted from all of us at once. What could have caused everyone in that village to leave? Had they left, or had they died? And how long had it been since someone had been here? Had they been killed off by disease or by other people or by animals? Or had they simply moved on? Was there a deadly plague on this island that we would now all be infected by?

This seemed the least likely possibility to me, but Kenya was convinced that the former inhabitants of this island had certainly been targeted by terrorists with some experimental biohazard, wiping them clean off the planet, leaving only their homes behind.

I was beginning to realize that Kenya was something of a dramatic.

Conjecture and speculation abounded in the group for several minutes until Kenya finally said, loudly, "Well, it doesn't matter what happened there. I am never going back. That place was..." she shuddered violently, "horrible."

Silence fell again. Each of us lapsed into our own thoughts. From the discussions, I surmised that our group was split nearly in half—with Kenya, Skippy, and Elodia convinced that the village was cursed, and the wind was a sure sign to keep away. Bridget, Howard, and I thought it was a coincidence. I couldn't get a solid reading from Jillian. She was tight-lipped with her opinion, but it was pretty clear that the scene had spooked her.

As though the universe had been listening and wanted to add its two cents to the conversation, the wind suddenly picked up, coming in cold and salty off the ocean. All of us looked out toward the watery horizon. My heart sank when I saw a wall of dark, angry clouds building in the middle distance.

Curse-driven or not, a storm was on its way to us, and judging by the strength of the wind, it was going to be a miserable one.

"We've got to get off the beach," I said. "We need to find shelter."

Kenya bristled. "If you think I'm going to go back—"

"I don't mean the village," I cut in, pushing to my feet. "We've got to get into the trees. Fast."

Another look at the fast-approaching hurricane was enough to spur everybody else to their feet as well. Jillian wrapped an arm around Captain Skippy and helped him to his unsteady feet. She murmured encouragement to him as she helped him up the beach. I turned to the others and urged them to follow Jill and Skippy.

Within minutes, the seven of us were tucked into the relative shelter of the trees—and just in time, too. The wind whipped at our clothes, tossing sand into our faces as it whistled and groaned through the trees. We pushed as deep into the trees as we dared, fearful of getting turned around if we got too far from the beach.

The storm came in faster than I ever would have expected. In total, it took maybe ten minutes from the time we spotted the clouds churning over the ocean for us to be drenched in rainwater. The trees around us were not as dense as they seemed from outside, and the canopy of palm fronds above us left ample gaps for water to find us. Within minutes, we were all soaked to the skin. With no better options, we sought out the thickest foliage we could find and huddled together beneath it, pressing tight against one another to retain some warmth in our quickly cooling skin. I made a sly move to allow Kenya to stand beside Bridget, whom she was still starstruck over, and I got to stand close to Jillian. She smiled up at me as I sidled in beside her, and I felt warmth spread in my chest that had nothing to do with sharing body heat with the group.

A strong gust rocked us on our feet, and Jillian shivered. Reflexively, I lifted my arm to wrap her up into my side. She happened to move toward me at the same moment, and I was knocked off balance, barely catching myself before toppling into her. So the move I'd made to appear gallant and heroic did nothing to comfort her and did a lot to embarrass me.

I think I yelped.

And that woman... She actually laughed! It was just a little snort, and she slapped her hand up to her mouth, eyes wide, and apologized right away. But I knew I was ridiculous, and it was kind of nice to have something to laugh about. I couldn't keep my own quiet laughter inside, and any attempt to try would have only hurt my side even more. Our laughs dominoed into each other, and soon we'd laughed back and forth so much that we were fully busting a gut. The others must have stared at us as if we were insane, and we probably were headed in that direction. But I had eyes only for Jillian. She was radiant with laughter, her cheeks rosy, her eyes crinkling slightly at the corners with mirth.

When our laughter subsided, she threaded her arm through mine and settled in close to my side, resting her cheek against my shoulder. Like we had planned it. Like we had done this a thousand times. Like she was meant for that very spot. I grinned like an idiot.

Come at me, rain! I'd take it all if it meant standing in it with her.

***

An hour into the punishing storm, my tune had changed.

The rain wouldn't quit. Our soggy group huddled close together, praying for relief. I was shivering violently, my teeth chattering so harshly that I was afraid I might shatter a molar. I stayed close to Jillian with my arm over her shoulders, but this did little by way of warmth or protection. Her grateful expression helped just a little, though.

We had given up on staying dry and sat down on the saturated undergrowth and sand, too exhausted and hungry to stand still any longer.

Captain Skippy sat on Jillian's other side, not speaking since she had asked after his well-being and he had barked, "I'm no worse off than anyone here, Jillian. Why don't you pester someone else?" I wondered why he was always so cold with his granddaughter when he was so genial with everyone else. Maybe it's just the head injury, I suspected.

Elodia and Howard sat a few feet away, Howard glaring at the captain relentlessly. Elodia just cried into Howard's shoulder, and when she was cried out, she held tight to him, shivering pitifully.

Kenya had taken up a position beneath a large palm tree that provided slightly more cover than the surrounding trees, and after a few minutes, Bridget crossed the group and sat beside Kenya, smiling at her shyly. I wondered if Bridget was embracing the idea that this island was a clean slate. Maybe this was an opportunity for her to make a real friend. I hoped so. I heard them talking in low voices under the drumming of the rain: they were the only ones brave enough to hold a conversation during the storm.

The afternoon was growing late, and I knew it would be impossibly dark after sunset. The previous night, we had had the moon and stars to see by, along with our campfire and some homemade torches. But it was far too wet to even think about a fire, and the clouds were so thick that we knew we wouldn't have moonlight to walk by tonight.

I sighed into the growing dimness, my eyes refusing to open and my brain refusing to calculate our odds of survival even one more time. All thoughts seemed to dust in and out of my mind like powdered sugar on a donut—not really sticking but not really going away, either. The one thing that I couldn't completely forget about, though, was the village.

We had discussed it at length, and we were divided in half about whether to even go explore it. But now, sitting in the elements for endless hours, I was having some serious second thoughts. I wondered how many of the others were, too.

Shelter from a storm... but the storm had driven them away from the village. There might be food nearby... all of the villagers might have died from disease. We could build a fire... evil spirits could use it to burn us up in our sleep. At least we'd be out of our misery.

I turned to Captain Skippy, who was sitting beside Jillian, his back against the trunk of a palm tree, eyes closed. The rain had washed the blood out of his bandage, and it was semi-opaque, showing bits of his skin and parts of the wound beneath.

He won't survive this.

That thought jolted me into action like nothing else had. I sat up, pulling away from Jillian. My movement got everyone's attention, and they all sat up a little straighter, as if they had been waiting for a signal.

"This is stupid," I finally said, my teeth still chattering and my numb lips making me slur. "We've got to go to shelter."

Howard Lovell gulped and said in an awed whisper, "The village?"

I nodded and looked at Jillian and Skippy for backup. Jillian returned my nod and gave me a reassuring half-smile.

"Why don't we build our own shelter?" Kenya tried, clearly still spooked by her earlier experience at the village. "We've got bamboo and stuff here..."

Jillian jumped in. "We don't have time. I don't know about you, but I'm numb, and we haven't eaten in days. I don't have the strength to build anything, and..." Her gaze darted to Skippy again. "If we don't get Skippy inside soon..."

Her unfinished thought needed no further utterance. First Kenya, then the rest of them, nodded solemnly. Visible relief washed over Jillian, and she reached out to take her grandpa's hand. "Are you up for a walk?" she asked him.

His eyes drooped and his face sagged, but he nodded brusquely and attempted to push to his feet. "Let's do it."

I stood up, blood rushing to my legs with needle-like irritation. "Then let's go. We'll have to hurry to make it there before dark."

Jillian explained where we could find the shortcut she and Kenya had created through the jungle. I was impressed with her foresight in marking the trail. Jillian stood up beside me and we helped assist Captain Skippy to his feet.

"To the haunted village, then," Elodia said with uncalled-for gaiety. Then she added in a lower voice, "I've always wanted to see a ghost in person."

# 10

*JILLIAN*

By the time we reached the village , the sun had completely set, plunging us into stormy darkness. Our trek had been painfully slow due to injuries and fear of the haunted village. Even following our tail markers, there was no path to speak of until we reached the overgrown road, and our journey had taken so long that I half-expected to never find it — that it had all been a hallucination or some Narnia come-and-go kind of land. So, I was relieved when we found the road at last. We traveled the last quarter mile quickly, finding the way easier and drier than anything we had encountered so far.

Grandpa was not doing well. His steps were slow and plodding, and a couple of times, he nearly went down over a gnarled root or fallen branch. The wind and rain pummeled us even through the overhead canopy. I couldn't help but wonder if we'd made a huge mistake leaving the beach. Would we ever make it to the village?

At last, we arrived. When we rounded the final curve and the huts came into view, I looked around reflexively, tensed to flee at the slightest increase in the wind or howl from the trees. But the rain just poured with no discernible change in ferocity. Still, I hesitated to cross the imaginary threshold into the village.

The seven of us stood together for a long moment, staring into the darkness, blinking to take in the hulking silhouettes of the huts. There was no sign of life—or afterlife. Nothing more than the drum of the rain and the whistling of the wind.

For as desperate as we had all felt to get into shelter, now that it was within throwing distance, it seemed none of us were quite brave enough to close the distance. What if it was unsafe? Were we simply trading one danger for the next?

Just then, lightning flashed, followed instantly by an ear-splitting thunderclap. Several of us flinched or even ducked at the intensity of the flash and bang.

When the rolls of thunder had echoed themselves to silence again, Howard stepped forward, breaking the stalemate at last. "This is stupid," he growled, striding toward the nearest hut. "I'm getting out of this storm before it's too late."

And that was all it took. Elodia followed directly behind her fiancé, pausing only briefly to take Kenya's hand and pull her along at her side.

Carter and I exchanged a look. His expression was impossible to discern in the dark, though, and I was too tired from the hike to put too much more thought into this. So, I shrugged, put my arm around Grandpa again, and followed the others to the hut. Carter and Bridget brought up the rear a few paces behind us.

Under normal circumstances, the interior of the hut probably wouldn't have been much more comfortable than the jungle, but when the seven of us entered—shivering and dripping and utterly exhausted—we might as well have walked into a five-star hotel. Though it was very dark outside, strategically placed openings in the roof allowed a little light inside but kept the rain from invading. The air was still and a few degrees warmer than outside, but mostly it was dry with a hard-packed floor and, to our shock, bed-like couches built into two of the walls. There was no mattress or padding of any kind, just bamboo shoots that had been tied together with strong cords to form a sturdy surface that was long enough for even a tall man to stretch out, and wide enough for two people to sleep comfortably side by side.

Since he had been the first to enter, Howard had taken the first test of the couch, sitting gingerly at first, but when it held him easily, he lay down with a mighty groan. Elodia sat down beside him and bounced up and down a little on the bamboo.

"Seems like it'll hold." She glanced at Howard, who had thrown his arm across his face and may have already been asleep. "Would you all mind if we take this for a few hours?"

Since Howard had clearly called "dibs" on the bed, arguing the point seemed useless.

"You girls should take the other bed," Grandpa said with as much chivalry as he could muster. I wasn't buying it.

"No way. You're about to faint. If anybody gets a place to lie down, it's you."

He was shaking his head before I'd even finished talking. "Not happening. I'll sit on the floor."

Before I could argue, he went ahead and lowered himself to the dirt floor, leaning his head back against the wall of the hut, trying and failing to mask the moan that escaped him as he finally relaxed.

Kenya and Bridget exchanged a look, and I glanced at Carter.

"Don't even think about it," he said. "I'll sleep on the floor, too."

I hadn't known Carter long, but I already knew better than to argue. So, I nodded at Kenya and Bridget. "You two go ahead and take it. I'll keep watch by the door."

"You will not," Grandpa growled from the darkness at my feet. "You need to rest."

At the same time, Bridget asked, "Keep watch? For what?"

Spiders. Mice. Jaguars. Evil spirits... I didn't say what was on my mind. Instead, I shrugged and said, "Someone might show up to rescue us. I don't want to miss them."

I could almost hear six pairs of eyes rolling at my ridiculous comment. It made me smile.

Sleeping assignments were sorted through, and so with four people off the ground and three people on the dirt, we settled into the quiet darkness. Howard's snores filled the space almost at once. Kenya fell asleep next, followed shortly by Bridget, Grandpa, and Elodia.

I could tell Carter was still awake by the way he kept fidgeting. I had taken up a sitting position by the hut's bamboo door, leaning the side of my head against the wall and watching the door crack like it might fly open at any moment. Grandpa had slouched down on the floor, and I had insisted that he put his head on my legs. Carter was on my other side, half reclined on the floor with his head and shoulders propped up against the wall. I think he intended to stay up with me. Stupid, honorable punk. He was so sweet.

The idea of keeping watch ended up being something of a joke. With so many sleeping people, the air warmed up quite a bit, and after a while, I felt my tired eyelids droop shut and my jaw slacken. I wanted to sleep so badly, but this village honestly freaked me out. Who knew when it would show its true colors? I lifted my head and shook it vigorously. Stay awake! The last thing I wanted was to be possessed in my sleep.

I felt a warm palm on my arm, then, and turned to see Carter smiling understandingly in the dimness. He pushed himself upright and slid over so our shoulders touched.

"Lean on me," he said, in a voice that didn't carry to anybody else in the room. "We'll take the watch together."

Too exhausted and emotionally strung out to argue, I leaned some of my weight into him and rested my cheek against his shoulder. He followed suit by allowing his cheek to rest on the top of my head. The warm, coziness was interrupted by my sudden awareness that I hadn't bathed in days. I really hoped my hair didn't stink too bad. Way to ruin a perfectly sweet and romantic moment, brain.

He was so warm and comfortable. Despite my aching backside, my grumbling stomach, my pounding head, and my troubled mind, I felt an unusual peace in that moment. I felt secure and content and peaceful.

Naturally, I fell asleep at once.

***

When I woke up again, blue light filtered through the upper windows. Moonlight. A low rustling stirred through the trees outside the hut, but the high winds and pounding rain had quieted. The storm had passed, and the skies had cleared.

A long breath escaped my lungs, and I felt tension ease from my shoulders. The storm was over.

It was still solidly nighttime, and I didn't pretend to be the kind of person who explores haunted island towns in the dead of night. So instead of exploring the other huts, I settled for studying the interior of the hut we'd piled into.

It wasn't terribly large—maybe 15 feet square. The ceiling was higher than I would have expected: about eight feet along the edges and reaching up toward twelve or thirteen feet at the center. The ceiling was constructed from woven palms and grass. I couldn't tell in the darkness, but I wondered if the weaving was tight enough to keep rodents from falling out of it onto our heads. I shuddered at the thought, then deliberately averted my attention to something else.

In the center of the hut was a small circular fire pit, and the skylights that allowed the moonlight to come in must have acted as a chimney for the smoke. The two low beds that the Lovells and Bridget and Kenya slept on were built directly into the walls, with the sturdy platform raised a foot off the floor. The walls were bamboo that had been trussed together with rough ropes, and small gaps between the poles allowed little speckles of moonlight to dance into the hut. The gaps also allowed a slight breeze to cross through the space, which felt pleasant now. The post-storm night had turned muggy and sticky-hot.

Carter shifted at my side, and I lifted my head from his shoulder to look at him. He was asleep. His head rested back against the wall, and his mouth hung open slightly as he dozed. He wasn't snoring, but his deep breathing told me that he was deeply asleep.

When I moved my head away from Carter's shoulder, a spike of pain ratcheted through my neck and up through the side of my head. I suppressed a moan and reached up to gingerly massage the tight muscles. Every part of my body was stiff, and even as I lifted my arm to ease the pain in my neck, my shoulder cried out in protest. The previous day spent hiking on an empty stomach with very little water had obviously not agreed with me.

I leaned forward away from the wall, gently allowing my back muscles to loosen. My movement made Grandpa stir where he lay on my other side. He had moved his head from my lap and lay with his face resting on his arm on the floor. He was snoring, and it made me smile. Grandpa was known in the family as a "buzzsaw," and tonight was the first time I had heard the notorious sound in quite a long time.

My worry for him hadn't let up from the moment I'd found him unconscious on the bridge. I'd spent the last six years working with him, and I knew his habits and his temperament better than any other person in my life. But the truth was that I longed for his acceptance, his approval. I had spent six years trying my best to prove myself to this man, but even with everything we'd been through the past two days, I didn't feel any closer to feeling like his true granddaughter than I did six years ago.

Feeling depressed, I rubbed my hands down my face to keep from crying. I knew that if I let my emotions out, I might not be able to stop them. And this was no place to have an emotional breakdown.

Get a grip, Jillian, I told myself. You can worry about your grandpa issues when you've got food and dry socks.

I adjusted my position on the floor, and it became apparent very quickly that I couldn't stay in this hut much longer—it was time to answer nature's call, and I needed to do so right away.

As quietly as I could, I pushed off the floor and got to my feet, ignoring the way my joints cracked and groaned as I stood up. The pain would have to wait: I needed to find some privacy. I stepped around the sleeping forms of my friends and let myself out of the hut through the bamboo door.

Exiting the hut into the moon-soaked night was like stepping into another world. The clearing was just as I remembered from the previous afternoon, but bathed in the soft light of the moon, the shadows stretched longer and deeper, making the small area seem to stretch out to infinity. Water dripped and splattered down from the trees, making the jungle feel alive and restless.

Trepidatiously, I walked a few yards from the hut and found a secluded area to conduct my business. I'd never been much of a camper, and I certainly was no Girl Scout like Kenya, so peeing in the woods was not something I was used to. Yesterday, Kenya had taken a few minutes to explain a few crucial skills for keeping one's shoes dry when squatting over a bush. But I've gotta say—it's not easy, and I had never wished for indoor plumbing more in my entire life.

When I was through, I walked back to the hut with fear-hastened steps. My heart galloped unsteadily in my chest, making my already aching head throb sickeningly.

Back at the hut, I cast one more look out into the village. Its emptiness yawned like an abandoned mineshaft. Like it was calling out to me from a memory or another life.

*You know this place*, it whispered to me. *You know this place.*

Another chill skittered down my spine, and I ducked back into the hut before I could conjure any spirits from my own imagination.

***

# CARTER

I was wide awake when the sun finally rose behind the storm clouds. I stood and stretched my arms above my head, wincing as the stretch pulled at my healing scrapes and cuts. I groaned a little, and Elodia shifted on the bamboo pallet. I looked at her and found her watching me with exhausted eyes. I raised an eyebrow questioningly.

Elodia responded by carefully sitting up, letting Howard's arm fall from where it had rested around her waist. With silent movements, she stood and walked to the door of the hut, looked back over her shoulder, and jerked her head toward the door. Her expression said, *Well, are you coming?* Then she stepped outside into the rainy morning.

I followed.

Elodia walked through the mud on bare feet, leading me across the clearing and circle of small huts to the shelter of some large overhanging palm trees. There she stopped, arms crossed over her torso, and waited for me.

She looked up as I stopped in front of her and released a little breath. "I'm not superstitious," she began. "But Howard is. I'm ready to poke around this place and see what we're dealing with. I just can't let Howard know I'm doing it until we prove there's nothing to be afraid of out here. Want to go exploring?"

"Sure," I said, still feeling a little confused. Why did it matter if Howard didn't want to explore? Why didn't she just explore on her own? Not that I was unwilling to look around, it just felt very 1950s for Elodia to not be allowed to walk around the jungle without her fiancé's approval.

"What are you hoping to find?" I asked, following her into the trees.

"Oh, I don't know," she said breezily. "Something to explain why this village is here. Or maybe some food." She paused briefly, looking around at the trees with her hands on her hips. With a nod to the left, she decided, "Let's look this way first."

There wasn't any discernible path, so we wove in and out of trees, scanning the trunks and underbrush for anything that might explain the oddities we'd found. After a few minutes, we found something just out of the ordinary enough to catch our attention.

"Is that a trail?" Elodia asked, stopping to examine a bare strip of sand. It was overgrown with sawgrass and vines, but as we moved them to the sides, we could see a small pathway, like a hiking trail. In one direction, it led in the general vicinity of the village. Crouched down beside the overgrown trail, my eyes followed the line in the other direction, winding into the jungle where it became thickly overgrown.

I looked up at Elodia. She was beaming and bouncing from one foot to the other. "Let's follow it!" she said gleefully, as if this was an elaborate escape room instead of a real-life wild jungle full of poisonous insects and snakes.

Her excitement was contagious, though, and before I knew it, I was grinning myself, brushing the sand from my knees and following her along the abandoned trail. It was slow-going because we had to stop every few feet to uncover the trail. More than once we wondered if this trail wasn't just a trick of our imagination—maybe a path for water runoff during the rainy season or a small game trail. But since there wasn't game on Bahamian islands like there is in, say, Wisconsin, we weren't likely to stumble upon a deer trail. But each time we were ready to give up and call our path a fluke, we would move one more palm frond and uncover the next section.

The path wasn't very wide, even in the clearest spaces—no more than the width of a shoe—but it was well-worn enough that it was constant as it wove deeper into the jungle. I kept my head on a swivel, watching out for vipers and hornets while Elodia talked nonstop about, seemingly, whatever popped into her head.

Without having to ask a single question, I learned that Elodia had just turned 40, had spent the last 18 years working in marketing, and created her own company two years ago. She hoped to have children someday, so she wanted her wedding with Howard to happen sooner than later because, as she said, her "clock was ticking." This led her down a rabbit hole of thought regarding freezing eggs and artificial insemination which, frankly, was more than I'd ever thought I'd learn from a woman I had never spoken to before yesterday.

Elodia didn't require much input from me to uphold the conversation, nor did she seem to care that she was spilling her soul to a man whose last name she remembered incorrectly. She kept calling me Dr. Brandson, for some reason. Eventually, I just asked her to call me Carter, which she switched to happily.

We followed the sparse trail for a long time. The jungle canopy over our heads was so thick it was difficult to see, and I wondered if it had stopped raining or if the cover was just thick enough to keep us dry.

I didn't have a watch, but I guessed that we followed the trail for close to an hour, clearing it off as we walked, which took up most of the time. Eventually, we reached a thick wall of shrubs that blocked the path perpendicularly, stretching to each side for as far as I could see. The shrub was taller than my head and so thick we couldn't see through it or push the boughs aside without being scraped by the rough branches.

Scowling at the plant, I studied the leaves while Elodia walked along the shrub, still talking about something. I had tuned her out, thinking.

The bush was a deep evergreen color with waxy pine needles and tiny blue berries scattered throughout the plant. My brain recognized the plant, but it was too tired to try to give it a name. I wasn't a botanist, after all. If this had been a reef, I would have been able to rattle off the species in a flash. But a bush... not so much.

But I couldn't take my eyes off of it. Something was wrong with it. It just... didn't belong here. It was darker in color than all the other plants in the area, and I knew I hadn't seen another plant like it in our journey so far. And it was enormous. And so straight. I imagined that with some pruning, it might even form a perfectly straight line... Why would it do that?

"Unless someone planted it," I answered myself out loud. "Like... as a fence?"

Elodia was back then, and she heard my muttering. "A fence?" she repeated. "Why would there be a fence in the middle of the jungle?"

I had no guess. "What are fences good for except to keep people out?"

Elodia's eyebrows rose and her mouth formed a little O. "I wonder what's on the other side!" She turned to the shrub and arced up onto her tiptoes, as if that extra inch would help her see two feet above her head.

"Here," I said, approaching the bush and dropping to a knee and forming a cradle with my hands. "I'll give you a boost so you can try to look over it."

She agreed immediately and slipped out of the high heels that had miraculously stayed on her feet. With one hand on my shoulder, she placed a foot in my hands and counted to three. I surged upward, pushing her skyward, and she gripped my head and shoulders even harder to keep her balance.

Hoisting someone up above your head looks a lot easier on TV than it is in real life.

Elodia wasn't heavy, but I wasn't exactly eating my Wheaties at the moment. I struggled to keep her aloft, holding my breath as my legs shook and my shoulders screamed in protest. "Do you see anything?" I puffed out with an un-macho moan.

"Oh my gosh!" she cried, tapping repeatedly on my shoulder. "Carter! It's an orchard!"

Whatever I had expected to find on the other side of the bush, it wasn't that. I dropped Elodia in shock, but she landed gracefully and hardly seemed to notice that I'd almost dumped her on her derriere.

"What kind of orchard?" I asked, my heart pounding against my sternum.

She shook her head. "Couldn't tell. But there was fruit on the trees, Carter. *Fruit!* We're saved!"

I was astonished, but not so dumbfounded that my stomach didn't growl loudly at the thought of actual food. "We've got to get in there! Did you see an entrance?"

"You dropped me before I got a good look," she said with playful chiding.

I cringed all the same. "Sorry."

She waved off my apology and studied the shrub. "The trail leads us right here, though. So maybe there's a gate hidden in the bushes." Without waiting for my response, she plunged her arms into the scratchy branches and began searching. There wasn't enough space where she was looking for me to dive in beside her, but she apparently didn't need my help anyway.

After just a minute, she cried out triumphantly. "I found it!" Branches cracked as she yanked them out of the way, and in no time she had moved enough greenery out of the way to reveal a neat wooden gate. It had a padlock on the latch, but years of rain had rusted through the mechanism and it crumbled beneath her hand.

The latch released with a little convincing, and with one excited glance back at me, Elodia pulled the gate wide. The hinges squealed and popped from misuse, and I stepped up to help her wrench the gate wide open.

The gate was open, and beyond the threshold was a thriving, overgrown orchard. "I can't believe it!" I said, awestruck.

"We've got to tell everyone!" Elodia cried, charging into the orchard and spinning a circle as if she was in a field of wildflowers. "Look—mangoes! And oranges. Apples, Carter, can you believe it?"

I really, really couldn't.

"Oh!" Elodia suddenly froze. "Do you suppose that this fruit might be tainted? Maybe that's how all the villagers died? Maybe that's why the gate was locked."

Her words repeated in my mind. I felt like my brain was in backwards. I couldn't think straight. Why did that locked gate seem especially strange?

Elodia approached one of the mango trees and tentatively selected a ripe fruit from a low-hanging branch. She studied it for a few moments, turning it this way and that before shrugging and taking a bite.

She had a mouthful of juicy fruit before I could even open my mouth to throw caution. She chewed slowly, then swallowed, licking her lips. Finally, she looked back at me with a shrug. "If this kills me, I guess I was dead either way. But it tastes fantastic."

My mouth watered at the sight of juice trickling down her wrist from the mango in her hand. She smirked then tossed the mango to me. I caught it reflexively, staring at the ripe flesh and nearly fainting from the urge to bite it.

Just then, a small yellow bird swooped over my head, calling out as it nearly scalped me. I ducked, and the fruit slipped from my fingers, landing with a soft thud on the vines growing beneath my feet.

My gaze followed the bird's flight as it soared up into one of the trees. It landed deftly on a high branch and began pecking at a gorgeous yellow mango. It ate the fruit until it had its fill, then it flew away again.

I swallowed and looked at Elodia. She had been watching the bird, too. "Well," I started, "you feel like you've been poisoned?"

She shook her head slowly, then a huge grin spread across her face. "If it's good enough for a Yellowthroat, it's good enough for me."

I couldn't help but grin as I picked up my fallen mango, brushed it off, and sank my teeth into the perfectly ripe fruit, juice spilling down my chin and leaking onto my arm. My eyes closed involuntarily. This was the best damn thing I had ever eaten.

Elodia was beside herself. "Everyone is going to flip out!"

I was absolutely sure that she was right.

***

When we returned to the village with our arms loaded down with mangoes and papaya, our appearance in the trees scared Kenya and Bridget out of their skin. They had been sitting outside the door of the hut we had spent the night in, and when they saw our movement, Kenya jumped up with a scream, pointing at us like she was seeing a ghost. Bridget cried out, too, but she recognized us a moment later.

"You're back!" she called, standing and jogging to us. "And are you kidding me?! You've got food!"

She took two mangoes from my arms and tossed one back to Kenya. They each took a luxurious bite of fruit, moaning with appreciation just as Elodia and I had done. Elodia scampered off to find Howard and share food with him, and I stayed back to talk with Kenya and Bridget.

When I looked at Bridget again, my brow furrowed with confusion. She looked different. Not just different because she was actually smiling for the first time in days, but something had changed about her. Was it... What was it?

She noticed me staring and shared a conspiratorial glance with Kenya before shaking her head dramatically, her shoulder-length brown hair swinging happily around her shoulders. "Do you like it?"

I blinked at her. "Did you... get a haircut?" I asked, flabbergasted. Don't tell me there's a secret barber shop on this island, too!

"Close," Kenya said, laughing and holding up what looked like a whole head of human hair in her fist. It was the same color as Bridget's, so I had to assume it was hers. But last I'd checked, scissors were not one of our few survival items, and Bridget's hair was cut perfectly straight.

"How did you do that?" I asked.

It was Bridget's turn to laugh. She took another bite from her mango then said, "They're extensions. Kenya untied them for me. I feel so much better."

My expression was enough to convey my confusion. "You have... fake hair?"

"Just the bottom half," Bridget said merrily. "And you wouldn't believe how hot it gets! I feel like I've lost twenty pounds."

I eyed the hair extensions in Kenya's hand, seriously doubting that fake hair weighed that much. But what did I know about beauty trends?

"When we get home," Kenya started, tossing the extensions away, "please don't tell anybody I did this for you. I don't need to be mobbed." She then finished her mango with finger-licking satisfaction.

"So, who else is awake?" I asked, walking with the girls back toward the hut and depositing my load of fruit next to the wall. Really, I wanted to make sure to tell Jillian about the food—she had been killing herself the last two days—and probably even longer than that—trying to make sure everyone else was taken care of. I felt protective, like it was my self-appointed task to make sure someone took care of *her* for a change.

Bridget was evidently able to read minds because she said, "She's still asleep. I think she might be having nightmares or something because she keeps moaning in her sleep."

"She needs to eat," I said, stating the oh-so-very obvious. "Should we wake her up?"

Bridget shook her head. "Let's let her sleep a while longer. You should take a drink of water, though. We're all dehydrated."

I was about to ask where I was supposed to get water when Kenya produced a bowl made from woven palm leaves filled with clean, clear water.

"It's just rainwater," she said apologetically. "But it's the best we've got."

It was the best thing I'd ever drank.

***

# *JILLIAN*

The next time I awoke, it was to the sound of familiar voices, murmuring softly but with serious tones. It was Grandpa and Carter, but I couldn't fully understand what they were saying. Thanks to sitting up on a dirt floor all night, my headache from the night before hadn't eased with the restless sleep I'd gotten. What had been a sharp pain in my temple now felt like a spike in my skull.

I moaned against the pain and squeezed my eyes closed again. I couldn't remember the last time I'd felt this terrible. Stress and dehydration were the likely culprits, but I couldn't see a likely solution to either of those problems right away. Go ahead and just add some more stress, there.

I sat like that for a long time, my mind reeling with possibilities, worries, worst-case scenarios and, with some insistence, hopeful feelings. We had survived another night, and we had a creepy place to keep safe and dry for a while. Those were positives. But the lack of food and drinking water were my topmost concerns, followed immediately by the question of rescue. We had to get home. Somehow... but how? How?

Someone's hand on my shoulder convinced me to finally open my eyes again. I'd expected Carter or Grandpa, but it was Bridget. She was crouched in front of me with concern plain on her face. And she was... sideways?

I blinked groggily and tried to look around. It was then that I realized that my face was pressed solidly against the dirt floor. I pushed myself upright, realizing that I must have fallen asleep again and slumped down onto the floor where Carter had been sitting before. He had obviously gotten up, and I didn't see him in the hut. In fact, there didn't seem to be anybody else in the hut except for Bridget, who sat on the floor in front of me. Her visible worry for me finally brought me back to the present.

"How are you feeling?" she asked in a low voice. "The guys said you were up and down all night, and then you were muttering in your sleep just now about some pain."

I just shook my sore head. "Just a migraine," I said. "I used to get them all the time. It's been a while since I've had an attack, though." I tried to reassure her with a smile. Then I noticed her hair. "You took out your extensions?"

She nodded. "Too hot."

I nodded. "Good choice."

She sat beside me on the floor. "Think you can drink some water?" she asked.

This surprised me. We hadn't come across any fresh drinking water since arriving on the island, and we had left the plastic suitcase we'd used to collect rainwater back at the beach. I hadn't had anything to drink since the storm began. "I'd kill for some, but..."

Bridget sat back on her heels and held out a bowl. An honest-to-goodness bowl made out of tightly woven palm leaves and made water-tight with the help of a large, broad leaf. Inside was the most beautiful water I had ever seen.

"Kenya decided to be a genius and collected some rainwater," Bridget explained with a grin. "We still don't have a way to boil it, but without a pan, we'll just have to keep taking our chances for now."

I took it from her with greedy, shaking fingers and carefully sipped the cool liquid, letting it soothe the fire in my throat and ease some of the gnawing hunger in my belly. I allowed myself two careful sips before handing it back to Bridget, thinking that someone else probably needed water just as much as I did. She stopped my hands, however, and shook her head.

"There's plenty where that came from. Have what you need."

So, I drank from the leaf cup until all that remained were a few stubborn dregs that refused to spill out into my mouth. I had never had such a delicious drink in my entire life.

When I was through, Bridget took the cup from me. "I can get you some more. Do you want to go back to sleep?"

I did, but I didn't think my anxiety would allow me to lay here any longer. I shook my head again, relieved that my headache seemed to have dimmed just a little.

"Migraine, huh?" Bridget asked, empathy in her eyes. "I get them, too."

I let my head rest against the wall and let out a slow breath. "It's a curse."

She agreed with a mild chuckle. "Do you get the light halo and vision stuff with them?"

"No, thankfully not. Just the pain. You?"

Bridget nodded with a grimace. "Yep. I get the works. Usually triggered by stress and fatigue, but sometimes bright lights and loud noise can cause it, too."

I clearly remembered that this woman had executed a nationwide stadium concert tour the previous year. What's brighter and louder than that?

"That must make it hard to perform."

Tucking a length of her shiny hair behind her ear, she shrugged one shoulder. "Sometimes. In fact, once, the migraine came on so suddenly I lost total vision in my left eye, and everything was spotty on the right. I was in the middle of a song and nearly fell off the platform I was standing on. Luckily, one of my dancers noticed something was up and grabbed me before I fell." Then she laughed again, "We took an unplanned intermission at that point."

"Just... in the middle of the song?"

"No, I finished the song. I sat down on the edge of the platform and kept my eyes closed. Total muscle memory. The manager said that I managed to pull it off and no one suspected something was wrong until they got me backstage, and I had to lay in the dark with noise-canceling headphones on for twenty minutes."

I had complete sympathy for the pain she must have felt, but I couldn't imagine the logistical stress that followed the headliner falling ill mid-performance.

"What happened to the concert?"

She fidgeted with her hair again, running her fingers along the ends. "They pumped me with meds and electrolytes, let the opening band showcase a few more songs, then I went back on stage. The nurse tucked an ice pack into a scarf at the back of my neck, and the manager had everyone alter choreography so I wouldn't have to move very much. By the end of the concert, I was sitting on a stool or on a piano to hide the fact that I couldn't dance anymore." She looked thoughtful for a moment then finished, "I don't remember the end of the concert... Next thing I knew I was waking up in the hospital with IVs and monitors everywhere."

My jaw dropped open. I had never heard this story, so her team must have worked a miracle to cover it up. I said as much, and Bridget kind of shrugged it off.

"It's what they do. They spare no expense to make sure I look perfect all the time."

The slouch in her shoulders and the scowl on her face clued me into the reality that her "perfect life" was just as much of a show as her concerts.

There was a lot I didn't know about Bridget's life, and I hoped that I might get a chance to know her—not as the famous pop star, but as the real person. I thanked her again for the water, inwardly realizing that that act alone made her a different kind of person than I would have imagined her to be.

"It was nothing," she said.

I cast another glance around the hut and noticed the bright sunshine through the upper skylights.

"What's everybody else doing?"

"We've all been up for a couple hours," she said. Bridget lit up, remembering something she had obviously meant to tell me before. "We went out to search for food, first of all, and Elodia and Carter found an orchard! We've got some food waiting for you by the fire."

Food? Fire? What the heck were we waiting for?

The throbbing pain in my head kept me from leaping to my feet at once, and my silence urged Bridget to continue explaining the morning.

"Captain Skippy's head is looking worse, so Kenya made him a new bandage. Howard wanted to go search the other huts right away, but Carter argued with him, saying we should wait for you, since you're the one who brought us here. Howard was just about to go ahead and go anyway, but Kenya threatened to sit on him if he tried it." Bridget giggled at that. "Not that she could have hurt him, but I think he was so shocked that someone would talk to him like that that he gave up. He's out there now eating his third papaya." She rolled her eyes.

I laughed. "I wish I had seen that."

"I'm sure there'll be more to come," she sighed. "He's starting to get back to his old self, and Kenya's not having it. If we're not careful, one of them is going to kill the other, and then we'll have to cover up a murder and get rescued from this island."

Another laugh bubbled out of my throat.

She went on. "On second thought, if he kills her, no cover-up. I'll totally let him take full blame. But if something happens to him... well, people get lost at sea all the time."

"Who knew you had such a mean streak, Bridget Foster?"

She shrugged one delicate shoulder. "I grew up with five brothers. I know how to hold my own."

I realized then that I didn't know very much about Bridget's pre-fame life, either. I wanted to ask a follow-up question, but just then the door to the hut opened, and Carter poked his head in.

"Sorry to interrupt," he said. Then when he caught my eye, he smiled and said, "Hey, Jill. How're you feeling?"

I didn't want to make Bridget gag by telling Carter that I felt better now that he was here, even though that was a little bit true. Instead, I just said, "Doing okay."

"Good. Hey, I just wanted to give you a heads up that it looks like another storm is coming in. Or maybe it's the same one just coming around again. Either way, looks like rain. If we want to explore the village and stay dry, we'd better do it soon. Feeling up for it?"

I nodded and got up. My head still screamed with pain at my movement, but I tried not to let it show on my face. Soon, Bridget and I followed Carter from the hut where we found Kenya and Howard shouting at each other on the threshold of the hut next door.

The eerie feeling from the night before suddenly returned. *You know this place.* The image of them fighting outside the hut was so familiar. The sense of déjà vu was stronger than I'd ever experienced before, and it made my head swim. Or maybe that was the hunger.

Bridget released a heavy sigh when she saw the fight and muttered, "They've been at each other's throats all morning." Then, striding confidently toward them, she shouted, "Hey, break it up, you two! Gosh, you're such babies."

I choked back a laugh, and Carter caught my eye with a smirk on his face. One might have thought that, if someone was going to be arguing all morning, it might be the engaged couple, but it seemed like Howard and Elodia were happy to sit together without speaking, more often than not. I wondered how well the two of them really got along. And come to think of it, Elodia was nowhere to be seen.

I spotted Grandpa sitting on a tree stump, leaning forward with his elbows on his knees and his fingers steepled together against his chin. His eyes were closed, and I couldn't tell if he was praying, thinking, or dozing.

Bridget had joined in the shouting match, all three of them gesticulating wildly. I felt that if this kept up much longer, someone was going to get smacked in the face—intentionally or otherwise.

I started toward them and Carter fell into step beside me.

"—not your private island," Kenya was shouting at Howard. "We have to decide things as a group. You can't just do—"

"I can do whatever the hell I please," Howard interrupted. "Do you know who I am?"

"Yeah. You're the pain in my—"

"Hey!" I hollered to be heard above their own raised voices. They stopped arguing and looked at me with varying levels of irritation in their postures. Rather than try to make any of them see reason or cool their obvious hot-headedness, I chose to do what I did best: gracefully shoulder the blame so everyone else could feel at ease. "Thank you both for waiting for me. Sorry I slept so long. Leave it to me to wreck everyone's morning." Never mind the migraine...

"So, are we ready to explore?"

Howard glared at me for two solid seconds before snorting derisively and turning toward the hut door. Kenya rolled her eyes artfully and followed directly behind him as he went into the hut.

Bridget muttered a few unladylike words under her breath, but she followed Kenya into the hut.

I rubbed my temple where the headache had resumed drumming its fingers on my nerves. Carter's heavy sigh pulled my attention back to him. He looked irritated, and that surprised me.

"What's the matter?"

"Why do you do that?" he asked, his voice low enough that the others wouldn't be able to hear.

"Do what?" I asked, playing dumb. I thought I knew what he meant.

"Take the blame for things that are clearly not your fault."

"I don't do that."

Lies. I did do that. All the time.

He gave me a level look that plainly told me he knew I was lying.

It was my turn to sigh. "I'm just keeping the peace."

"At your own expense."

"It's a trade-off."

"You allow others to think you're incompetent in exchange for peace," he summarized, not sounding reassured.

I gave him a half shrug. "Regularly. It's part of the job."

He blinked at me, his mouth dropping open slightly. "What job?"

"My job." I gestured at our surroundings. "This."

He shook his head, eyes narrowed as he folded his arms across his chest. "This is not your job."

Now I blinked at him. "Yes it is. I'm in charge of making sure everyone is comfortable and taken care—"

"I think that responsibility ended right around the time you got dumped into the ocean. And it certainly didn't start up again when we washed up on a deserted island. You don't have to be a stewardess here, Jill."

"But—"

Bridget popped her head out of the hut then, calling to us. "You two coming, or what?"

I responded that we would be right there, and Carter sighed again. "We can talk about this later."

He walked to the door of the hut and held it open for me. I attempted a grateful smile, but it probably looked more like a grimace. This day just got better and better.

***

As it turned out, this new hut was identical to the one we had spent the night in, right down to the built-in beds and skylights. The space was small, and it didn't take long for us to get the grand tour—especially since we had seen the exact setup right next door. We left that hut and moved down to the next one. It, too, was identical to the first hut. The beds and door were even constructed of the same amount of bamboo poles, and they were bound together with the same knots in the same places.

"Did they make these huts all at the same time?" Kenya wondered as we left cabin three and found the same things in cabin four.

"Maybe they were all designed by one person," Bridget theorized, "that oversaw all the work."

"Micromanager," Howard grumbled, even as he studied the intricate ties that made up the door's hinges.

Carter scrubbed his hand through his hair as he looked up through the skylight. "Does something about this feel weird to anybody else?"

I ran my fingers along the edge of a bamboo chute on the door. It was slightly bent in the center, creating a gap just like the one I had watched moonlight filter through in the first hut. Something about its placement nagged at me.

"Yeah," Kenya agreed, "almost like this is too perfect."

The crooked bamboo on the door wasn't perfect, though. The imperfection was small but noticeable. Why had the meticulous architect allowed a crooked bamboo pole to take such a prominent place in one of his huts—much less two of his huts? And was it just a coincidence that they happened to be in exactly the same place?

When we left hut four, I looked back at the doors of huts two and three. They didn't have the obvious gap in the door, but standing back and looking at doors one and four, it was clear that they had exactly the same hole. I turned and let my eyes skip forward to the next several huts. Five and six—no hole. But hut seven's door had the same hole.

I pointed out this oddity to the others, but no one could attempt to explain it. With the puzzle itching at my brain, we moved forward and continued our exploration.

There were nine huts in all, each one made just like the first. Our collective superstition about the village being haunted had relaxed in the light of day, replaced as it was with bigger questions. Namely, where had the inhabitants of this village gone? There was nothing left behind in any of the huts—not so much as a pot or rubbish in the corner. And all the while, something in the back of my mind continued to shout, *You know this place. You've been here before.* I countered that thought with the rational notion that I certainly had not been to an abandoned village in the middle of the ocean before, but my gut feelings had no patience for rational thinking.

When our tour concluded, we returned to where Grandpa still sat on his tree stump, and we sat in the sand around him. A glance at the sky proved the earlier prediction that the storm was returning.

Grandpa handed me a leaf cup with cool rainwater inside, and I guzzled it down without protest. It's always wise not to argue with your elders.

Elodia returned then, carrying two coconuts and... My eyes widened and I sat up straight. "Is that a machete?"

"Where did you find that?"

Elodia deposited her armload of goods next to the small pile of fruit she had gathered earlier that morning. She held the machete in front of her so we could all see it at once. It was rusty, and the wooden handle was cracked down the center. I wondered if it would be good for anything in this state of disrepair. "I found it stuck in a tree out by the orchard. Looked like it had been there for a long time."

"I wonder if we could sharpen it," Bridget said, gingerly running her finger along the rusty spine. "Could be really useful to have around."

"We're going to need some kind of protection," Howard said, nodding approvingly at Elodia. "Good work, dear."

Kenya scowled at him. "Protection from what?"

Howard gestured toward the village and said, "From whatever killed off whoever lived here before. Animals, another tribe. Whatever it is, I'll feel better knowing there's at least one weapon around here."

Carter interjected, "We won't see any big animals on an island in this region."

"What about pumas?" Howard challenged. "Jaguars?"

Carter shook his head. "Not native to the Bahamas. And I don't know how much good a machete will do against a spider or a snake."

"Snakes?!" Kenya cried, launching to her feet. "There are snakes here?"

"Snakes are a vital key to an ecosystem like this," Carter explained, clearly unperturbed by the prospect of slimy, creepy creatures slithering around him. Then he scowled. "But it is weird that we haven't seen any." He looked around at the trees, tilting his chin in thought. "In fact, I haven't seen any predatory animals at all since we landed."

"But you said there weren't any," Bridget countered.

"Not any large ones," he clarified. "But I haven't seen anything more than birds and bats."

A puzzled silence fell over our group. I didn't know what to make of this information, so I had nothing to add to the conversation. I think most of us felt the same way.

I looked back at the village, standing proud with its secrets. My mind conjured up images of the seven of us settling into these huts, creating a little community. With the orchard, we would have food to survive indefinitely. We could live here, if we needed to. Sheltered in the trees, protected from the storms. But hidden from view of the sea.

"We can't stay here," I said. Everyone turned to look at me. "We've got to stay close to the beach. For when they come to rescue us."

A general murmur met this remark. They understood that our surest source of rescue would come from the water, but there was a great deal of appeal in the thought of sleeping under a roof.

As if it had read my mind, the sky rumbled then, grey-black clouds churning above us once again. I felt a cold raindrop on my arm. The storm had returned. And maybe a roof wasn't the worst invention after all.

With faces inclined toward the sky, we sat together in silence for a few moments, caught between the desire for comfort and the real need for rescue. Grandpa finally spoke up and settled the question for us all. "Sitting out in the rain won't get us rescued. It's not likely anybody will be out searching in a harsh storm like this, anyway. So I say we all go get some rest in the hut and come up with a plan."

Though he had not been speaking as the ship's captain, his suggestion was taken as a direct order, and I was grateful that there was no argument, even though his suggestion had directly contradicted my own inclination to get away from this village. Something about it just didn't sit right with me. I couldn't put my finger on it precisely, but something was definitely off about this place.

# 11

## *CARTER*

The storm returned with vengeance. If there was a god of rain, he was certainly irritated that we had found shelter away from his forces. Wind and rain swatted and clawed at the huts, icy rainwater finding the smallest cracks in the roof and dripping down on our heads. The wind slashed at the trees, making them moan and groan like Dickens' ghost of Marley.

Eerie feelings or not, I was glad to be at least somewhat sheltered from this storm.

And now I had my own bed to stretch out on. It wasn't a Serta by any stretch, but the bamboo was a level up from lying on the ground. I had left Jillian and Captain Skippy in the first hut to rest and recover from their ailments. Since none of the other buildings were filled with skeletons or zombies, the others had deemed it safe to spread out. Howard and Elodia had elected to move into a hut three doors down, and Kenya and Bridget had decided to be roommates right next door. I ended up in a hut on my own, which most bachelors would probably be thrilled about. And since I wasn't man enough to admit that I was scared to death to be alone in this village, I went into the hut right next to Bridget and Kenya's.

Honestly, I didn't feel like moving in just yet. I still held out hope that we would be staying only a night or two more. At the same time, it was nice to have a place to lie down and to have a few private minutes alone that didn't include relieving myself in the jungle. Of course, living in a primitive, bamboo hut didn't eliminate that necessity. We'd established a makeshift privy about fifty yards into the trees. It was a dense enough cluster of trees to give anybody privacy, but it was a far cry from indoor plumbing. If we got home, I would never take Charmin for granted again.

It had been a few hours since it had started raining again, and I had spent most of that time alone in this hut, lying flat and staring at the ceiling. I kept replaying a conversation I'd had with Jillian right before we had all split up to take refuge in our separate spaces.

She pulled me aside with apprehension on her face. "Maybe I'm crazy, but... does this village seem... I don't know..."

"Convenient?" I supplied, speaking what I'd already been feeling.

"Well, that, but something about these huts feels weird. Like they're too perfect to be real."

Too perfect to be real. She had pointed out the similar gap she had seen in three of the nine doors, and I agreed that it was strange that all of the cabins had identical layouts. At the same time, though, it didn't feel nefarious. Just odd.

But now that I had been thinking things through for several hours alone, I could feel what Jillian meant. The path leading to this village was wild and overgrown, making me think that it had been years since it was regularly used. But the huts were in perfect condition. No weeds grew where they shouldn't, none of the roofs had any damage from the frequent storms the area received. Not a hair was out of place, so to speak. Almost as though the area had some charm around it to keep it from aging. Or, more realistically, it wasn't what it appeared to be.

My mind tumbled through a list of possibilities that did not include magic spells. Honestly, it wasn't a long list. And it included aliens. So, it wasn't a good list, either.

I gave up. My brain was fried, and my body was exhausted from hunger and dehydration. The fruit and water we'd collected that morning had been heavenly, but satisfaction from eating the sugary fruit had worn off quickly, and I was hungry and lightheaded again.

I turned onto my side, facing the wall, and tried to find a comfortable position to relax, using my arm as a pillow. It was not comfortable, but I was too tired to care. I stared at the wall, thinking sluggishly, wishing that I would just drop off to sleep and wake up only when the storm was over.

As I stared and thought, my mind drifted a few doors down to Jillian. And our kiss from the other night. I wished that I had the power to go back in time, just to that moment, and freeze it forever. I hadn't wanted to let her go then, and I badly wanted to take her in my arms again now. But, circumstances being what they were, it didn't seem like a good setting for romantic advances.

I vividly recalled the warmth in her brown eyes when she gazed up at me and the feel of her hand on my shoulder, her fingers toying with the hair at the nape of my neck. I sighed, hoping that I would get to feel that touch again soon.

My eyes were trained on the bamboo wall but not focused on any certain thing. After a few minutes, I realized I had been staring at a scratch on the wall's surface. It wasn't long or deep, but what finally caught my attention was the color of the scrape. A scratch like that should have been yellow or white inside, showing the inner layers of the bamboo. But this scratch was a dark, grayish brown.

Pulled back into the present, I lifted myself onto my elbow and reached out with my other hand to touch the scratch. The dark material felt rough and grainy beneath my fingers. Nothing like bamboo.

My brow furrowed, and I sat up. Using my thumbnail, I pried away a sliver of the exterior bamboo. Underneath was more rough black stuff.

"What the—?"

I dug at the wall some more, finally able to get access to a large enough piece of the black substance to get a good look at it. I pulled out a chunk the size of a marble and turned it between my fingers.

It was firm and brittle and seemed to be filled with tiny air bubbles. I had seen this kind of thing before, but not in nature.

Realization dawned on me like a slap across the face. Foam.

"You're made of foam?" I asked the hut, not expecting an answer. Turning now to the bench I sat on, I scratched at it, but it did not give way like the wall had. The bench at least appeared to be made of real bamboo. So why was the wall made of foam and then covered to look like bamboo?

My brain hurt. Was this a dream? It felt dreamlike. What other explanation was there for this madness? Any second now, I was going to wake up in my own bed in my apartment in Sarasota, and I'd realize that all of this had been in my imagination. No cruise, no wreck, no deserted island, no Jillian, no stupid huts made out of stupid foam for no stupid reason.

I counted out a few seconds and held my breath. The scene around me didn't change.

Well, at least Jillian was still real.

"If the walls are fake," I thought aloud, "I wonder what else isn't real." Time to conduct an investigation.

Making the project science-y was an uncool move, but it helped me keep my mind on track. This wouldn't be the first or the last time I'd started a project in less-than-ideal conditions. Hey, I'd been a college student once, too.

I just wished I had a notepad.

To make sure that the wall by my bed wasn't an anomaly, I went across the hut and scraped the wall over there. I was able to remove a few layers of paint with my fingernail, and sure enough, beneath the paint was the same dark foam as I'd found before. Another test revealed that this second bed was also genuine bamboo. The door was made from real bamboo, too, but upon closer inspection, I realized that the bamboo had been secured to a board on the inside. I pried two of the bamboo shoots away and found plywood beneath. The nails were small with a square head—the kind used in a nail gun. And the rope hinges were artfully tied around narrow pin hinges.

I sat back on my heels and stared, slack-jawed, at the door. It was a mask, an illusion. Someone had built this structure using modern tools and supplies and then made it up to look like an authentic island hut. Were all the huts like this? I couldn't imagine why they wouldn't be, but then I also couldn't imagine why this one was.

With this new information, I sat in the center of the hut and slowly scanned the walls, looking for other oddities. The thatched roof caught my attention. I wondered how the roof was really made, if the normal rules apparently didn't apply in its construction.

So, standing on the bamboo bed, I reached up to tear down a sample of the thatching. A sheet of grass came off with a few small tugs, popping as I pulled it downward, breaking away from the staples that had secured it to more weather-treated plywood. The wood was not water-tight, though, and it allowed rainwater to leak in and drip through the thatching.

I hadn't given any thought to the skylights in the roof before then, but now I wondered how I hadn't noticed anything odd before. The crown of the roof was raised away from the rest, held up by 2x4s that hadn't even been disguised with bamboo. And now that I was closer to the ceiling, I could see that square metal brackets had been screwed into the wood. They were empty, but there were scratches in the black paint that told me they had held something up at some point.

My mind reeled with the many possibilities of what could have hung up here. Both innocent and... less so. Torture devices? Pottery? A clothes rack? Security camera?

And then I saw something that froze me where I stood. Was that... a power outlet? Mounted on the opposite side of the hut from where I stood was a box that jutted out from the top of the wall. It was disguised on the bottom, so looking at it from below, it blended in perfectly with the wall and ceiling. But from my vantage point, I could clearly see that it concealed a secret power box.

I jumped from the bamboo bed and ran out into the rain, slopping through the mud around the outside of the hut to the spot where the outlet was hidden on the inside. I craned my neck and squinted through the rain, searching for what was sure to be some well-camouflaged evidence. To my surprise, the thin metal conduit that jutted out of the wall wasn't trying very hard to hide. It had been painted the same color as the bamboo around it, but it was otherwise obvious.

I swiveled in the mud, studying the exterior of the hut behind me. There was no conduit on that hut. But the huts had been identical inside in every way, so maybe there was something on the other side. My feet slapped through puddles as I ran to the other side of the hut, and my breath whooshed out of my lungs when I saw it: conduit. A pipe to house an electrical wire.

Both pipes had elbowed out of the side of the hut and gone directly down into the ground. So that meant the outlets were getting power from somewhere else. I jogged toward the center of the village, thinking fast and considering where I would have routed electricity to, if I had been the designer of this nightmare-inducing village.

The low platform caught my attention first. It was only a foot or two tall, and the top was covered with a bamboo lid and tied down to heavy rocks. I hadn't given it much thought before, but now everything felt incredibly suspicious.

I didn't think twice before racing toward the rock wall and dropping down to my knees in the mud to begin untying the cords.

"What are you doing?"

My heart leapt into my throat, and I jumped so badly I nearly fell backward in the mud. Regaining my equilibrium, I whirled around to see who had spoken.

It was Kenya and Bridget, standing in the door of their hut, peering out at me through the rain.

I didn't quite know how to answer that, so I just shouted back, "Hold on a second." Then I turned back to my task of loosening the lid. The ropes had been fastened tightly, and the rain had shrunk the fibers, making it nearly impossible to free them from around the rocks. I fumbled with the knots for several agonizing minutes, feeling the rough fibers bite into my fingertips, and I worried that I'd be a bloody mess by the time I finished.

I had almost decided to bend down and use my teeth when the knot finally gave a little. It was all I needed. I unwound the rope in a few quick movements, and within a minute, I had removed the bamboo cover and revealed a large hole within.

By this time, Kenya and Bridget had emerged from their hut and stood beside me in the rain, watching, open-mouthed, as I revealed the hole and its secrets.

The lid dropped to the ground, and the three of us stared breathlessly down, down into the hole.

"Woah," Bridget whispered.

Kenya was just as flabbergasted. "Holy. Crap."

"What..." Bridget was nearly speechless. "What is that?"

I looked at each of them before returning my gaze to the tangle of wires and pipes inside the hole. "I wish I knew."

***

# *JILLIAN*

We spent the afternoon discussing the hole and the village and the road and all the super weird things we'd found. This island just keeps getting stranger!

When Carter had hollered for me and Grandpa to come outside, I was sure that someone had been badly hurt, but what he revealed about the hole and the huts was more than I could wrap my mind around.

He showed us the outlet in his hut, the walls made of foam, and the building supplies that held it all together. I was stunned. It felt like this information changed everything, and yet nothing about our situation was changed at all.

We fanned out through the village and checked each hut, and each one held the same secret as Carter's: they were replicas. And now this hole in the center of it all. It seemed to be a power hub, with the conduit and wires from each hut leading here and connecting to a metal breaker box, like the spokes of a wheel. In addition, there was a water pipe standing vertically from the ground, and around it was the framework for something. I could only guess that it used to hold a sink or basin that the water would connect to. But why would there be only one water source for the whole village, if modern amenities were a possibility?

"Maybe it's like a camp," Kenya theorized. "You know, they have camps set up in the mountains and stuff with one water source. This could be like that. Like 'glamping.'"

"Why would they run electricity but not water?" Bridget countered.

"And why," I inserted, "would someone pay hundreds of thousands of dollars to come to a remote, private island just to semi-rough it?" I worked in the travel industry—I knew how expensive it would be to get passage to a remote location like this. "If I was going to spend that kind of money on a trip, I'd at least want a bathroom."

"Maybe it isn't a leisure place," Elodia said with wide, fearful eyes. "Maybe it's a prison. Or a POW camp! I think I saw something like that on the History Channel. Maybe it's haunted by the victims."

Howard rolled his eyes. "That was a documentary about Vietnam, not the Bahamas."

Elodia didn't seem fazed by his derision. "People are people all over the world, Howard. Vietnam isn't the only place in the world that has had wars."

Grandpa interrupted the argument. "I don't know about a POW camp, but this place doesn't feel like it was built for comfort."

"But why go to the trouble of building something this elaborate to only go halfway?" Carter wanted to know.

"And," Bridget chimed in, "foam is a good insulator, but it's not going to keep anybody caged in for very long. It would be easy to break out of a hut like this if you needed to."

The group lapsed into silence for a long moment. I mulled the conversation over in my head, something niggling at the back of my mind. There was something about this that felt so familiar, almost like I'd been here before... or seen this before... or...

I jolted upright as realization zinged through my body like a lightning strike. "Oh my gosh—I know where we are!" I turned a circle, seeing the village with new eyes. I couldn't believe it had taken me this long to figure it out.

I turned back to my friends, grinning. "*Shudder Island!*"

Bridget gasped and jumped to her feet, studying the surroundings just like I had. "You're right! This is *Shudder Island!*"

"What the hell is *Shudder Island*?"

"It was a reality show that ran for a few years, but it was canceled four or five years ago," I explained. "It was one of those elimination games where all the participants had to live together with just the basics and perform challenges. They're eliminated one by one until one person wins the grand prize."

"Is the grand prize a plane ride home?" Howard asked dryly.

Kenya seemed to remember the show now, too. "Wasn't it a million dollars?"

"I've got that," Howard said flippantly. "I'll gladly trade it for a private helicopter and a glass of whiskey."

Grandpa spoke over him, ending his unhelpful line of conversation. "So what's with the hole? Was it some kind of ritual or something?"

"They called it the water well. It was the hub for gossip and backstabbing, as well as the center of the village. On camera, it looked like a real well. I guess the water was piped in here, and all the electrical stuff was run here, too, for convenience."

Bridget clapped her hands together with a gasp. "Oh! The electricity must have been for the lights and cameras! It would be too obvious to have extension cords running all over the ground."

Silence fell over us again as we looked around at the village, understanding now. No wonder this place had felt so eerily familiar. I had never been here before, but I'd seen a hundred episodes of that show, so I knew the village well—at least, from the angles they'd shown on TV.

"Wow," Kenya breathed at last. "I've always wanted to be on a TV set. I never thought I'd have to live in one, though."

Suddenly, Carter slapped his palm to his forehead. "That's what was bugging me about the orchard!"

We were all duly confused. "What?"

"When we got into the orchard, the gate was padlocked. I was too tired and hungry at the time to put my finger on why a machine-made Master Lock was out here in the jungle. But if this island was used for a TV show, they probably grew some authentic food close by so they didn't have to ship it in for the cast."

"That makes sense."

He gasped again, eyes wide. "If this island is where they used to film this show, then someone else has to know about it."

Grandpa sat up straighter then, too, showing the first signs of enthusiasm I'd seen in him in days. "Yes! And if nothing happened to the other lifeboat, the others might have already been rescued by now. The authorities will be looking for us in this area."

"You think they're okay?" Bridget asked, breathing unevenly as she worried about Patrick and the others.

"What are the chances that both lifeboats had broken antennae?"

"So, if the other boat was found," Elodia said tentatively, "it's only a matter of time before someone comes looking."

"We should be standing out on the beach, then! Not hiding in the trees. If a boat comes, we need to be able to flag them down. We can't even see the beach from here."

"I am not going to sleep on the beach again," Elodia said stubbornly. As if sleeping on an unpadded bamboo platform in a hut was the Ritz. "And if this storm keeps up, I don't want to catch my death sitting in the rain, either."

"We can figure all of that out when the weather clears," Grandpa said. "It won't do us any good to go to the beach in a storm. For now, let's get out of the rain and try to get some rest and make a plan."

# 12

## *JILLIAN*

Kenya started a fire using her lighter and some of the faux thatching as kindling. Knowing that the roof was made of decorative grass and plywood made us extra cautious about it catching fire, so we kept the blaze small.

The sky seemed to never run out of rain. While we were holed up in the huts, we came up with a plan. It was absurdly simple: For safety and comfort, we would sleep in the village, and in the daylight, we would always keep at least one person on the beach, watching for a rescue ship.

Because the huts were small, we decided to divide up again into four cabins as we had before. I felt bad that Carter was the odd man out, but truthfully, he would probably only go to his hut to sleep. Otherwise, my hut was the hangout spot.

Howard and Elodia kept to themselves, even when we were all crammed together in my hut. They sat together on one of the beds and talked quietly to each other or silently listened to the other conversations in the room. I didn't get much chance to talk to either of them, but it seemed Elodia and Carter had become friends during their voyage into the jungle that morning.

Where Howard was abrasive and outspoken during group discussions, Elodia was talkative and friendly. I wondered how the two of them had met, and later that evening, when all the men had gone out looking for more firewood, I got the chance to ask her. All three men were absent for the moment, so the four of us ladies had a rare few minutes to ourselves to discuss our personal lives. I started the conversation rolling.

"Elodia, how did you and Howard become an item? You two seem so different."

"We met at church," Elodia said with a little shrug.

Kenya, who was eating a mango nearby, goggled at her. "You're joking."

Elodia laughed a little. "We get that reaction a lot. Most people are surprised that Howard is religious."

I had to admit that I fell into that group. "He doesn't seem like the pious type."

"Church takes all kinds."

"Good point."

Kenya wasn't swayed. "But Howard is so... unpleasant. I thought church people were nice."

"You can't make a generalization like that," Elodia countered, "any more than you can claim that all non-church people are nasty. Besides, Howard isn't always like this."

Kenya huffed. "You're not going to try to tell me that he's actually a softie, are you?"

Elodia laughed again. "No, he's not soft. He's not sentimental, and he can be insensitive sometimes. I think he gets wrapped up in his own thoughts, kind of trapped in his own world. It's hard to get him out of that mindset at times. But when he is really himself, when he's really paying attention..." she trailed off, her eyes dropping to her lap. After a breath, she finished quietly, "He's one of the best people I know." She looked up at us again then. "It takes time to get to know him; I won't deny that. I just know that it's worth it. At least, it is for me."

Elodia was a beautiful woman in her early forties, and Howard was a grouchy middle-aged man with salt-and-pepper hair and a bad attitude. I had assumed all along that she was something of a "trophy wife" for him, and that she was marrying him for his money. But this conversation gave me cause to rethink my hasty assessment. And also to realize that my opinions on their relationship did not matter. Whether I thought she was too young for him or he was too grumpy for her—it didn't change the way they felt about each other. Who was I to judge them?

"Will you tell us the story?" I asked, feeling contrite. I needed to erase my perceptions of their relationship and allow her to tell me the story herself.

She smiled then, a grin that lit up her eyes. I wondered how often people asked her for this story. The excitement on her face gave a hint at the answer: not often enough. "I'd love to."

To my surprise, Elodia and Howard's story was sweet and romantic—the complete antithesis of the person I perceived in Howard himself. They had both attended the same church for several months. She had joined the congregation soon after moving into her new home in Rochester. She had made a few friends in the congregation, and she was invited to a Christmas party at a friend's home. Howard had been at the same party. She had known of him before that point, but she had never officially met him. They were introduced by a mutual friend, but Elodia had already decided that she had no interest in him romantically. He was interested right away and asked her out, but she politely declined. That began a six-month friendship in which he never gave up on her and, eventually, she got to know him well enough to see his true self beneath the business-like exterior. She had finally agreed to go out with him for a 4th of July church social, and they had been together ever since. That was five years ago. "And ever since then," she concluded, "he's always been there for me. He keeps me grounded and makes me happy, and..." she shrugged in a girlishly helpless way, "I just love him."

"I never would have guessed that he had it in him," Kenya said, a little too honestly.

For the first time, Elodia turned a little frosty. "Lucky for me, I don't depend on you to make my decisions for me."

Kenya put up both palms in a show of surrender. "No offense meant. I'm just saying I misjudged him, that's all. Apparently, I'm good at that."

"What do you mean by that?"

Kenya tried to wave the words away. "It's nothing. I've just had too much time to think, that's all."

We fell silent for a few moments. Then Bridget released a long sigh. She hadn't said much during the previous conversation, and I had nearly forgotten she was there. "I think I know what you mean."

Kenya's head snapped in Bridget's direction, her eyes wary. "You do?"

"I'm a bad judge of character, too, sometimes. And I'm especially bad when it comes to men."

My mind flitted back to the altercation I'd witnessed between Bridget and her bodyguard on the first day of the trip. "Do you mean when you were dating Patrick?" I asked.

She winced at the mention of his name. "There were lots of stories about that online. Only parts of it are true. Me and Patrick were never a couple, but we did go out a couple of times. We were friends, though, and I wasn't interested in more than that."

"But he was, I'll bet," Elodia guessed, leaning forward slightly. "He'd be crazy not to be."

"Oh, he definitely was," I agreed. I could see that Bridget wanted to deny the claim, but I knew more than she thought I did. "I heard him say so."

Bridget's chin was downturned, but she cast her gaze upward at me. "How much of that conversation did you hear?"

"All of it." We shared a long, loaded look, and Bridget swallowed hard, tears swimming in her eyes.

Kenya and Elodia's eyes bounced back and forth between the two of us. "What did you overhear?" Elodia asked, as Kenya demanded, "What happened?"

I looked to Bridget before responding. She rolled her eyes but gave me a "go ahead" wave. "Might as well hear it," she said.

"It wasn't a deep, dark confession," I explained. "I just heard him tell you that he wished you would change your mind and give him another chance. He said he was sorry for something, and he just wanted to see if things would work between the two of you. But then, when you said no, he got... cold."

Bridget stilled and cast her gaze to her lap. "Mean is more like it." She drew in a long breath and released half of it before saying more. "Patrick has a temper. He always has, but for as long as I've known him, he has always had it under control. And he's always been upfront about it. He told me before I even hired him that he saw a counselor for anger management. But he hadn't had an outburst in years. Since I've met him, he's always kept his temper under control. But he started to change lately. He started running with these guys that just give me the creeps. And he even told me that he got into some trouble with a gang..." She looked up at Kenya. "Does the name Giovanni Accardi mean anything to you?"

Kenya shook her head, but Elodia nodded tightly. "He's been wanted worldwide for like a year," she said knowingly. "He escaped from some prison in Italy and has been on the run since then."

I scowled. "Is Patrick mixed up with Giovanni Accardi?"

Bridget's lips tightened. "I think so. I ran into them together once. I recognized him from pictures online."

Elodia interrupted, "Isn't he the one with the long-ish black hair?"

Bridget nodded. "That's him. He was threatening Patrick, and when he saw me, he gave me this look like..." she shuddered. "Like he saw dollar signs instead of a person."

Silence fell between the four of us for a few moments.

Then Bridget finished her description of the altercation between her and Patrick on the ship. She rubbed her upper arm unconsciously. "He grabbed me, hard, and kept telling me I didn't understand."

My blood chilled again then, just as it had when I'd witnessed the encounter. "He kept yelling, 'It's not too late.' What did he mean by that?"

Bridget shook her head. "Just that he'd asked for a second chance so many times, maybe he wanted me to know that he was still interested if I changed my mind."

"I hope you never do," I said firmly, clearly remembering the anger and hurt in his eyes as he'd lifted his arm to strike her. "And I hope you fire him."

She laughed mirthlessly. "I already did. He came to my door after I went to bed that night and he begged me to reconsider. I told him I'd had enough. I told him that he was to get off at the next port. I would pay for his trip home, but I never wanted to see him again."

Kenya's jaw hung slack. "I'll bet he was not happy about that."

"Actually, he looked more hurt than angry. I felt like I was kicking a puppy. He was so crushed. He..." her voice lowered, "he even cried, begging me to change my mind. But when I stood my ground, he went back to his room. And I didn't see him again until we were getting on the lifeboat the next morning. I feel terrible that we left things that way. What if their lifeboat sank? What if I never see him again? The last thing I told him was that I never wanted to see him again and... now I never will. You'd think I'd be happy about that, but..." she brushed away a tear that escaped from her shimmering eyes, "I'm not. Even though we didn't see eye to eye, he was still my friend for a long time. I care about him."

Elodia put her arm around Bridget's shoulders, and Kenya immediately followed suit. "They're going to be okay. You'll see. We'll all be okay."

Bridget wiped the last of her tears away and broke free of the embrace with a small laugh. "It's someone else's turn, now. Kenya, you tell us about your love life."

Kenya shook her head sharply. "Nope. Nothing to tell."

"Bologna," I cried. "I know you were going to bring your fiancé on this trip."

She eyed me warily and pointed a finger at me. "I'll get you for this, lady." Then she shook her head in fast surrender. "That's what I get for trying to do something nice."

We were all properly confused by that remark.

"I was going to bring my ex-fiancé on the cruise," Kenya explained. "But when I found him making out with another girl the night before our wedding, I dumped his sorry butt and came by myself. I forgot to take his name off the roster, though," she cut a look over to me, "so that's how Jillian knows about him."

"Wait, wait, wait," it was Bridget's turn to be irate. "You're telling me that your fiancé cheated on you right before your wedding? And this was supposed to be your honeymoon, so this was all, like, five days ago?"

"Has it only been that long?" Kenya stretched her arms over her head in mock nonchalance. "Feels like I've been free for a lifetime."

"You'll find someone better," Bridget said with a firm nod. "And in the meantime, you and me can be BFFs and eat chocolate and watch movies together to heal our broken hearts."

Kenya laughed. "I'm so in."

"Now," Elodia turned fully toward me. "What's going on with you and Dr. Buckley?"

My face flushed so hot that even the tips of my ears burned. "Nothing," I squeaked.

My three friends laughed at my outright lie.

"Right. And I've never seen the ocean before," Bridget said dryly.

I rubbed my forehead. "We're just..."

"You say 'friends,' and I'm going to hit you," Kenya threatened.

"—just getting to know each other," I finished instead.

"Mmhmm."

"As Bridget pointed out," I defended, "it's only been four days."

Kenya wasn't having it. "Four very intense days that, as I pointed out, feel like years."

Elodia's eyes sparkled as she leaned toward me. "Has he kissed you?"

"No."

All three of them deflated.

Then I couldn't help but add mischievously, "But I kissed him."

Bridget squealed.

"No. Way!" Kenya hollered.

Elodia clapped her hands, grinning hugely.

I looked at the three of them and felt myself bonded with these women in a way I hadn't experienced since high school. Had I really known them for only a few days?

"Tell us everything."

So, feeling the first slivers of normalcy I'd had in days, I did just that.

***


That night was freezing. No matter where I moved, it always seemed that a raindrop would hit me in the face just as I dozed off. So, when the third morning in the village dawned with sunlight and clear skies, I nearly cried for joy.

During our meager breakfast of two coconuts and three bananas, I was the first to volunteer to go back to the beach to start our signal fire. Carter offered to go with me. The rest of the group agreed to strike out into the woods to look for more food and possibly the source of water or electricity that the pipes in our hole were connected to.

Carter and I fashioned torches and gathered up some of our remaining dry firewood so we wouldn't have to start from scratch once we reached the beach. Then we set off along the road, careful not to drop any wood or ignite the jungle around us with our open flames.

Residual rainwater continued to drip from the overhead trees, and the air was muggy and thick with humidity and mosquitoes. Overhead, we heard birds calling to one another, probably telling each other that the useless humans had somehow survived the storm.

Neither of us spoke much as we trekked through the overgrown path. We had had only a few bites of fruit, so I felt weak and lightheaded. The hike would have been easy after a normal meal, but with my starvation diet, I was panting and shaking by the time we cleared the trees and saw the ocean once again.

We dropped our wood into a pitiful pile in the sand, far enough from the water that it wouldn't be doused at high tide. We stuck our torches into the sand and agreed to gather more supplies to create our bonfire—just as soon as we both caught our breath. I was gratified to see that Carter, for all his muscles, looked just as exhausted as I felt.

I sat beside him in the sand, resting my arms on my knees, and stared, bedraggled, out at the crashing waves. "Carter," I finally said, "we have got to get out of here."

He nodded. "And what do we do in the meantime? We're going to starve to death if we don't find a better food source."

I agreed. "And one of us is going to get really sick if we don't find a better water source." It seemed like only a matter of time before our questionably clean rainwater brought one or all of us down with a stomach bug or worse.

"So, we need to go home," he concluded. Then he rubbed his hand over his face, his palm scraping against the stubble on his chin. He looked every bit the handsome castaway then. Scrubby beard, dirty face, torn shirt, no shoes.

We lapsed into silence again. We had spent the past three days talking of nothing but escape from our predicament. There wasn't much more to say. Our only hope was the signal fire or the appearance of a miracle. I hadn't even been a believer in miracles before, but I was willing to convert.

We rested for a few minutes before trudging back to the jungle to find the driest wood available. Then, with a nice little pile, we formed the start of our signal fire, and Carter did the honors of setting it ablaze with Kenya's lighter. The warmth from the flames washed over my skin, and I closed my eyes to enjoy it.

When he finished adding wood to the fire, Carter sat down once again in the sand, grabbed my hand, and pulled me down beside him. I laughed and bumped my shoulder into his before getting comfortable. I slid my feet through the sand, bringing my knees toward my chest and resting my chin on top of them. My thoughts drifted, my brain too tired to hold on to any one thought for more than a moment.

After several minutes, Carter interrupted my scattered ruminations. "What happens next?"

Without lifting my face from my knees, I turned my head to look at him, my brow furrowed in confusion.

He sat, relaxed, with his legs stretched out before him, crossed at the ankles, and his elbows supporting his weight. His face was angled toward the crashing waves, but his eyes were on me. If you ignored the dark circles of fatigue beneath his eyes, he could be the cover model for a beach resort pamphlet.

I realized that I was staring, and I blinked quickly. "What?"

"After we go home," he said, "then what? What will you do?"

I hummed a little laugh. "Check myself into a Vegas hotel with an endless buffet and then spend a week on the world's softest mattress."

He nodded. "I'll be right behind you." Suddenly his cheeks flushed bright red, realizing what he had said. "I—I meant at the buffet. Not ... on the ... m-mattress."

A laugh escaped me before I could even consider fighting it back. "As much as I like you, Carter, I'm so exhausted, I wouldn't even know you were there."

His blush didn't fade, and he ran his fingers through his hair. Then he grinned and reached over and linked his pinky with mine. "I like you, too."

I bit my lip, and it was my turn to blush a fiery red. "Good."

"I never got to thank you. For the other night."

I cocked my head to the side, feigning ignorance. "What happened the other night?"

His eyes widened slightly, and he blinked a couple of times. "Uh, when you, I mean, when we ... had our moment on the deck." He cleared his throat. "That was really nice. I've never had a beautiful woman hit on me before."

I laughed again. "You rotten liar. Every woman on that ship was half in love with you after two hours."

He smiled, embarrassed. "Even if that was true, what I meant was: you're the most beautiful woman I've ever known, and I just can't believe you would give me the time of day."

I slid my hand around, unlinking our pinkies and threading my fingers through his. I couldn't think of a proper response to his beautifully simple compliment, so I just whispered, "Same."

He squeezed my fingers and gave me a grin that completely erased every tired line from his face. "Did I mention that I like you a lot?"

I nodded, scooting a little closer to him in the sand. "Yeah. I have a confession, though."

His brows rose. "Oh yeah?"

"I kissed you on a dare."

I was surprised by the flash of hurt I saw in his eyes, but when he spoke, his voice held forced aloofness. "Oh yeah? Who dared you?"

"Alexis, my coworker." I watched his face closely for any change of expression or chink in his armor. "She gave me $100."

He winced but tried to cover it with a laugh. "Glad you got something from it. I wouldn't want it to be a waste of your time." He stood then and took a few steps away, his back turned to me.

I had expected a negative reaction, but somehow I hadn't expected to hurt his feelings. I'd selfishly assumed that he would have thought negatively about me, not about himself.

I stood but didn't follow him, letting him have space to feel whatever he needed to feel. Except ... "It doesn't mean I didn't want to kiss you."

He hummed an unconvincing assent. "But it took someone paying you to make it happen."

This was going poorly. "It wasn't about the money, and I wouldn't have done it if I didn't want to. It was just a push, you know? I'm usually kind of shy and, according to my ex-fiancé, dull and prudish."

Carter looked back at me again, a scowl still creasing his brow. "So you regret it? That's why you feel like you had to confess?"

"No, I just didn't want you to find out some other way and get hurt."

"Well, guess what," he said, his voice getting louder, "I'm hurt anyway."

His words rang between us, thudding against my heart, wounding with each beat. Tears of regret and exhaustion pricked my eyes, and I could only stare at him, unable to keep the sorrow from my face.

I stepped forward slowly, extended my hand, and waited to see if he would take it. At length, he did.

"I'm sorry," I said, locking my eyes on his and trying to infuse sincerity into my apology. "I never meant to hurt your feelings. Honestly, I never expected to see you again after the cruise was over, so I figured—who would get hurt?" I stopped, at last letting my gaze fall to the sand. "I'm sorry that you did."

He was silent for a moment. Then, at last, he took a step and closed the distance between us. I peeked up and saw that his gaze was on the sand, his head bowed sadly.

"Can you forgive me?"

He lifted his gaze and met mine. "Yeah," he said at length. "But no more gambling about our relationship, okay?"

I nodded firmly. "Deal."

Then he straightened and his brow furrowed. "I can't believe anybody would say that about you. You're the funniest, most vivacious ..." He broke off with a scoff and a sharp shake of his head. "Prudish. Ha! That guy must have been raised by wolves."

"So, you don't care that I kissed you on a dare?"

He considered that for a moment, then watched me carefully as he asked, "Did you want to?"

"Yeah," I breathed.

He smirked. "Then I don't care why you did it. I'm just happy you did."

I couldn't hold back my grin. "How are you the sweetest man on the planet?"

He leaned toward me, and I mirrored the movement until our faces were close and I could feel his breath tickle my cheek. And then I ruined it by talking again. "I had an ex-fiancé."

Carter didn't move away; he just looked into my eyes and nodded slowly. "You mentioned that."

I swallowed.

"Do you want to talk about it?"

I closed my eyes briefly. "I never talk about it."

"How come?"

"It hurt for a long time, and even now that I'm over it, I'm afraid of what other people will think when I tell them about it." I drew in and exhaled a quick breath. "I messed up. No one wants people to know about their screw-ups."

"Because they might think that you're an imperfect human being?" he correctly guessed.

"Something like that."

He nodded and turned his gaze out to the ocean again, but I kept my eyes on him as he said, "I'm divorced. Did you know that?"

I shook my head.

"Even though she was the one who ended things with us, I am not blameless." He turned back to me with a sad little smile. "Everybody's got their baggage and crap to sort through. It wouldn't be fair for me to judge your failed relationship, and it wouldn't be fair for you to judge mine. My only question is: Do you feel like you're a better person than you used to be? Did you learn from what happened?"

My answer came immediately and honestly. "Yes, I do. And I did."

"Me too." He squeezed my hand again. "If you want to talk about what happened in the past, I'll listen. If you don't, that's okay too."

"You're not curious?" I teased.

"Of course I am. I want to know everything about you."

His honesty touched my heart and made me feel brave enough to say, "I haven't told anybody about this since it happened. So don't make fun of me, okay?"

"Never."

"I got left at the altar. Seven years ago. I was really young, and I think I was looking for stability. I dated my fiancé, Joel, for less than six months before we got engaged."

"Fast movers," Carter remarked.

"Too fast. There was a lot I didn't know about him before I said yes. The biggest thing was his tendency to run scared at the thought of getting married." I cut Carter a look, then admitted, "I found out later that he had been engaged three times before me. So I guess I wasn't exactly the problem, but being ditched right before the ceremony gave my confidence a blow. It's not a story to write a book about, but ... I guess I'm just embarrassed by it."

I sagged backward and lay down on the sand, staring up at the clouds that drifted above.

It was a long time before either of us spoke. During all the time I talked, Carter had held my hand, not interrupting. Just listening.

Now that he knew my bad track record, I wondered if his opinion of me had changed.

Finally, he broke the silence. "I'm sorry you had to go through that." Then he gave me a sweet look and said, "Thank you for telling me. That guy ... he's really missing out. And I'll bet he knows it. But I can't say that I'm sorry it happened."

That surprised me. "Mean!" I cried.

He chuckled. "If you had married him, I wouldn't have gotten the chance to meet you. And you definitely wouldn't let me kiss you again."

He wanted to kiss me again.

"There's that, I guess."

He finally let go of my hand and stood up, stretching his arms over his head. "We probably ought to gather more wood," he said, tossing a spare branch into the flames beside us. "Who knows how long it'll be before someone comes for us." He reached a hand down to me, and I grasped it, letting him help me to my feet. When I was almost up, he gave me a playful little tug, making me fall forward into him. He wrapped his arms around me, and I gulped as I gazed up into his face.

"Hey," he whispered.

I grinned, feeling my heart fluttering madly. "Hey."

We locked eyes. He looked serious but happy. His eyes dipped down to my mouth, and I felt myself blush. I took a tiny step closer. He accepted my invitation. His right arm cinched around my waist, pulling me close so my thighs pressed against his. With each breath, I could feel his abdomen rise and fall against my own. My hands rested on the soft, damp material of his torn shirt, my traitorous fingers curling into the fabric, savoring the firm tension of the pectoral muscles beneath. His hand was warm at my waist where he wrapped his fingers in the material of my own shirt.

My breath hitched as I heard him swallow. The green of his eyes jumbled my mind so no thoughts could penetrate the fog. I forgot how to inhale, perfectly content with the understanding that I may never breathe again, just so long as I could remain hypnotized by this man's stare.

His left hand cupped my cheek, gently angling my face upward and tugging me even closer. I didn't resist. In a movement as slow and deliberate as a rising tide, we closed the distance between us. My eyelids fluttered closed as I touched my lips to his. The kiss was soft, feather-light, just a brushing of our lips. We moved apart, a fraction of an inch, and let the tension buzz between us. One breath. Two. I felt his fingers twitch at my side, and I lost the stalemate. I grinned and vanquished the distance between us yet again, allowing his lips to wipe my smile away.

His fingers wove into my hair, and mine slid down his chest and around his side. Each of us held tight to the other, pulling and yearning to be nearer. There was no space between our bodies anymore, yet neither of us released the tension. He kissed me, and I kissed him, and the waves roared around us. And my stomach swooped, and my heart pounded, and my spirit soared.

I had never felt like this. I had never been kissed this way. A true connection where both of us wanted it just as much as the other. But it wasn't selfish. I knew he was thinking about me, and I was thinking only of him. We could have been the only people on this island, or there could have been a million—it would have felt the same way. Just about us. Just Carter and Jillian. Just this kiss in this moment. And oh, it was decadent.

A bird cried above our heads, and we let each other go at last. I dropped onto my heels, not even aware I had been up on my toes. I grinned at him, and he laughed, tucking my hair behind my ear before bending down to give me a final, searing kiss.

When he stepped back, his hand slid from my hair, down my shoulder, and along the outside of my arm until he linked his fingers with my own again. He used his free hand to tap my nose as he said, "We'd better get back to work."

I couldn't wipe the smile from my face. "Okay, Professor. Lead the way."

# 13

## *JILLIAN*

**W**ith the fire burning merrily against the tropical blue sky, painted with bright blue with fluffy white clouds, I found a driftwood log to sit on to look out at the water. Carter sat beside me, bracing his hand around the log behind me and leaning his side into mine slightly. It was comfortable and warm. I was so glad he was there.

Our conversation had left me feeling refreshed and clean, like my soul had been caught in a summer rainstorm. I released a long breath and let my head rest back against his shoulder.

"Can I ask you something?"

"Mmhmm," he hummed. I glanced up and was gratified to see that his eyes were closed in contentment.

"Would you like to talk now? About your divorce?"

His eyes didn't open, but I felt him slowly sigh. "I don't usually like to talk about it. But I'll answer any questions you have."

I thought carefully. What did I want to know about his divorce? Being separated from a past relationship didn't change the person I had beside me right now. It didn't discount or change anything that

I knew about him. So I supposed I was just curious. "How could any woman in her right mind let you go?" I finally asked.

He smiled again, eyes still closed. "You aren't the first person to ask me that. But, like I said, I'm not blameless."

I sat quietly, inviting him to continue in any way he wanted to.

"Her name is Melanie. We met in college and dated for a long time. She was comfortable. Being with her was easy, and when it was time to graduate and head out into the real world, I guess I was scared to go alone. So we decided to get married and face the real world together. We got engaged the night of my graduation, then she left for the summer for an internship in British Columbia. We called and texted and saw each other a couple of times, but our relationship changed a lot over that summer. Our wedding was set for the first week in September. She came back from Canada, and we were so excited to 'start the next chapter' that neither of us stopped to really ask ourselves if that was what was going to be best for us.

"We got married and afterwards found out that we hadn't talked about a few important things. Like how she had fallen in love with her job in Canada and wanted to relocate there, but I had just started grad school in Miami and needed to be close by the ocean in order to keep up my studies. As you can guess, we fought about that. I was stubborn and I wouldn't let her change my mind about where I thought I needed to be. So after a year of back and forth, she ended up leaving. She sent me divorce papers from Canada." He paused for a minute, squinting out at the waves as they crashed onto the sand. "I haven't seen her since."

I placed my hand on his knee and squeezed once to get his attention. "You miss her?" I guessed.

"Yeah, but not in the ways you might think. Mostly, I wish I could get that time back and do things differently. Every one of those situations could have, and should have, been handled better. By both of us. It's a great regret of mine. That I was too immature to handle my own life." He shook his head. "I'd like to think that I've changed since then, that I would do things better if I had another chance. But it scares me, too. I mean, what if I'm still the same selfish person I was ten years ago?"

I cast my eyes upward toward the heavens, seeking the right words to convey just how impressed I was with this man. "I think just the fact that you recognize your own mistakes, that you don't blame everything on someone else … that says you've matured. And you know what?" I turned toward him a little, looking into his warm eyes and smiling, "I'm glad I get to know this version of you. The one who has learned and decided not to get in your own way. I can learn a lot from you."

His smile crinkled the corners of his eyes. "I feel the same way."

"Good," I said, leaning forward to press a kiss to his cheek. "Thank you for telling me."

"Anytime."

I rolled my stiff shoulders back and shook out my hands. "Now, can we go back to the village? I can't feel my booty anymore."

Laughing, he stood and helped me to my feet, giving me a proper kiss before threading his fingers through mine. "As you wish, my lady."

I liked being his lady.

We put some more wood on the signal fire before turning back to follow the road to the village. When we arrived, we emerged from the trees to find Kenya hanging upside down in the stone hole, her backside up in the air, one foot planted on the ground, and the other kicking ridiculously at the sky.

I jogged over, worried that she had somehow fallen in, but as I approached, she lurched back out of the hole and shouted toward the trees, "I felt it. I think that's the one!"

My gaze followed the direction of her shout, expecting to see someone standing in the tree line, but no one was there. I stopped beside her.

"Who are you yelling at?"

She started a little when she saw me. "You're back!" Her eyes swung around behind me where Carter was closing the distance. "You two get lost?" Then she winked at Carter, and I thought my face might catch fire.

"Something like that," Carter said with a smirk, bumping his shoulder against mine as he stopped at my side. "What's going on?"

Kenya beamed as she hooked her thumb over her shoulder at the pit. "We found where the electricity runs."

I gasped. "No way!"

"What did you find?"

She started to walk toward the jungle. "Come on, I'll show you." Obediently, we followed her out of the village and into the jungle. A few hundred feet into the trees, we came to the orchard that Bridget had found on our first day here. It was overgrown, like the road, but the trees were clearly hand-planted in their straight, even spacing with room to walk comfortably between them. Mango, coconut, and papaya grew in abundance, in varying levels of ripeness. Its presence was lifesaving.

We didn't stop in the orchard, though. Kenya led us through it and out the other side, back into the dense, disorganized trees for several hundred more feet. Then, just as I was sure Kenya had brought us back here to murder us for our shares of tropical fruit, the trees broke, and we stepped out into a small clearing. There weren't any more huts here—no structures at all, actually. But there was something even better.

"Is that a generator?" Carter gasped.

Sure enough, Bridget and Grandpa Skippy stood on either side of a large, gas-powered generator that looked like it had once been powerful enough to light up a small city. The red paint was peeling and the metal beneath it was rusty. Bridget showed us the conduit they had found next to the generator, sticking up out of the ground. Inside was a thick, black wire.

The pieces fell into place in my mind. "Does this connect to the breaker box in the hole?"

Kenya nodded, bouncing excitedly on her toes. "You know what this means? If we can get this running, we could have light and heat!"

"Not exactly," Grandpa cut in. "Even if we do get it working, we don't have anything to plug into it." His eyes moved to me. "We haven't found a shed full of lamps and heaters. Yet."

"This is still encouraging," Bridget protested. "Maybe we can't use the generator, but I can't help but wonder what else was left behind. And maybe we can find the water source that used to connect to that pipe. I, for one, wouldn't mind a nice drink of clean water."

The look on Grandpa's face spoke plainly of his doubts that the water on the other end of the pipe would be nice and clean anymore, but he didn't say it out loud.

Grandpa had been improving the last two days. Being inside the huts had done him a lot of good. The fact that he was out here in the jungle hunting down abandoned generators spoke volumes about his physical state of being. I felt like a brick load of worry had been lifted from my chest. He had removed the bandage from his forehead, and I was glad to see that his cut was healing, especially that it wasn't bleeding anymore. In all, he had bled through five or six makeshift bandages before the wound closed. In an unknown jungle full of mosquitoes and lizards, profuse bleeding is discouraged.

We stayed by the generator for a while, searching through the tall grass and bushes for any other items the television crew might have abandoned. But apart from the last remains of an old cigarette and a crushed beer can, we came up empty-handed.

Once we were satisfied that there was nothing else to find in the small clearing, the five of us gathered the ripe fruit we could find on the trees and returned to the village. Howard and Elodia were back by then, and they joined us for a papaya and stale rainwater lunch. When we were done eating, Bridget volunteered to take the next watch out at the beach and asked if Howard and Elodia would go with her. Her choice of companion surprised me. It seemed like she and Kenya had become fast friends. But when I saw Kenya's face and the dark circles under her tired eyes, I understood her friend's compassion. Kenya needed to rest. And come to think of it, so did I.

We broke up again, and I went into the hut I shared with Grandpa Skippy. He followed and lay down on his bed without a word. I followed his example and lay down, thinking only how grateful I was that it wasn't raining anymore before falling deeply asleep.

***

When I awoke again several hours later, I walked out of the hut and found Bridget returning to the village by herself. I waved to her, and trepidation crept up my neck when she grunted in response. As she brushed past me, she muttered, "They're unbelievable."

I could only assume that they were Howard and Elodia. I turned and followed Bridget to the hut she shared with Kenya. "What happened?" Her irritation surprised me—I thought we had turned a corner with Elodia, at least.

Bridget stopped and whirled around, tossing her hands up. "We're stranded on an island, right?"

This was not a promising beginning. "Right..."

"Right. And this uppity rich man has the audacity to start in on how my last concert series was a disappointment. And how he thought that I had better sense than to talk about religion in public. As if talking about my beliefs was the same as murdering puppies on stage. And then he starts giving me career advice." She scoffed. "As if I need advice from someone like him." She pointed back toward the beach. "Do you know that, last year, he publicly called out the president for something that happened like thirty years ago? It's like he thinks he owns the world just because he has a couple successful businesses. And you know what? He even told me that he hasn't ever listened to any of my music. So, I'm thinking, why don't you just go ahead and back off then, huh, buddy?"

I had my share of knowledge about how aggravating it was to be talked down to by entitled rich people, but that wasn't what Bridget needed at that moment. Sometimes I felt like the only neutral party in the middle of a fistfight. Being a referee to everybody else's disagreements wasn't foreign to me, but it became tiresome after a while.

I tried to say the right things to help her cool down and rethink her notion to go back to the beach and punch him in the gut. She called him a few choice words and finally decided he wasn't worth it.

She crossed the village center to where Kenya was sitting on a chair she had fashioned from logs and rocks, shaded by the gold sequined dress. No one had found a better purpose of that garment, so Bridget and Kenya had strung it up to be a sun shade.

Bridget collapsed onto the ground beside Kenya, and I heard Kenya ask what was wrong. That was all it took to get Bridget fired up again. With a sigh, I turned away so I didn't have to hear it all for a second time.

I had nothing else to do, so I started down toward the beach. A few steps down the road, I ran into Carter, who was returning to the village with an armload of firewood. His face lit up when he saw me, and I felt my sagging spirits buoy up considerably.

"What are you up to?" he asked as we stopped together in the road.

I rolled my eyes back in the direction I'd come. "Running away."

He winced. "From Bridget? Yeah, she gave me an earful, too."

"She's telling Kenya all about it now. And with the way the two of them get each other worked up, it could be hours before they cool down again. So, I'm going to see if I can get the other side of the story from the Lovells."

His eyebrows rose. "You're going to talk to them about it?"

"Well, yeah. If we're going to solve this, we need to let everybody have their say."

He shifted the firewood in his arms. "Solve this?" he repeated. "What's to solve?"

I pointed back and forth between the village and the beach. "They're fighting. I don't want them to fight. It just makes it bad for everybody."

He hummed in the back of his throat, and something about the look on his face told me that he knew I wouldn't really like what he was thinking.

But I knew I wouldn't be able to just let it go, so I pressed him. "What?"

"Nothing." He lifted his armload of firewood slightly then nodded toward the village. "Let me put this away, then I want to show you something." He hustled to the place where we'd been stashing extra firewood then came back to my side and took my hand.

I was intrigued by the excitement in his eyes as he led me off the road and into the jungle. The seven of us had explored the area around the village a little, but it seemed like every day someone found something new in the trees. Elodia had found a broken bongo drum that we thought might be an authentic tribal instrument until Howard saw the "Made in Indonesia" sticker on the inside. We were still on the lookout for a fresh water source, so I hoped that Carter was leading me to a pristine waterfall.

He hadn't found fresh water, but it was only a minor disappointment when he brought me to another sloping hill that transformed into a pillar of intriguing rocks. We circled around the rocks to find a cliff face that revealed several openings.

"There are caves back there," Carter explained, pointing out the largest opening. "That one goes back a few hundred feet. I didn't go too deep because some bats flew out at me as soon as I got in there." A shudder rocked through him, and I suppressed a laugh at his theatrics. "Wildlife aside, I thought it might be fun to explore them. You in?"

"Definitely." Exploring a cave with Carter sounded much better than picking a fight with Howard and Elodia. "We should have brought a torch though," I added, squinting as I stepped into the dark mouth of the cave. It was pitch-black inside, and my skin prickled as I imagined what kind of bugs and vermin might call that place home.

Carter grinned and held up Kenya's lighter and showed me the makeshift torches he had made and stowed just inside the cave. "Gotcha covered. Let's explore."

He handed me a torch, took one for himself, and lit both of them with the lighter. He had become our resident expert on torch-making, knowing just how much kindling was needed to start a light and what kind of material would burn the longest. It was a weirdly specific talent that I'm sure he never thought he had.

Duly warned by Carter's previous experience, we grabbed some sticks and knocked them against the rock walls to create a racket and scare away bats and mice and man-eating iguanas. Nothing leapt out at us from the darkness, so we took our lives into our own hands and stepped into the cave.

The torches worked really well, but I wished we had a floodlight anyway. The entrance to the cavern was a few inches shorter than I was, so I had to duck to get inside, but after a few feet, it opened up dramatically. The ceiling soared upward to maybe thirty feet, and the light from our torches danced on sparkling minerals embedded in the walls. This cave didn't go very deep, maybe seventy feet, before it ended in a solid rock wall. The firelight caught on some etching on the rock, and we stepped closer to investigate.

My stomach flipped when I saw the long, deep grooves carved into the rocks. It looked like a grizzly bear had sharpened its claws here. The span of the marks was wider across than my hand, and I looked at Carter with wide eyes. "Whatever made this was huge!" I said.

The scratch marks marred the wall from my eye level all the way down to the stone floor. Carter crouched down and gently ran his fingers over the mark, studying it intently. After a few moments, he looked up at me and said, "I don't think this was an animal."

"Then what could it be?"

"I'm not sure." He turned to the wall again and traced his fingernail along one line. "It's deep and really even all the way along. I'm wondering if it was some kind of equipment."

I cocked my head to one side and looked around the room again. As I examined the other walls more closely, I found more scratches of the same kind and a couple of horizontal scrapes as well. One section met at a right angle at knee-height. Like a metal shelf had sat here, rubbing against the stone anytime something was placed on it. "Maybe the TV people used this cave as storage space," I theorized. "That might explain why we haven't found any storage buildings or anything."

"Makes sense to me. Only, how would they get stuff in here? The doorway is too small to fit anything bigger than a person."

I pondered this while taking another tour of the room. When I reached the farthest corner of the cave, I noticed that my torchlight created a deep shadow, and when I got closer, I saw that a wall jutted out into the space, creating a false end to the room. The deep shadow behind it hid a passageway that was wide enough for a car to fit through. I called Carter over, and we cautiously walked into the passage together. It led us to another large cavern, this one double the size of the first, and on the opposite side from our entry point, the cave wall yawned open wide to allow sunshine to peer inside. This opening was largely blocked by boulders and a thick cluster of vine-covered trees. I doubted if we would have found it coming from the outside.

Unlike the first cavern we explored, this cavern's walls were rough, leading to smaller chambers and a labyrinth of tunnels.

"It would be so easy to get lost back here," I observed after Carter and I found the sixth tunnel leading off of the cavern.

"Probably easier to see with floodlights," he shrugged. "I think you're right, though. I'd guess that this is where they stored their equipment. It'd keep it all out of the elements and they wouldn't have extra buildings they'd have to hide from the cameras during their reality show."

I sighed. "Wish they had left some of their stuff behind. I could use an espresso machine right about now."

He hummed his agreement, and we continued to poke around until we were certain that there was nothing in the caves to find except cobwebs and bat droppings. We found our way back to the first cave we'd explored, and my torch finally gave out. I figured we had been exploring for forty-five minutes, and such was the state of my general exhaustion that I was ready to take a nap. And eat an entire Thanksgiving dinner by myself.

Without the light from my torch, the cave was dark, but it had lost the spookiness from before. I felt I understood it now. It was a forgotten place that had a lot to offer and no one to take advantage of it anymore. That feeling resonated with me, and I suddenly felt like crying. I dropped my torch to the ground then slowly slid down the wall until I sat on the floor beside it. Without a word, Carter joined me, propping up his torch against the stone then relaxing beside me with a sigh.

We reached for each other's hands at the same time, and I smiled. I never knew that being with somebody would ever be simple. Easy and uncomplicated. I wondered if, had I chosen a more normal lifestyle, the simplicity of this relationship would seem dull to me. Maybe that's why my previous romances had failed. I didn't appreciate simplicity. I was waiting for a dramatic life-changing spark, but maybe I didn't need my whole life to change. Maybe I just needed someone to sit next to me and hold my hand while I figured stuff out. I needed someone who got me.

"Have you ever wondered what your great flaw is?"

His out-of-the-blue question derailed my train of thought. "Pardon?"

"Your big flaw. Everybody has one. I mean, everybody has a thousand little flaws, but usually we have one big one that tries to ruin our lives time after time."

I narrowed my eyes at him. "Okay... and, what, you think you know what my big flaw is?"

He shrugged. "Maybe. I'm not trying to offend you. I just noticed something."

"Tell me."

His gaze dropped. "I don't want to."

I rolled my eyes. "Now you have to tell me. What's my great flaw?"

He sighed and then let me have it. "I've been thinking about the group and how everyone always expects you to solve the problems. It makes you think that you aren't useful if you're not making other people happy."

My worried scowl changed to one of confusion. "You say that like it's a bad thing."

"It's not bad, but—" He bobbed his head back and forth.

I felt my hackles rise. This wasn't the first time I'd been told that. I tried to keep my ire at bay, though. "It's literally my job."

"It goes beyond your job. Do you think that, while we're shipwrecked on an island in the middle of nowhere, you should be expected to serve cocktails and wipe up people's spills?"

"That's ridiculous."

"Only because there isn't anything to serve. You bend yourself so far over backwards that it's a wonder you can't kiss your own feet."

"Hey!"

I couldn't see his expression in the darkness, but his voice was mild and tired. "All I'm saying is: what about you?"

I blinked at him, struggling to keep up with the thread of this conversation. "What about me?"

"What do you want?"

I gestured to the caves. "To get off this—"

He didn't let me finish that overused phrase. "Out of life," he cut in. "What do you want to do with your life?"

That was easy enough to answer. "I'm doing it. Working with Grandpa, sailing, adventure. What's not to like?"

He was unconvinced. "Really? Sailing from port to port, catering to other people's needs while never making lasting connections or planting roots? That's what you want?"

"Hey, everybody has to have a job." I shrugged. "This is mine."

I felt his body move as he shook his head. "This is way beyond a job, Jill. This has become your life. When was the last time you did something that wasn't directly, or indirectly, related to this job?"

I didn't have a ready answer for that. Truthfully, I worked nonstop. Even Grandpa had said he worried about how absorbed I was in his business. "Uh..."

"I'll wait."

Irritation flared in my chest, and I poked a finger at him. "That's not fair. You're probably the same way, but we're not currently at your job. If I was to come into your lab or whatever, you'd be just as focused on work as I am when I'm working."

"But at least I go home at night. At least I eat breakfast and scroll through Instagram for a few minutes before I head into work. At least I have a few hours a week that I could spend on a relationship or a hobby or something—if I wanted to. You work like an oil-rigger—nose to the grindstone, never at home, no connections."

I pulled my hand out of his and pushed to my feet, my blood boiling with righteous indignation. "You're attacking me because my life looks different from yours. Not everybody wants 'roots' or to have boring days. Some people want to sail the world and find their next adventure day after day."

He stood up, too. "Are you one of those people?"

I tossed up my hands. "Of course. Why else would I work this job?"

"I'm surprised."

"Surprised I want to see the world?"

He bent over and picked up his torch. The flame had nearly extinguished, and its light was pitifully dim. "No. I'm surprised that you would lie to me."

That brought me up short. "I didn't lie. I really do love my job."

"I think you love your grandpa so much that you're willing to center everything in your life around his dream so that he doesn't fail or get disappointed. You feel like his success is up to you." He paused for a moment, then cleared his throat and continued in a softer tone, "Plus, it's pretty clear that Skippy doesn't give you the... appreciation you deserve. Much less grandfatherly love. But apart from all of that, yes, you are amazing at your job. You put your whole soul into it, but your heart isn't in it."

No one had ever summed up my situation quite so succinctly before. I stared at him, jaw agape. "How do you know that?"

"I can see it on your face when you talk to people about their lives. About their dreams and their goals. You get this fire in your eyes that I didn't see when you were serving drinks or handing out schedules. You have a dream, too. And I want you to be honest—with me and with yourself—and tell me what it is."

I glared at him as his words pinged around in my brain, sparking anger and hurt and then something much more painful—realization. I didn't want to admit that he was partially right. I had come into the business just for Grandpa, and if he wasn't doing this anymore, would it be something I wanted to continue on with?

That was a real possibility now—since his yacht was sitting on the ocean floor by now. Would he want to buy a second yacht and keep going? And after everything we'd been through over the past few days, would I want to stay?

My immediate answer was yes. I wanted to be with Grandpa. I wanted to help him and make sure his business grew and did the very best it could. For him. To make his dream a reality.

But Carter was right. Wanting something for Grandpa Skippy did not make that thing my dream. So, if the yacht wasn't my dream... what was?

In my agitation and anger, I walked toward the light at the mouth of the cave, ducking out into the filtered sunshine of the jungle, leaving Carter behind. I could hear his footsteps a ways behind me, but I was grateful he let me leave him behind and think for a while. Just because he was right didn't mean I wasn't mad at him for it.

Before long, I reached the road again. I turned toward the beach and stalked down the path until I reached the beach. I found Elodia and Howard sitting in the sand by the signal fire. He had his arm around her shoulders, and she rested her head against him. They spoke quietly together, and I couldn't understand what they said. I cleared my throat as I approached, not wanting them to think I was eavesdropping.

Elodia sat up and turned around. She nodded when she saw me, but I saw exhaustion ringing her eyes. Initially, I had planned to play referee and try to fix things between them and Bridget. But after my talk with Carter, I didn't have the energy.

"I can sit by the fire for a while if you want me to," I said instead. "You can go rest."

Howard nodded and got slowly to his feet. Then he extended a hand down to Elodia and helped her stand. They brushed the sand from their pants, thanked me for relieving them, and walked back into the jungle.

I watched them go, surprised that Carter hadn't emerged from the trees yet. Maybe he was going to ambush them with their worst qualities as well. Best of luck to them.

# 14

*JILLIAN*

Carter must have known I was mad at him and gone back to the village after all, because he didn't emerge from the trees. So, I sat alone and stared out at the ship-less horizon, wishing to see a boat at any moment, but knowing in my heart that I would not.

A long time passed. I never would have imagined that while in a life-or-death situation there would be space to be bored. But there was only so much worrying my brain could stand before it got used to it and shifted over into boredom. It had been a very long time since I had felt boredom—I typically kept my schedule so packed with work that by the time I went to bed at night, I fell asleep instantly, only to wake up the next morning and work myself to the bone all over again. Sitting on a beach had never been my ideal vacation—why would I want to laze around on my rump staring at the same ocean I spent every working day arguing with? I'd rather vacation on a mountain. Or maybe a desert. At least there I'd have something new to look at.

Waves rolled in and out at the same menacing volume that hadn't let up since the storm, but my ears had grown accustomed to the roaring. My skin, however, had not gotten used to the ocean's chilly spray or the breath-catching winds, nor would I ever learn to ignore the annoying scraping and clawing of sand, wedged into every crevice and plane of my body.

The sun crawled across the sky, birds flew above my head, and crabs scuttled along the edges of the water. I swatted at bugs. And I thought, and I thought, and I thought.

I replayed my conversation with Carter about a dozen times. And by the thirteenth repeat, I had accepted that he made good points, and that maybe he hadn't set out to attack me. Maybe the shipwreck could be the springboard for me to change careers. Assuming we got rescued, of course. I had not dreamt of being a yacht stewardess before Grandpa started his business. So, what had I wanted to do? And did I still want that now?

Truthfully, I had hoped to prove myself to Grandpa—show him that I was just as worthy of his love as the other grandkids. To change his mind about me. But that was like repeatedly banging my head against a brick wall. Every day, for six years, waking up and doing my best and praying that that day would finally be the day that Grandpa showed me I was worthwhile. And every night, going to bed exhausted and secretly disappointed, knowing that to Skippy, I would never be more than just another set of hands to take care of.

When would it finally be time to give up my childish fantasy of having the love of my grandfather?

Just before sunset, I heard the approach of footsteps from the jungle. I turned, expecting to see Carter or Kenya coming to relieve me of watch duty. But instead, approaching sheepishly across the sand, was Skippy. He had his hands in the pockets of his white captain pants and his eyes downcast. He sat beside me on the sand and let out a long breath.

I waited for him to speak.

"Hey, kiddo," he finally said, his voice low.

"I'm surprised to see you out here," I said. He hadn't been well enough to take a watch before. He had hardly been out of the hut most of the time we had been here. I was glad to see that he felt well enough to make the walk through the jungle. But he looked drawn and pale from the exertion.

Skippy stared out at the water, blinking slowly and rubbing his palms together. "I've been thinking, Jilly," he began without looking at me. "Being laid up and all... I've been thinking about my life and my priorities."

I hardly dared to hope that he had come to apologize. "Oh yeah?"

"And I think my business is focused on the wrong clientele."

My heart drooped: guess I'd gotten my hopes up after all. "Uh huh?"

"Once I get a new ship, I want to do more giveaways, give this kind of experience to more people like Kenya and Carter. People more like us. Sure, I've liked working with the rich people, but they can get a good trip anywhere. I want more people to be able to experience this."

I looked at him blandly. "What? Wrecking and getting stranded on an island?"

"Don't you start on me," he answered curtly. "I've had just about enough of that kind of thing from Howard. I would never do this on purpose—you know there's nothing more important to me than that boat!"

On a normal day, in normal circumstances, I would have let this comment glance off of me, trying not to let it hurt my feelings. But the wound was too fresh, the exhaustion too deep, and the sorrow too real. Unbidden tears filled my eyes, and I had to bite my lip to keep it from trembling.

Skippy kept talking, not noticing my tears or my sadness. Not noticing me. Like always.

The pain became too much to bear, and I dropped my face into my hands and finally let myself cry. I was so tired. Tired of being the joke of my grandpa's ship. Tired of being his errand girl, of getting no respect, of getting the blame for every little problem. I was tired of being a doormat for every person to wipe their emotional shoes on. And beyond all of that, I was sick and tired of trying to please a man who would never accept me as one of his own. Through no fault of my own, I would never be a granddaughter to Scott Hamilton. And I was tired of trying.

Skippy finally noticed that I was crying. "Jillian? What's the matter?"

I dropped my hands and looked up with an overemotional huff. "You'll have to do it without me," I said as calmly as my streaming tears would allow.

He blinked at me. "Do what without you?"

"Run the business. Run the ship. If you buy another yacht... I'm out. I can't do this anymore."

"You want to give up on our dream?" He looked confounded. Like I'd thrown a conch shell at his face.

I shook my head. "It was never my dream, Grandpa. You know that."

"Then... what are you still doing here?" he asked, seeming honestly confused. "If you don't want to be part of the business, why have you stuck around for all these years?"

I turned my gaze out to the ocean, where the sun hung low over the horizon, a mere hour away from setting. When I answered, my voice was low and soft, but I couldn't keep the hurt out of it, even though I tried. "If you don't know why I've stayed working with you for six years... killing myself to make you proud of me... then I guess you never will. I'll never make you proud."

Silence fell between us. I knew he was staring at me, but I couldn't look at him. I'd said the words that I'd known were true for years. I finally spoke aloud the truth that I had always refused to acknowledge. My chest felt a little lighter, the tension in my back eased. But my heart still hurt. I was beginning to understand that, in this case, it always would.

Moments passed without a word. I had half-expected a rebuff of some kind. It wouldn't have been unusual for him to tell me off, to stop being selfish, to think about who I'm hurting. But he didn't say any of that.

Eventually, I stood up and walked away, leaving him sitting alone on the sand. It wouldn't have surprised me if he decided never to speak to me again. And part of me still felt that I deserved it.

***

I made it ten steps onto the road back to the village before emotions flooded through me. Sobs broke through my resolve, and I ended up crouched on the path, pressing my palms against my eyes, crying irrationally. I knew it wasn't just my conversation with Grandpa, but everything I'd been through for the last week. The wreck, the abandonment, my conversation with Carter, the utter exhaustion and fatigue, hunger, the creepy-crawly feeling all over my body from not showering for a week. My teeth had never gone so long without flossing, and I was ready to shave my head because my hair was so greasy and awful.

So I broke down in tears, sobbing into my hands until my shoulders stopped shaking and my breathing finally settled down. I looked up with a heavy, shuddering sigh. It was only then that I realized I wasn't alone.

Skippy sat beside me on the path, his face in his hands. If I wasn't mistaken, I thought I saw a tear on his own cheek.

"Grandpa?" I whispered, shocked to see him beside me.

He looked up with an expression so sorrowful it broke my heart all over again. He reached out, took my hand, and locked his eyes on mine. "I'm sorry, Jillian," he whispered. "I've been unfair to you. Your parents and I didn't see eye to eye about their situation all those years ago, and I've taken all of my disappointment out on you." He cleared his throat and squeezed my fingers tighter. "I was wrong. Taking you for granted... I don't have an excuse for it. But I need you to understand that..." Another tear slid down his cheek. "This business would be nothing without you. I... I couldn't have made this dream come true if it hadn't been for your imagination and hard work. I'm so grateful for you, Jillian. And I..." His voice broke. "It's hard for me to say this. You know I'm a stubborn old man."

I laughed lightly through fresh tears, wordlessly agreeing with him.

"I love you, Jillian. I couldn't love you more if you were my flesh and blood. And I should have shown you that all this time. I hope you can forgive me."

I didn't hesitate. I threw my arms around his neck in a hug. He wrapped his arms around my back and held me tight. It wasn't the first hug I'd gotten from my grandfather, but it was absolutely the best.

"If you really don't want to be on the boat anymore," he said into my shoulder, "then I'll do anything I can to help you do what you want to do. You being happy... that's more important than anything I could do on the ocean."

That got me crying all over again. "Love you, Grandpa."

"Love you, Jillian."

***

Grandpa and I talked for a while more, wandering together back out to the beach. We discussed our individual future plans and our hope that we could improve our relationship. We talked about the family and shared funny stories. It was the first time I could remember sitting with Skippy and feeling like he was not my boss or my teacher, but just my grandpa.

I felt like my heart was glowing.

When he finally left to go back to the village, the sun was just setting over the ocean. I knew someone else would come soon to take my place by the signal fire, so I settled in contentedly to wait.

The sun was fully set when Carter appeared on the beach. He took the same path Grandpa had and came to sit beside me by the fire. I gave him a sideways glance. I wasn't mad at him anymore, exactly, but I knew we needed to have another conversation. I just hoped this one didn't blow up in our faces.

"Skippy told me you two had a long-overdue conversation," he said. "How're you doing?"

I took a deep breath, feeling lighter after my conversation with Grandpa. "You'll be glad to know: You were right."

He sat up, surprised. "I never get tired of hearing that," he said cautiously.

"I do want more for myself than being a glorified waitress-at-sea. I talked to Grandpa about that, and he agreed that it's time for me to pursue my own career. And that he'll support whatever I do."

"I'm so glad to hear that."

I had more to say. "But you're wrong to say that being a people pleaser is a bad thing. In fact, I think that is what I ultimately want to do."

He nodded slowly. "Go on."

I hunched forward and traced my fingers through the sand. "I want to make people smile. But not just because I did something for them, but because I helped them to... find some kind of spark in themselves." My gaze drifted to the signal fire, and a metaphor formed in my mind. "If happiness was like a flame, I want to help someone learn to light a bonfire, not just strike a match for them and walk away. If I could do anything in the world, it would be something that lets me help others see the light that is already inside themselves."

I glanced over at him to see that he looked impressed with my insight. "That's a different kind of happy from serving drinks."

"Yeah... So, what do I do with that? I've never been able to take this nebulous desire to make people happy and turn it into something that'll, you know, pay the bills and crap. No one is going to pay me to stand on street corners shouting that they're taking themselves for granted."

He chuckled lightly, then we both fell silent for a few minutes. At length, he said, "What about therapy?"

I rolled my eyes. "I know I'm messed up, but I think I can figure it out without a shrink."

"No, I mean you be the shrink," he said earnestly. "Have you considered becoming a psychologist or a psychiatrist? Sure, they work with people with a lot of problems, but isn't that their whole goal: to help people learn how to find happiness through hard times?"

My brow furrowed, and I stared at him for a long moment. "I actually thought about doing that. Once."

His eyebrows rose with surprise. "And?"

I shrugged one shoulder and went back to drawing abstractly in the sand. "And it's appealing. In fact, I even started to apply to school for it, years ago. I picked out a school and a program and everything. I was starting to get really excited, but then..."

"Grandpa Skippy won the lottery?" he finished for me.

I shook my head. "Eventually, but that wasn't what kept me from the program." I exhaled a long breath, deflated. "My parents talked me out of it."

"How come?"

"A lot of reasons, probably. The biggest one was money—I couldn't afford tuition at a nice school, and I didn't get good enough grades to get a scholarship. There were other reasons, too, but that was the main thing."

He weighed that in his mind, nodding slowly. "Is that what you're trying to do working on the yacht? Earn enough money for tuition?"

I laughed darkly. "No. Well, ideally, yes, but... I haven't thought about that in years. Life got in the way, and I'm probably too old to start in on it now anyway." I picked up a smooth white stone and tossed it toward the waves.

We sat in silence for a long time. He picked up several smooth stones and handed two to me. We took turns tossing them, quietly competing to see whose rock would hit the water first.

When my fourth rock was the first to plop into the water, Carter let the rest fall to the sand, and he brushed his hands on his pants. Then he looked at me with sincerity in his gaze. "I would never presume to tell you your business. But I hope that, someday, you look into it again. You know, when life gets less crazy. Hey, I'd hire you if I needed serious psychiatric help."

I smiled at last, letting the tension between us melt away, and hoping that we would be able to resume our closeness with even more honesty between us. "Who says you don't now?"

We laughed for a little while together, then I reached out and placed a hand on his knee. I waited for him to look at my face before saying, "Thank you. I don't know what'll happen, but... it's nice to know someone believes I can do great things."

"You can do anything you set your mind to—whether it's waiting tables or changing the world. I have total faith in you." He cast his gaze downward, contritely. "And I'm sorry I hurt your feelings before. I guess the professor in me sneaks out sometimes, and I use the 'tough love' method a little too well."

"I needed to hear it," I conceded.

He leaned toward me, stopping when his lips were only an inch from mine. I reached up and ran my fingers along his scruffy jaw, letting my nose rest against his for a few breaths. And then I let him kiss me.

He was such a good kisser.

After a few wonderful moments, he pulled back, grinning. "Is that what it's like to make up after a fight?" he asked cheekily. "Maybe I should buy us a set of boxing gloves."

I laughed, and he reached out to take my hand.

Then he reclined back onto his elbows and said, "Now, it's my turn. What's my flaw?"

I answered automatically. "You're too good-looking."

He shrugged. "Well, sure, but you've got to give me something I can actually work on."

"I could hit you. That'd help."

His eyes sparkled with mischief. "Then we could make up again. Cool!"

I shoved his shoulder playfully. "You're such a dork."

***

Our days in the village passed mostly in the same way. We took turns going to the beach to keep up the signal fire, and in our off time, we collected wood, searched for food, and roamed the surrounding jungle in search of anything that might help us get home. As we found more food and got better rest in our shelters, I found I had more energy, and I felt a lot better.

Then, one afternoon, I saw a boat.

I was taking a watch duty on the beach, tending the signal fire and trying not to fall asleep in the hot sunshine. Though my achingly empty belly was keeping me awake. Kenya and Bridget had joined me by the fire and were gabbing cheerily, burying their toes in the sand while they exchanged stories about their vastly different childhoods. I had largely tuned out of their conversation, since they seemed to get a real kick out of each other, and sometimes it was more effort than it was worth to insert myself into their fast-paced conversations.

So I stared out at the distant horizon with my imagination playing tricks on me. Each time a large wave came in, breaking up the monotonous blue landscape, it caught my attention with a jolt, making my heart trip in my chest. *Is that a ship?*

When the wave settled back into the uninteresting ocean, I'd be let down all over again.

The heat was making my head swim, and the migraine I'd been fighting back for days was inching into the corners of my brain. There had been a rainstorm that morning, and as I sat there, the dark clouds were blowing out, being replaced with kinder-looking white ones. On the very edge of the horizon, just where the water blended into the sky, I imagined one of the clouds taking the shape of a little white speedboat.

I hmphed to myself as my mind played tricks on me. A speedboat of that size would be tossed around mercilessly out here in the middle of nowhere. No one in their right mind would take a small craft like that out this far all alone.

*Unless it's not alone...* I thought vaguely.

I sat up, blinking at the boat-shaped cloud. It was getting larger and moving faster. *Was it real?*

"Is that..." I shot to my feet and ran toward the ocean. I squinted into the distance, the sun blinding me. I couldn't see the boat anymore! Shading my face with my hand, I scanned the ocean.

*It must have been a trick of light...*

Kenya and Bridget ran up beside me. "What is it? Is it a boat?" they asked.

I stammered with my heart pounding in my throat. I was sure I had seen something, but now... now...

"There!" I screamed, pointing out at the white blur that was speeding across the water, perpendicular to the island. I couldn't see any details about the boat from that distance. But it was small enough to fit only 12–14 people, I guessed. Certainly not large enough to feel comfortable at sea.

It had to be a search party sent from a larger island. They were looking for us!

Jumping and waving my arms, I screamed, "Help! Over here! We're here! We're here!"

My friends joined in immediately, and we raised such a din that it would be impossible for someone not to hear us. The boat's path never wavered.

"The fire!" I cried, spinning around and running back up the beach to where our fire burned moderately. I grabbed armfuls of firewood and threw them into the flames, piling the wood higher and higher until I had used the entire stock of firewood. The signal fire transformed into a bonfire.

Surely they had to see the fire.

*Please. Please see our fire!*

If they were out there looking for us, they would surely turn around. They would see our signal. They would come rescue us!

I ran back to the water, not stopping until I was ankle-deep in the surf, eyes trained unfailingly on the boat.

"Come on," I breathed. "Look over. Come on!"

The boat was nearly out of sight. *Look on the beach! See our fire!*

They passed us by. They hadn't seen the fire. They were leaving...

My heart sank, and I desperately ran farther into the water, screaming myself hoarse, barely even noticing Kenya and Bridget beside me doing the same.

Then, miraculously, the boat slowed.

"They're turning," Kenya hollered, jumping up and down like a woman possessed. "They're coming!"

We kept screaming, waving, calling, and yelling until our throats ached. The boat turned and raced the other direction.

But it never got closer. The white blur faded to a speck and then, just as suddenly as it had come, it was gone.

Mouth agape, my last scream for help silent on my tongue. I couldn't believe it. They hadn't seen us. They hadn't seen the fire.

Unbidden tears washed over my cheeks, and my knees buckled. I knelt in the surf, staring dumbfoundedly at the ocean.

Kenya hadn't given up. She ran farther out into the water, still waving her arms and screaming. Eventually, Bridget followed her, put a soft hand on her shoulder, and convinced her to come back to the beach.

I wouldn't move. Foolishly, I thought that if I stayed still, if I just waited a minute longer, they might come back. Maybe they were going back for reinforcements. Maybe... maybe...

I don't know how long I knelt there. My clothes were soaked with seawater, and I cried until there were no more tears left to fall.

We never saw another boat after that.

***

On the fifth morning we woke up in the village, I sat alone, looking up at a rocky peak at the center of the island. I studied it for a long time, mulling over an idea and thinking through the logistics of the plan that was forming in my mind.

Grandpa was the first to notice that I was a million miles away, and he called me back to the present. "You have that look," he said knowingly.

I blinked at him as I came out of my reverie. "What look?"

"The one that says you're about to be brilliant." He looked at Kenya and Elodia, who sat nearby, and added, "She had that same look on her face just before she gave me the idea to start The Flying Honeymoon business."

Kenya was impressed. "I didn't know the business was your idea, Jillian. Captain Skippy, I thought this was your lifelong dream."

"Owning a yacht and spending my golden years at sea was my dream," Grandpa corrected. "But it was Jilly who suggested I make it into a touring company. If not for her great ideas, I would have squandered my money away on myself. And I wouldn't have made nearly so many friends." He patted my shoulder fondly. He didn't have to say he was proud of me; I could see it in his eyes.

"Wow, Jillian," Howard said, surprising me by joining us from where he had been sitting alone, "I had no idea that all of this was your fault."

His remark cut, but I tried not to take it personally.

Grandpa was not so forgiving. "Watch your mouth, young man," he growled at Howard. "I've about had it with your bad attitude."

"What are you going to do about it, old man?" Howard ground out in response. "Leave me stranded on an island to starve to death? Oh wait, you've already done that."

I jumped up and physically stood between the two snarling men. "That's enough, you two. Knock it off."

Howard muttered indistinctly, and Grandpa just shook his head and turned in the other direction. Men.

Kenya brought us back to Grandpa's original question. "So, what were you thinking about just now, Jillian? Were you being brilliant like Captain Skippy said?"

I sat down again, watching the two men warily in case either decided to jump up and start swinging. "I don't know about that. But I was just thinking about how we've been sitting on the beach, watching the ocean—"

"And not seeing jack squat," Howard grumbled.

He wasn't wrong. "And I was just wondering if we'd be able to see something more if we got higher up." I pointed to the peak I'd been studying. "I was just trying to see if it might be possible to climb up there to get a better look."

Kenya sat up straight. "That's a great idea." Then she turned to Elodia and asked, "Why didn't we think of that?"

Elodia shook her head primly and said, "I blame the humidity."

Grandpa said, "I'd volunteer to hike up there with you, but"—he cut a look over at Howard—"I'm afraid some people would think I'm too old and frail to make the trip."

I happened to be one of those people, but I kept that to myself. "I'd be willing to try." I eyed the distant ridge skeptically. "I'm sure it'll be harder than it looks." That was saying something, because it looked pretty hard.

"I'll go with you," Kenya said. "And I'm sure Bridget will, too. It'll be nice to have a change of scenery." She cast a scornful glance at Howard.

It would be nice to get a break from spending so much time together. There was only so much negativity a person could take in one day. I wondered how Howard lived with himself, or how Elodia did, for that matter.

"Ask Carter to join you, too," Grandpa suggested. I didn't miss the way his eyes twinkled at the idea of letting me and Carter spend some time alone together. I'd made the mistake of mentioning our kiss the other day, and he had been trying to shove us together ever since. It was sweet—in a slightly annoying way. But I agreed to ask him, and I knew Carter would say yes.

When everyone was back together, and we all agreed that climbing a mountain was the best use of our time, Carter and Bridget agreed to the idea, and the four of us made a plan. I guessed that it was four miles away or so, and with the thickness of the trees and no path to speak of in that direction, the journey there and back would likely take us the better part of the day. So, we gathered up some of the food and stowed it in a woven palm bag that Kenya had fashioned in the previous days. I led out with Carter behind me, Kenya following him, and Bridget bringing up the rear.

The trek toward the mountain was harder even than I had anticipated, and after only a few minutes, we were breathless and sweating. As we moved further inland, away from the ocean, the ground began a gradual but discernible incline. After an hour of walking, we reached the first true hill. The incline was rocky and steep. I was already winded and tired, but we knew that we didn't have a lot of time to stop and rest. We each had a swig of coconut water, took a few deep breaths, and started up the hill.

Time passed at a crawl even slower than our progress. The vegetation was so dense and unstable that at times it felt like we fell back two steps for every one we took forward. But it wasn't in any of our natures to give up without laying everything on the table, so we pressed on. We reached the top of the first hill and paused to breathe, or pant as the case may be.

Ahead of us, the hill met a low space that immediately rocketed skyward. I groaned when I saw it, and Kenya looked like she was about to cry. Bridget dropped down in the tall grass, and Carter stood with his hands on his knees, taking long breaths as he struggled to calm his breathing. I placed both hands on my head and turned a slow circle, the realization sinking in that climbing a mountain in our condition was going to be impossible. One of us was going to faint if we kept this up, and someone was sure to get badly hurt.

*Damn, this island,* I thought. With the exception of finding the village and the orchard, everything seemed to be working against us. We were no closer to rescue today than we had been when we landed on the beach. We wouldn't be able to summit this mountain, and I couldn't help the despairing feeling that everything we tried was destined for failure.

Emotion washed over me, choking my constricted windpipe, and tears welled in my eyes. I had never felt more trapped or hopeless than I did right then. Facing an impassable cliff before me and an uncrossable ocean behind me. We were stuck here.

I sank to my knees, pressing my palms against my eyes, and a sob burst from me, followed by another, and another. I felt a hand on my shoulder, and the dam broke loose in my heart. "We're never going to get home," I cried. "We're going to die out here."

"Jillian." It was Carter, speaking to me gently, squeezing my shoulder.

But I couldn't stop the flow of despair now that it had begun. "There's nothing more we can try. No one is looking for us. They probably assume that we died already and now... now we probably will. We're going to die out here, and it's all my fault."

"Jillian—"

"No!" I looked up at him, tears streaking down my face. "You can't tell me that I didn't do this. I should have checked on Grandpa and Eric. I should have paid more attention. I should have checked the lifeboats the night before the crash. I should have known that the radio didn't work. I should have known all of that. That was my job, and I didn't do it good enough, and now we're all going to die, and it's all my fault!"

Bridget knelt beside me then, placing a comforting hand on my arm. "Hey. Hey, look at me." She waited until I looked into her face before going on, "We're all beyond spent. We're exhausted, and you are, too. Listen to me when I tell you that none of us blame you or Captain Skippy for the accident. It was a freak thing. It happens. The only thing we can do is fight our way out of this. Have your breakdown if you need to, but then you'd better get right back up again and help us find a way home. I won't take 'no' for an answer."

Her tough-love approach was exactly what I needed to hear. So, after a few minutes, I calmed myself down enough to take a few steady breaths and get up again.

She patted my arm twice and said, "Atta girl. Now, let's figure out what's our next try."

Carter put his arm around my shoulders and gave me a tight squeeze. "Well, I don't think trying to climb that cliff is a good idea," he said, nodding toward the rock face in front of us. "And I don't see another way to continue upward unless we start from the other side of the island."

"We can't do that today," Kenya interjected.

Bridget shook her head in agreement. "No, and I don't know if it'd do us much good. We can see enough of the horizon from here to know that we're not in sight of another island. And unless we plan to hike up the mountain and keep a watch every day, I don't know what more we can do."

I rubbed my hands down my face. "I'm sorry, you guys. I should have known better than to waste our time and energy with this. It was stupid."

"It wasn't stupid," Bridget countered with a stern look. "It just didn't have the results we wanted. You don't call an experiment a failure just because it didn't turn out the way you thought, right, Dr. Buckley?" She turned to Carter with a teasing smirk, but he didn't see it.

In fact, he seemed to have stopped paying attention to us altogether. He had turned away from us and was staring out at the ocean. "Carter?" He didn't react. I would have thought he'd be sick of staring at the sea by now. I said his name again and put my hand on his arm. My touch finally jarred him from his thoughts, and he turned to me with wide eyes.

"Do you see that? Or am I imagining things?" He pointed at the water, and I followed his finger with my heart in my throat.

"Where?" I scanned the horizon, but I didn't see anything other than clouds and distant waves.

"Do you see a ship??" Kenya and Bridget looked out, too, squinting in the direction Carter pointed. "I don't see anything."

"Look about halfway to the horizon," he said, still pointing.

I peered at what I thought he meant, but I didn't see a rescue boat. All I could see was—

"Rocks?"

"Big rocks. They've got to be at least a league out."

Kenya chimed in again, "Can you speak land-lubber for us dumb folks?"

"About three miles," I translated.

Carter nodded. "And do you see what I see?"

My heart leapt, knowing at last what he must have spotted. I couldn't see it myself, so his eyesight must have been stronger than mine. But Kenya and Bridget realized what it must be at the same time I did.

"The ship!"

I could barely discern a white smudge against the black and gray rocks. That must have been where our yacht wrecked, and it was still there, pinned against the rocks.

"Wow," I breathed. "I never thought we would see her again."

"Neither did I."

Bridget let out a low whistle. "It's so crazy. It seems so much closer than I thought. When we were on the raft, we didn't see this island at all. I thought we had drifted for a hundred miles."

"Well, that explains why you washed up on the beach, Jill," Carter said. "You didn't really have all that far to go."

"But why didn't we see the island from the wreck?" Kenya asked, dumbfounded.

"It was really stormy," Bridget deduced. "I'll bet the island was hidden behind the clouds and rain. Plus, we weren't really looking for land. We were just trying not to die."

"Still trying not to die," Kenya muttered.

The four of us stood together, staring out at the cause of our woes. I didn't know what to say or do. We had found a ship at last, but it was a useless one. It's not like we could swim out there, patch the hole, and then sail back home in the lap of luxury.

My mind's eye was captured by memories of the soft beds and the plush couches, the comfortable air conditioning and the generously stocked—

I gasped and slapped a hand to the side of my face. "The kitchen!" I turned to Carter, eyes wide with excitement. "What if there's still food on board? We always pack plenty of non-perishables. And tanks of drinking water. Not to mention water bottles."

Bridget gasped, and Kenya goggled at me. Carter's mind went back to planning mode.

"We could fix up the lifeboat, don't you think? One or two of us could go out there, gather supplies, and bring them back."

"It wouldn't be a rescue," Kenya said, "but it would keep us alive for who knows how much longer. And, hey, there's probably a first aid kit on board, right? Captain Skippy could definitely use some new bandages."

Bridget jumped up and down, pumping her fists in the air. "That's a great idea. Let's do it!"

My thoughts had snagged on Kenya's words though. First aid kit... Then it was my turn to scream.

"A radio." I grabbed Carter by the shoulders and shook him in excitement. "The ship has a working radio!"

# 15


*JILLIAN*

**W**ithout waiting for a response, I grabbed Carter's hand and started running. He stumbled a few steps before straightening up enough to keep up with me. I heard Kenya and Bridget's shouts for me to wait and explain myself, but I felt frantic desperation surge through my body.

*The ship has a radio.*

It was suicidal to consider running down the steep incline we had just climbed, so I slowed to the fastest downhill hike I could perform safely, still clutching Carter's hand with my heart pounding in my ears.

"Wait, Jill," Carter said, his voice bouncing in the fast rhythm of our feet on the slope. "I thought the radio was disconnected. That's why Eric couldn't send an S.O.S. as soon as he realized we were lost."

"It was," I answered in a breathy voice, panting with adrenaline and exertion now. "It is. But I just remembered." I quit speaking until we reached the bottom of the hill. I was ready to take off running again, but Carter held me back until Kenya and Bridget reached us. Bridget clutched her side, her breathing labored, and Kenya put her hands on her knees, gasping like she'd just emerged from the deep end of a pool. I sucked in a few deep breaths, trying to keep my heart from banging right out of my ribcage, before trying to speak again. "I remembered that there's an old emergency radio on the ship."

"What?!" all three of them shouted.

"I forgot about it until you mentioned a first aid kit. He kept it with the big first aid kit in the galley. The radio belonged to Grandpa Skippy's first boat, and he brought it over as a spare. We haven't ever needed to use it, and since it's been years since we got it, we both just forgot about it. But I'm sure it's there. I'm positive it'll work!"

We had to get that radio. It had to work.

Halfway back, Bridget called for another rest, and we stopped in the shade of a large palm tree and opened the last remaining coconut with a sharp rock Kenya had fashioned into a primitive knife. We each got a single sip of the coconut water, then she set to work cracking open the nut so we could divvy up the white fruit inside.

As I sat in the weeds, a sharp rock digging into my thigh, too tired to do much else other than chew the coconut, I began to construct a plan. "We need to go back to our first beach and get the lifeboat," I said.

"What for?" Bridget asked.

"To get us out to the wreck," Carter deduced. "Right?"

I nodded. But Kenya thought of something I hadn't. "But the motor doesn't work anymore," she said. "It got busted when we capsized after the wreck. And there's no emergency oar. Captain Skippy said there was one, but it must have fallen out when we capsized. That's why it took us so long to drift to the island. We were at the mercy of the waves."

I rubbed the back of my hand across my forehead and grumbled, "It's always something, isn't it?"

I let my head fall back and my eyes close, thinking. I didn't know anything about repairing a boat motor. What could we use to make an oar?

"I'll bet Howard could fix it," Bridget said after a moment.

The three of us looked at her blankly.

She nodded, undeterred. "The other day on the beach, before he started demanding favors, he told me that his dad was a mechanic and that, before he went to business school, he had worked as his dad's assistant for a few years."

"You're kidding," I breathed, dumbfounded. In my whole life, I never would have guessed that Howard Lovell used to be a mechanic.

"But we don't have any tools," Bridget pointed out, deflating a little.

"There was a little tool kit in with the first aid kit," I suddenly remembered. "It might not have everything he'll need, but at least it's something."

Kenya jumped to her feet. "Well, then what are we waiting for? Let's go get the lifeboat!"

We didn't waste any more time. We hastened back to the village and found Elodia, Howard, and Skippy sitting in the shade of a large palm tree, talking sedately. They started when they heard us tramping into the village, and before anybody could properly catch their breath, we were headlong into explaining our discoveries and realizations.

Skippy was especially surprised to learn how close the island was to the shipwreck, and he dropped down to the sand and began drawing a map from memory, trying to figure out just where we were in relation to our original course. While he was doing some mental gymnastics, trying to figure out velocities and distance over time, the rest of us discussed the best options for fetching the lifeboat and repairing the engine.

We decided that the lifeboat was large enough that it would take at least four people to lift and carry it, but even so, it was too wide to fit through our marked jungle path. We would have to bring it over via the beach.

Kenya was not on board with carrying the extremely heavy and awkward raft across the island with no water. As a testament to our collective cognitive deterioration, she suggested the most obvious idea ten minutes into our discussion: "Why don't we just fix the motor there at the beach? Then we won't have to carry it anywhere."

Carter and I looked at each other with mirrored expressions of idiocy. Why hadn't we thought of that sooner?

Because it was the "no duh" obvious thing to do, we altered our discussion and finally asked Howard if he would take point on the motor repair. In the back of my mind, I was already devising a plan to build oars out of wood borrowed from these huts, if he refused.

To my surprise, Howard agreed easily, and Elodia volunteered to go with him to assist in the repair.

"I'm ready to do something," Elodia explained, stretching her arms over her head. "Let's finally get out of here!"

Kenya volunteered to go, as well, but I guessed that her motives had more to do with making sure Howard didn't fix the engine then ditch the rest of us than it did with being truly helpful.

To ensure that Kenya and Howard didn't kill each other, Carter and I said we could come, too. And so, the five of us set off toward the beach with our mini tool set and the first aid kit—just in case.

It felt good to have a plan, and even better to feel the first inklings of hope. Maybe we'll make it out of this after all...

***

If I was to guess, if we had asked Howard Lovell to repair mechanical equipment that did not have a direct relation to saving his own life, he probably would have pretended that he had never even heard of motor oil before. As it was, he agreed to try repairing the motor under the condition that we never speak of his hidden skills to anybody. Everyone agreed, but I had a sneaking suspicion that Kenya had her fingers crossed behind her back.

The reason for Howard's secrecy regarding his mechanical skills soon became evident: he was not very good. Sure, he knew more about engine repair than I'd ever heard of, but when it came to the actual work, he was all thumbs. He blamed it on never having worked on a boat motor before, but I privately thought it was more to do with lack of practice.

It was nice to have something productive to do, but it was even better to have a surge of hope in the group. The despair in the air had been a choking hazard, and now that some of the gloom had abated just a little, it felt easier to take a deep breath.

The tool kit was bare bones, with an adjustable wrench, a pair of pliers, and a screwdriver with a bit that could be flipped to either standard or Phillips head. Howard removed the motor cover and started poking around at the engine, muttering to himself. I watched for a little while, but before long I became bored of staring at metal parts that I didn't understand, so I sat beside Kenya and Elodia on the sand and let Carter be Howard's assistant. The two of them didn't have much to say to each other, but they worked well together as they showed off their macho bravado and repaired the motor.

Kenya sighed slowly and turned her face up toward the sky. "What's the first thing you'll do when you get home?" she asked us dreamily.

I pondered that question as I watched the cotton-candy clouds drift lazily across the blue-blue sky. "Shower," I answered after brief consideration. "Then eat an entire pizza and drink three gallons of water." I smiled to myself. "After that I'm going to sleep in my own bed for a week, and then maybe I'll call Carter and see if he wants to, like, get a sandwich or something."

Kenya snorted a laugh and Elodia grinned broadly. "I'm going to move up my wedding date," Elodia announced.

With her brow scrunching down into a scowl, Kenya asked, "You're still going to marry Howard? He's not even... very nice. You see that, right?"

Elodia cocked her head to the side, impressing me by not becoming offended. "I'm more sure now than ever." She cast a loving gaze at her fiancé, who was banging on a bolt with the wrench and swearing heavily. "The best thing about Howard is that he always gives it to me straight. I never have to wonder what he's really thinking. And yeah, sometimes he doesn't say things with much tact. But he usually says what anybody else would be too afraid to. I like that about him. I like knowing where I stand. Not playing games. That's important to me."

A shadow flitted briefly across her face, and I wondered for the first time what Elodia's past must have been like. Had she been hurt by someone's games and lies? I couldn't help but guess that must be the case. But the way she looked at Howard as she talked about honesty made me realize that there must be more to her relationship with Howard than I could understand. And that was okay.

"How soon do you want to get married?" I asked her.

Still looking fondly at Howard, she grinned cheekily and said, "I think we're going to elope."

Kenya looked startled, but I just laughed. "You know, if you're that desperate to get married, Skippy is a sea captain. So he can marry people."

Elodia chuckled. "I hadn't thought about that! That would be something though, huh? Show up back home—Surprise! We're not dead and we got married without all of you!"

We were laughing lightly at that when Howard's voice cut in, "Will you girls quit giggling? I'm trying to concentrate over here!"

And then, knowing more about Howard and Elodia than I did before, his gruffness didn't bother me so much. After all, he was just being honest. Right?

"Sorry, Howard," I said for the three of us. Then I pushed up from my relaxed posture in the sand and stood up, dusting the sand from my pants. I walked over and stood beside Carter, who was holding tools out for Howard, waiting for him to request one.

"How's it going?" I asked sotto voce.

"No idea," Carter replied with a minute shrug. "He stopped swearing a few minutes ago, though, so that's got to be progress."

He had been tinkering with the engine for over an hour by that point, and there seemed to be more pieces on the ground than there were left in the motor case. My hopes for using the motor to get us out to the wreck were beginning to dim. Time for Plan B...

Just then, with a pop and a final curse, Howard pulled something free from the motor with a triumphant grunt. "Gotcha," he said, holding up a shard of metal between his fingers and examining it in the sun.

To my untrained eye, the metal shard looked like a thick spring, curling around itself, but it was too jagged and uneven to be a real spring. "What is that?" I asked, peering at the metal shard.

"Who knows?" Howard said. "I'd guess it's part of the wreck. It was caught around the impeller here." He pointed to a small fan-looking thing. "It was twisted up in there and stopped the motor from pulling in water to cool it down. The motor must have shut itself off when it started overheating."

He handed me the twisted metal, and I studied it. It was unremarkable in itself, but it was amazing that something smaller than my finger could have such a catastrophic effect on the boat's motor. "So, now that you've got this out—will it work?"

Howard frowned at all the pieces on the ground. "Only one way to find out. Let's put it back together. Elodia," he called over to his fiancée, "keep praying."

"Never stopped, baby!"

Elodia's prayers must have done the trick, because after another hour, Howard had reassembled the motor and we all worked together to push it and the raft into the water so he could try to start it.

We watched with bated breath as Howard turned the key once. Twice. Three times. And then...

*Vroooomm.* The five of us cheered, Kenya and Elodia hugged each other and jumped up and down, and Carter clapped Howard on the back. "You did it!"

Howard nodded, satisfied. "Let's get out to that ship and get the hell out of here."

***

By the time Howard got the engine running and had successfully proven that the raft was still seaworthy, it was late afternoon, and the sun was moving toward setting over the horizon. Though we were anxious to get out to the wreck and get whatever help we could, we didn't know exactly how far it was offshore, and it would be terribly unwise to venture out into the ocean just as the sun was going down. Being stranded on an island one more night was better than losing any of us to drowning at sea because we got turned around in the dark.

So we pulled the lifeboat back onto the shore, this time tying it to a sturdy palm tree to make sure it would still be there in the morning, and then we made our way back through the jungle to camp for a dinner of tropical fruit and rainwater.

I was so ready to go home.

# 16

## *CARTER*

That night, it was my shift to watch the signal fire, so I walked alone back to the beach and prepared for a sleepless night as I set up a little camp. And by set up camp, I mean that I gathered the softest-looking bamboo shoots I could find and made myself an uncomfortable cot and covered it with palm fronds. One of the fronds surprised me with a brilliant orange spider that both frightened the hell out of me and fascinated me. I never was much of an insect nerd, but in the absence of coral reef to study, spiders would suffice.

I didn't let him get on me because I didn't know if he was venomous, and I was more than confident that we didn't have a vial of antivenom back in our made-for-TV huts, but I watched him for a few minutes before finding a nice long stick to pick him up and escort him off to other adventures in the jungle.

It was nearly sunset when I settled down on my little cot beside the fire, and I knew that sleep was just about the farthest thing from a possibility. I didn't feel much like sitting and staring at the horizon for hours, though, either, so after checking that the signal fire was plenty bright, I got up again, brushed the sand from my pants, and decided to burn some nervous energy by walking the shoreline for a while.

The weather was magnificent, and if I wasn't stranded on an island, I might have even enjoyed my time on the beach. I found a stone to perch on while I looked out over the sunset-lit ocean and pondered my life.

After a deep inhale that sharply reminded me that our island was lacking a shower, I decided to use my atypical moment of privacy to take a bath in the ocean water. Seawater had to be better than dirt and sweat, and no ocean smell could ever be worse than the stench that was now likely a fundamental element in all my clothing.

Feeling like a twelve-year-old, I stood and looked all around me before disrobing and plunging into my bath. The lack of soap and shampoo did not deter me from scrubbing. Using handfuls of the fine white sand, I gave a thorough exfoliation to every inch of my body that could handle such rough treatment. For my face and other more delicate areas, I found a semi-soft palm leaf that I used as a washcloth to more gently cleanse my sore, sunburnt skin.

I gave the same treatment to my mangy clothes—or rather, what was left of them. My shirt had gotten a huge rip down the side upon arrival at the island, and my tan pants had received just as much punishment since then. Every inch of each article was stained with sweat, blood, and mud, stretched and snagged beyond recognition, and torn to shreds in some places. Still, some clothing was better than none, so I scrubbed them up and rinsed them out as best I could, then set them out on a rock on the beach to dry in the warm, humid air. When I got back to the fire, I planned to string up a branch or pole near the flames so I could hang the clothes and let them dry a little faster. They would end up smelling like smoke, but that was still an improvement over the Castaway Perfume I'd been enjoying to that point.

The cool water had taken some of the ache from my tired muscles, so when I finally finished my bath and laundry adventure, I was able to walk back to the signal fire feeling refreshed.

When my underwear was tolerably dry, I wriggled back into a semi-clothed state and stretched out on my bamboo and palm leaf cot, tucking my hands behind my head as I gazed up at the picture-perfect twilight sky.

I let my mind wander as I watched a few birds soar overhead. Before long, the birds were replaced by bats, their unfamiliar screeches drawing my focus as they dove and swooped in and out of the palm trees, nipping up any flying insect they came upon. I decided that bats were given a bad reputation. They were fascinating. I watched them carefully, studying the frantic motion of their wings, a blur in the twilight, trying to memorize the sounds they made as they called to each other. I imagined what they must have felt as they hunted their dinner, knowing, as they must, that with their bellies full, they would get to return to their homes to rest and relax. I missed that feeling. I longed to go home.

A long time passed, and the sun set beyond the watery horizon. A million million stars appeared in the blue-black sky, winking to life one at a time until suddenly it was impossible to imagine that they had been there all along, hiding in plain sight, veiled by a mere sheen of atmosphere and light waves. I stared at the heavens, feeling small and helpless, more lost than ever. Alone, yet not alone. Insignificant, yet still breathing. Was there a purpose in all of this? How could there be? And yet how could there not be?

My mind twirled thoughts like a drummer using a well-loved set of sticks, and I lost myself to thought, fully, for the first time in ages.

So I was startled when I heard footsteps on the rocks behind me. I sat up with a start and turned to find Captain Skippy stepping off the jungle path. He had his hands tucked into his once-white slacks. He wore no shoes, and his white captain's shirt was more hopelessly stained than my own clothes had been. Even so, his clothes made him stand out in the darkness, lit up by the firelight and the spotlight of stars.

Feeling my shoulders relax after my surprise at his arrival, I waved him over and made room for him to sit beside me on the cot. He accepted my wordless invitation and sat heavily at my side. He dropped his elbows onto his knees and stared into the fire.

"What are you doing up so late?" I asked him, guessing that it was nearly midnight by then.

He released a long breath, not taking his gaze from the flames. "I remembered."

Spine straightening, I turned to more fully face him. "You remembered what happened on the bridge?" I guessed.

"I think so. But I'm not... maybe it was just a dream." His odd answer surprised me.

Confusion and eagerness warred for attention. "What did you remember?"

"It might have been a dream," he hedged. "Because I didn't expect..."

"What?"

The firelight etched shadows into the wrinkles on Skippy's brow, and concern speared through me at the look in his eyes. "Someone else was there. On the bridge that night." He looked up at me at last. "I didn't just hit my head. Someone attacked me."

My mouth went dry. "What are you saying?"

"I don't think this shipwreck was an accident after all."

My pulse jumped from its lazy plod to a gallop. My jaw hung slack and my baffled mind couldn't come up with anything to say besides, "What?"

Skippy shook his head. "I don't remember all of it yet, but I do remember that. Everyone had gone to bed. It was late and I had just gotten a fresh cup of coffee to help me stay awake. I had the radio up, listening to some chatter between cruise ships that were not too far out from us—nothing terribly interesting, but it was enough to keep me alert. Then, someone opened the door and two men ran inside. It was pretty dark, so I couldn't see them well, but I didn't recognize them, even in the dark. I shouted at them, and they seemed surprised to see me at the helm. One of them ran at me with a club, but the other had a gun. What happened next is a blur. I think I tried to fight them off, but one of them got me..." he reached up and gingerly rubbed the bandage on his temple. "Next thing I remember, I was lying on the floor on the bridge, kind of wedged beneath my chair, and I saw another man's body right beside me. He was dead. Then I heard two men talking to each other, so there must have been another guy on the ship somewhere when the first two came in and jumped me. They were saying something about their skiff. I think I must have hurt the dead guy when we were fighting, but I don't remember that." He blinked at the fire. "You would think I'd remember killing someone..."

I gulped but couldn't form any words.

He continued his spotty recollection, "The two other guys lifted the dead guy off the floor and talked about getting him back to their skiff before coming back to get 'her.'"

My blood turned icy. "Who?"

He shook his head. "They didn't ever say who—just 'her.' But from what had happened so far, I wasn't about to sit quietly while they attacked someone else on my ship! After they dragged their dead friend off the bridge, I pulled myself up to the helm. My mind was already foggy—they hit me pretty hard, and I was going in and out..." He cleared his throat then shook his head. "This is the part that's most blurry, so I don't know if I dreamed it, but considering we ended up on rocks and nowhere near where we were supposed to be, it's probably real."

"What?" I asked, feeling breathlessly desperate to hear the end of Skippy's story.

"I waited until I thought they would have had enough time to get back onto their own boat, and I just prayed that there were only three of them, and then I grabbed the throttle and just gunned it, hoping that we'd be able to get away from them before they got back on. And then... I blacked out." He released a long, heavy sigh. "That's all I remember, but if that's true, the wreck is completely my fault. I steered us to get away from those men, but I didn't steer us toward anything."

"We just took off out to sea," I summarized for him, imagining the scene he'd described and seeing the ship in my mind's eye, hurtling out across the black ocean toward the rocks that violently ended our cruise.

We lapsed into silence for a few minutes after that. I replayed Skippy's tale in my head, each element snagging new feelings of dread and concern. Someone had boarded the yacht in the middle of the night, in the middle of the ocean. Whoever it was might have followed The Flying Honeymoon from the port. And they were looking for someone—with obvious ill intent. But who would they have been looking for? And who were "they" to begin with? And the fact that Skippy had surged the ship forward into the unknown in an act of self-preservation changed the nature of this shipwreck from a mere accident to a... what? A crime scene? Still an accident, but not for the reasons we had suspected.

Goosebumps rose over my skin. What does that mean for us now? Were the men who had attacked the ship still looking for us—and their victim, whoever "she" was? If someone arrived on the beach to rescue us, would we even be able to trust them? Skippy hadn't seen his attackers' faces, and he had sustained an extreme wound after, so he couldn't be depended on to identify potential wolves who might arrive in sheep's clothing.

My brain churned through this information, coming up more concerned and confused each time I sifted through it.

Fundamentally, the information didn't change our situation: we were still stranded with no way to communicate and no way home. But did it mean we should be more cautious when we send out a distress signal, once we get ahold of the emergency radio from the ship?

I scratched the stubble along my jaw then expelled a heavy breath. "There's one bit of good news," I said, breaking the long silence. When Skippy looked at me with confusion, I couldn't help smiling a little as I said, "Your memories are coming back. That must mean you're healing. No lasting damage."

He hmphed with a shake of his head. "I'm sure that will make Jilly happy. But what's the point of healing up if we're just going to die out here? Or worse—get rescued only to have one of us hurt by pirates?"

His use of the term pirates amused me, but it seemed fitting for the situation. "We've got to tell everyone first thing in the morning," I decided. "Maybe someone knows something about these guys. Maybe she even knows who might be after her?"

Skippy shook his head slowly but didn't dispute my conclusion. "Never a dull moment out here, huh?" he grumbled, turning a smooth stone between his fingers. "I'll bet this isn't the kind of adventure you signed up for, eh, Professor?"

I chuckled with little mirth. "Being shipwrecked wasn't ever on my bucket list."

Skippy dropped the stone and went back to staring at the fire. "I just can't believe this is all my fault."

I didn't pretend to understand the complexity of what he must have been going through, so I just patted his shoulder. "You had limited options. You did what you thought was best. It's better than doing nothing."

"That's debatable."

I pushed to my feet and tossed a few more logs onto the fire. "Want me to walk you back to your hut? You'd better try to get some sleep."

Skippy stood but shook his head. "I can manage the jungle. See you in the morning."

I bid him farewell, then went back to my cot, staring out at the ocean with more questions than ever. Finally falling asleep sometime later and waking with the first blush of sunrise in the sky. With our plans to go out to the ship and Skippy's revelations, it was sure to be a full day.

***

# *JILLIAN*

The next morning dawned with pink and red clouds on the east horizon. I didn't know how late I had stayed awake the night before, tossing and turning with anticipation to get out to the wreck and finally start making some progress to get home. After only a few hours of sleep, the fatigue I felt would normally have made me want to roll over and hit the snooze button a few dozen times. But we had a plan. I sat up on my bamboo bed, wondering if this might be the very last time I'd sleep here. What a thought!

Grandpa was still soundly asleep and snoring raspily, so I left the hut as quietly as possible and went out to our makeshift bathroom—hoping that this would be the last time I used that, too. My skin ached for a shower and my teeth sobbed for a toothbrush.

When I returned to the village circle, I saw Carter returning also. He had told me before I went to sleep the previous night that he was going to sleep on the beach and get the signal fire going—since it had been neglected the day before. From the look of him now, I gathered that he hadn't slept well. He looked awful.

He grinned when he saw me, and I was grateful that I'd taken a moment to take a bite of papaya to chase away most of my morning breath. The distance between us closed within a few steps and, without requesting an invitation, I put my arms around his waist and held on tight.

"I missed you last night," I breathed into his stiff shirt. It was slightly damp, and I wondered if he had taken a midnight swim. Suddenly I was jealous of the ocean.

A chuckle rumbled through his chest, making me smile up at him. "You did not. I'll bet you were sawing logs all night."

I didn't suppress a little laugh at his accuracy and opted to snuggle into his chest again instead. "Bet it would have been more comfy with you there."

He hummed and gave me a firm squeeze before releasing me. "All in good time, Jilly." Then his expression turned unexpectedly serious, and he said, "We need to gather everyone together. Skippy has some news, and everyone needs to hear it."

Surprise hummed through my skin. News? What kind of news came in the middle of the night on a deserted island?

We didn't waste any time going to each cabin and waking everybody up to gather at the well for Grandpa's big news. After I woke up Grandpa, I tried to convince him to tell me his news before everybody else, but he wouldn't hear of it.

Kenya was irritated to be awoken at the break of dawn, but Bridget had already been awake. From the looks of the dark circles beneath her eyes, she hadn't gotten much sleep. I wondered what had kept her up, but there wasn't time to get into it before everyone was grumpily gathered around the well and all attention was focused on Grandpa Skippy. He had removed the bandage from his head, and I was relieved to see that his wound was healing remarkably well, and his eyes were clearer and sharper than I had seen since we left Florida.

"Our wreck was no accident," he began with no lead-in, eliciting gasps from everyone in the group except Carter and, oddly, Bridget. Demands for explanation rang out from the group, and Grandpa held up a hand to silence the outrage. Then he explained that his memories from the night before our wreck were slowly returning, and he revealed his experience with the strangers on the bridge. This revelation sent a ripple of shock through me and my friends. An attack? Who would do that? And why?

Evidently, Grandpa had talked all of this through with Carter the previous night, so when Grandpa was done recounting his story, Carter took the lead over the meeting. "The attackers said they were looking for a woman." His eyes studied the four of us women. "Do any of you know anything about that?"

Kenya reared back slightly, eyes wide with alarm. She looked to Elodia and Bridget, mouth agape. "Not me," she said, flabbergasted. "I'm just a kindergarten teacher. Nobody is looking for me!"

Elodia had the same shock and fear in her expression, and she shook her head slowly. "I don't know. I mean, we sometimes get threats from people because they're after Howard's money." She shot a fearful glance at Howard, and his expression mirrored her own confused anxiety. "But that hasn't happened in over a year. Not since we hired Tyron as our bodyguard."

"Can't rule it out," Howard interjected gruffly. "But it's news to me."

Accepting this, all eyes turned to me, and I shrugged. "Nobody would be after me, either," I said, not even having to search back in my memories to know this was true. "I don't have any enemies, and I don't have enough money for someone to go to much trouble to rob me."

"What about Skippy?" Howard asked, eyeing the captain assessingly. "He's got money. Maybe someone was after Jillian to try to get a ransom from the captain."

"That would be more likely to happen to you than to me," Grandpa countered hotly.

Howard didn't take that lying down. "Anybody with an internet connection knows that you stumbled head-first into your fortune, and it'd be just as easy to trick you into losing it."

"That's enough," Bridget said, surprising the men into silence as she stood, hands clenched into fists at her sides. "Fighting isn't going to help anything. And besides, I think they were after me."

Kenya was the only one to gasp at that. Bridget ignored her friend's theatrics and addressed Howard, "No offense, Mr. Lovell, but I'm pretty sure I've got more money than you, so a kidnapping and ransom attempt wouldn't be out of the ordinary."

"Are you serious?" Kenya cried.

Bridget continued to pretend not to hear her. "Besides that," she went on, her gaze now dropping to the ground, "I think I know who might want to hurt me. He warned me that something like this might happen."

"Who?" All six of us might have demanded this at the same time.

Bridget licked her lips. "My bodyguard. Patrick."

# 17

## *JILLIAN*

**N**one of us could make heads or tails of the revelation that Patrick had been involved in Grandpa's attack the night before the wreck. Bridget told us days earlier that Patrick had gotten mixed up with some criminals and had racked up a significant debt. According to Bridget, it was possible that Patrick had used Bridget's fortune as a bargaining chip as he got himself in deeper with the criminals.

"Do you think he'd really be willing to hurt somebody over money?" Kenya asked with wide eyes.

"I don't know," Bridget said miserably. "But I wouldn't put anything past his new buddy, Giovanni."

This part of the story was news to Carter, Skippy, and Howard. "The gangster?" Grandpa asked with a scowl. "What's he got to do with Patrick?"

Bridget explained Patrick's gang affiliations and his threats to her. "He warned me that if I didn't do what he asked, I might be in trouble. I think this is what he meant."

Howard shook his head. "This is just sick. Twisted."

I ran my finger through my hair. "Do you think... maybe Giovanni was in that boat we saw the other day? Do you think maybe he's looking for you? Or Patrick?"

Bridget looked just as confused and unhappy as the rest of us. "I guess it's possible. I mean, he can't exactly collect thousands of dollars from a man who's lost at sea."

Carter shook his head seriously. "If Giovanni was looking for us—even if it was to hunt down Patrick or something—he would have come to the shore if he had seen us out there. On the off chance it was one of them."

This did nothing to improve the spirits of the group. If someone was looking for one of us—hunting her down—we had to do everything we could to protect her. "That boat was close," I said after a few moments. "And if that much money is really on the line, I doubt that whoever is out here will give up easily." We had previously hoped that the boat would return, see our signal on the beach, come close enough to rescue us. But now... I shivered. I never thought my anxiety to see a ship on the horizon would shift to anxiety about who might be on it—and whom they might have wanted to harm.

"You're right," Skippy said. "They'll be back. It's only a matter of time."

The color had drained from Bridget's face. "So what do we do? Just sit tight and wait to be found?" This question had been asked repeatedly since we washed up on the shore. Never had it sounded so menacing.

Carter ran his fingers through his hair, then reflexively reached up as if ready to pull his glasses out of the pocket of his shirt. His hand stuttered slightly when he found no pocket and no glasses. He ran his fingers through his hair again instead. "We've got to come up with a plan. We can't just be sitting ducks, but we can't give up on getting rescued, either."

"Why don't we just give her up?" Howard cut in, standing and glaring at Bridget. "If handing over a celebrity is going to save the rest of our lives, that seems like good survival odds. Eight people wreck on an island and only one of them didn't make it back."

"Howard!" Elodia gasped at the same time Kenya growled, "How'd you like it if *you* didn't make it back?"

Skippy was on his feet now, too. "We aren't sacrificing anybody," he commanded in a booming voice. "We haven't made it this far just to turn on each other now." He looked at Howard with a steely gaze. Howard held the look for three full seconds before dropping his gaze to the ground and sitting down again on his rock.

"Carter's right," Skippy continued. "Rescue is still our top priority. In order to do that, we've got to get supplies from the shipwreck and find a way to call for help." He looked around at us, making a moment of eye contact with each castaway, silently impressing on us the seriousness of our situation. "We need to hurry to the wreck. Who wants to go?"

Everyone volunteered. The urgency in the air and the promise of hope spurred all of us into action. It was finally time to act, and the faster we did, the faster we could go home.

Because we didn't know how much we would be able to salvage from the wreck or what we could bring back, we concluded that not everyone would be able to go. In the end, we decided that Kenya, Bridget, and Skippy should go out to the ship. Skippy knew the ship best and would be best able to find what we needed, even if everything inside was scattered and broken.

Howard and Elodia stayed back at the village, and Carter and I decided to walk to the beach with the rest of the group to watch their progress. It was hard to stay away from the only interesting thing happening on the island.

Howard hadn't been any friendlier after his contribution yesterday than he had been the whole time we'd been on the island. I hadn't expected him to turn into Santa Claus after being included in a group breakthrough, but it was like nothing about him had changed at all since the wreck. Was it possible to go through a life-changing event like this and not allow your life to be changed?

He and Elodia went back into their hut and closed the door, to go back to sleep or plot our demise.

I took Carter's hand and followed Kenya, Bridget, and Skippy through the jungle to the beach where our lifeboat was still tethered to a tree. Relief swept through me like a warm wind: with our string of rotten luck, I wouldn't have been surprised if the lifeboat had been destroyed overnight. But everything was in order, and after we shoved the raft into the water, Skippy was able to start the motor on the first try.

I wanted to throw my arms around Grandpa and wish him luck and urge him to be careful and not take unnecessary risks, but I knew from experience that such an outpouring of affection would not be well received or reciprocated. Instead, I opted for his customary handshake and terse words of well-wishes.

He accepted my handshake, but then he shocked me to my core and wrapped his arms around me and pulled me in tight. "I love you, Jilly," he murmured into my hair. "And I'll be back real soon."

Tears pricked my eyes at his affection. This was the kind of love I'd longed for from him and... here it was. I squeezed him tight then pulled away before he could start to regret his decision to hug me.

"Be careful," I said, blinking back a tear.

He ruffled my hair, then turned to clamber into the lifeboat with Bridget and Kenya.

The lifeboat and three passengers departed from the beach without fanfare, each of them waving briefly to us before heading out into the choppy waves of the ocean. Before long, they were out of sight.

Carter and I sat together beneath the shade of a palm tree, each of us lost in thought as the morning wind blew around us and the birds sang above us in the treetops.

Wordlessly, he reached over and took my fingers in his hand, giving me a little grin before closing his eyes and relaxing against the tree trunk.

I watched him, a smile playing at the corner of my mouth as I thought about how remarkable it was that, amidst all the fear and craziness of this week, I had found someone to truly care about. Someone's hand to hold. An anchor in a chaotic sea of problems.

I might have thought that spending the last week stranded on an uninhabited island would have given me enough time for self-reflection, but nothing changed my perspective about my own life as dramatically as developing a relationship with Carter. His words echoed in my mind for hours, growing stronger with each reverberation.

Connections. Roots. Someone to come home to.

I knew that he hadn't been speaking of himself when he'd said those things, but as I'd contemplated the future—and a potential future without Carter in it—the words adhered to my soul alongside the image of his face. The memory of his hand in mine, his lips on my skin, his laughter in my ears, and his comforting presence in my heart.

It had only been a week since I'd met Carter, but I felt bonded to him with stronger cords than I had in any previous relationship. In my heart, I knew that I could love him. Easily. It would be effortless and wonderful. All I had to do was let go of the tight control I'd kept over my heart and let myself fall. For the first time since closing the door to love all those years ago, I thought I was ready to do it. I was ready to open up and share my life with someone else.

I wanted it to be Carter.

We sat in companionable silence for a long time, just watching the clouds and basking in the hope that, soon, we could call for help. Soon we could return to our normal lives.

***

They were gone for hours.

Since we had nothing better to do, Carter fashioned a spear out of a branch and waded into the water to try spear fishing. I stayed on the shore and built a small campfire that we could either use to cook a fish if he caught one or help Carter warm up after his swim.

He returned a while later with no bounty and tried to justify his failure by not having goggles or swim fins. I didn't argue.

We sat together and talked quietly about nothing of importance, periodically glancing up at the horizon, hoping to see the raft return. They had set out mid-morning, and the sun was on its way westward by the time we heard the motor in the distance. I got to my feet and walked toward the waves, straining my eyes until I saw them returning from the south. Kenya stood at the front of the raft and waved when she saw us on the beach.

All the stress of hours of anxious waiting dissipated at their arrival. Skippy steered the lifeboat expertly up to the shore, killing the motor before they bottomed out on the sand. Carter and I waded in to help pull the boat up onto the beach. I was itching to learn what they had found at the wreck.

Kenya jumped out of the lifeboat first, holding a sack full of canned goods and a can opener. "Feel like peaches? Or lima beans?" she asked with a huge grin.

I'd never been a fan of lima beans, but the thought of eating something other than coconuts or mangoes made my mouth water.

Bridget came next with an armload of blankets and sweaters.

I eyed her load with a dry mouth. "Did you get water?"

Bridget produced another sack from beneath the blankets, stuffed with bottled water. "Gotcha covered."

"Bless you."

Grandpa Skippy stood and lifted from the bottom of the lifeboat a radio. It was the size of a toaster and simpler than the models he regularly used as the yacht captain, but with the right touch, it would get the job done.

I took the radio with tingling fingers, holding my breath as I held the cool plastic casing in my hands.

"Does it work?" I asked breathlessly.

Grandpa's mouth pulled into a tight line, and he gave a minute shake of his head. "It won't complete a signal," he murmured, keeping his voice low enough that the others wouldn't hear.

My heart sank. "Can you fix it?"

He didn't look optimistic. "I can try."

"Did you tell them?" I asked, nodding toward Bridget and Kenya, who were busy showing Carter the goods they'd scored from the wreck.

"No. And if I can get it fixed fast, I hope I won't have to."

I nodded my approval then returned my gaze to the radio. It was old and worn—several of the textured knobs had been worn smooth from years of use. But I knew that it had worked last time Grandpa tested it. I wondered if it had somehow been damaged in the wreck. I didn't have a chance to discuss it with Skippy before Kenya returned to my side, eager to share her experience on board the waylaid *Flying Honeymoon*.

"I couldn't believe how much damage was done," she told Carter and me as we walked up the beach toward the jungle. "There's this huge hole in the side, and it's already covered in seaweed—"

"And birds!" Bridget interjected. "There must have been a hundred seagulls on it. The mess was unbelievable."

Kenya nodded excitedly. "And there were crabs and fish and stuff swimming down inside of it, too."

"How much of the ship was underwater?" I asked, directing the question at Grandpa Skippy.

He shook his head, looking like he'd just identified the body of a loved one. I supposed, in a way, he had. "The whole lower galley and cargo spaces are submerged. There was some water in the lower staterooms, too, but the sun decks and the bridge are all above the surface. But"—a shadow passed across his face—"there'll be no saving her. We might be able to get some equipment out, but she's a total loss otherwise."

A lump formed in my throat at the sorrow Grandpa felt over losing his precious gem—the ship he had worked for and dreamed of for his entire life. I didn't know a proper way to console this man, so I just patted his arm and said, "I'm so sorry, Grandpa."

He looked at me with eyes that were downturned in sorrow, but one side of his mouth lifted in a smile. "At least no one got hurt." He put an arm around my shoulders and gave me a quick squeeze. "And I've still got my granddaughter by my side. So it could have been worse."

The weight of that statement touched my heart, and I had to look away to keep from dissolving into a blubbering puddle of tears.

Carter gave me an encouraging nod, and we turned back to Kenya, who was explaining what the damage looked like from inside the ship and, in particular, how all of her belongings had been destroyed and sucked out to sea when the rocks had punctured the wall directly into her stateroom.

Their descriptions of the ship made me realize, once again, just how lucky we were to have survived without greater injury. And now we had a radio in hand! If we could get it working again, I would never again doubt the power of miracles.

***

When we reached the village, Grandpa took the radio into his hut and got straight to work. Kenya and Bridget ran to Elodia's hut to tell her about the food and blankets they'd scored, and I sat down on a log, staring at Grandpa's closed door, wishing him luck in fixing the radio.

The girls prepared dinner, and Carter convinced Howard to help him clean up. The evening stretched itself long in the sky, the light slowly fading, and it had been ages since Grandpa had sequestered himself in his hut.

Finally, I couldn't stand the suspense anymore, and I went into his hut. It was dim inside, and Grandpa knelt on the floor in front of the radio. He had gotten a screwdriver from our little tool kit, and the radio was in pieces on the bed.

I blinked at the mess. "What's wrong with it?"

Grandpa answered without taking his eyes off a little cluster of wires in his fingers. "Water damage. I found the first aid kit and the radio in the galley, completely submerged. I had to swim five feet deep to reach it."

I gulped. "Can it be fixed?"

"I think so." His eyes darted up to me at last. "But it'll take me all night."

I rubbed a hand over my face. Another night sleeping on a bamboo cot. Yippee. "Do you need anything?"

He shook his head. "No, just get some rest. I'll let you know."

***

He worked all night. He built a fire in the center of the hut and worked by its light. I didn't want to disturb him with obsessive questions, so I excused myself from our hut and bunked with Carter. It was a restless night, and I didn't sleep much, but spending the night alone with Carter wasn't half bad. My feelings for him

229

were deepening by the day, and I was in real danger of falling in love with him. We talked most of the night, then we kissed for a while longer than that, and eventually fell asleep side by side on his cot.

In the morning, I went to Grandpa's hut just after sunrise. I expected to find little parts strewn all over the floor and the radio sitting, gutted, on the bed. Instead, I was pleased to see the radio resting primly on the bamboo, perfectly reassembled. The microphone was in Grandpa's hand, and the speaker box was contentedly hissing.

My heart stammered and I rushed into the room. "Is it working?"

He looked up at me with a grin and a nod. "I'm close to getting a signal. Just a few more adjustments and I'll be ready to make the call."

I couldn't believe it: We were going to get help. We were going to go home! "I'll go tell everybody!" I swiveled and raced back out the door, halting when I was two steps away, then retracing my steps at once. I opened the door and stuck my head back in. "Can you wait to call until we get here?"

He barked a laugh and waved me out. "If you hurry. Go, already!"

I did.

After running around the village, I found everyone except Kenya, who was down at the beach by the signal fire. Grandpa set up the radio with careful, practiced fingers, kneeling on the floor beside the empty bed where the radio now lay. He turned dials slowly, and I could see the slightest tremble in his weathered hands. He needed this as much as any of us. Everything was on the line.

When it was time, Grandpa looked up at each of us and nodded solemnly. The five of us held our breath as we stood around Captain Skippy, watching him work his radio. The hissing changed in tone as Grandpa fiddled with the knobs, then suddenly a dull buzzing noise began. Grandpa's head twitched up, and the room held its breath. He'd found a channel. It was time.

He depressed the button on the side of the microphone and waited a second and a half before attempting to call out. "Mayday.

Mayday. Mayday. This is Flying Honeymoon. Repeat, this is Flying Honeymoon. Mayday. Mayday. Mayday."

He released the button, and we waited.

Static met the call. I saw Grandpa count to thirty under his breath before trying again. "Mayday. Mayday. Mayday. This is Flying Honeymoon. Does anybody read?"

More static. Grandpa started counting again.

My heart hammered against my chest, and I squeezed Carter's hand so tightly it was a wonder he hadn't shaken me off yet. I heard muttering to my left and glanced over to see Bridget clutching Elodia's arm. She whispered a prayer while tears streamed down the other woman's cheeks.

More seconds passed with no answer. My throat constricted until I felt like I couldn't breathe. All the energy of my soul was focused on the radio. On that static buzz. On the fleeting hope that someone would hear our distress call. Someone answer, I pleaded. You've got to answer!

The captain did not give up. He tried again. And we waited.

Tears burned my eyes, and my anxious breaths were transforming into heartbroken sobs. This had to work. It just had to work!

"Mayday. Mayday. Mayday. This is Flying Honeymoon. We've run aground. Does anybody copy?"

And then the static broke. It crackled, and a voice spoke over the speaker. "I copy you, Flying Honeymoon. It's good to hear from you. What is your location? We've been looking for you."

Elodia burst into tears and flung herself at both Howard and Bridget at the same time. I pressed my free hand over my tear-streaked face and looked at Carter. His eyes were wet with tears, and his chin trembled with overwhelming relief. Someone heard us: Someone is out there!

"We're going to get out of here," I whispered to him, my voice breaking at the end. "We're really going to go home!"

***

The biggest complication in calling for a rescue was that we didn't know precisely where we were. But the good news was that we had connected with someone who had GPS and a map and a working knowledge of the islands in this area. And the even better news was that we were located on the former filming location of a well-known television series. So, someone had to know the coordinates for that, surely. Grandpa spoke with the man on the other side of the radio waves for many long minutes as they tried to pinpoint where we had landed. With our physical description of the land and the dead giveaway of the filming location, Grandpa and the man on the radio nailed in our coordinates in no time.

We were near the Bahamas, on the southwest side of the largest island, and about sixty miles from land. Since we had been sailing toward Nassau the night before the wreck, we could only guess that when Grandpa had had his episode and collapsed at the helm, he had inadvertently turned the wheel and dramatically changed our direction from eastbound to southbound.

And, most important of all, our new friend on the radio was going to call for help.

I didn't know if there were boats out actively searching for us, or if help was nearby, but I guessed that, if the rescue ship was coming from the Bahamas, it would probably take six or seven hours for them to reach us.

"I guess we'd better start packing," Bridget said, her eyes bright. That set us all in motion. Excited energy surged through us, and I saw more life in my new friends than I had in a week. Grandpa had been recovering so well over the last few days, but the mental energy of fixing the radio plus the emotional strain of remembering the trauma of our wreck sapped him of his energy. He sat with the radio on the rock wall and watched all of us hustle and gather the minimal items we had seemingly strewn all over the village. Seriously, we had washed up on the beach with nothing and yet we had crap all over the village.

About an hour after we got in touch with help over the radio, Bridget suddenly remembered that Kenya didn't know that we'd had contact, and she set off at a run down the road to tell her the great news.

It took us about twenty minutes more to gather everything up, but then we were ready to go. And we only had five hours to kill. I sat next to Carter on the wall, and Grandpa and the Lovells joined us. We didn't have much to say, so I spent some time looking around the village and the lush jungle that surrounded us and felt weirdly sentimental. Who would have ever guessed that I might be sad to leave this place?

That may have been the wrong word. I certainly wouldn't miss the uncertainty and fear that came with being a castaway, but now that I knew that I would never be here again after this... I guess I just wanted to commit its beauty to memory. I learned a lot about myself during this journey. I fell halfway in love with an incredible man, and I had made new lifelong friends. So, I guess it wasn't all bad.

"We might as well head down to the beach," Elodia said, standing and brushing her hands down the front of her pants. "I won't be sorry to leave this place." She cast a look around and shuddered theatrically. "It still gives me the creeps."

Howard stood and, in a move that surprised us all, extended a hand to Grandpa Skippy, helping him to his feet and then giving his arm two firm pumps. "I want to thank you for taking care of us, sir. You did more than you needed to, and... I'm sorry for the things I said. I didn't mean it."

Grandpa nodded and gave Howard's hand one final shake. "Apology accepted."

The moment was serious but sweet, and it was one of the few times I'd seen Howard as a real person and not a business tycoon. It was refreshing to see the human side of him. It made me hate him a little bit less.

Howard released Grandpa's hand and took Elodia's instead, then they walked together toward the road. Grandpa, Carter, and I exchanged looks. "I guess it's time to go."

I nodded and took Grandpa's hand with my free one. "Let's go home." So, with Carter on one side and Grandpa at the other, we followed the Lovells toward the beach. I could already imagine the sweetness of our rescue. We would all be there, huddled around the signal fire when, at long last, one of us would spot a ship on the horizon. It would be a distant, gray speck, and we would wonder if it was an illusion, a mirage, or a product of our imagination. But then it would get bigger, we'd see the colors of the rescue flag—would it be from the U.S. or from the Bahamas? It would feel like ages, but it would only be a matter of minutes before the boat would be close enough to see people onboard. They would wave at us and call out. Everything would be okay. They would send out a little skiff and a doctor on board who would finally get Grandpa the help he badly needed. They would take us back to their rescue boat where there would be hot tea and donuts on board. And running water and a bathroom. They'd let us use their satellite phone. I could call my mom and dad. We would be safe. It would be over.

It was coming soon, and I picked up my pace a little, unable to wait a moment longer than necessary.

We walked less than a quarter of the way down the road toward the beach, when we heard someone up ahead. I craned my neck until I could see around the trees enough to spot Kenya running toward us, her hair flying out behind her. She spotted us about the same time I recognized her, and she sped up, waving at us as she approached.

"A boat!" she cried. "The boat is here. They're here! We're saved! Come on—hurry!"

Already? The thought flitted, unbidden, through my mind.

Howard and Elodia didn't need to be told twice. They took off at a dead run toward the beach. Kenya hung back just long enough to repeat her message to the three of us before dashing back the way she had come.

"Wow," Carter said, voicing the apprehensive surprise I felt. "That was fast."

"Someone must have been closer to us than we thought," Grandpa surmised, not sounding surprised. "It's common for a ship to come rescue if they determine that they're closest. It may be the Coast Guard, or it could be just a Good Samaritan. Either way, I'll be glad to see them."

What about the attackers? What about Patrick and his ties to that gang? What if it's not our rescue?

I pulled on Carter's hand to slow him down. His expression told me plainly that he was concerned about the new boat, too. "We'll go meet them," he said, "but move with caution."

Without a better alternative, I agreed, and we followed Skippy to the beach.

At last, we rounded the final bend in the road and our view to the beach opened. The sliver of the ocean we could see didn't hold a boat, but I continually scanned the horizon as we neared the water. We found the rest of our group standing around the signal fire, waving at the water. When we cleared the tree line, I finally caught my first look at our rescuers.

It wasn't any wonder I hadn't seen the boat from the road. I had expected a large vessel—a freighter of some kind or even a cruise ship. Instead, a dark speedboat cut through the water, heading toward our signal fire.

Something twisted in my gut at the sight of the boat. Why was I nervous? It's not like our rescuers would care that I hadn't brushed my teeth or combed my ratty hair for a week. They knew what they were getting into.

Ignoring the squirmy feelings in my tummy, I walked with Carter onto the beach, joining the others as we waited for the boat to get near enough to see the people on board. Kenya came to my side and wrapped her arms around my neck, her face wet with tears.

"I can't believe it's finally over," she wept.

I returned her embrace, grinning widely. "We made it."

"Hey, look at that," Howard's voice sounded above the rest of the chatter, "there's a second boat."

We all turned again to the ocean. Sure enough, coming into view behind the first boat was a second. Both were dark-colored and neither had any markings or flags flying. "They must be private vessels," Grandpa said, scowling out at the sea. "But they're not fishing rigs."

I watched them, feeling a knot form in my stomach. "Don't they seem kind of small to be this far from the mainland?"

The first boat was within a hundred yards of the shore now, and the noise of the engine died. They coasted for a ways, leaving white wake churning behind them until slowing to a smooth crawl through the waves.

At last, we could make out a person on the deck. He wore dark clothes, but he waved his arm over his head, calling out something we couldn't understand. We all waved in return. A second person joined the first on the deck, followed by two more. They were close enough now that we could almost make out their features. Then a fifth man joined the first four and he held a long, thin object vertically in his hand. It was thin at the top, but thick and boxy on the bottom.

My heart thudded in my ears. "Is that a gun?" I breathed.

Why would our rescuers be armed? Did they think we were a threat?

Then, a thickly accented voice shouted through a megaphone, the crackly words beating against the serenity of the beach. "Bridget Foster?" the voice asked. "Do you have Bridget Foster with you?"

All heads swiveled toward Bridget, and she took a step backward, narrowly missing stepping into the signal fire.

Howard snorted. "The joy of being famous," he grumbled, unkindly.

Bridget's brow was furrowed, and she looked at me and Grandpa. "Why would they single me out?" she asked. "The man on the radio was worried about all of us."

That was true. The man we had spoken to had had the passenger and crew list that Grandpa had entered into his computer at the office back in Florida. Our names had been publicly broadcast for the last week as Coast Guard and military ships had searched in vain for us. Sure, Bridget was the most famous among us, but from what the man had said, it seemed like we were all household names by now.

The megaphoned voice repeated the question then added, "We need to know Bridget is alive before we can bring you on board."

Okay, now that didn't make any sense. "This feels weird," I finally admitted aloud. I looked at Grandpa, and he had a scowl on his brow and concern in his eyes. "I don't like this."

"Neither do I."

"That makes three of us," Carter added in a low voice.

The second boat pulled up alongside the first and four more men were visible on the deck. I saw two more rifles.

Acting purely on adrenaline-fueled impulse, I grabbed Bridget by the arm and hauled her backwards, away from the water. "Everybody back into the jungle," I shouted. "Now!"

Confused but equally concerned, the seven of us turned from the fire and ran up the sand toward the trees. The men on the boats recognized our retreat for what it was, and they began shouting at us. I heard splashes as a few of them jumped into the water to pursue us. Then, to my right a section of sand exploded upward just as a gunshot echoed from behind us.

"Run!" I screamed. Turning to flee, I felt Carter's hand slip from my grip, and I looked back to see him hunched, doubled up over his left side. He looked up at me with wide, terrified eyes. And then I saw a bright crimson stain seeping through his T-shirt between his fingers.

Carter had been shot.

# 18

## *CARTER*

I hit the **sand face-first**, lava-hot pain slicing my side wide open. A cry was strangled from my lungs as I hit the ground. Shock stuttered through my body. I had been shot. *Shot!*

A scream sounded somewhere above my head and soon I felt hands on my shoulders, turning me over in the sand to look up at the sun. Fiery pain erupted anew from my right side, and I gasped, choking on the pain.

Jillian dropped to her knees beside me, clutching my shoulders and crying my name.

"I'm okay," I ground through my teeth, never having uttered such a bald-faced lie before. "G-go on without me. I'll catch up."

"Like hell," Jillian breathed. "Get up. Can you get up?" She looked back over her shoulder, eyes wide. "They're coming, Carter! We've got to move!"

With a herculean effort, I turned over again and pushed to my feet. Before I knew it, we were running into the jungle.

Pain clawed at my side as I fought to keep up with the group. Jillian stayed at my side, tugging me along, not ditching me to save herself like she should have done. All the while, she threw wide-eyed glances over her shoulder, cussing under her breath. I didn't have the spare energy to waste looking behind me, so I didn't know if we were being chased, but the shouts from the incomers and the gunfire had been plenty of motivation for me to run as fast as my injuries would allow.

The seven of us rushed into the jungle, and at Skippy's urging, we left the path and scattered into the trees. I wouldn't have made it very far without Jillian. With each step we took, the pain in my side ratcheted, and before too long I felt hot blood creeping over my hip and down my leg.

I hissed in a breath through my teeth to fight back a howl of pain. Jillian clutched at me and pulled me into a tight group of trees that offered more shelter than the rest. She helped me lean against a tree as I fought to catch my breath and not scream and remain conscious.

"Keep running..." I finally said in an agonized whisper. I suppressed another groan as a fresh wave of pain stole through me. "I'll catch up in... just a minute."

Jillian's eyes were wide and frightened as she split her attention between trying to help me not die and watching for pursuers. "We've got to find a place to hide," she whispered on a quick breath. Her eyes flicked around the space. When she had settled on a plan in her mind, she took my arm once again. "We're not far from the caves. Do you think you can make it?"

Knowing arguing was going to be pointless, I nodded and struggled back to my feet, feeling my consciousness slip at the edges. "Just h-hold on to me," I stammered, grabbing at her shoulder. "I can make it."

She slung my arm over her shoulders and wrapped hers around my waist, taking on most of my weight. I was so tired already and getting weaker. She pushed us forward, and I could feel her panting, but she didn't complain. I fought to keep my focus and put one foot in front of the other.

Our progress was painfully slow, but we didn't see another person in the trees as we made our way toward the caves. Time passed in a red haze. I couldn't catch my breath, sweat poured from my face, and I began to tremble so fiercely that I could scarcely keep myself upright.

Finally, my legs gave out on me, and I collapsed to the forest floor. Jillian dropped to her knees beside me, pulling at me to try to help me get up again.

"I-I can't. I'm sorry." I swallowed hard as I huffed for breath, struggling not to vomit all over Jillian. "Go without me. Find somewhere safe to hide."

"I am not leaving you," was her immediate, stubborn reply. "I can... carry you."

Delirious as I was, I still managed a quiet laugh. "I love you, Jill, but you are not carrying me." Strong as I knew she was, I had four inches and sixty pounds on her. "You've gotta keep safe until help comes."

When she spoke, her voice was a broken whisper, and I looked up to see tears pooling in her eyes. "I don't know if help is coming. What if these guys, whoever they are, are the only ones who know we're here? What if they're the ones we've been talking to all morning?"

I adjusted my position so I could rest my head on the ground. I couldn't think straight and keep my head up at the same time. Thinking alone was a supreme challenge. "Find Skippy. And the radio. We've got to try again."

I hadn't realized my eyes had closed until she shook me and whisper-shouted my name. I tried to look at her, but my eyelids wouldn't respond. She shook me again. I used my remaining energy to lift my arm and place my hand on her thigh. "Help..." I didn't remember what else I'd wanted to say. I felt my hand drop to the ground again, and my world went dark.

***

# JILLIAN

A dark, wet stain had spread from Carter's side, soaking his shirt from armpit to hip and through his pants halfway down his thigh. I had no idea if the bullet had hit any organs, but his bleeding was so profuse I doubted he could survive this much loss. My breathing was close to hyperventilation as I knelt beside him, pressing my hands against his side, feeling his blood seep between my fingers.

I looked around frantically. I don't know what I hoped to see—a hospital, maybe? A helicopter? But there was nothing around me but trees, grass, and vines. I held still for a moment, straining my ears to see if anybody might be nearby—friend or foe. Nothing.

I knew that I couldn't do anything to help Carter by just sitting here. When we packed up the village, I had stuffed a roll of gauze into my pocket. Thank my lucky stars! I fished it out, unspooled a length of the bandage, and pressed a square against the bleeding hole in Carter's side, just beneath his armpit, hoping to staunch the bleeding. I then tore off another long strip of bandage and wrapped it around his chest, tying it tightly to hold the packing in place over the wound.

With that done, I sat back on my heels and tried to make a plan. I had no ideas.

Then from behind me, I heard a shout followed by a burst of rapid gunfire. A woman screamed—was that Kenya?—and then I heard pounding footsteps. Someone was running toward Carter and me.

In a split-second decision, I jumped to my feet and ran away from Carter, knowing that I would draw attention away from him. If these men were shooting at innocent, unarmed castaways, I wanted to give them no chance to take a shot at an already fallen man.

I heard a shout. Someone had spotted me. I didn't recognize the voice, so I ran faster, dodging around trees and ducking beneath vines. My evasive tactics made me lose my bearings quickly, and by the time the sounds of running behind me had faded away, I was well and thoroughly lost. Stopping to catch my breath, I pressed my back to a tree, squeezing my eyes shut and praying that Carter would be okay—my heart breaking that I had left him defenseless.

When I could breathe again, I cautiously leaned out from behind my tree and looked around. I couldn't see or hear anybody else. I needed to get to higher ground so I could figure out where I was—and how to get back to Carter. I decided that my best choice was to try to go back the way I'd come but avoid being spotted, so I began walking again, trying to keep my steps as quiet as I could. After I'd gone a few hundred feet, I heard a voice—distant and low, but familiar. Grandpa.

I adjusted my course and headed the direction I'd heard the voice. The trees began to thin, and, with great relief, I realized that I'd made it to the caves. I saw Grandpa first, standing at the mouth of the largest cave with Howard and Elodia. They had heard me coming, and their relief was visible when they realized who I was.

Grandpa hurried out to greet me with a hug, then we walked back into the cave together. Howard and Elodia followed, and soon I saw that Kenya and Bridget were here too. Everyone was safe, except...

"Where's Carter?" Grandpa asked, reading my mind—or maybe just my stricken expression.

"He was shot," I explained breathlessly. "I couldn't move him, and someone saw me, and I had to run so they wouldn't find him. But I've got to go back for him."

Grandpa agreed without argument. "I'll go with you."

To my surprise, Howard stepped forward. "I'll go, too. You'll need the extra help to lift him."

I nodded, too tired and worried to look a gift horse in the mouth. I just hoped that I could remember how to get to the place I'd left Carter. We struck out again into the trees and, to my relief and slight annoyance, I realized that we had been only a few hundred yards away from the caves when Carter had fallen. We'd been so close!

Thankfully, we found Carter just where I'd left him. He was out cold, but he began to rouse when Grandpa and Howard lifted him up. I would have helped, but I was so exhausted from running through the jungle that I was useless. I was halfway through thanking the two men again for their help when a loud crack sounded from behind us, shocking us all into silence.

I whirled around to see four men approaching from behind. Each wore black clothing and each held a rifle, all of them aimed at me and my friends. On reflex, I backed up a few steps.

"Don't move," one of the men growled in a low voice. He stepped closer and the rest of the men held their positions, all aiming their weapons carefully.

I raised my hands, palms forward, and noticed that my fingers trembled violently as I stared down the barrel of the gun. "W-what do you want?" I breathed. "We don't have anything."

"We're shipwrecked," Howard joined in.

Grandpa added, "We're just trying to get home."

The man who had spoken took a few more steps until he was directly in front of me. He wasn't very tall—maybe an inch or so shorter than me. He had black hair, a thick beard, and olive skin. His eyes were dark beneath thick eyebrows that were set in a scowl. I knew I had never seen this face before.

"Bridget Foster," he said in the same accented tone we'd heard from the loudspeaker. "Where is she?"

I spread my arms to the sides, looking around pointedly. "She's not here," I said, amazed at the defiance in my voice.

His patience ran out. In a flash of movement, he closed the distance between us and grabbed me by the throat with one meaty hand. A strangled scream escaped me, and my hands flew up, clawing at his grip. He shook me, making my body jerk backward. "Where is she?"

"Let her go!" Grandpa shouted. He darted forward and lunged at the man, shoving his shoulder with both hands, offsetting his balance. Still holding my throat, the man pulled me down on top of him as he fell sideways, and Grandpa landed on top of both of us.

Air whooshed from my lungs as Grandpa landed on my back. A commotion sounded all around us as the other three men closed in. Before I could catch my breath, Grandpa was yanked upward, and the man who had held me in a chokehold rolled out from beneath my weight.

Having had the air knocked out of me, I felt paralyzed as my body fought to breathe again. Tears poured from my eyes, and I felt like I was choking on my own throat as I wheezed and sputtered for breath. The man took advantage of my distraction and placed his knee on my back, shifting his weight onto my body.

I scratched at the ground, squirming and crying out, unable to breathe or think straight or see anything. From above me, Grandpa yelled something, and I heard a loud crack followed by three gunshots.

I screamed, throwing my arms over my head and pressed my face against the dirt.

"What about you?" the man shouted. "Do you want the same, or are you going to tell me—WHERE IS BRIDGET FOSTER?"

"Th-that way," Howard's voice stammered meekly. "At the caves."

The man's weight lifted from my back, and I finally drew a full breath. The man had gotten to his feet and he and the three others were walking away. "Stay here, if you know what's good for you."

I lifted my head from the ground as the four men jogged away in the direction of the caves. Howard, Carter, and Grandpa were all on the ground. Howard knelt beside Carter, who was lying on his side, awake now and blinking in shock. Grandpa was several feet away, halfway between Carter and Howard's position and mine. He lay on his back. A bright red stain blossomed on his once-white captain's shirt.

"Grandpa." I sprang to my feet, the memory of the gunshots played a delayed echo in my brain. One. Two. Three. Had he been hit once? Twice? Three times? "Grandpa!" I collapsed to my knees beside him, one hand pressing against the wound on his chest, the other grasping his hand.

His eyes were open, and he was breathing, but the sound was rough and raspy. He coughed violently, and when he was done, his gaze raked over my face. "Help Bridget," he whispered on a breath so faint it hardly moved. "Don't let... them..." he broke off in a fit of wheezy coughing. His fingers gripped my hand fiercely.

"We're going to get help for you, Grandpa," I promised wildly. "Just hang on. Help is coming." I looked up to see Howard and Carter staring at us, frozen in place with terrorized expressions.

"Where is the radio?" I demanded of Howard. "Where did Grandpa leave the radio? We've got to call for help."

Howard's mouth opened and closed soundlessly several times. Carter shook his arm and repeated my question. The physical roughness finally got an answer from Howard. "I-in the cave. He was using it before you found us."

"Did he have contact with someone?"

Howard looked lost. He began turning his head, looking all around us as if watching for an incoming invasion. "I-I don't know."

I looked back at Grandpa who was struggling to draw breath now. Panic flooded my body. I had to get him help. I had to call for help!

"Howard. Howard! I need you to put pressure here." I waited until he knelt at Skippy's side and replaced my hand over Grandpa's wound. I handed him what remained of the roll of gauze and quickly packed Grandpa's wound. With the bandage in place, Howard reached out obediently and placed his hand over the bullet wound, applying pressure even before I took my hand away.

Limbs shaking, I got to my feet. Carter still lay on his side, bleeding through the bandage I'd applied minutes before. Howard was as pale as a sheet, and Grandpa Skippy was unconscious.

I licked my lips, desperation clawing at the back of my throat. It was time to move, to act. I needed to save my friends.

"I'll be back as soon as I can." Without waiting for a response from any of the men, I found the direction I needed to go and began jogging through the jungle again.

The mouth of the cave was empty when I approached this time, and my chest constricted with terror. Had the men found Bridget and the others? Had they taken her? Had they found the radio?

"Hello?" I called, my voice breaking on the single word. I stepped into the dimness of the cave and blinked to let my eyes adjust. "Bridget? Kenya? Elodia?"

I heard a scuffling sound to my left and whipped around, afraid my attackers had returned. Kenya's head poked out from a large crevice in the rock face that had been hidden in the darkness. When she saw me, she rushed forward and threw her arms around my neck.

"We heard gunshots, and some men were poking around here. I was so worried they were going to find us," she cried, her body trembling. "Are you okay?" She pulled back and saw the blood on my hands and clothes. "Oh my—!"

"It's Grandpa," I interrupted hastily. "And Carter. They've been shot." I couldn't let myself pause to feel the weight of that reality. "Is the radio still here?"

Kenya took half a second to process this then nodded briskly. "Back here." She led me toward the crevice she had emerged from a moment ago, and after we slipped through the tight walls, we entered a large open cave. Light came in from an opening overhead, and I saw Elodia sitting with the radio next to—"Bridget, you're okay!"

She nodded, but tears and dirt streaked her face. "I heard you say Captain Skippy was shot. Is he—?"

"He needs help. Right now." I pointed to the radio. "Do we have someone on the line?"

Elodia drew in a ragged breath. "Captain Skippy was talking to someone for a little bit, but then another voice interrupted and started yelling at him, demanding that we give up Bridget or... or they would kill us all."

My thoughts flicked back to Grandpa's body on the ground, and I had no reason to doubt that these people had no qualms about making good on that threat.

I dropped down beside the radio and examined it. It was switched off. I wasn't an expert, but Grandpa had taught me enough to use it if I needed to. I knew from his tutoring that Channel 16 was universally understood to be a distress channel, so I wasn't surprised that the radio was set to that now. I reached for the receiver to send out another distress call, but my hand paused before I touched it.

If the men who had come for Bridget had communicated with Grandpa, they were likely listening to Channel 16. If they had been looking for Bridget all along, it was a simple thing for them to eavesdrop in on Grandpa's previous conversation with our real rescuers, since the radio used open waves that anybody could tune in to. If they were listening to Channel 16, any information I used to contact help would be heard by the bad guys, too. I didn't know enough about the radio to start turning knobs and hope someone might hear me in time to help. I also didn't know any codes that would be helpful in this situation either.

How could it be that I finally had a radio to call for help, and I couldn't use it?

Think, Jillian, think.

I rubbed my fingers against my temples, trying to remember everything Grandpa Skippy had ever said to me about radios.

My radio instruction had begun long before Grandpa had won the lottery and purchased his dream boat. Ever since he was a young man, Grandpa had been a HAM radio enthusiast, and I never knew a time when he hadn't spent evenings hiding out in the garage, listening in to the radio chatter. He'd always joked that he wouldn't be able to pick his best friends out of a lineup—unless they spoke through a crackle-voice filter.

One of my earliest memories of Grandpa involved sitting with my sister in Grandpa's garage, perched high on a metal stool, chin resting on my elbows on the stained workbench, listening to Grandpa as he played with his radio.

Even back then, he hadn't liked paying much attention to me, so the instructions were given to my sister, but I was allowed to listen in. I closed my eyes and delved into those memories.

What had he told us? What could I do now?

Emergency. If professionals used Channel 16, what line did amateur radio users go to in an emergency?

The answer came to me in a burst of clarity. How many times had he told me? If I wasn't so panicked, I would have felt embarrassed that I hadn't remembered sooner. "If you're in a jam," he'd said countless times, "your first option is always Channel One. Someone might redirect you, but start with One. It's as easy as that."

"Gosh, I'm so stupid," I muttered, finally adjusting the dial and finding Channel One where I knew I'd find HAM radio users, just like Grandpa, who sat in their garages, just waiting for someone to need them.

It was still possible that the men who had come looking for Bridget would hear my call on this channel, but hopefully they wouldn't think we would use amateur stations. All I could do was hope and try.

I took a quick breath and pushed the button. "CQ, CQ, CQ, this is Flying Honeymoon, Flying Honeymoon calling for a contact. Over."

Bridget, Elodia, and Kenya were crouched beside me, and the four of us held our breath as we listened to the low static, praying for a response.

Ten seconds passed. Twenty. Thirty.

"We might be too remote for anyone to pick up our signal," I said, my voice strained and quiet. "If we had a longer antenna, maybe—"

A voice crackled through the speaker then. The signal was weak, but the male voice was friendly when it said, "Flying Honeymoon, this is Shark18. I hear you. Over."

Kenya let out a whoop then slapped her hand over her mouth, having suddenly remembered that we were in hiding.

My heart raced, but I tried to keep my voice even as I spoke, "It's good to hear a friendly voice, Shark18. We're in some trouble. Is there a better channel we can talk?"

The radio was silent for two beats before Shark18's voice returned. "Your signal is weak, Flying Honeymoon. Let's try a new channel." He suggested a channel, and I agreed to the move, adjusting my dial as soon as I finished saying, "Over."

When I'd locked into the new channel, I spoke my call again, praying that my small antenna would be enough to reach Shark18, wherever he was.

The tension in my shoulders released dramatically when Shark18's voice answered my call, loud and clear, on the new channel. "Got yourself in a jam, huh, Flying Honeymoon?"

"You would hardly believe it," I said with a relieved laugh. "What is your location, Shark18?"

"Nassau, Bahamas. Over."

My gaze flew to Bridget, Kenya, and Elodia. He was close. It made sense, considering the short range of this radio, but it was still nice to know he might be able to send help.

Shark18 continued before I could respond. "Are you the lost cruise ship? Over."

I locked eyes with Bridget, hesitating. How did we know we could trust this stranger on the radio waves? She nodded once, surely thinking the same thing I was—we've got no other choice.

"Affirmative."

"Is Bridget Foster with you, over?"

I gulped. We had heard this question so many times over the last hour. Had we just walked into another trap?

When I didn't answer, Shark18 spoke again. "She is a friend of mine. I've been so worried about her."

Bridget leaned forward, hope sparking in her eyes. A friend. "Who is it?"

I shook my head once. "We are having trust issues, Shark18. Can you identify yourself?"

"10-4. She'll know me best as little Aussie Bear."

Bridget gasped, her eyes alight and excitement palpable. "It's Austin Holmstead."

Kenya's jaw dropped. "The NFL player?"

Bridget nodded. "I've known him for years." She took the microphone from my hand and commandeered the call. "Aussie! It's Bridget."

Austin sighed into his microphone and swore lightly. "I can't believe it's you. I've been so worried!"

"Why are you in Nassau?"

"I'm at the family island," he responded, as if having a family island wasn't outlandish. "Where are you?"

I took the microphone back. "Shark18, we are stranded on an uninhabited island, southwest of the Bahamas." I finished by telling him the coordinates that Grandpa had figured out that morning.

At my businesslike tone, he returned to radio-speak. "Copy. I know the location. That island is owned by a movie studio, I believe. Have you been able to contact authorities for assistance, over?"

"Affirmative, but we've run into trouble." I explained the situation as best as I could, for as little as I understood about what was really happening. "Our captain and one other man have been shot and need urgent evacuation. We are in immediate danger from the gunmen."

"Copy. Stand by."

Silence fell over the line, and Elodia clutched my arm. "What does that mean?"

"I don't know. He just wants us to wait a minute."

"For what?" she demanded. I did not have an answer.

Minutes passed by, and the tension mounted. I kept thinking back to Grandpa, bleeding out in the jungle. Hurry, Austin.

At long last, the radio crackled, and Austin's voice returned to the conversation. "Flying Honeymoon, this is Shark18, come back. Over."

"Copy, Shark18. It's good to hear your voice. Over."

"Apologies, Flying Honeymoon. I have arranged emergency transportation from your location. Can you identify a rendezvous point on your island? We can get a chopper to you within the hour, over."

A landing space for a helicopter. My first thought was the beach, but with the invaders out there, it wasn't a great choice. The village didn't have enough flat space for a landing, and most of the rest of the island was covered in thick trees. Then I remembered the flat clearing we found two days before that had given us a sightline to the shipwreck.

"Stand by, Shark18." I consulted with my friends before answering Austin. "We can have them land on the big hill, but we'd have to try to get there without being seen. The last thing we want is to have someone else get hurt."

"It's our only choice," Bridget said. "We'll make it."

"We've been here for a week," Elodia added. "We know this place better than they do. That's got to be worth something."

Kenya nodded. "It's worth the risk. And, in the meantime, we'll keep Bridget hidden here until help comes."

Bridget took umbrage with that. "I'm not hiding in a hole while everyone else risks their necks."

Elodia was more clinically minded. "Having you safe is our only advantage," she reasoned. "If it's you they're after, our best move is to keep you out of their hands for as long as possible."

"I'm not letting everyone around me get killed while I sit back here on my hands," Bridget growled.

"I'd rather not get killed," Elodia said, "which will definitely happen if we don't get to that helicopter."

Bridget conceded the argument. "Fine. I'll do whatever you say."

I finally answered Austin's last question. "We know a place."

# 19

*JILLIAN*

I hated to leave Bridget behind , but Kenya agreed to stay with her and the two of them were to keep conversation going with Austin. Our plan was desperately bare bones: sneak out without being seen, find the boys, make it up the hill, meet the helicopter, get Bridget out, go home.

Easy peasy.

This would have been a lot simpler if we had any kind of weapon to defend ourselves with. Not imagining that we would be attacked by our rescuers, we had left the machete back at the village. Why didn't we keep a crossbow in our First Aid kit? Elodia and I each picked up the sharpest, fist-sized rock we could find. But when it came down to it, I didn't know if either of us would have it in us to actually hurt someone with a rock.

I emerged from the cave first, slowly peering out and around to make sure we didn't walk into the arms of our enemies within two seconds. The area was clear, so I motioned for Elodia to follow, and we crept out of the rocks and into the trees. Keeping quiet and moving cautiously, we wended our way through the jungle until we reached the place where I knew I'd left the men.

When we reached the place, my heart sank to my toes. No one was here. I found blood on the ground and leaves where Grandpa and Carter had lain, so I knew we were in the right spot. I stood, trying to ignore the way my breath had gotten very shallow. I could barely breathe around the lump that formed in my throat.

Elodia asked the obvious, "Where are they?"

I shook my head, turning and scanning for any clues. There was a lot of blood on the ground, and if the men were still alive—please let them still be alive—then they would still be bleeding, and there should be a blood trail on the ground. I dropped to a crouch and began searching the dirt for blood. Just then I heard a twig snap from behind me, and I jumped around, rock at the ready.

"Jill?"

"Carter!"

I hastened to where he stood, leaning against a broad tree for support. His face was ashen, and he shook at the effort that it cost him to stand. I hurried to his side. "Where's Grandpa?"

"And Howard," Elodia added, jogging up beside me. "Are they okay? Did those men get them?"

"No, we haven't seen anybody come back. We moved Captain Skippy somewhere less open."

Breath rushed from my lungs in relief. "Thank goodness. What about you, though?" My eyes scanned his blood-stained clothes and didn't miss the way his skin had gone a deathly kind of gray. "How are you even standing right now?"

"I think it was a through and through," he said with a wince. "The bullet went through my side and out the back."

Elodia let out a quick breath. "You got lucky."

Carter nodded. "Hurts like hell. The captain's in worse shape: he's bleeding bad. I think the bullet hit some organs."

I gulped. Even without a medical degree, I knew that was a devastating injury.

Carter took my hand and squeezed my fingers to get my attention again. "Were you able to call for help?"

Blinking past the emotion that threatened to drown me, I nodded. "Yes."

As I explained the incredible radio conversation we'd just had with Austin Holmstead, Carter led us through the trees. Carter was duly amazed at the turn in our luck—who would have guessed that a famous NFL wide receiver, that also happened to be a friend of Bridget's, would have a private family island nearby?

But he was less relieved. "Doesn't that seem suspicious?"

I hadn't considered what an incredible coincidence it was. My mother's lifelong advice flooded my mind: "If something seems too good to be true, it probably is."

"Do you think it's a trap?"

Elodia gasped. "Could these men be working with Austin Holmstead? Maybe Austin was the one who intercepted our call in the first place."

"Crap," I muttered, then said with more feeling, "Crap."

Carter put his hand on my arm and the three of us stopped for a moment. "Jill, you should know, Skippy's... bad. If we don't get him help soon, I'm worried he's not going to make it."

That cinched the deal for me. Whether or not Austin Holmstead was the mastermind in this attack, if he was going to send us a helicopter to get us off this island, it was a risk we had to take. I couldn't do nothing and let Grandpa die. "Where is he?"

We found Grandpa Skippy with Howard in a little hollow surrounded by thick brush and grass. If Carter hadn't known to stop here, we would have walked right past. It was the perfect hiding spot. Skippy was unconscious, but from the looks of things, the guys had taken the last of the bandage roll and wrapped Grandpa up to try to stop the bleeding. The bandage was red with blood, but it appeared to be helping slow the blood flow.

Kneeling on the jungle floor beside my grandfather, I looked up at my friends. "Austin Holmstead is sending a helicopter," I began. "He might be conspiring with whoever is after Bridget, though." I darted a glance at Carter. His expression was grim, but he nodded to encourage me to continue. "But we can all agree that Skippy won't make it out of this alive without getting him to a hospital ASAP." And maybe not even then.

It was Howard that spoke next. "It's a gamble we have to take," he said. Looking at Elodia, he went on, "I know that if it was you that needed help, I'd risk anything." He looked at me then. "I don't want Bridget to get hurt, though. What can we do to protect her and still get help for Skippy?"

Carter let out a frustrated breath. "There's nothing else we can do. We've got to get Skippy on that helicopter."

"We can keep Bridget hidden in the caves until we know for sure that Skippy is at a hospital," I proposed. "One of us can go with the helicopter and then give a signal that everything is okay."

Elodia, Howard, and Carter all nodded solemnly.

"I think it should be you, Carter," I said with a nod toward his bleeding side. "You need a doctor, too."

Howard cut in before Carter could answer, "Elodia is going, too."

Elodia squeezed his hand and gave him a loving look. "You, too."

"If there's room for all of us," Carter said, "then I'll go. But if not, I'll stay here and help Bridget."

"You are not staying," I said, a flare of anger lighting through my chest. "I'm not letting you bleed out in the jungle just for the sake of stubborn chivalry."

Carter had the gall to actually laugh at my outburst. "Easy, tiger. I don't want to die any more than you do."

"Gosh, you're so stubborn. Just let me help you!"

The levity he'd forced a moment before was gone. "I don't want you to help me. I want to be the one to help you!"

"Hate to break it to you, but that hole in your ribcage is making you not very helpful right now. So just... stop being right all the time and let me take care of things."

He scoffed. "I didn't know you could be so mean."

"Yeah, well I never asked to solve everybody's problems and be in charge of getting us all out of an impossible situation, but here we are! I'm sick of everyone fighting me and everything blowing up in my face, okay? So just sit there and let me love you, damn it!"

I wanted to sit down and cry myself to sleep, but there was no time for that. I took a deep breath and spoke once again to my stunned audience. "Grandpa is priority, and we'll need all of us to carry him," I said, moving around to cradle Skippy's head and shoulders. "And we'd better hurry. It's about a mile up the hill and we'll have to move slow."

Carter agreed and crouched down at Skippy's side, ready to help lift him. I worried that his own bleeding would increase with the effort, but I knew better than to argue with the man. "Stay quiet and stay hidden as much as possible," he instructed us. "We don't know where those men have gotten to."

Howard and Elodia agreed, and we each got a good grip on Skippy and lifted him after a count of three. With Skippy in our arms, we struck out for the hill. It was painfully slow-going, and when we had made it only a few hundred yards after half an hour, we knew we had to come up with a better plan. We couldn't carry Skippy up the hill, exhausted and injured as we were.

"I'll go ahead to meet the helicopter," I said as we lay Grandpa on the ground to catch our breath. "You all stay here and stay hidden, and I'll bring help."

Howard looked up from his doubled-over position, scowling. "How do we know you won't just get on the helicopter and leave us?"

I might have thought I was too tired to be offended, but that was not the case. I felt like all the energy and life had been sapped from my body. The fact that, after everything we'd all gone through, and how hard I had tried to fix everything, Howard still thought so little of me... it stung. I realized that I would never be able to please him or people like him, not completely. I would never be good enough. Nothing I did would ever satisfy. And I was sick of trying.

"Fine," I hissed. "You go ahead and meet the helicopter. Do whatever you want. Just don't forget about Skippy."

Howard's haughty expression darkened, and he straightened his shoulders, stepping away from Skippy and reaching out for Elodia's hand. They left without saying another word, but Elodia looked back at us over her shoulder as Howard pulled her away.

After they'd gone, Carter and I moved Grandpa under the cover of some thick palm trees and brush, and I checked on the wrapping around his torso. The bandage was soaked with blood, but I was heartened to see that the flow seemed to have lessened. If we hurried, if we were able to get him help, he had a chance.

Once we were sure we were hidden, I hunkered low beneath the foliage and rested my head against the trunk of a tree. Carter stretched out beside me and reached over, grasping my hand in his.

"I'm sorry," I said, meaning my outburst from earlier. "I'm so sick of this," I whispered. For the umpteenth time that day, my throat clogged with tears, and it hurt to swallow. "I just want to go home!"

He squeezed my fingers with warm, reassuring pressure. "I know. We're close, though."

A few tears escaped my eyes, and I released a sad sigh. "Do you think we can trust Austin Holmstead?"

"I didn't talk to him," Carter returned with a shrug. "But if he knows Bridget, and she recognized his voice... I guess it's either trust him or turn Bridget over to the armed psychos down at the beach."

He was right, and I hated that our options were both so disastrous. "Austin Holmstead is the lesser of two evils, I guess."

"Maybe we just have to keep hope alive—maybe there are still good people in the world?"

We fell silent again for a few moments, listening to the jungle around us, straining to hear any sound that was out of the ordinary. At length, I broke our quiet by asking, "What do you think they want Bridget for, anyway? I know we've only known her a week, but she doesn't seem like the type to be wanted by, well, let's just call them 'pirates.'"

Carter smirked at the 'pirate' label, then he shook his head, looking as confused as I felt. "I can't imagine."

"How's your side?" I asked.

"Terrible. But I'll live."

I closed my eyes, replaying the events of the day. The sun was centered above us overhead, so it had only been a single morning since I had awoken to help Grandpa fix the radio. It felt like a lifetime. Hope, rescue, armed gunmen, running through the jungle, Grandpa and Carter were both shot, Bridget was hiding in a cave, the Lovells were hiking up a mountain to meet a helicopter. Had there ever been this much excitement in my life before?

Carter shifted, and my gaze wandered over to him. I was so grateful he was here with me. I didn't know how I would have gotten through any of this without his support. Then, almost as if my brain had been trudging through swamp water, my thoughts finally caught up to something Carter had said before the world had turned completely upside down.

I turned to face him straight on. He perked up at my movement and his brow arched quizzically when he saw my expression.

"You said, 'I love you' earlier."

The corners of his mouth turned up ever so slightly. "Do you want me to take it back? Because I'm not planning to do that."

"No," I said with a breathy laugh. "I just didn't get a chance to acknowledge it before."

He nodded and his expression turned a little sheepish. "I hadn't meant for it to come out like that. I usually try to be more suave."

That made me want to burst out laughing, but since we were trying to keep a low profile, I just rolled my eyes and shook my head instead. My gaze fell to our interlocked hands then, and I asked, "Did you mean it?"

"Yeah." He squeezed my hand again until I looked up into his eyes. "I mean it."

My gaze dropped again, and I licked my lips. "I really care about you. A lot." I peered up at him. "Is it okay if I don't say... that... yet?"

"I don't want you to say anything you don't feel. And it's only been a week. I'm not in a hurry." He shrugged. "I've always been a quick study, though." Then he winked at me, and it was all I could do to keep from jumping on him and kissing the smirk from his mouth.

"If we were home, and I met you at a party or something—"

"Yes," he cut me off. "Yes, I would have noticed you. Yes, I would have talked to you. Yes, I would have gone home and thought about you for hours until I finally fell asleep. And then I would have dreamt about your smile and your laugh. And I would have called you the next day because I have no chill, and I would have spent my whole day thinking about you. And I still would have known, in only a week, that I love you, Jillian Preston. On any continent, in any circumstances, I would have fallen in love with you."

I pressed my free hand to my blushing cheek, grinning. "You are so adorable."

He grinned. "I try." Then he leaned close, his eyes asking for a kiss. My heart sang out in acceptance.

"I might need more than a week," I whispered.

"I can wait."

I had never before considered that the perfect time to sneak up on someone was while they were involved in a heart-to-heart. Now I know, for the future. I was so deeply focused on Carter and our touching conversation that I had stopped listening for approaching pirates.

They seemed to appear out of midair, surrounding us from all sides. They shouted to get our attention then started barking orders, guns aimed at our chests and at Grandpa. Carter's arm had been around my back, and when the men appeared, he pulled me into his chest, wrapping both arms around me defensively.

"Give us the girl," a man growled roughly from behind me. "No one else has to get hurt."

Carter tightened his hold, and my fingers curled into his shirt as I clung to him. "You don't want to do this," he said to the man. He might have said more, but the man pressed the barrel of his gun to my shoulder, and Carter fell silent.

"Let her go. Nice and easy."

He thinks I'm Bridget, I realized in a flash. We had similar coloring, so it wasn't completely outside the realm of possibility. I could have turned around right then and cleared the confusion, but since that likely would have resulted in a bullet to my head or Carter's, I went along with it.

I gave Carter the barest nod, and I pulled away from his arms. I didn't have a plan—I didn't even have a notion of what to do next. Decisions were made for me, though. As soon as I was out of Carter's arms, two men grabbed me by the arms and hauled me to my feet. I screamed instinctively. Someone slapped me across the face, cutting off my scream and sending me scuttling sideways. The men behind me jerked me upright again, then a bag was placed over my head, and my hands were bound in front of me. They gave Carter the same treatment, and I heard him shouting even as I fought to free myself.

I struggled against them, kicking and fighting, but there were too many attackers. They had me tied up and marching within minutes. I heard Carter shout somewhere behind me, but I couldn't understand what he said.

"Move it." Someone shoved me between the shoulder blades, and I stumbled forward.

In front of me, another man grumbled, "Let's get her to the boat. Radio the boss—tell him we've got her."

# 20

## *CARTER*

**I** **fought against the ropes** around my wrists and ankles, straining until my skin was torn to pieces. As soon as the men hauled Jillian away, I began yelling, hoping that Bridget and Kenya or the Lovells would hear and come to save Jillian. I yelled until my throat was hoarse, but no one came.

Captain Skippy was still unconscious in the brush, and the men hadn't seen him. I was grateful for that. Who knows what they would have done if they'd found him?

My ropes were tied around a tree trunk, so my range of mobility was limited to two feet in either direction. Using my toes, I searched through the sand and plants for anything sharp enough to cut my bindings. Nothing.

When Jillian was taken, all I felt was panic, but after a few minutes, the adrenaline began to wear off. My heart pounded against my ribs, but I forced myself to sit still and think. How could I get out of this? How could I untie the ropes? I had to get free to help Jillian.

*You're a scientist,* I thought firmly. *They pay you to think. So, think.*

I didn't have the brute strength, or the leverage, to go ahead and break the ropes, so that was out. I couldn't find anything to cut them with, so that idea didn't hold water either. I stared at the ropes, my brain moving like an elephant through bubble gum. My gaze trailed the length of the rope from the tree to my wrists and back. I needed to pull the rope tight somehow then somehow loop my wrist bindings around the taut rope and then rub it briskly. The friction would eventually wear away the fibers and break. The problem was that I couldn't think how to do that without removing one of my own arms first.

There was some slack in the long rope, but not enough for me to put my foot on it for tension. I wondered if I could get it with my mouth. I lifted my arms over my head and started trying to catch the rope in my teeth, feeling like a piranha and an idiot. Plus, it didn't work. There wasn't enough slack for me to get it in my mouth and then rub my wrist ropes against it. I stared down at my wrists again.

Suddenly, I was glad that I was all alone. "Buckley, you are an idiot."

I lifted the ropes on my wrist up to my mouth and used my teeth to turn the ropes around enough that I could reach the knot. It took a couple of minutes, but I got it untied. And it was much faster than sawing through rope with friction would have been.

*Moron.*

I threw the rope aside and untied my ankles. Getting to my feet gingerly, I shook out my hands to return blood to my fingertips. My wrists and ankles were raw and bleeding, but I hardly noticed. I scrambled back to where I had left Captain Skippy. He hadn't moved, but he was beginning to stir. I knelt beside him and lifted his head a little, calling his name until he opened his eyes.

He gasped and tried to sit up, coughing violently as he did so. I pressed a firm hand to his shoulder to keep him down. "Jilly?" he groaned, his eyes pinching shut again as he thrashed against my hold. "Where's Jilly?"

"We've got to help her, Skippy," I said, seeing no benefit in lying to him. "She's in trouble."

He gritted his teeth and nodded. "Help me up. Let's go get her."

I kept my hand on his shoulder. "I don't think you ought to move."

He grimaced. "What do we do, professor?"

Not ready with an answer, I thought fast. We needed reinforcements. I didn't know how long it had been since Jillian had spoken to Austin, but I guessed that we were close to the one-hour mark. If that was true, the helicopter would be arriving on the hill soon. Hopefully, the Lovells had reached the meeting point and would be able to meet up with the helicopter without any issue. I needed to find Kenya and Bridget.

The echo of a gunshot echoed up from the beach. Skippy and I froze, looking at each other, terrified.

Knowing first that these men had no qualms about shooting innocent people, my blood ran cold. Had they realized Jillian wasn't Bridget? Had Jillian been shot? Killed?

I helped Captain Skippy sit slightly upright, propped against the base of a tree. "Do you think you'll be okay here for a few minutes? I'm going back to get the girls, and we'll make a plan to rescue Jillian."

Skippy nodded. "I'll be fine. Hurry!"

***

# *JILLIAN*

The men guided me with rough hands, pushing me along until the ground changed beneath my feet, shifting from hard dirt and undergrowth to shifting sand. The sound of the ocean waves intensified, and without seeing, I knew they were taking me to their boats at the beach.

As we had walked fast through the trees, the unruly jungle plants had scraped and clawed at my skin, and I was unable to protect myself. I had twisted both ankles and fallen several times onto my knees. I'd thought I ached all over before my blind hike through the jungle.

My eyes were tightly closed beneath the hot hood over my head. Sweat poured from my face, and the confining interior of the suffocating sack made it difficult to breathe.

Somewhere down the beach, a man shouted, and the pirate on my left yelled, "We got her!"

A rough hand grabbed the back of my collar. "Keep moving," the man growled at me, shoving my shoulder. I couldn't tell how far we walked through the sand, but before long I heard the unmistakable sound of another set of footsteps on the beach.

"Bridget," someone said. "I warned you this might happen. You should have listened to me."

I knew that voice.

Patrick.

A hand grasped the top of the hood and yanked it from my head, pulling a handful of hair along with it. I yelped and staggered away, blinded by the sudden rush of direct sunlight.

"Jillian?" Patrick gasped, recognizing me instantly. He turned to one of my captors and hit him solidly on the back of the head. "That's not Bridget, you morons."

Through my watery vision, I saw the two men blink at me stupidly. Clearly they hadn't considered this outcome of their kidnapping scheme.

Patrick reached out and took my chin in his hand, pulling my face so close to his that I felt spittle hit my cheeks as he growled, "Where is she?"

I tried to pull back from his painful grasp, but he held tightly, threatening to fracture my jaw. "I don't know," I cried.

"Liar!" He shook me.

"N-not here," I invented wildly. "She never made it to the island."

Patrick roared, "WHAT?!"

I didn't have to fake the tears that flowed freely down my face. "We thought she was in the other boat with all of you."

With a scream of rage, Patrick tossed my face aside with enough force to send me tumbling to the sand once again. The men on either side of me did nothing to break my fall. I landed on my elbows and tried to crawl away, but a heavy boot came down on the back of my knee, pinning me down.

Patrick had regained his composure. "How do I know you're not lying?"

I had no response; I just huddled my face into my arms. Patrick grabbed me by the back of the neck and pulled me back, my legs scrambling against the sand to prevent my back from breaking.

"How do I know?" he yelled in my face.

I couldn't think of a thing to say that would satisfy that answer even if I wasn't lying. He shook me a few times then shoved me away. This time, one of the pirates caught me.

"Back to the boats," Patrick barked. "We've got leverage now." He cast a hateful look back at me before turning on his heel and stalking toward the boats that had moored on the beach. The pirates bullied me along after him.

When we reached the boats, I counted eight men. That meant that all the pirates were here at the beach. The tension in my chest slackened a bit. At least I knew no one was out killing my friends at this very second. I hoped that the helicopter would come before any of the pirates decided to return to the jungle to search for Bridget again.

Upon returning to the pirates, Patrick walked directly to the one man in the group who looked nothing like the rest. With the exception of Patrick, all the other men wore black clothes in varying states of shabbiness—none nicer than a banged-up pair of sweatpants. Patrick wore the same black T-shirt and jeans he had worn the morning of the wreck. This eighth man, though, wore pressed brown slacks, deck shoes, and a short-sleeved white polo shirt. The only thing his preppy outfit lacked was a cardigan tied by the sleeves around his shoulders. He had an olive complexion and dark, dark eyes. His black hair was long and oiled to a shine, combed straight back away from his face, curling at the ends around his ears and collar. I had never met him, but I knew who he was right away: Giovanni Accardi. He had been in global news recently as he was wanted in multiple countries for espionage, extortion, gang affiliation, and assault.

I gulped. Could this day get scarier?

Giovanni watched me closely as the men brought me along behind Patrick, depositing me in the sand.

"Who is this?" he asked, his voice heavy with an Italian accent.

Patrick scowled at me, as if I was personally responsible for being kidnapped incorrectly. "She's nobody. These idiots grabbed the wrong person."

Giovanni's demeanor turned scary, his upper lip pulled up in a sneer and his eyes flashing with impatience. "Where is the pop star?"

"We haven't found her yet."

Giovanni stepped around Patrick and towered over me, his face cast in shadows as he glowered down at me. "Where is she?"

I shook my head and started, "I don't—"

"Don't tell me," he took a large step forward then swung his other foot forward, connecting solidly with my stomach, "that you don't know."

The air rushed from my body so fast I couldn't even scream. I curled in on myself, clutching my abdomen. Pain rocked through my body; I could hardly pinpoint where it began or ended. The sole of his shoe collided with my side when he kicked me again, and the third kick glanced off the side of my head.

The world seemed to curl in around the edges as I gasped for breath, pain ricocheting through my abdomen and bouncing through my skull. I couldn't catch my breath, and tears streaked down my face as I sobbed into the sand.

"Stop!" Patrick cried after the third kick, jumping between Giovanni and me. "I'll talk to her. I'll... she'll talk to me, okay."

"You?" Giovanni shoved Patrick. "You are weak," he said. "Gutless. You want something done, you do it right the first time. Your plan," he said the word with disdain, "was ridiculous, and I should have taken matters into my own hands." He shoved Patrick back, making him trip over me and land on the ground, his legs landing hard on my hips.

"I'm done playing games." He raised that black handgun and aimed at Patrick, not hesitating a moment before he pulled the trigger.

# 21

*CARTER*

I hadn't made it sixteen feet away from Captain Skippy when I heard movement ahead in the trees. With my heart in my throat, I ducked behind a tree, looking around for anything I might be able to use to defend myself and Skippy. Then I heard a shout.

"Carter? Jillian?"

My shoulders relaxed and I stepped out from behind the tree. It was Bridget.

I saw them a short distance away through the trees. Kenya carried the rusty machete from the village and Bridget had a mean-looking rock in one hand.

I waved my arms to get their attention, and they jogged over to me, relief clear in their expressions.

"We've been so worried!" Bridget cried as Kenya demanded, "Who got shot? We heard tons of gunshots."

I led them back the short distance to where Skippy was still taking cover in the brush, and I filled them in on Jillian's abduction.

"They thought she was me?" Bridget asked with a furrowed brow. "But... I don't understand. Why are these people looking for me? What did I do?"

"Nothing to warrant this," Kenya said in her friend's defence. "I don't care who you might have pissed off, no one comes after my BFF with guns and gets away with it!"

Bridget dropped the rock in her hand and threw her arms around Kenya's waist. "I'm so glad I have a BFF," she said emotionally.

Kenya returned the hug and said, "Girl, you deserve one."

Their hug lasted longer than I expected, and I cleared my throat. "Uh, girls?"

They broke apart, laughing, then in a flash returned to being serious. "Okay," Kenya said, "What's the plan?"

My injuries and the weight of the day were catching up to me, and I just shook my head helplessly. "I don't have one."

Kenya exchanged a look with Bridget and they both nodded. "Okay then. Let's make one."

Because neither of them had been recently injured, they had much clearer heads than Skippy or I did. I was glad to let them form a rescue plan. Kenya was an unexpected strategist and was unafraid of guerrilla warfare. After they had finalized a plan, we watched in surprise as Skippy grabbed onto a tree and pulled himself up with a determined expression.

"I'm coming with you," he said.

All three of us looked at the blood stain on his clothing and the way he held onto the tree for balance.

"But, Captain..."

"Jill is my granddaughter," he said in a gruff voice. "I haven't always treated her the way I should, but she's mine, and I'm not giving her up. She deserves better. And I'm not about to sit by when she's in trouble."

Without a word, Bridget stepped up and looped his arm over her shoulders. Kenya did the same on his other side. "Let's go get your girl, Skippy."

It was time to move. Though we were closer to the helicopter meet-up site than we were to the beach, we knew that Skippy wouldn't make it up the steep slope, and there wasn't time to waste. Austin Holmstead's helicopter would just have to wait. For now, all we could do was hope to make it to the beach without being seen and take the pirates by surprise.

We set off toward the beach, the girls supporting Skippy's weight while I followed carefully behind them. Though my own wound was not life-threatening, I felt like death-warmed-over as I followed my friends through the humid jungle, sweat pouring from my brow and soaking my blood-stained clothes.

It felt like we walked for hours by the time we had gotten halfway from our position to where we knew the boats had arrived. Kenya, who had been leading our trek, pulled up short and put up a hand to stop us in our tracks. I froze, my ears straining for sound and eyes scanning for movement.

There, coming through the trees ahead, was a man in black clothing carrying a rifle.

I dropped to a crouch and shouted for the others to get down. A gunshot reverberated through the trees, and I heard a bullet impact a coconut tree behind me and to the left. At the jolt of being shot, the tree dropped several coconuts to the ground. The motion drew the gunman's attention, and he fired again in that direction. From my hunched position in the ferns, I made eye contact with Kenya and gave her a slight nod. We had discussed this possibility, and we both knew what to do.

I had a few pebbles in my pockets that I'd gathered along our hike, just for this purpose, and I fished them out, keeping them in my tight fist as I watched Kenya silently creep to our right. She disappeared into the foliage, and I kept low, awaiting her signal that she was in position.

I counted to sixty, barely blinking. If our plan worked, Kenya would creep around behind the man, and when she was ready, she would wave a palm frond to signal me.

After a few more seconds, I saw the palm leaves rise slowly above the rest of the ground cover. I watched the gunman carefully as he stepped slowly through the jungle. He hadn't seen the palm. It was go-time.

My handful of stones sailed through the air, clattering against the trees, fifteen feet from our position. The gunman whirled in that direction and opened fire at the innocent trees where the rocks had fallen. Kenya took full advantage of his distraction and sprang from her hiding spot wielding a thick tree branch. She swung it as well as any pro baseball player I'd ever seen. The wood made a sickening crack when it struck the man's head. He collapsed in a heap without another sound.

Bridget jumped up and whisper-yelled, "Home run!"

"Grab the gun," I told Bridget, taking Skippy's arm so he didn't fall as she walked away. When she'd picked up the rifle, she tried to hand it to me, but I shook my head. "I won't be able to use it," I said, indicating my injured side. "Have you used one before?"

"No. How about you, Kenya?"

Kenya rejoined us then, and she eyed the gun warily. "I don't know how."

"I'll take it," Skippy said then. He didn't say it, but I couldn't help but guess what he was thinking: if it came down to it, he would use the gun to draw attention away from us and Jillian, risking his own life in the process. I hoped it wouldn't come to that.

We continued cautiously through the jungle, wary of more gunmen, but didn't meet anybody else. When we finally reached the beach, we took cover behind a large rock outcropping to finalize our plan. We'd selected a spot that was on a small cliff that overlooked the beach. We had the high ground and the element of surprise.

The two black boats were moored in the sand, and five men moved about on the beach, calling things out to each other as they readied weapons.

"Looks like they're getting ready to go to war," Kenya whispered.

My mouth was dry as I agreed. "They're coming in after us."

Bridget nodded once. "Then we don't have much time. Let's go."

Our plan relied heavily on the machete, coconuts, and rocks, since we didn't have much else at our disposal. While we had walked through the trees, we had picked up as many coconuts as we could carry, repurposing Skippy's jacket into a makeshift sack.

We divided up: Kenya and Bridget took posts near the cliff's edge, and I headed down to the beach, leaving Skippy alone to keep watch with the rifle.

If we had had time, we would have gone *Swiss Family Robinson* on these guys and made booby traps: a tiger in a big pit covered with leaves, tripwires with large boulders on the other side, alarm bells and catapults—the works. But since we had only minutes instead of days to prepare, the best we could do was arm ourselves with what we had and utilize our only advantage: our knowledge of the island and the element of surprise.

Skippy, from his position in the middle of the ridge, worked a ham-sized boulder free from the rest and pushed it down the cliff. It crashed as it fell, causing a terrible din and making every one of the pirates turn in that direction.

Skippy added to the confusion by hollering nonsensically to give the pirates further incentive to go over there. They took the bait, and four of the five men ran toward the cliff, guns at the ready. When they were within range, Bridget and Kenya hurled coconuts at them. Kenya had a killer arm and even better aim. She beaned two men right on the head before they even knew what was coming. They fell like sacks of potatoes to the sand. The other two men turned their guns toward the cliff and began to fire.

That was my cue. From the other side of the beach, I ducked out from my hiding spot in the trees and ran as fast as I could toward the boats. I was armed only with rocks, but I held them like live grenades, ready to fling them at anybody who looked my direction. I sprinted toward the boats, watching the last man who stood guard there. He had his back to me and didn't hear my approach.

When I was within throwing distance, I hurled a rock up the beach where it thudded in the sand. That caught the man's attention, and he drew a pistol, turning it menacingly toward the rock. I took advantage of his distraction and dove behind the hull of the nearest black boat.

I flattened myself to the sand in the waves, using the shadow of the boat in the water as further cover.

Skippy, who had been watching from the clifftop, fired the rifle twice. From my hidden position by the boat, I couldn't see where the shots had landed or if he had struck anybody, but the shots had the desired effect. It was a dual signal that we devised beforehand, letting the girls know that I was in position to search the boats for Jillian, and that they were to move on to phase two of our hastily constructed plan. The shouts stopped, the coconuts stopped raining down on the pirates, and Bridget and Kenya fell back to the village. Skippy stayed, since he was not able to move fast enough.

Keeping my eyes peeled for the lone man who remained by the boats, I scooted backwards into the ocean waves. I had somehow forgotten about my fresh wounds and the salty nature of the sea. When the water met open flesh, it was all I could do to keep from screaming in surprised agony. The dirty saltwater in my wound felt like poison-tipped sandpaper. I inhaled three quick breaths and bit my wrist to hold back my agonized growl.

Then I heard something that pulled me out of my pained distraction. A scream.

Jillian. She was in the boat right beside me. I was so close!

Doing my best to ignore all the pain, I got my feet beneath me and waded deeper into the ocean, so the boat blocked me from view of the pirates before standing up. I timed a jump with the inward rush of a wave, and I was able to grasp the edge of the boat and haul myself upward. Fiery agony ripped through my side, but I refused to let go. With a grunt, I hoisted myself into the boat. I found two people lying on the deck, hands zip-tied behind their backs and black hoods over their heads. I recognized Jillian and knelt beside her.

"Jill, it's me," I whispered, touching her arm.

"Carter," she breathed.

I started to work on cutting the zip ties with my sharpest rock. "We're all okay. Time to get you out of here." When I'd freed her hands, she pulled the hood from her head, and my attention fell to the other person in the boat. "Who is that?"

Jillian rubbed her liberated hands over her tear-stained face then looked over at the person at her side. Tears flooded her cheeks anew and she sobbed, "It's Patrick. He's dead!"

There was an ominous click from behind us, and I froze as a harsh voice said, "And so, it seems, are you."

# 22

## *JILLIAN*

Giovanni Accardi held his pistol to the back of Carter's head, but his hateful glare was fixed on me. "So, it's a rescue party?" he asked sardonically. "I wondered why you lot would be stupid enough to make such a scene." He dug the gun barrel further into Carter's scalp. "Get up. Keep your hands where I can see them."

Carter's gaze never left my face. His expression was cool and unfazed, and he got smoothly to his feet, hands aloft at his sides. He didn't say anything, but his gaze spoke volumes. *Stay calm,* he seemed to convey, *don't give him a reason to hurt you.*

"Let him go," I said to Giovanni.

The criminal didn't even acknowledge me. "Go to the front of the boat," he barked at Carter. "I'll deal with you once I get Bridget."

"Now, how long do you think it will take for Bridget to come to your rescue?" Giovanni asked. He pretended to be thoughtful for a moment before adding maliciously, "Do you think she would be hurried up if she heard another gunshot?" He re-centered his aim at Carter's chest. "I don't really need two hostages."

"No!" a voice screamed from the beach.

I swiveled to see Bridget running across the beach toward the boat, waving her arms. My heart clenched in my chest. "Bridget! Get out of here!" I screamed.

Giovanni whipped around and grabbed me by the back of my collar, pulling me in front of him and pressing the pistol to my temple. But when he spoke, his voice was silky smooth and utterly calm.

"Bridget Foster. It's so good to finally meet."

Bridget reached the edge of the boat and stopped. "Let my friends go," she demanded.

"Gladly," Giovanni answered amiably. "I don't want to hurt anybody." Here he stepped over Patrick's prone body and dragged me with him toward the edge of the boat.

"What do you want?" Bridget yelled, her hands balled into fists at her side.

"Get in the boat," he said, "and we'll talk."

Bridget shook her head. "Let them go."

"You are not in a position to negotiate," he said, cocking the pistol near my ear, "if you want your friends to live, you will do what I say."

Bridget's poker face was impeccable. She took a single step toward the boat but didn't react to his threats. "Why are you here?"

Giovanni's demeanor suddenly shifted, and he ground his teeth with irritation. "I am the one people call when they want to get things done. I am the one who takes care of problems no one else can solve." He stepped forward again, pushing me with him. "I'm the one who collects debts and turns worthless addicts into millionaires." He cast the barest glance back at Patrick's body. "So, I'm here to solve a problem.

"Your idiot bodyguard owed me a great deal of money, and this was his stupid idea to pay me back. Sneak onto the yacht at night, kidnap the pop star, and use her for a ransom. The family would pay—everybody wins."

Bridget looked pale, and her brow shone with sweat. She took another step toward the boat. "This doesn't make sense. How did you expect to get me from the ship?"

Giovanni sneered. "Patrick was the one who suggested you take the cruise. I picked *The Flying Honeymoon* because it was a small boat with a small crew. I knew my men would be able to take over the ship without much of a fight." He scoffed then. "Captain Skippy is about a hundred, so I thought it was a sure thing."

*Take over the ship?* Those were the men Grandpa had fought off that night.

I finally spoke as the pieces fit together in my mind. "The first night at sea ... you had a boat tailing the yacht, and after everybody went to bed, Patrick helped them get onboard. They were just supposed to go to Bridget's room and scoop her up, but Skippy caught you."

"Shut up," Giovanni hissed at me, digging the gun into my temple.

Bridget continued the explanation, still inching closer to the boat as she spoke, "They fought with the captain, and eventually one of them hit him over the head and knocked him out. They were both bleeding so bad they couldn't finish the job. So, they went back to their own boat to get help..."

"Then Patrick went through the whole yacht and broke every radio and threw out every phone," Giovanni finished. "Yes. He thought if the ship had no communication, it would be easier for us to get away with the kidnapping."

I had nearly forgotten that Portia had complained about her phone being missing the morning of the wreck. It hadn't registered with any significance at the time.

"Patrick got in over his head," Bridget said. "You took advantage of that."

Giovanni was evidently done talking. He tightened his grip around my throat and pressed the gun deeper into my temple. "Get in the boat now, Miss Foster. Unless you want to see the inside of your friend's head."

I gulped convulsively, barely breathing. My eyes dipped to where Carter still lay at the bow of the boat, curled in on himself, clutching his side. His wound was bleeding heavily again, probably from when Giovanni had pushed him over. His eyes were wide and his face was gaunt. It looked like our time was up.

"I'll get in the boat," Bridget said, putting her hands up in the air, palms forward in a show of surrender. "If you let them out first."

Giovanni's body jerked as he shook his head. "I don't think so. I could just kill them both right now and then get you in the boat. My generous offer to leave these two as lone survivors on this island won't last forever. Get in the boat, now, or I start shooting."

Bridget didn't hesitate any longer. With a determined set to her jaw, she closed the remaining distance to the boat and climbed the metal ladder. She stood before Giovanni Accardi with a proud set in her shoulders and a stubborn look in her eyes.

"Good girl," Giovanni said in a tone that made my skin crawl. "Now go sit at the front of the boat by him." He gestured to Carter with the gun. Bridget did as he instructed, sitting beside Carter on the deck.

Giovanni nodded once, lowered the gun, then in an unexpected motion, shoved me sideways. I lost my balance and tumbled off the boat, falling head-down into the water. I just had time to hold my breath before being submerged in the waves. My feet found the sandy bottom, and I pushed myself up to the surface just as the boat's engine started.

I had fallen in the water near the outboard motor, and I was barely able to swim out of the way before Giovanni put the motor in reverse and hit the throttle.

The boat careened backward away from the beach. I heard Bridget scream just before Giovanni steered the boat around and motored away toward the open water.

Helpless, I watched the boat race away, leaving a foaming white wake behind it. But as it left, I thought I saw a person on the back, perched on the swim deck beside the motor.

"Kenya!" I breathed.

She was ducked down out of sight, holding on to the lip of the boat with one hand, and in the other, she held the handle of our trusty machete. She was ready to make a move.

I held my breath as the boat got farther away. I prayed she was able to help our friends. "Make your move, Kenya," I whispered. "And don't miss!"

***

# *CARTER*

Teeth gritted, I clutched my searing abdomen. My side screamed with such intense pain that I could barely breathe. My wound was bleeding freely again, the bandage had slipped down and was no longer keeping my blood in my body where it belonged. My arms and legs felt limp as noodles, and I couldn't keep my head up. My vision was fading, and the sounds of the motor and the waves turned to mush in my ears.

I felt a hand on my shoulder and someone was saying my name above the roaring of the sea. "Carter, look at me."

I cracked an eye open, not even realizing that I had closed them. "Bri-idget? Wh-where's J-Ji-ill?" My tongue refused to help form the words, and my lips felt frozen in place.

"He threw her overboard," she said in a voice just loud enough to hear. "She's safe for now."

"You hurt?" I managed to grumble through my uncooperative mouth.

"I'm okay. You've got to stay awake, though."

I think I nodded. I tried to, at least. "W-what do we do now?"

I watched her throat constrict with a hard swallow. "Don't worry. We have a plan."

*We do?* I meant to say that out loud, but the world was getting dim again. Bridget shook my shoulder and urged me to stay awake, and I blinked at her. Satisfied that I was awake again for the moment, she turned to look over her shoulder. I followed her gaze, letting my eyes take a few seconds to adjust.

Giovanni Accardi stood behind the helm of the boat, glaring in our direction as he steered us away from the island. Focused as he was on driving the boat and keeping his eyes and his handgun fixed on me and Bridget, he did not see Kenya Adamson sneaking up behind him with a machete held in both hands, cocked over her shoulder like a baseball bat.

I stared, open-mouthed, as Kenya crept behind him on bare feet, ocean water dripping from her saturated clothes and hair, and a fire burning in her eyes. She was three steps away from him when Giovanni sensed her presence.

He turned, abandoning the helm and throwing up his arms as she charged him, swinging her machete. But she was farther from him than she thought, and he dodged the blade. Her momentum spun her away from him, and he acted fast, leaping at her with a furious yell.

Giovanni landed on top of Kenya, flattening her to the deck as he pulled back a fist. He delivered a blow that might have knocked her out cold, but she saw the swing coming in time to evade. His fist glanced off the side of her head and struck the deck.

He howled in enraged agony, and Kenya took her chance to wriggle out from where he pinned her to the floor. By this time, Bridget was on her feet, stumbling back along the still-speeding boat toward the scuffle.

The boat hit a wave, and with as fast as we were going with no one at the helm, the boat rocked dizzyingly, setting my stomach spinning with nausea. The motor roared and the boat threatened to capsize, righting itself just in time to catch the water again and continue its charge.

Bridget stumbled and fell onto one of the side seats during the boat's unsteady progress, and Kenya lost her balance as well, falling to her backside on the deck, the machete falling from her hand with a clatter.

Giovanni had already been on the floor when the boat tipped, so he kept his balance better than the girls, and while Kenya was trying to get off the floor, he was already on his feet, gun drawn from the holster at his hip, and aiming it at Kenya.

Showing no restraint, he pulled the trigger.

Bridget screamed at the sound, throwing her arms over her head. The boat hit another choppy wave at that same moment, and the bullet missed its target. Kenya scrambled away from Giovanni.

He raised the gun again with a snarl, hissing in Italian as he prepared to fire again.

Seeing her new best friend in the crosshairs of an international criminal, Bridget leapt to her feet. "No!" she screamed, launching into a dive directly toward Giovanni.

Her full-body tackle knocked Giovanni off balance. He yelled as they both fell on the deck, and the gun fired. Bridget landed on his legs and received a knee to the ribs as he fought to get out from under her.

I took advantage of the chaos and jumped to her aid. Crawling across the deck, I reached out and snatched the gun from where it had fallen from Giovanni's hand. Meanwhile, Kenya scrambled upward onto Giovanni's torso and pinned his free arm down so he couldn't strike any of us again.

With Kenya on his arms, Bridget on his legs, and me holding the gun, Giovanni cursed and screamed at us.

"Put his arms behind his back," I told Kenya, spying a discarded packet of zip ties. Pushing up to my knees, I tied the man's hands together, giving the strap an extra-tight pull before finally letting go.

Just then, over the water, we heard the unmistakable sounds of beating helicopter blades. I whirled around, squinting into the distance. Sure enough, a few moments later, a shiny white helicopter appeared over the treetops. Kenya jumped to her feet, screaming and waving her hands over her head. Bridget stood stoically beside me, staring at the helicopter as though she could determine just by sight if this newcomer posed a new threat.

The spike of adrenaline that had gotten me across the boat deck wore off, and I slumped down against a bench, pulling the handgun from the deck and into my lap. Bridget at last turned to the helm of the boat, pushing up the throttle control until the roar of the engines died, and we coasted to a stop.

The helicopter approached fast, the thundering pound of its rotors immediately replacing the roar of the boat's motor. The craft came in low, creating a mini hurricane of ocean spray and rough wind all around the boat.

Huddling down on the deck of the boat, I peered up at the helicopter as it slowed and hovered above us. The side door of the helicopter was open, and after a moment, a helmeted head looked out over the edge, shouting something that we couldn't hear and making a gesture with the hand that I didn't understand.

Kenya, Bridget, and I exchanged bewildered looks, not knowing what to do now. We were at last face-to-face with someone from the real world, but we felt just as stranded and confused as ever.

Realizing they couldn't be heard, the person retreated back into the helicopter and after a moment lifted higher into the sky. And then they left.

Bridget stood again, watching the helicopter fly away.

What did it mean? Was it Austin Holmstead and rescue? Was it more bad guys making sure Bridget was on board the boat? Was it another stranger who had decided we weren't worth the trouble and left us after all?

My fingers were tingling, and I realized I had lost sensation in my toes. With effort, I turned my head to look at Kenya. "Hey," I said, feeling consciousness slipping, "I think I need help..."

And then my vision went black, I felt my body slump to the floor, and I heard nothing else.

***

# JILLIAN

With the boat out of sight, I waded out of the water, sloshing my way onto the sand where I collapsed in a soggy heap, panting and staring out after my friends.

Kenya and Bridget must have seen that I was in trouble in the boat and altered our previous plan to come to my rescue, using Bridget as bait. I hoped that Kenya was able to make good use of that machete and save them all from Giovanni's ransom plans.

A few minutes later, the thunder of helicopter rotors came from behind me, up on the hill on the island. I turned and watched as a white helicopter crested the far end of the island then lowered into the trees. A few minutes later, the helicopter lifted into the air again, cleared the treetops, then careened my direction, pausing to hover over my head.

A person in a black helmet leaned out of the open door, waving to get my attention. I stood, staring upward at the helicopter, waving my arms with nothing better to do.

The person in the helmet pointed out toward the water, obviously trying to communicate something that was beyond my current level of comprehension.

I followed the direction they pointed, and my eyes landed on the second black boat on the shore. I had nearly forgotten it was there! I looked back up at the helicopter and the person was making some sort of gesture with a gloved hand next to their face. It took way too long for me to realize that they had one pinky extended toward their mouth and the thumb pointed up to the ear: the universal "phone call" motion.

*There has to be a radio on board that boat,* I realized. I gave an OK sign with my hand, and the person up there returned it, ducked back into the helicopter, and the craft flew away, out over the sea. I pushed to my feet and staggered a few steps before jogging back into the water to board the empty vessel. Dripping onto the fine interior of the speedboat, I hastened to the captain's chair and reached for the radio.

Just as I was about to lift the receiver to make another distress call, the radio crackled with noise and a voice: "Flying Honeymoon, this is Shark18—do you copy?"

It was Austin Holmstead's voice—I half-wondered how many times he had asked that into the void of radio waves. I forewent all radio etiquette and breathlessly answered, "Austin, this is Jillian Preston from the *Flying Honeymoon.* I copy you."

"Glad to hear your voice again, Jillian," Austin replied with relief in his voice. "Are you with Bridget at sea?"

This question twisted my tired brain. "No, I'm on the shore."

"Good. Glad you understood my sign language. It's harder than you'd think to talk to people from a helicopter."

His dry humor surprised a laugh from me.

He went on, "We've got three passengers on board, and we just flew over another boat about a league from your position. I recognized Bridget on that boat."

"Is my grandpa with you?" I asked breathlessly.

"Affirmative. I have Captain Hamilton, Elodia Francom, and Howard Lovell on board. We are *en route* to the hospital in Nassau."

I blinked back the tears that had suddenly pooled in my eyes. "Is he…"

"Captain Hamilton is unconscious but still breathing. We're going to get help as fast as we can, Miss Preston."

My tears fell hot and fast down my cheeks as I slumped into the chair behind me. "Thank you."

"You're welcome. From what Elodia tells me, it sounds like you've got a bunch of bad guys on the island with you."

*How could I forget?* "That's right. One of them is with Bridget and Kenya and Carter on the other boat. I don't know if they were able to subdue him. And there are six or seven more men on the island. Presumably armed, but I haven't seen any of them for a while."

"I've called in reinforcements," Austin informed me. "Giovanni and his gang are wanted internationally, so the military is on their way to scoop them up. In the meantime, it's a good idea for you to get out of harm's way. Do you think you can operate that boat?"

I glanced at the speedboat's controls—child's play compared to the control board of the beautiful, sunken *Flying Honeymoon.* "Yes."

"Good. The Marine captain in charge of the troop on the way—Captain Sullivan—instructed you to motor out far enough that you'll be out of range when any action goes down. They'll let you know when it's safe to come back to shore."

I nodded, numbly. "What about the others?"

"My helicopter pilot just got them on the radio. They are to stay put until help comes for them."

I swallowed hard, ready to weep again from relief. "Do they know about Carter's gunshot wound?"

There was a pause in the radio conversation before Austin replied, "Affirmative. They are sending a helicopter out to extract him as we speak."

Now I really did start to cry. "Thank you, Austin. I don't know how we could ever repay you."

"No thanks necessary. We'll be in touch soon."

"Take good care of Grandpa," I added worriedly.

"He's in bad shape," Austin replied in a serious tone, "but we'll get him into good hands. We are arriving at the hospital in a few minutes."

I acknowledged this news and we ended our conversation. Replacing the radio back on the control board, I fell back into the seat, staring out at my island—our disastrous home for the past week—awash with feelings. Fatigue, worry, fear, relief. Hunger was a big one. Was our adventure really over? Was it really almost time to go home?

As I stared, contemplating, I saw movement through the trees. Two men materialized onto the beach, running toward the boat with upraised guns.

*Time to go!*

I started the motor in one swift move, reversing the engines away from the sand and launching away from the beach just as the men got within firing range. I ducked down behind the side of the boat, steering blindly away from the beach and the vicious pirates. After a minute or two, I peeked over the side of the boat and saw the pirates and the island shrinking into the distance.

I was safe.

Expelling a breath I hadn't realized I'd been holding, I pushed up the throttle control to reduce my speed, and as I coasted across the ocean waves, I saw another black boat, bobbing placidly on the waves, and two women aboard waving to me from across the distance. I adjusted my course and headed toward my friends.

When I neared their boat, I cut my engine and let the waves pull us together. I found a rope in one of the compartments and tossed it to Kenya, who tied it to the side of her boat, and I pulled the two vessels together. In a move that was dangerous only because I was dangerously exhausted, I crossed the span between the two boats and joined my three friends and one notorious criminal in their boat.

Kenya and Bridget wrapped me in a three-person squeeze as soon as I was on board, and they spoke animatedly over each other as they explained what had happened after Giovanni threw me overboard.

Giovanni glared at us hatefully from the floor of the boat during this reunion and explanation, and when I looked at him, he started spewing at me in Italian. I never knew that romantic language could sound so ugly.

Thereafter ignoring Giovanni, the mastermind of our whole misadventure, I crossed to the front of the boat where Carter was lying, unconscious, across a bench.

"I found a first aid kit on board," Kenya explained, "so I added some more bandages and tried to slow the bleeding again. We've been taking turns keeping pressure on the wound." She winced when she realized they had abandoned him when I came aboard.

I crouched beside him and placed my hand over his injury, pressing firmly and praying that this would be enough to keep him alive.

When I touched him, Carter's eyes opened—deep and blue as the ocean that he loved, warm as his embrace, and sweet as the love I felt for him. "You're here," he whispered.

I nodded and stroked my free hand along his brow. "Help is on the way, Carter. You just hold on, okay? You are absolutely not allowed to die today."

He managed to chuckle. "I don't plan on it."

I pressed a kiss to his forehead then rested my own against his shoulder. "Help is on the way," I repeated, still not fully able to believe it. "We're going home."

He hummed in the back of his throat then murmured, "I've never been happier to leave a place in my life."

Bridget came and sat beside me on the floor. Kenya perched on the bench beside Carter's head. "Do you think you'll miss this place?" Kenya asked, looking back at our island.

"It *is* paradise, after all," Bridget added with a smirk.

It was a beautiful place. The sunshine struck the waves and created an almost unearthly shade of teal. From this distance, the sand was pristine and white. The trees were lush, green, and full. Birds called from the jungle and as they swooped overhead. This place was paradise.

"No," I didn't have to think twice. Paradise was overrated. I was ready for reality, and for the first time in my adult life, I felt ready to commit to permanence. I squeezed Carter's hand then looked at my friends with a smile. "No, I'm ready to go home. And I'm taking the best parts home with me."

# 23

## CARTER

### four weeks later

The warm evening breeze felt good on my face as I stepped out of the funeral hall. The service had concluded an hour before, but this was my first chance to step away from the thick crowd. I was impressed by how many people had come. It wasn't lost on me how Jillian's face had lit up when she saw the large gathering. It was exactly as Captain Skippy had wanted.

It had been a long day—a long month, really. The wreck, the week on an island, the assault, the rescue... and now the funeral. I released a long breath and combed my fingers back through my hair, stopping just outside the front doors to take in the evening air.

It was twilight, and the streetlights were just coming to life. Directly before me, the sky stretched itself out luxuriously toward the ocean, its color changing to a bright reddish orange just before kissing the sea on the horizon. This building had a breathtaking view. I had to commend Skippy's family on their choice to host the funeral here; the sweeping ocean view provided the perfect backdrop to the day's theme: *A Life at Sea.*

Across the street, silhouetted against the sky, a woman sat on a large boulder, the ocean breeze lifting strands of her hair off her shoulders. Even in the poor light, I recognized Jillian, and I crossed the street at a sedate pace, coming to a stop just beside her.

She looked up at me and offered a half shrug. Her eyes betrayed the fatigue I knew she fought. She hadn't had a full night's sleep since before we had set sail, five weeks before. Since returning to the States, she had elected to stay by her grandfather's side in the hospital. At the expense of her own well-being, she upheld a personal oath to look after Skippy until he no longer needed her. That day had come sooner than she had expected, just one week ago. Since then, she had spent all her free hours planning this funeral and making all the arrangements.

From what I understood, every guest who had ever been on board *The Flying Honeymoon* was invited to the funeral, and an astounding number of them had accepted. With celebrities and billionaires flying in from all corners of the globe, this funeral was as star-studded as the night sky. There were well over three hundred guests, including Skippy's own family members and friends. And, most surprising of all, these famous people seemed just as enthusiastic to meet me, Jillian, Kenya, and Elodia as they were to see Bridget Foster and Howard Lovell. Our disappearance had been headline news, and when we finally got back home, we were all micro-celebrities. (My class enrollment had never been more in-demand.)

We were reunited at last with the other passengers of our ill-fated cruise:

April Yung gave me quite an earful about how worried she was about me, and she told me that she hadn't been able to sleep not knowing that I was in trouble. She confessed some long-harbored feelings for me, and I had to awkwardly explain that, while she was sleepless over my wellbeing, I was busy falling in love with Jillian. April's tune changed after that. She let it slip that she had spent the time relaxing in an upscale resort, and I heard her mention to someone else that she had never had a better vacation. So I didn't feel quite so bad for letting her down.

The entourage that had boarded the ship with Elodia and Howard also attended the funeral. Portia had apparently started a fling with both of the bodyguards. I didn't think they knew they were being played, so I backed away from that tangled web as soon as I was able to.

Alexis had gotten in contact with Jillian as soon as we were back in civilization. She and her husband, the chef Mikey, were evidently the only people who lost any sleep about our wellbeing. I was grateful that Jillian had these loyal friends. And now, I was lucky to call them my friends, too. From Alexis, we got a blow-by-blow recounting of what had happened to their lifeboat after they'd abandoned ship. They had watched our lifeboat capsize just as they were taken away by a huge wave, and none of them saw us again after that. Their lifeboat had been tampered with in the same way ours had, but, luckily, their boat was blown into the path of a passing cruise liner, and they were rescued and taken to Nassau.

I witnessed the tearful embrace between Jillian and Alexis before the ceremony began, and I even spotted a tear sneaking down Mikey's cheek. I thought he and I might become good friends.

But everybody knew that the real reason they were gathered was for Captain Scott "Skippy" Hamilton, a friend to everyone he'd ever met. When they'd heard about the funeral, his friends dropped everything to be there for him.

I sat beside Jillian on the boulder, and she reached out to take my hand without saying a word. We sat in companionable silence together for several long moments, watching as the sun stole back its last rays of light from the horizon.

She let out a little sigh and leaned forward so her elbow rested on her knees. "Did you see my cousin come chew me out?" she asked glumly.

I shook my head. "I spent the last half hour trying to get away from Kenya's mom. Apparently, I'm 'irresistible.'"

Jillian laughed once. "She's not wrong."

"What happened with your cousin?"

Rolling her eyes, she looked back at the ocean. "Apparently, he's all bent out of shape because he thought the funeral is a waste of money because of the 'burial at sea.' So, he took it out on me, of course."

I scowled. "Skippy wanted the funeral," I said, telling her nothing she didn't already know. "It wasn't your choice. He arranged everything."

She lifted one shoulder in a shrug. "Apparently I should have talked him out of it because I'm his favorite."

I didn't buy that. "This was all he talked about while he was in the hospital. If this was such an issue, your cousins should have brought it up then."

"I'm not really surprised. This is the same cousin that wouldn't speak to Grandpa for a year after he bought the yacht because he felt like he was being cheated. As if Grandpa's money should automatically be handed over to his grandkids."

"What a piece of... work," I grumbled, censoring my original phrase because a family with young kids walked by just then. I sent them a little wave, and the little boy gave me a grin that was missing two front teeth.

I returned my attention to Jillian. "Don't let him spoil this for you, though. It was a really nice presentation."

"I know. I just feel bad for Grandpa. I hope no one said anything like that to him. He's been through enough."

"I saw him in there chatting with a former Senator and a movie star. I don't think a disparaging word from your cousin will do much to bring him down today."

"I can see Tedd's point," Jillian said after laughing at her grandpa's charm. "Holding a funeral for a ship does seem silly. But I think Grandpa just wanted something like a retirement party. And Tedd should be happy, anyway, since Grandpa announced that he wasn't going to use the insurance money to buy another yacht."

"Do you think he's had enough adventure for his old age?"

Here she squeezed my hand. "I think we've all had enough adventure for several lifetimes."

I feigned shock. "Miss Adventure I-Don't-Need-No-Roots has had enough excitement? I never thought I'd see the day."

She bumped me with her shoulder. "Adventure is probably not the right word. I wouldn't mind going on a nice trip to—"

"Bermuda?" I supplied.

"I was thinking Seattle."

I laughed. "You've had enough beach time, I guess."

"I also wouldn't say no to a weekend in a mountain cabin." She snuggled a little closer to my side.

"That could be arranged."

"Kenya was telling me she wants to plan a reunion trip for the seven of us. I think the only person on board so far is Grandpa."

"He's recovering from a head injury. Among other things... Clearly his judgment is impaired."

She gave a wistful smile, and her eyes sparkled a little in the streetlights. "It was nice to see everyone again, though. Don't you think? I kind of missed them."

I scowled playfully. "Did you hit your head, too?"

"Har har." She stood up and pulled me to my feet beside her. Then she linked her fingers with mine again and we began to stroll along the road. "I heard back on that job in Miami," she told me.

My heart skipped a beat. She had been doing some soul-searching since returning home from the island. We had talked for hours about her options and what she would like to do next. She ultimately decided that she would like to go back to school and finish her degree and ultimately pursue a career in counseling. But for now, she wanted to get a new job, and when I suggested that I would be glad to have her live in Miami so we could see where things went between us, she agreed that that was something she would be willing to consider. Next thing I knew, she was applying for jobs in Miami, and I was thrilled that she was serious about moving somewhere close by.

"Good news?" I asked.

"I've got an interview next week."

"Congratulations! When you get the job, I'll take you to dinner."

She grinned. "Deal."

Up ahead, we saw a man and woman leaving the building Skippy had rented for his Yacht Funeral. It was Howard and Elodia. I caught Jillian's eye then nodded in the other couple's direction. "Do you think those two are going to make it?"

"As a couple? I don't know. If I was her, I would have dumped him a long time ago, but she really loves him. Plus, he's absolutely loaded. I'm sure that doesn't hurt."

Shaking my head, I said, "I guess I just don't get it."

"Not everyone can find a great guy while stranded on a deserted island," she said with a little shrug.

I laughed then wrapped my arm around her waist, pulling her into my side. "Totally worth it." We stopped walking and turned to face one another. My arms fit perfectly around her, and she fit against me like my embrace was made just for her. "If I had known that I had to be shipwrecked and stranded in order to make you fall for me, I would have sabotaged the boat myself."

"I hope you don't mean that." A voice came from behind, bringing a little scream from Jillian. I turned sharply to see Captain Skippy approaching from the building's entrance. He still walked with ginger steps, but his recovery since leaving the hospital had been remarkably swift.

"You scared me," Jillian scolded, swatting his arm as he stopped beside us.

He chuckled and put his arms around both of our shoulders. "Well kids, we did it. I got to attend my own funeral and enjoy the food, too."

"I really enjoyed your slideshow," I told him. I wasn't too proud to suck up to my girlfriend's family. "I had no idea you had taken your boat so many different places."

"Oh yeah, she saw the world," Skippy said with a melancholy smile. "She led a real good life. Just wish it could've been longer. But," he clapped me on the shoulder, "I'm glad you got to sail on her, even if it was... uh..."

"A disaster?" Jillian supplied innocently.

Skippy hmphed as though that word wasn't precisely accurate. "I was going to say 'short-lived.'"

"I was surprised you didn't want to use the insurance money to buy another boat," I said honestly. "It sounds like being a ship captain has been your lifelong dream."

"Oh, it was," Jillian answered for him. "My whole life, all I've ever heard from him was how he'd missed his calling."

"The good thing is that, now, I've lived that calling," Skippy said. "I don't have any regrets. And now I can give the money to you kids and go build a mansion somewhere." He stepped back and looked up and down the street we stood on, his expression thoughtful. "Maybe even somewhere like here. I could get used to a view like this."

"That sounds nice, Grandpa." Jillian's eyes were filled with affection. I loved how much she loved her grandfather.

"What say we go back inside and wrap things up?" Skippy suggested. "Then you two can sneak off and get back to making eyes at each other." He winked at Jillian.

I took her hand, grinning. "You're a smart man, Captain Skippy."

"That's Grandpa Skippy, to you." He clapped my shoulder again.

"Grandpa," Jillian scolded, "you'll scare him away."

"No offense, Jilly, but he spent a week with you smelling like bad fish. I think if he was going to be scared away, he would have hightailed it by now." Skippy looked at me for confirmation.

I shrugged and said simply, "I'm not going anywhere."

"Except inside," Skippy corrected. "Kenya and Bridget are waiting to say goodbye to you two."

Jillian rolled her eyes and started toward the building. "Why didn't you lead with that?"

"I'm an old man," he cried. "I can't be expected to remember everything all at once."

When we got inside, Skippy excused himself to chat with Austin Holmstead and his teammates. Jillian and I found Bridget and Kenya standing together looking at a phone. Bridget looked up as we approached. "Hey guys, did you hear? Giovanni's trial date was moved up."

Kenya took over the explanation. "If things go our way, he'll be behind bars for the rest of the decade."

"Clearly, we're not that lucky," Bridget interjected.

Kenya rolled her eyes. "Some of us are." She turned to Jillian conspiratorially. "Austin Holmstead just asked Bridget to stay with him and his family at their island next month." She cast her friend a knowing look. "He's totally smitten with you."

Bridget blushed and tucked her hair behind her ear. I'd never seen her look so shy. Was she as smitten with him as he reportedly was with her?

"You're one to talk," Jillian said. "You've been getting new secret admirer love notes every day since we got home."

Kenya just shrugged, no embarrassment. "Yeah, but none of them are as dreamy as Austin Holmstead."

"If I go, you're coming with me," Bridget said firmly.

Kenya's jaw dropped. "Seriously?"

"Of course. I've gotta have my BFF with me." Bridget turned back to us. "I'd love to have you two come, too. It could be a romantic getaway for you." Her eyes shone with dreamy mischief.

Jillian shook her head, though. "Thanks, but I've vowed never to set foot on an island again."

"That's fair," Kenya and Bridget said together.

We chatted with them for a few minutes before Jillian made an excuse for us, and we stepped away. The crowd had thinned, and it was time to clean up. I helped Jillian pick up the photos that Skippy had set up on a display table in the lobby. And before I knew it, it was time to go.

I left the building with Jillian by my side. Captain Skippy had put us up at a nearby hotel that was close enough to walk. The evening was warm but breezy, and it was the perfect setting for a peaceful walk with a beautiful woman.

I settled my arm around her waist and held her close to my side again. She stopped and turned to face me, smiling up at me with an invitation I couldn't ignore. I put my hand to her jaw and leaned down for a kiss. She responded by sliding her arms around my neck and eliminating all space between us. Just before she let me kiss her, she whispered, "I love you, Carter. I'm so glad you were here tonight."

"I'll be anywhere you want me to be. Anytime." I was hypnotized by the tender look in her eyes and by how amazing she felt in my arms. I traced my fingers over her shoulder blade and grinned when she shuddered slightly.

She rested her forehead against mine, forestalling our kiss even longer. "I'm ready, you know."

I did not. "For what?"

"Ready for permanence. I'm ready to make a real life. And I want to do it with you."

I beamed and tightened my arms around her. "I'd love that. And I love you."

"Good." She touched her lips to mine in a quick peck. "This would be really awkward if you didn't say it back."

I didn't bother with a reply. Instead, I showed her just how I felt with a long kiss. And I was suddenly grateful for all the time we'd been given. There would be time for jobs, for love, for a family, for a future. I was glad to know that, no matter what came next, I would spend it with Jillian.

# THE END

# *Bothered, and Bewildered*

# *BRIDGET*

It was barely nine o'clock when Kenya excused herself to go to bed early. That left me and Austin sitting alone together by the fire pit. He was lounging in a pose that would make any photographer itch to whip out a camera and start a photoshoot: hands clasped behind his head, muscled arms perfectly highlighted and shadowed by the firelight, long, strong legs stretched out on the sand in front of his chair, feet crossed at the ankles. His eyes were closed, and that enchanting little smirk was playing at the corner of his mouth, flirting with his dimple in a way that made me want to press my lips to his mouth. It would be so easy to be swept away by him.

"You're staring at me," he said without opening his eyes.

If it was anybody else, I would have demurred, claiming that he was up in the night, but this was Austin, and I knew he knew better. "Yep," I said, letting my lips pop on the 'p.' "You're doing a *Sports Illustrated* pose, and I'm the only one around to enjoy it."

He cracked one eyelid open, and his smirk transformed into a grin. "Is it working?"

It was, but admitting that would ruin the game. "Depends on what you're trying to sell."

I had his attention then.

"If you're trying to sell cologne or something... meh. But if you're wanting to convert me to be a Jaguars fan? I'm tempted."

He leaned forward, bracing his elbows on his knees, and I couldn't help copying his posture. Too late, I realized that sitting like this brought our faces dangerously close together. But I didn't move away.

His grin threatened to melt my bones. "Would you believe me if I told you I've had a crush on you since the day I first saw you?"

I quirked an eyebrow. "At the playoff game?" Because that's when my crush on him started.

"Before that," he said, still grinning as the ocean breeze tousled his dark hair. "When I first saw one of your music videos in high school."

A laugh burst indelicately through my lips. "Back when I was sixteen? Right. Who wouldn't think that skinny little toothpick was hot?"

He just shrugged. "I thought you were hot, yes. But I also knew you were spunky and fun. I spent a lot of time imagining what I would say if I ever got to meet you."

I hummed thoughtfully, finally leaning away to give myself a little more room to breathe. "And did our disastrous little meet-cute live up to your expectations?"

His laugh was a warm, low rumble in his chest that sent chill bumps over my arms. "Nah. It was even better."

I swirled the ice in my glass, feigning indifference even though my heart was hanging on his every word. "How so?"

"My teenage-boy fantasy included you thinking I was amazing and, I don't know, letting me make out with you right then and there. But by making a fool of myself, you got to see that I was a real person, and you didn't forget me right away. That was better than anything I could have dreamt up."

That answer rang with sincerity I hadn't expected. I didn't know what to say.

"I thought I had a crush on you before that, but it was nothing compared to how much I thought about you after. And then you actually kept in touch with me and..." he shrugged theatrically. He sat back and placed his hands behind his head again. "I've been falling for you ever since."

I wiped my clammy palms against my pants and licked my lips, breathing slowly to try to ease my thickly pounding heart. "You're telling me you've been pining after me all these years?" I asked, forcing a teasing lilt into my voice.

He laughed. "I wouldn't go that far." I knew that was true. The man dated a lot, from what the gossip circles claimed. "But I never gave up the idea that someday you'd come around and we'd end up together." His expression was serious, his eyes fixed on me with a burning focus.

"As another one of your four-week flings?" I asked, trying to insert more levity back into the conversation. Things had taken a heavy feel.

He paused before answering, but his eyes never left my face. "No. Not you. If you and I ever got there..." his throat tightened as he swallowed hard, "that'd be it for me."

*Me too...*

And suddenly my mind whirled away from the heat of this moment with Austin and hurled down a path of repercussions.

If I started dating Austin, the media and the internet would go berserk. Our friendship wasn't exactly a secret, especially since he had been instrumental in our rescue from Shudder Island. And there had been more than one article already written, speculating if we were a couple and how such a move would benefit both of our careers. This fledgling flame between us would be used to spark a maelstrom of publicity.

I could handle that. I had been dealing with the press since I was sixteen years old. But did I want the rest of my life to be one giant publicity stunt?

Say I started seriously dating Austin: I would go to his games and there would be people watching me the whole time. It would pull focus from his sport and put it on me. I didn't want that for him. And honestly, I didn't want that for me either.

And, more than anything else, my recent discoveries about myself couldn't be shunted to the side. If what I really wanted, long-term, was a quiet life, then being in a relationship with a mega football star was *not* the move to get me there.

Austin thrived in the spotlight, loved being the center of attention, and sought out opportunities to be in the public eye. There wasn't anything wrong with that, and my publicist would have loved nothing better than if I were more like that. But the fact was, I wasn't—I never really had been—and I knew that I didn't want that for myself in the future.

I liked Austin. A lot. I could see myself loving him, but what was the trade-off? A life in the spotlight all the time—a life that made me miserable. And it wasn't like I could shut myself off from the world in a vacuum if I was attached at the hip to a man who constantly sought attention. It just wouldn't work.

I pulled away slightly, keeping his face a safe two inches from mine. He stroked a finger over my jaw. "What's wrong?"

I let my forehead rest gently against his, keeping my eyes closed. "You know I like you, Austin."

"I'm getting that picture, yeah," he said. I could hear the smile in his voice.

"But..."

He pushed softly against my shoulders so he could see my face. "But?"

"I've been doing a lot of thinking lately, and I'm not sure this is what I want anymore."

"'This' being...? Making out with me? Because we just started doing that."

I laughed despite the grave feeling in my chest. "No. I mean, being Bridget Foster. Being in the limelight all the time. I'm thinking about retiring."

He studied me with a guarded expression. "That's a huge decision," he observed. "What would that look like for you?"

"I'm not entirely sure yet. Not touring. Not releasing new albums every year. Not being so public... not seeing my face every time I open an internet browser."

Austin scratched his neck. "What would you do instead?"

I released a long, slow breath. "I'm not sure. I'm interested in writing songs for other people. Maybe producing. I don't mind doing film stuff—I might look into that somewhere down the road. The point is, I just don't know. I feel off-kilter and like I'm at this huge crossroads. Not just professionally, but personally too. And I don't want to start a new relationship when everything is up in the air."

He cocked his head to one side, still watching me closely. "But this isn't a new relationship," he pointed out evenly. "This would be the progression of a previously existing relationship. I think that might be an exemption."

I chuckled at his joke, but my heart didn't feel any lighter. "I need some time to myself," I concluded, my gaze dropping to somewhere near his collar. "Out of the news, out of the world's eye. I need to just be me again. Does that make sense?"

I could see from the pucker in his brow that it did not. "So... you don't want to make out with me because you don't want to be front-page news?"

"Essentially."

"That's kind of stupid."

I winced at his bluntness, but then my temper flared at the insult. "It is not. Not everybody likes being the center of attention all the time."

"Bridge," he interrupted in exasperation, "you're the most famous woman on the planet right now. You were even before you disappeared, and now you're all anybody can talk about. You can't just shut off being famous because you don't want it anymore. It doesn't work like that. People will still care, they'll still talk and write about you, whether you want them to or not."

"Yeah, but that'll cool down after a while if I lay low," I protested. "If I don't put out music or do any interviews, eventually I'll become one of those, 'Hey, whatever happened to that one girl?' celebrities."

He looked skeptical. "That's really what you want?"

I thought about telling him that if I could go back in time, I would have done things differently, would have never made myself famous at all. But I knew he wouldn't understand. He thrived in the spotlight, craved the attention and approval of strangers. He clearly didn't understand why I would want out of that life, and he certainly wouldn't understand my wish that I'd never gotten into it in the first place.

But I could only give one honest answer to that question: "Yes. That's really what I want. Maybe not forever, but for now... I just want to figure out who I am."

"And you can't do that with a boyfriend?" he asked dubiously.

I stood up and began pacing. It was time to be blunt. That was the only way he would understand. "I can't do that with a boyfriend who jumps in front of every camera he sees. You are a pro athlete.

You're a household name, and you have more commercials on TV right now than I can keep track of. You do interviews constantly, every time you walk down the street someone asks for your autograph. Do you think that, as your girlfriend, I would be able to just hide against the wall while you're giving a press tour? No one would ask about me or want my autograph because I'm with you? Austin, we'd never be able to go outside! Between your fans and mine, we'd never get ten minutes' peace. That's not a great way to start a relationship, and it just doesn't sound like something I want to do anymore."

He looked a little thunderstruck. "I'm too famous for you? I'm a football player. You're Bridget Freaking Foster!"

I threw my hands up in frustration. "I know! And I don't want to be Bridget Freaking Foster anymore!"

He stared at me for several long moments, eyes narrowed, his elbows on his knees and hands in tense fists. "You're sure?" he finally asked in a voice so low it was nearly lost on the breeze.

Nodding 'yes' to that question was one of the hardest things I had ever done. "I'm sure."

He studied me a moment longer before, at last, dropping his gaze to the ground. "That's disappointing, and I'm not going to pretend to understand. But I..." his eyes lifted up to my face again, "I respect you. And if this is what you want, I respect that."

My mouth was dry, and my heart hammered in my ears. *This is what I want... Right?* I licked my lips. "Thank you, Austin."

A single nod was his only response, then he pushed up to his feet, stepped over, and pressed a warm kiss to my forehead before walking, wordlessly, back to the house.

And that was that. We were on the same page. No relationship. No *BridgetandAustin*. No chance for the paparazzi to splash our faces all over the world wide web with obnoxious headlines and endless questions. This was my chance to rediscover myself, and I couldn't do that with Austin.

*Right?* ...

## About the Author

**Kimberly Webb** earned an English degree from BYU-Idaho, but her true education came from the countless books that swept her away on grand adventures. When she's not writing, Kimberly can be found jogging, getting lost in a good book, or chasing a bit of everyday magic with her husband and three children. She still believes in the wonder of Disneyland, the thrill of a well-told tale, and the idea that the best adventures often begin with a single, unexpected detour.